STAY OR GO IN DEADWOOD

A.L. LONG ANN SCHREIBER
CHARLES BROWN JESSA AARONS
LYNN DONOVAN MELISSA NAATZ
NORY WOODS V.J. LEE VIA MARI

Twisted Teacup
PUBLISHING

These stories are a work of fiction. The events and characters described herein are imaginary and are not intended to refer to specific places or living persons. The opinions expressed in these manuscripts are solely the opinions of the author and do not represent the opinions or thoughts of the publisher.

Cover art by Wicked Smart Designs.

Ebook ISBN: 978-1-968014-08-7

Print ISBN: 978-1-968014-09-4

STAY OR GO IN DEADWOOD

A Chord of Destiny by A. L. Long

After weeks of touring, country music's newest sensation Sage Grayson watched the endless asphalt ribbon unfurl beneath his bus wheels, until his bus breaks down. The nearest mechanic is in Deadwood, South Dakota, an hour away. When he explores this little town, he finds more than just a place to stretch his legs. That unfortunate stop turned out to be the best thing to happen to him.

The House Always Wins by Ann Schreiber

Two years after losing her fiancé, traveling nurse Brooke Cassidy arrives in Deadwood, South Dakota, determined to focus on work and keep her heart guarded. But a chance encounter at a local casino brings her face-to-face with Dane Walker, a powerful businessman whose presence is impossible to ignore.

Their connection is immediate and unexpected, pulling Brooke into a world far more complicated than she planned. As their relationship deepens, tension builds when a jealous physician begins to interfere, stirring up secrets and forcing Brooke to question who she can trust.

Set against a town built on risk and reinvention, Brooke must decide whether opening her heart again is worth the gamble, because in Deadwood, the house always wins.

Return to Deadwood by Charles Lemar Brown

Two days out of Deadwood, Jack Abbott had nothing on his mind but finding a place to ranch and the beautiful woman who was traveling with him. All that changed in an instant when, during a shooting, Violet Daniels was seriously wounded. Now, even though Jack was told he was not welcome, he must return to Deadwood, for that is where the closest doctor is, and he fears that even with proper care, she may not live.

A Real Trooper by Jessa Aarons

Even though I'm no longer an agent with the FBI, when my former mentor calls in a favor to keep an eye on a woman in Witness Protection, I drop everything and am on my way to Deadwood in a flash.

Being an outlaw biker has really honed in my radar of when something isn't right, so it doesn't take long to see that this "favor" won't be as easy as he said. And then when danger shows up at the ranch and tries to take her from me, I realize I need to reevaluate my next steps very carefully to get us both out alive.

Drawn into Danger by Lynn Donovan

In 1882, Brynn Ellison arrives in Deadwood chasing a mail-order promise that collapses the moment she steps off the coach. Deceived and penniless, she finds refuge in a small church, trading labor for shelter. By lamplight, she returns to the one skill that still feels honest—drawing faces with uncanny precision.

Gideon Carver, a soft-spoken printer's apprentice burdened by a scandalous past, spends his days pressing wanted posters for the sheriff. When he notices Brynn's sketches, he recognizes her talent. Their partnership soon breathes justice into the lawless town--her drawings identify outlaws, while his press spreads their faces across the territory.

But when one of her portraits helps hang a man, vengeance comes looking for the unknown artist. As bounty hunters and bandits close in, Brynn and Gideon retreat into the Black Hills, where survival depends on trust neither has fully dared. Confronted by ghosts of his father's mysterious death and her own shame-shadowed past, both must choose whether faith and forgiveness can outlast fear.

Together, they will test the truth that art can illuminate—even when it's drawn in darkness—and discover that courage, once pressed to paper, can rewrite both their lives.

How It Began by Melissa Naatz

Before Las Vegas. There was Deadwood.

Sixteen-year-old Wyatt Halliday believes she's found her escape in Bodie Vega—a boy with big dreams and promises to match.

But first love doesn't always last.

One reckless summer changes everything, forcing Wyatt to face a choice that will shape who she becomes.

This is where it began.

Deadwood's Killer Brew by Nory Woods

Starr Kona and her spirited corgi companion, Bean, embark on their first true vacation adventure. As a computer analyst she always stayed close to home but now she wanted to see all the Americas had to offer. Their first stop is Deadwood, South Dakota. Everything seemed to be running smoothly, that is, until Bean found that pesky dead body. Will her innate curiosity and Bean's corgi charm be the keys to solving the case or will they end up stepping on everyone's toes?

Deadwood's Killer Brew is Book One in *The Perfect Blend Cozy Mystery Trilogy*

Finding Hope In Deadwood by V. J. Lee

It was love at first sight between Nico Marino and I. He showed me every day how much he loved me. No gift was too extravagant, and flowers were "just because." All my favorite things were always readily available. He gave me his attention and time, until his best friend died in his arms on the side of the road. Nico promised he'd take care of Dorian's little sister, Heather. Then his time and attention turned entirely to her. I understood and helped care for her as well. But when she showed up at my wedding in a wedding dress, I was done. I gave her the ring and ran to the place I knew he'd never come looking for me, the place where his friend died: Deadwood, South Dakota.

I learned too late that my attention had shifted from Hope Walker to my best friend's sister, Heather. Now, the only woman I have ever loved and will ever love is gone. I had once vowed never to lose Hope. She can run, but I'll always chase her until I find Hope again. I will make amends. She may never take me back, and if that's the case, I'll care for her from the shadows, because there is only one woman for me.

Ferocious Protector by Via Mari

Blake

When I come along with my elite bodyguard team for the double wedding in Deadwood, South Dakota I was expecting a quiet weekend under the big blue sky.

But the Chicago boys, a mafia family who doesn't listen to the word no, uses the opportunity to make their claim.

And when they mess with Patti Ann, they cross a line with no return. They messed with the wrong women.

Unfortunately for them, I plan to protect what's mine, this town, her and anyone in it.

Because the blue-eyed blonde with a special little smile she saves just for me, is going to be mine.

Furious Protector is the explosive fifth book in the Ruthless Guardians series by International Best-Selling Author, Via Mari. You will love these spicy, instalove bodyguard novels set in Deadwood, South Dakota, where the passion is fiery, the loyalty is fierce, and the stakes are high. Each book is a standalone featuring different couples. All have a guaranteed happily ever after.

A CHORD OF DESTINY

A.L. LONG

A Chord of Destiny

1

The engine sputtered and died. Like something inside Sage, it had finally given up too. Then came the silence—eerie and absolute—pressing against the luxury upholstery of the tour bus, making him aware of just how accustomed he'd become to constant noise: wheels on asphalt, roadies laughing, his own thoughts screaming for attention. Beyond the windows stretched nothing but the long black line of County Road 83, shimmering under a merciless sun. The air conditioner gave one final, pathetic wheeze before surrendering, letting the heat creep in like an unwelcome guest.

"Perfect timing," Sage said bitterly. The universe's punchline to his joke of a career.

He pressed his forehead to the window, feeling the last vibrations of the dead engine through the glass. How long had it been since he'd felt anything real? The stadiums blurred together—faceless crowds screaming his name, lights so bright they blocked out everything else, applause that had once been his addiction but now felt like hands around his throat. The fans wanted pieces of him he no longer had to give. His creativity had abandoned him months ago, leaving him hollow-eyed in hotel rooms at 3 a.m., staring at blank notebook pages. The man on magazine covers, the voice on the radio—that wasn't him anymore. That was just the empty shell, still going through the motions. He closed his eyes, trying to conjure any feelings of inspiration, the fire that used to ignite his songwriting. But all he found was exhaustion, a lost desire that seeped into his bones. This breakdown, he realized with a bitter twist of irony, was as much his own as it was the bus's. It was an internal crisis, a roadside confession of a man on the brink. He'd been chasing a feeling, an escape he couldn't quite name, a quiet place away from the road of his own making. And now, fate, in its own peculiar, inconvenient way, had delivered him to it. A desolate road, a broken-down machine, and the dawning realization that this unexpected detour might just be the only way back to himself. This was more than just a pause; it was a disruption, the first, jarring note of a song he hadn't yet composed, a melody born from silence and solitude.

He closed his eyes, fingers drumming a phantom melody on his thigh. Nothing came. The well had run dry months ago, leaving only dust where inspiration once flowed. The irony wasn't lost on him—both he and this metal beast had finally given out on the same desolate stretch of nowhere. His throat tightened. How long had he been running on empty, cranking out hollow echoes of songs that once meant something?

Gary burst through from the driver's cabin, sweat beading his forehead, phone clutched like a lifeline.

"We're screwed, Sage," he said, mopping his brow with a crumpled tissue. "Engine's fried. Need a tow to some place called Deadwood. About an hour away. Could be hours before a tow truck gets here."

Deadwood. Like something from an old Western movie his grandfather would watch. Sage managed a nod, surprising himself with the relief that flooded his chest. The endless highways, the identical hotel rooms, the sea of faces blurring together night after night—all temporarily halted by a blown gasket or whatever the hell had finally given way. Maybe this breakdown was exactly what he needed. A forced stop. A chance to breathe air that wasn't recycled through arena vents. Maybe here, in this unplanned pause, he might remember what it felt like to have something genuine to say.

Two hours later, the tow truck hauled the massive tour bus across the dusty landscape like a wounded animal being dragged to shelter. From the passenger seat of the cab, Sage watched his rolling sanctuary—or was it his prison—shrink in the side mirror as he rode ahead in the pilot car. He inhaled deeply, trading the familiar recycled air of the bus for the truck's bouquet of motor oil, burned coffee, and the driver's pine-scented air freshener dangling from the rearview mirror. Earl, a mountain of a man with hands like weathered leather, navigated the winding road in silence, broken only by occasional grunts about the road conditions.

When Deadwood, South Dakota, finally materialized through the heat waves, Sage felt his expectations crumble. No wooden boardwalks or swinging saloon doors greeted him—instead, a blend of modern storefronts stood alongside scattered historic buildings. The town didn't announce itself with gunslinger bravado but rather whispered its history through the faded brick and timeworn façades that punctuated the main street.

Deadwood tugged at Sage in ways he couldn't articulate. The town stood defiantly unpolished compared to his regular haunts—the five-star luxury suites, the faceless first-class lounges, the manufactured experiences crafted to anticipate his slightest desire. Here, despite the large hotel casinos and tourist accommodations, something genuine persisted in the weathered buildings and unhurried pace. Among these streets steeped in frontier lore, Sage felt his celebrity shrink to proper size, offering a rare reprieve from the constant demands of fame.

Earl maneuvered the bus into a parking space behind an unexpectedly sleek garage. Sage barely noticed, his attention captured by "The Coffee Grind" across the street with its whimsical hand-lettered sign. Golden light poured from the windows while the rich scent of fresh-roasted beans drifted toward him like an invitation. At outdoor tables, locals lingered in easy conversation, no one checking watches or phones. The scene promised a simplicity his gilded life had long ago sacrificed.

"Think I'll wander a bit," Sage said, his voice scratchy from hours of silence. "Get some real coffee. I'll find you after the mechanic's verdict."

Earl hardly looked up from the tow mechanism. "Fine by me. Just remember—no gunfights at high noon. This ain't exactly Tombstone."

The corner of Sage's mouth lifted. Tombstone. That hardly tracked with the renovated storefronts and paved streets of Deadwood. Loose gravel popped beneath his Italian leather boots as he made his way to The Coffee Grind. A bell jingled overhead when he pushed through the door—the coffee-scented air wrapped around him, laced with vanilla and warm sugar.

Inside, the café felt like someone's living room that happened to serve coffee. Rough-hewn beams stretched across the ceiling. Faded photos of stern-faced miners and saloon girls hung beside watercolors of the surrounding hills. No two chairs matched, and the counter showed decades of elbow marks. Nothing like the antiseptic white-and-chrome cafés where the baristas knew his order before he spoke. This place had absorbed the stories of everyone who'd ever sat here, and now it waited for his.

And then he saw her.

Behind the counter, she expertly whipped hot milk into a frothy ecstasy, her back temporarily hidden from his view. The steam wand hissed seductively, synchronized with the low bass notes pulsating in the background. Even from a distance, there was an arresting allure to her movements, a certainty that magnetized his attention. As she pivoted, hands sensually wiping across her apron, Sage's heartbeat stuttered. She sported a waterfall of lush, chestnut hair tied back nonchalantly, a few rebellious strands framing a face that was drop-dead stunning and alluringly kind-hearted. Her eyes, a piercing hazel that held a spark of mischief and intellect, danced at the corners when she gifted a departing customer a sultry smile; it was one that lit up her eyes and oozed raw, genuine warmth, much like a sunbeam slicing through his constant fog of exhaustion.

He felt himself drawn into her magnetic field—a beacon of genuine warmth radiating irresistible sensuality in the rough-hewn café ambiance. Her movements were an enticing dance as she navigated through the charming disorder of the café with comfort and ease. There was an earthiness to her—an unspoken power—that emitted from her like heated whispers from the espresso machine. The quality stood stark against the flighty and often damn superficial vibes thrown by the women who usually swarmed around him—the groupies, the handlers, and all those industry vultures. He saw within her an aura of satisfaction and self-assurance that somehow eluded him despite his global fame.

What he wouldn't give to have just a taste of such contentment... and, indeed, her.

2

Harley had picked up on the presence of the mysterious stranger the very instant he'd sauntered in. He perched by the window; an intriguing specimen poised among the usual cascade of Deadwood's dwellers and nosy sightseers. A distinct sexual aura radiated from him, a sultry weariness that clung to him like his expensive clothes, but also an undeniable lustful intensity that echoed within her. His eyes, when they dared to meet hers, held a depth that hinted at carnal experiences far beyond the confines of this quaint, historic town. He was no ordinary Joe. There was a seductive melancholy about him, a tantalizing whiff of something both mysterious and possibly a little shattered.

Every aspect of him was alluringly masculine—from his rugged jawline to the broad set of his shoulders. She couldn't tear her gaze away as he ran his fingers through his disheveled hair so nonchalantly. Harley caught herself wondering how those strong, calloused hands would feel against her bare skin—a magnetic pull toward him, seemingly out of her control. It was as if invisible threads were weaving their way between them, drawing her closer with each passing minute. As she moved hesitantly toward him to serve his coffee, she caught a whiff of his scent—a heady mix of musk and something unfamiliar yet intoxicating. The proximity was electric, sending a thrill coursing through her veins.

His gaze seared into her eyes, heavy-lidded with unspoken promises and breathless secrets. They held a raw promise, an assurance of untamed, passionate encounters that transcended the boundaries of this small-town existence.

She was acutely aware of her heart pounding in her chest, ensnared in his hypnotic presence. As she retreated back to the safety of the counter, Harley found herself unable to shake off the intoxicating essence of the handsome stranger resting by her café window.

He was so wildly different from the calloused cowboys she usually dated. He was more suited for silk sheets than saddle sores—a polished mystery in her homely sanctuary. And yet, when their gazes locked, even if only for a sizzling split second, a spark exploded between them; an unspoken recognition of this electrifying connection that vibrated beneath their skin.

~

Coffee and cinnamon perfumed the air—rich, earthy scents that Sage breathed in like oxygen after too long underwater. Nothing like this existed in his world of tour buses with their filtered air systems or the artificial food aromas wafting from backstage buffets. Around him, murmured conversations blended with the percussion of cups meeting saucers and the steam wand's sighing. These ordinary sounds struck him as extraordinary—a revelation after years of carefully engineered noise.

His gaze drifted across the room. Behind the counter, a woman's eyes crinkled as she slid a mug toward a man in faded overalls, their wordless exchange conveying years of morning rituals. Near the window, sunlight caught the concentrated frown of a young woman hunched over her sketchbook. An elderly couple sat with fingers loosely tangled between their plates, speaking in voices too soft to hear but with a rhythm suggesting decades of practiced dialogue. Sage watched their unhurried movements with something like hunger. No one here performed their connections or guarded their words. They simply existed together, something he had almost forgotten was possible.

Sage cleared his throat before stepping up to the counter and ordering a black coffee, the words catching slightly in his unused voice. The barista looked up, her smile genuine, eyes bright with a hint of mischief—but no recognition. No widening eyes, no subtle double-take, no smartphone appearing from a pocket. Just a nod and the clink of a mug against the counter.

His shoulders relaxed a fraction. Here, the platinum records and magazine covers meant nothing. The tour bus breaking down outside town had forced this unscheduled stop, but as he wrapped his fingers around the warm ceramic, he couldn't summon any real regret. Deadwood seemed to exist in its own pocket of time, unhurried and unconcerned with the world beyond its borders.

He found a seat and sipped slowly, watching the locals move through their morning routines. A gray-haired woman with laugh lines teased the postal worker until they both doubled over. Three men leaned against a hitching post outside what appeared to be an actual saloon, their conversation punctuated by easy nods and comfortable silences. No one performed here. No one posed or calculated their expressions for maximum effect. They simply existed, weathered and real, their lives unfolding according to rhythms established long before Sage had ever stepped onto a stage.

He found himself magnetically pulled toward the barista, the sultry temptress who had served him his morning vice. She wasn't merely pouring out caffeine; she was dishing up a serving of solace, an intoxicating touch of warmth amidst the often-bitter tides of existence. Sage couldn't tear his eyes off her from his secluded corner, trapped in the allure of her radiant energy, a stark sensual contrast to the always-hurrying, impersonal bustle that dominated his world.

Burned into his memory were her delicate features—full, pouty lips that held a promise of sin and secrets, eyes that sparkled like an espresso with a swirl of caramel, promising to drown him in their depths. Her figure was nothing short of sinful—curves that could make a saint sway and legs that seemed to run for miles, encased in tight denim. He couldn't help but savor the sight of her, every damn time their paths crossed.

Her chestnut hair fell in tousled waves over her shoulders, wild and uncontained despite her attempt to tie it back, just as he imagined her to be between silken sheets. Her skin, fair and unspoiled, shone under the dim café lights, making Sage yearn to trace every hidden secret etched into her. Each time she moved—graceful yet filled with unspoken promises—his heart pounded in his chest like a loaded gun.

His imagination painted vivid scenarios. Their bodies tangled together in a heated dance of desire under the sheets—the sound of their heavy breaths and hushed whispers echoing in the room—the taste of her soft skin against his eager lips.

Shit! She was more than just a barista delivering coffee; she was becoming his erotic safe-hold and he was ready to worship devoutly at her altar. He needed to get his head out of the gutter.

As he sipped his coffee, the café's silence eased his perpetual anxiety. He noticed things he usually missed—sunlight through dusty windows, wooden beams overhead, the rich aroma filling the room. After years of concert spotlights and amplifiers, this quiet felt like medicine.

He'd often fantasized about escaping fame—a cabin in mountains, a seaside cottage—never a Wild West town with his tour bus broken down miles away. Yet this unplanned detour brought unexpected peace.

Opening his notebook, he sketched the town and its people rather than his usual lyrics. His pen captured worn wooden surfaces, weathered faces, and Deadwood's rugged authenticity—so unlike the manufactured world he inhabited daily. When he glanced up at the barista, he found words and melodies flowing again, awakened by something real.

The barista with hazel eyes approached, coffeepot in hand. "How's that brew treating you?" Her voice carried the slight lilt of someone who'd grown up elsewhere but had long ago chosen this place as home.

Sage glanced up from his notebook. "It's exactly what I needed," he said, surprised by the sincerity in his own voice. "Reminds me of something I've been missing."

"All that in a cup of coffee," she said, setting the pot down. "I'm Harley. This little piece of heaven is mine."

"Sage," he replied, offering his hand and savoring the anonymity.

Her grip matched his, calloused and certain. "You've got that look about you—like you've been running too long without stopping."

A laugh escaped him, rusty from disuse. "Mechanical problems about three miles east. Wasn't exactly planned."

"Nothing ever is around here," Harley said, leaning slightly against the neighboring table. "Deadwood has its own gravitational pull. Catches folks when they need catching."

"I can feel it," Sage murmured, noticing the easy rhythm of the place, so different from backstage chaos. "Like time moves differently."

"That's what keeps me here," Harley said, straightening. "You should stick around for Wild West Days this weekend. The whole town transforms—live music in the streets, the works."

"Sounds tempting."

"Think it over," she said, retrieving her pot. "Coffee is on the house next time."

He found himself aching to prolong the sultry dialogue, captivated by the desire to delve deeper into the mystery of this woman, this town, this unexpected haven of temptation. The relentless grind of his career, the merciless deadlines, and the insatiable cravings of his fans now seemed a faint murmur in the backdrop. They were replaced by the intoxicating allure of an uninhibited conversation with a woman who had ignited a fire within him. It was an honest conversation that took place in a town that felt inexplicably like home, despite being uncharted territory.

3

Harley found herself glancing his way between customers, curiosity warming her cheeks. Most visitors blew through town like tumbleweeds, leaving no impression. But this man—Sage, she'd learn when taking him a refill—sat differently. He watched the world with a stillness that felt like gravity. Their second shared look lasted three heartbeats, something electric passing between them, as surprising as her truck breaking down had been last Tuesday, yet infinitely more welcome.

Across the room, Sage couldn't stop watching her. After months of chaotic touring, her methodical movements behind the counter steadied something in him. He noted how she double-knotted her apron strings, the way she nodded at the mailman without interrupting his usual order, how she bumped hips with her barista during the morning rush. Here was someone anchored in place, while he'd been adrift for years. Her presence hummed like a perfect chord he'd been searching for but couldn't compose himself.

Sage felt an almost magnetic pull toward Harley. Her presence was a soothing balm to his frayed nerves, a stark contrast to the chaotic energy of his life on the road. He found himself dissecting her every move, not out of an obsessive gaze, but out of a deep-seated curiosity. The way she tied her apron, the small, almost imperceptible nod she gave to a customer she clearly knew well, the easy camaraderie she shared with her staff—it all painted a picture of a woman who was deeply rooted, completely present. This was a form of music he hadn't composed, a melody he hadn't written, yet it resonated with him on a profound level.

When Harley caught him staring, she didn't look away. Her eyes met his without flinching, without the usual flutter of recognition he'd grown accustomed to. Instead, she studied him with the same quiet focus she gave to measuring coffee grounds or balancing her ledger. Something in his expression must have betrayed him—the weariness behind his careful composure—because her gaze softened slightly before she turned back to her work.

His pencil moved across the page almost without his direction. Not lyrics this time, but the slope of her shoulder as she reached for a mug on a high shelf. The slight furrow between her brows as she concentrated on steaming milk. The practiced efficiency of her movements as she navigated her domain. He hadn't drawn anything but stylized album art in years, but now his hand remembered how to capture something real—the way light caught in her chestnut hair, the quiet confidence in her stance. For once, he wasn't creating for an audience. He was simply seeing.

Harley glanced over his shoulder, a dish towel slung over her arm. "Got a good eye, don't you?"

Sage snapped his notebook half-closed, heat crawling up his neck. "Just... noticing things," he managed, clearing his throat. "This place has character."

"Deadwood's got stories in every corner." Her smile reached her eyes as she tucked a strand of hair behind her ear. "What's that you're drawing?"

His fingers hovered over the page. Truth seemed easier than lies here. "Impressions. The café. The people." His eyes met hers briefly. "You've got something about you."

She cocked an eyebrow. "Something, huh? Care to elaborate?"

"Rootedness," he said finally. "Like you belong exactly where you're standing."

A soft laugh escaped her. "Ten years pouring coffee will do that. You get to know every creaky floorboard." She leaned against his table, arms folded. "Meanwhile, you look like you fell off a moving train."

"Bus trouble," he corrected with a wry smile. "Though this is the longest I've stayed put in..." He trailed off, taking in the mismatched mugs hanging from hooks, the sun-faded local photographs. "There's something peaceful about it. Unexpected."

Harley's lips quirked. "That's Deadwood for you. Folks who try to rush through here end up staying the longest." She absently rolled a sugar packet between her fingers. "So, what storm blew you into my café?"

Sage's thumb traced the edge of his notebook. The whole truth seemed both too much and the only answer. "Fate, I guess. And then my bus trouble did too."

"Mmm." She nodded, the corners of her eyes crinkling. "Funny how the universe throws up roadblocks exactly when we need them. Especially for people who'd drive themselves into the ground otherwise."

His eyebrow lifted. "What makes you think I'm that type?"

"Those calluses on your fingertips. The way you keep glancing at your phone even though it's dead. The three empty coffee cups." She shrugged. "You've got that hungry look. Like you're searching for something just beyond your reach."

Her words landed with unexpected precision. Not an accusation—just clarity. Sage felt a sudden urge to tell her everything: the soulless stadium tours, the label executives dictating his sound, the hollowness of being "Sage Grayson" when he barely remembered who that was anymore.

"Peace has been... scarce lately," he admitted, the words barely audible.

Something in Harley's face shifted. Not pity—recognition. As if she'd walked similar roads, just on different terrain. Her life here wasn't glamorous—the worn edges of her apron and the stubborn coffee stain on her sleeve told that story—but it was authentically hers.

"Well," she said, tapping the table twice, "you're here now. Good coffee, better pie, and conversation that won't end up on social media." She winked, sliding a fresh mug toward him. "Sometimes breakdowns lead to the best discoveries."

For the first time in months, Sage's smile felt real, not the practiced one he'd been using like armor. "I could get used to this place, Harley."

"Most people do," she said, not breaking eye contact. "Deadwood is like that old song you can't get out of your head—before you know it, you're humming along without even realizing it."

4

Something shifted in the air between them, a silent understanding taking root. For the first time in what felt like forever, Sage's shoulders relaxed. The weight of fame—the constant scrutiny, the expectations—seemed to lift in this little corner of The Coffee Grind. The gentle clink of mugs and low conversations around them created a cocoon of normalcy he hadn't realized he'd been craving. Maybe the bus breaking down wasn't the catastrophe his manager would claim. Maybe it was exactly what he needed.

Sage settled deeper into his chair, uncrossing his arms. With most people, he measured every word, calculating potential headlines or social media storms. But watching Harley move behind the counter, he felt no need for his usual verbal chess game.

"So," Harley said, wiping circles on the countertop, her eyes meeting his occasionally, "musician, right? The whole tour bus situation kind of gives it away." Her smile held no trace of the star struck gleam he'd grown wary of, just genuine amusement.

A laugh escaped him—not his practiced interview chuckle, but something real. "Singer-songwriter, actually. And yeah, the bus comes with the territory." He shrugged. "Though apparently so do unexpected stops in small towns."

Sage studied her movements—the slight crease between her eyebrows when she focused, the way she cocked her head while listening. Something about her struck him as authentic, grounded in a reality he rarely encountered anymore.

"Singer-songwriter," she echoed, eyes lighting up. "Making something from nothing. That must be quite a life." She looked up. "What's your style?"

The simple question landed with unexpected weight. Music wasn't just his career; it was his refuge, his confessional, his blessing and curse rolled into one. It had also built the very walls that now separated him from people.

"It shifts," he answered, measuring each word. "Reflects whatever is... happening. Whatever I'm going through." He took a breath. "These days it's mostly... chaos. Pressure. Not much... peace."

Harley set down her cloth, meeting his gaze directly. Her eyes held no pity, just recognition. "Sometimes the noise drowns everything out," she said quietly. "You need stillness to hear what matters." She resumed wiping; the soft rhythm of her movements punctuated her words. "This town has plenty of stillness. And stories. If you listen, you can almost hear the whispers of what came before."

Sage leaned forward, suddenly captivated, imagining gold-seekers and gunslingers, a world utterly removed from his carefully curated existence.

"I bet," he said, genuinely intrigued. "Like the history is woven into everything here. Not like the temporary world of tour buses and concert venues."

Harley's laugh rang out, bright as a bell. "Don't get me wrong—we get our share of drifters. Tourists with their cameras and their Wild Bill Hickok fantasies." She wiped her hands on her apron, eyes crinkling at the corners. "But underneath all that? There's bedrock. These walls," she said, tapping the wooden counter with her knuckle, "they've stood while empires rose and fell. Same with the families here—some have roots deeper than the mine shafts. My grandmother poured coffee in this exact spot when Eisenhower was president." She glanced around the room with quiet pride. "If these floorboards could talk..."

He scanned the room again, this time letting it sink in. Floorboards worn to a satin finish. Tables bearing the marks of a thousand conversations—rings from wet glasses, initials carved by pocketknives. Photographs in amber tones lining the walls like preserved memories. "You're right," he conceded. "There's something solid here."

"Solid is good," Harley said, settling her weight against the bar, forearms resting on the burnished counter. "Keeps your feet on the ground when everything else wants to blow away." Her eyes held his. "I get the feeling you've been chasing a lot of things that blow away, Sage. Maybe it's just a matter of finding what you're looking for and holding on to it."

The familiar armor slid into place—deflection, distance—but something in her straightforward compassion made him hesitate. Suddenly, he had a name for the turmoil that had become as familiar as his own reflection. Emptiness. Loneliness.

"It's funny," he started, measuring each word. "You spend your life climbing toward some imagined summit, desperate to be heard. Then you reach it and realize you've built yourself a beautiful prison. You're too busy oiling the gears to remember why you constructed the damn thing."

Harley tilted her head, considering him like a difficult chord progression. "Always wanting more. It pulls you like a riptide. What exactly are you chasing, Sage, that's turned into such a trap?"

Her question floated between them, simple and unavoidable. He could dodge it with some practiced line about creative vision or artistic growth. But in this quiet corner, the truth felt like the only currency worth spending.

His voice caught. "Connection, I suppose," he said finally. "My songs are all about what makes us human—falling in love, having your heart broken, wanting something you can't have. But I live on a tour bus and in hotel rooms and green rooms. I write about life while barely living it." He exhaled slowly. "It's like standing at the edge of a canyon, singing as loud as I can, but the echo that comes back doesn't sound like me anymore."

He studied his hands, running a thumb over the hardened skin where flesh met string night after night. Strange how something so familiar could suddenly feel borrowed. Harley didn't rush to fill the silence that followed. When she finally spoke, her words came soft as a lullaby.

"That must be a lonely place to be," she said. "To be surrounded by people, by noise, and still feel utterly alone."

Something hot and unexpected welled up behind his eyes. Sage blinked rapidly, throat suddenly tight. "Yeah," he managed.

She rounded the counter, her footsteps gentle on the worn floorboards. She stopped a respectful distance from his table, hands clasped loosely at her waist.

"You know what my grandmother used to say? That the universe puts detours in your path when you need to change direction." A half-smile softened her face. "Maybe a broken-down tour bus isn't just bad luck."

Sage looked up at her, this woman who somehow saw through the carefully constructed armor he'd spent years perfecting. Not the magazine covers, or platinum records, or the carefully curated public persona. Just him—tired, confused, and completely lost.

The words spilled from him before he could catch them. "I think... I think I needed this. I've been running so long I forgot what it felt like to stop."

"Running from what?" Her voice remained gentle, inviting rather than demanding.

He weighed the question. The emptiness. The expectations. The gnawing fear of inadequacy beneath his success.

"From myself, I suppose," he said, his smile crooked and knowing. "Or who I've become."

Harley's expression softened. "Then you've stumbled into the right place. Deadwood has a way of catching runners. Makes you plant your feet, face your reflection. Sometimes you even like what you see." She nodded toward his empty cup. "More coffee? Or should we try that pie I mentioned? Nothing clarifies existential dilemmas quite like a good piece of apple pie."

His laugh came easier this time. "Pie sounds perfect," he said, something tight in his chest beginning to unravel. "An excellent first step."

5

The mechanic's wrench whined persistently from the garage down the street, grating on Sage's nerves like a reminder of the inevitable end to his stopover. His tour bus—that gleaming chrome monster that had carried him to chaos across state lines—sat defeated by a single missing part, stranded for who knew how long. The first day, he'd paced and made frantic calls, rescheduling shows and placating managers. Now, three days in, something strange had settled over him. The silence no longer felt like absence; it had texture, substance, almost a melody of its own.

Deadwood revealed itself slowly. Walking its streets at a pace that felt foreign to his body, Sage traced his fingers along sun-warmed brick that had witnessed a century of winters. The town wasn't preserved so much as it was continuing—each building standing not as a museum piece but as a chapter still being written. He found himself lingering at corners, watching the afternoon light transform ordinary windows into blazing gold. The locals nodded as they passed, their conversations unfolding without awareness of an audience. Their genuineness struck him as revolutionary—no one trying to be seen, to be validated, to perform. But most of all, he always found himself at The Coffee Grind.

Yesterday, he'd watched Harley chat with Mrs. Keller (he knew her name now) about her grandson's college acceptance. Harley had leaned across the counter, her face lighting up at the news, asking questions that showed she'd been following this story for years. Sage had felt something twist inside him—not quite jealousy, but recognition of something precious he'd misplaced along the way. For all his practiced stage banter and carefully timed vulnerability in lyrics, he'd forgotten how to simply exist in a moment without shaping it for consumption. He watched Harley carefully slide a slice of apple pie, identical to the one he'd devoured with such relish, onto a plate. The aroma, even from a distance, was intoxicating. He'd found himself developing a rather significant appreciation for her. It was more than just her baking; it was tangible. It was everything about her: the way she smiled, the way she talked or pressed her brows together when she was concentrating hard.

Harley set the pie on the counter and watched the woman walk away. "Another satisfied customer," she said in a voice like warm honey.

Sage's lips curved upward. "Can't blame her. I think I'm becoming a pie junkie myself."

Harley's laugh brightened the room. "Happens to everyone eventually. Grandma had a theory about that. 'Two ingredients make these special,' she'd say with that little wink of hers. 'Love and pure stubbornness.' Meaning she'd remake a batch until it was perfect."

"Stubborn perfection," Sage echoed, turning the phrase over in his mind. He recognized that quality—the same force that kept him hunched over a guitar at 3 a.m., repeating a passage until his fingers bled, chasing that perfect sound. But while his perfectionism had built walls, Harley's seemed to build bridges.

Harley wiped the counter in smooth, practiced arcs. "Have you explored those quiet corners of town I mentioned?"

Her direct question caught him off guard. "Actually, yes," he said. "I've been walking—real walking, not the backstage-to-tour-bus shuffle I'm used to. Taking my time."

"And?" Genuine interest filled her eyes, refreshingly different from the calculated attention he usually received.

"I'm discovering..." Sage paused, searching. "It's layered, like geology. Beyond the tourist-friendly gold rush tales, there's something deeper. You see it in how buildings nestle against hillsides, in conversations at street corners. This place isn't scenery—it's alive. And the people belong here in a way that..." He hesitated. "In a way I've forgotten how to belong anywhere."

Harley gave a knowing nod. "That's our little corner of South Dakota for you. The gold's mostly gone, but what remains is something more valuable—grit. The pioneers who settled here passed down more than just buildings. They left a blueprint for living." She held her arms out toward the other patrons. "Nobody here expects easy. They expect real—real coffee, real conversation, real pie with lard in the crust."

Something loosened in his chest. "Back in L.A., everything's about the next hit, the next tour, the next..." He trailed off, the weight of expectations momentarily stealing his words. "In music, we're taught to push toward the climax, but lately I've been wondering if I've been missing everything that happens before."

"The pause between notes," Harley said softly, meeting his gaze. "That's the breath of the song."

Her words resonated through him like a perfectly struck chord. When had his music—his life—become so cluttered with noise that he couldn't hear his own heartbeat?

"I've forgotten how to just be," he admitted, voice barely audible. He motioned to the café with its mismatched mugs and worn wooden floors. "This place has a different tempo. Slower. Steadier."

Harley's eyes crinkled at the corners. "Sometimes engines break down exactly when they need to. The universe has its own timing." She leaned in, lowering her voice. "Word around the garage is your bus needs parts they don't stock locally. Could be here another week, maybe longer."

Something fluttered in Sage's chest, a sensation he hadn't felt in years—not anxiety, but possibility.

"A while longer," he echoed, tasting each syllable. His earlier irritation had dissolved like morning mist. In its place bloomed something unexpected: relief. The weight of being Sage the Icon had slipped from his shoulders, if only for these stolen moments.

"You don't sound disappointed," Harley noted, her eyes crinkling at the corners.

"I'm not," he confessed, his lips curving upward. "Getting stuck here might be exactly what I needed. A forced pause. I've been running so long that I've forgotten how to stand still. And I get to spend more time with you."

His mind flashed to the life he'd left behind: cities blurring into one another, the thunder of crowds, the exhausting cycle of creation and performance that had consumed him. Sage wasn't just his name anymore—it was armor he'd forged, a character he'd inhabited so completely that he sometimes forgot where the role ended and he began. But in this unassuming corner of Deadwood, that armor felt unnecessary. When Harley looked at him, she wasn't searching for the rockstar. She was simply seeing him.

"I'd like that." Harley's face lit up with a smile that could light up all of L.A.

6

The café's ambient noise, which had soothed Sage for days, now energized him like a springboard. He'd immersed himself in this place—the coffee scents, Harley's pastries—finding an unexpected serenity. Yet within this calm, something stirred: creativity awakening after a long hibernation. His fingers moved across a battered notebook pulled from his suitcase, tracing not melodies but the sharp edges of buildings opposite and the weathered silhouettes of hills beyond.

"You're unusually quiet today," Harley said, her words flowing gently as she collected his empty mug. She remained his steadfast connection to this unexpected reality.

He glanced up with a slight, self-conscious smile. "Just lost in thought... and sketching. Seems this place sparks more than just deep musings." He nodded toward his notebook. "Trying to preserve some impressions."

Harley's hazel eyes wrinkled with interest as she examined his work. "That's talent right there. You've perfectly caught how sunlight falls across the old courthouse. Few people get that right."

"Thanks," Sage said, feeling a small surge of satisfaction. "I think it's about capturing the depth—not just structures, but their narratives. They seem to exhale their past."

"They do exactly that," Harley agreed, resting against the counter. "The entire town does. You've been out wandering, haven't you? Discovering?"

"More than I expected," he confessed. "Back in L.A., 'discovering' meant finding new agents or record labels. This feels different. More... exhilarating."

He'd started his wanderings with an intoxicating hunger, a lustful yearning to become one with the bare bones of Deadwood because he wanted to learn everything about it for Harley. A brutal contrast to the ephemeral shows and skin-deep flirts that had served as poor substitutes for real intimacy in his career. He'd found himself irresistibly drawn to the cobblestone paths less traveled, the shadowy alleyways that murmured with unspoken desires, the age-old buildings that seemed to sway under the weight of their sinful pasts. Everything Harley loved so much. He'd envisioned a life with kids giggling in the background, Harley, his chestnut beauty, displayed at his side. He fantasized about fueling their passion each night, with nothing but the moonlit silhouette of the Black Hills serving as their sultry stage.

"There's a raw energy here," Sage purred, his voice laced with a newfound respect resembling sensual worship. "You can almost taste the residual heat from lovers who lived and loved fiercely here... it's so damn tangible. So lasting, in a way my superficial world rarely achieves. A hit song is here today, gone tomorrow. But here is where stories of love are made."

Harley nodded, a soft smile playing on her lips. "That's the magic of Deadwood. It's not just a collection of old buildings; it's a living testament to romance. People came here with nothing but a dream and a shovel, and they built this. They faced hardship, danger, and they carved out a life. And that spirit... it's still in the air."

"I've been trying to translate that feeling into something," Sage confessed, tapping his notebook. "I've been humming little melodies, sketching out ideas. It's like the history is seeping into my bones and reawakening something inside me I haven't felt for a long time. The creative block that's been plaguing me for months... I've started to come alive, all because of you."

He'd always been a conduit for sound, his music a reflection of his experiences, his emotions. But the constant demand, the pressure to produce, had stifled that connection, turning his passion into a chore. Here, in the quiet embrace of Deadwood, the muse was returning, not with a thunderous roar, but with a gentle, persistent whisper, and Harley made it happen.

"That's wonderful to hear. I doubt it was all me, though," Harley said, her genuine pleasure evident. "You know, my great-grandfather was a prospector. Came here in '76. Never struck it rich, but he loved the grit of it, the sheer possibility. He used to tell me stories about the boomtown days, about the characters who walked these streets. He said every creak of a floorboard, every gust of wind through a saloon door, had a story to tell. He met my great-grandmother here at this very café. This is where he fell in love with her."

Sage's eyes lit up. "Tell me more. Tell me everything you can remember."

Harley perched on a stool behind the counter, her eyes wandering to the window like she was pulling memories from the dust motes dancing in the sunlight. "My neighbor, Mrs. Gable—she's pushing ninety-three now—told me about when these streets were paved with only brick pavers. They are actually still there today. She remembered the beautiful automobiles that would line the streets. The ladies would dress in their Sunday finest for church, then rush home to change before the elements ruined their good clothes. And that old building down the way? That was the miner's union hall. Men would gather there, planning strikes and arguing late into the night. They weren't just digging for gold—they were laying foundations for a community, fighting tooth and nail for something better. Anyway, Mrs. Gable would sneak behind the Old Style Saloon No. 10 with one of the miners and make out. She was so afraid of getting caught since she was only fifteen at the time. She ended up marrying him. They built a life here."

Sage leaned forward, entranced. These stories weren't the Wild West shootouts plastered across tourist pamphlets—they were the quiet heartbeats of love, the kind that made a place real. In his mind, he saw those miners with their rough hands and grime-streaked faces, their voices echoing off the union hall walls fighting for what they loved. The same reason young Mrs. Gable tiptoed through the streets to meet her boyfriend.

His chest tightened. How had Harley read him so clearly? He'd arrived empty, hollowed out by his own success, creativity dried up like a desert streambed. Now this unexpected stop was filling something in him—anchoring him, rekindling purpose, coaxing melody from silence. His fingers found his pencil, eager to translate her words, her animated expressions, into music. Notes began to flow across his page, intertwining with text, a composition blooming that honored both her stories and his awakening.

"I think I lost my way," he admitted softly. "Chasing applause, I forgot what it feels like to build something true, one note at a time." He glanced from his scribbled composition to the weathered buildings outside. "This place... it's survived by holding on to what matters. It reminds me that worth doesn't always announce itself. Sometimes it just... exists."

Harley smiled, a gentle, knowing smile. "That's the Deadwood way. You learn to appreciate the sunrise after a long, hard night. You learn to find strength in the community, in the shared experience. And you learn that sometimes, the most valuable treasures aren't the ones you dig out of the ground, but the ones you find in your own heart. Maybe you'll even find love."

She picked up a cloth and began to polish a glass, her movements practiced and unhurried. "It's a lesson I think a lot of people, myself included, are still learning."

Sage watched her, a warmth spreading through him that had nothing to do with the coffee. He'd been surrounded by people who wanted something from him—his music, his fame, his attention. But Harley seemed to offer something pure, a connection devoid of expectation. He was starting to hear the music again, not in the amplified echoes of a stadium, but in something that had meaning. *Who was this woman?* The melodies that had been dormant within him began to stir, inspired by the rugged beauty of the woman who stood before him.

Sage cleared his throat. "I think I've been missing something," he said. "All this time chasing after the spotlight, the standing ovations. But you—you remember if someone takes sugar in their coffee. You ask about their kids. It's like you're composing something, one conversation at a time."

Harley set her rag down on the counter, a half-polished glass forgotten in her hand. "I never thought about it that way," she said, meeting his eyes. "But I suppose that's right. Every regular who walks through that door adds another note." She swept her arm toward the café—the scarred oak tables, the chairs that didn't match, the pastry case with its flaky croissants and lopsided muffins. "No grand symphony here. Just the quiet rhythm of people coming back, day after day."

Something clicked into place for Sage. After years of orchestrating stadium-sized emotions, he'd forgotten the power of simplicity—a single pure tone that cuts straight to the heart.

"Last week I was at this charity thing," he blurted. "You know the drill—photographers everywhere, everyone air-kissing, calling me 'Sage' like we're old friends." He winced. "My shoes pinched, my smile felt plastic, and the whole time I kept thinking, 'Who is this person they're all looking at?'" His laugh was hollow. "My manager just kept whispering about 'exposure' and 'networking opportunities.'"

Harley's eyes softened as she put down the glass she'd been polishing. She leaned forward slightly, really seeing him. "That sounds like its own kind of exhaustion."

Sage's shoulders slumped. "God, yes. Exhausting is exactly the word. I used to feed off all that—the screaming crowds, the fans. It was better than any high. Now..." His fingers traced invisible patterns on the countertop. "It's like I'm reading lines in someone else's play. And when the curtain falls, I can't remember which character is actually me."

He caught Harley watching him, her head tilted slightly, eyes soft with something that wasn't pity. A tightness formed in his chest. Fame had built walls around him so gradually he hadn't noticed until now—until this woman who poured coffee and baked scones looked at him without wanting anything.

"That's why I keep coming back," he said, voice dropping to nearly a whisper. "This café. You." He gestured vaguely between them. "You're like... hearing perfect pitch after years of distortion. You don't see platinum records or magazine covers. You just see..." He swallowed hard, meeting her eyes directly. "Me. Just me. And I'd almost forgotten who that was."

Harley's smile was gentle, understanding. "It's easy to get lost in the noise, Sage. The world is very good at amplifying certain things—fame, wealth, success—and drowning out the quieter, more meaningful sounds. The sounds of connection, of community, of simply being present." She picked up a stray sugar packet from the counter, her fingers tracing its edges thoughtfully. "I've seen it happen to people before. They get caught up in the whirlwind, and then one day, they wake up and realize they don't recognize the reflection in the mirror."

"That's exactly it!" Sage exclaimed, leaning forward. "I feel like I'm looking in the mirror and seeing a stranger. A very successful, very tired stranger." He ran a hand through his hair, a gesture of exasperation. "My music... it's started to feel like a chore. Like I'm just going through the motions. I used to pour my soul into every note, every lyric. Now it feels... manufactured."

"And that's a terrifying feeling, I imagine," Harley said, her voice soft.

"Terrifying," he agreed, the word heavy with unspoken emotion. "Because music is all I've ever known. It's how I communicate, how I process the world. If I lose that... I don't know what's left." He looked down at his sketchbook, at the unfinished drawings, the unfinished melodies. "But here... it feels different. It feels like the music is coming back, not from a place of obligation, but from a place of genuine feeling. From the stories I'm hearing, the landscapes I'm seeing, the... the quiet strength I'm witnessing." He glanced at Harley, a hopeful light in his eyes. "From the simple act of a conversation, with no agenda."

Harley reached across the counter, her fingers brushing his lightly as she steadied his sketchbook. The brief touch sent a surprising jolt through him. "Sage," she said, her voice low and sincere, "you came here looking for a solution to a broken-down bus. But maybe you found something more. Maybe you found a place where you can just... breathe. And listen. Not to the applause, but to the rhythm of your own heart."

He held her gaze, captivated by the earnestness in her eyes. In her simple, unadorned world, he saw a profound truth that had eluded him in the glittering chaos of his own. He saw the beauty in the ordinary, the strength in vulnerability, and the quiet power of genuine human connection.

"I think you might be right," he admitted, a genuine smile finally gracing his lips. "I was so busy trying to write the next stadium anthem, I forgot how to appreciate the quiet melody of everyday life." He gestured to the café, then to the street beyond. "This is a different kind of performance, isn't it? One that's not about capturing attention, but about building something real. Something that lasts."

"It is," Harley agreed, her smile widening. "It's about being part of something. Contributing. And finding joy in the simple act of living, moment by moment." She picked up her polishing cloth again, her movements regaining their practiced rhythm. "You know, I was going to invite you over for dinner tonight. My parents are in town, and my mom makes the best pot roast. It's nothing fancy, just... family. Good food. A lot of comfortable silence mixed with easy conversation."

7

Harley's words lingered between them, shifting the air like a change in weather. "Dinner tonight?" Sage found himself repeating, testing the weight of it. Not the choreographed spectacle of industry dinners with their hidden agendas, but something altogether different—plates passed around a family table, voices overlapping, no cameras in sight.

His pulse quickened in a way that had nothing to do with spotlights or critics. "Honesty," he said, surprising himself with the word that surfaced. It felt unfamiliar on his tongue, yet right somehow. "I've been searching for that again." When he looked up at her, his own candor caught him off guard. "I'd love to, Harley. Really."

Stepping outside the café's familiar boundaries meant shedding the armor he'd worn for so long. This was Harley offering him a glimpse behind her curtain—the everyday rhythms, the genuine connections, the unguarded moments he'd watched her navigate with such natural ease. The kindness she showed everyone, now extended to include him.

"Don't expect anything fancy," Harley said

matter-of-factly. "Just dinner, conversation. Dad will bend your ear about the good old days, and Mom will keep refilling your plate." Something softened in her expression. "It's simple, that's all. Thought you might need a little of that these days."

"Simple," Sage repeated, feeling the smile form before he was conscious of it. "That sounds perfect." He pictured it: warm kitchen light, the scent of home cooking, conversation without an angle. Miles from the cold precision of hotel suites and hollow applause he was used to. Here, in Deadwood, he was slowly shedding the layers of his celebrity, allowing the man beneath to emerge. And Harley, with her quiet perception and unwavering authenticity, seemed to see him, not as the polished product, but as the raw man he was underneath.

Sage cleared his throat. "What time would you like me there?"

"Six works," Harley said, her smile crinkling the corners of her eyes. "The little blue house with the porch swing, just down that way." She pointed vaguely south. "You'll smell my mom's bread before you see the place."

He committed the details to memory, another pin in his mental map of Deadwood. "Six it is. And Harley... thanks."

"You're welcome," she said with a smile that lit her face. "See you at six."

Stepping into the afternoon sunlight, Sage felt pounds lighter. The chaos of his old life—the constant demands, the shallow conversations—receded like a tide going out. In its place came Deadwood's gentler cadence, its weathered buildings and unhurried pace setting a tempo his soul recognized. He wasn't just another musician mining small-town America for material anymore. He was becoming someone else entirely, breath by breath.

The prospect of dinner at a family table, of conversations that didn't revolve around him, awakened something he'd nearly forgotten. As he walked, notes for a new composition began arranging themselves in his mind—not the arena-filling anthems he was known for, but something intimate, built from porch swings and bread-scented air and the feeling of being truly known.

The Dakota evening painted the sky as Sage walked to Harley's house—blues deepening, oranges flaring at the horizon, stars piercing through like distant stage lights. No arena show could match this. Something about the vastness made him feel both small and somehow exactly where he belonged. A tune formed in his throat, rising and falling like the hills around Deadwood, coming from somewhere genuine inside him.

The blue cottage appeared just as Harley had described, complete with a porch swing. Smells of dinner drifted out—roasted meat, herbs—homey and inviting. With each step toward the door, Sage felt less like the performer everyone knew and more like himself, whoever that was becoming.

Harley waited on the porch, backlit by warm window light. When she turned, her smile hit him like a spotlight.

"Sage. You made it."

"Wouldn't have missed it," he said, his voice unexpectedly quiet. Her hazel eyes took him in—not the celebrity, just him. He'd grown to treasure that look.

Eleanor and Robert matched Harley's description perfectly. Her mother's hands never stopped moving as she talked, making conversation feel as natural as breathing. Her father watched more than he spoke, but when he did, his dry comments caught Sage off guard, pulling genuine laughter from him.

The pot roast melted against his fork, its rich aroma mingling with the earthy scent of fresh herbs. Sage closed his eyes at the first bite, savoring the contrast between the tender meat and the snap of green beans. Around the oak table, Eleanor refilled water glasses while Robert passed the gravy boat without being asked. Between mouthfuls, Sage found himself recounting the time a Tokyo sound engineer had stayed three hours past midnight to perfect a single note, and how a barista in a tiny Italian hillside café had remembered his order after a year's absence. He caught himself mid-anecdote about Nashville, realizing he hadn't mentioned record sales or stadium sizes once.

After a comfortable silence, Robert cleared his throat. "Harley mentioned you're a songwriter and sing as well, Sage." His tone was matter-of-fact, neither impressed nor dismissive.

Heat crept up Sage's neck. "It's what keeps me sane, really."

"We catch your songs sometimes," Eleanor said, the corners of her eyes crinkling. "When we turn the dial." She tilted her head. "Strange, though—how music that fills stadiums isn't always what stays with you at night. Like comparing thunder to rainfall."

Sage's chest tightened. Thunder and rainfall. The words crystallized something he'd felt but couldn't name: the gap between his stadium self and whoever sat here now, in this kitchen that smelled of cinnamon and honesty.

"That's... exactly right," he managed, swallowing hard. "I've been chasing thunder so long I've forgotten how much I need the rain."

Harley's fingers grazed his knuckles—brief, electric. "We're rain people here," she said, holding his gaze. "The quiet stuff that sinks in deep."

Robert nodded, lifting his water glass. "The spotlight follows you everywhere, son. But remember—plants don't grow from applause. They need what falls softly, when nobody's watching."

Robert's words struck Sage like a tuning fork, vibrating through him until everything else fell silent. For years, he'd been chasing applause so loudly he couldn't hear his own melodies anymore.

The porch swing creaked beneath them after dinner, keeping rhythm with the crickets' night song. Eleanor's coffee still warmed Sage's hands through the mug as he watched stars puncture the darkness above the farmhouse. He breathed in air that tasted nothing like tour buses or green rooms.

"Mom and Dad really took to you," Harley whispered, her voice barely disturbing the night.

"I can see why you love when they visit," Sage said, meaning it.

"They're my foundation," she said, settling her head against his shoulder with a naturalness that surprised him. "We live in different worlds, don't we?"

"Mine's all movement—venue to venue, song to song, always chasing whatever's next." Sage watched the silhouettes of distant hills. "Yours has... permanence."

"Both have their place." Harley traced the rim of her mug. "You've seen corners of the world I can't imagine. I just have... this. Solid ground when you need it."

"I haven't truly seen anything in years," Sage admitted, the confession rising unbidden. "When everyone's watching you, you stop seeing. When everyone's listening, you stop hearing. I've forgotten how to be present somewhere without performing it. Except when I'm with you."

He looked at her, at the way the starlight caught the highlights in her hair, the gentle curve of her profile. He felt a profound sense of connection, a feeling that transcended the superficial differences in their lives. "With you, Harley," he continued, his voice hushed, "it's different. It's like the noise fades away. I can actually hear myself think. I can... breathe."

Harley turned to him, her eyes searching his in the dim light. "That's what I hoped for. I saw you, Sage, not the rockstar, but the man beneath the fame. The one who was lost, searching for something real." She hesitated, her gaze softening. "And I... I'm starting to think I'm falling for that man."

The confession lingered in the air, intoxicating as a melody strummed on a solitary guitar in the midnight silence. Sage's pulse hammered wildly in his chest, a raw, teetering hope burning in his veins. He hadn't dared dream of something so damn real amidst the fabrication of his own existence.

"Harley," he began, his voice husky with unleashed desire, "I'm right there with you. This two-bit town, this ordinary life... and you." His eyes drank her in; wanderlust etched in every line. "You're that elusive tune I didn't know I've been craving. You're the whisper that ignites my soul." His hand drifted to her face, fingers tracing a spicy trail along her cheekbone. "I've spent years banging out anthems for unknown faces, but I believe I've found my goddamn favorite song right here..." His voice trailed off as he closed the gap between them.

Their initial kiss beneath the infinite Dakota sky began tentatively, exploring before morphing into an urgent blend of tongues and teeth. Their bodies spoke a silent language of intertwined destinies, their shared longing blooming into something far more potent under the cloak of night. It was a kiss laden with starlight and shared secrets, the intoxicating thrill of falling headlong into lust.

~

As days turned into weeks, Sage found himself drawn into the pulsating rhythm of Deadwood like a moth to a flame. His sketches remained constant, yet took on an entirely new focus—the enticing curve of Harley's hips, the irresistible swell of her breasts under her thin shirts. The vivacious camaraderie he shared with Harley's friends sparked more than just idle banter—it stoked a smoldering desire that threatened to consume him entirely.

Their stolen moments escalated from tender, discreet kisses to heated, passionate explorations of each other's bodies. Harley's hands traced the contours of his muscles with careful yet confident strokes, her fingers exploring every inch of him. Sage responded by running his fingertips down the curve of her spine, causing a shiver to run up her body.

He marveled at the way she moved against him—her breaths coming in quick gasps as he trailed kisses down her neck. Their eyes locked for a moment, an unspoken permission granted before he suddenly flipped her onto her back, straddling him as their movements became more urgent.

Harley arched beneath him, her nails digging into his shoulders as she bit her lip in an attempt to stifle a moan. Their bodies found a synchronized rhythm, their passion building until it threatened to consume them both.

Through it all, Sage saw Harley in a new light—her untamed passion mirrored in the way she clung to him and the intensity with which her body responded to his touch. It was crystal clear to Sage—this woman's passion and emotions matched his own.

Yet, the reality of their contrasting worlds remained. The relentless demands and global reach of Sage's career constituted a force that Sage couldn't ignore forever. There were phone calls from his manager, reminders of looming deadlines, tours to be planned. The world of noise was always waiting, a siren song he couldn't entirely escape.

One evening, as they sat in Harley's living room, the conversation turned to the inevitable.

"What happens when your tour starts again, Sage?" Harley asked, her voice soft, tinged with a hint of apprehension. "When do you have to go back out there?"

Sage watched the flames dance, the question heavy in the air. He'd been avoiding it, clinging to the peaceful bubble he'd found in Deadwood. But he knew, deep down, that he couldn't stay in this quiet harbor forever, not without a plan.

"I don't know," he admitted, his voice low. "It's... it's a different planet, really. The travel, the schedule, the constant performance. It's hard to reconcile that with... this." He gestured around the cozy room, then reached out to take her hand. "With you."

Harley squeezed his hand, her gaze steady. "I know it's not easy. Your life is... huge. Mine is small in comparison. But it's real, Sage. And I'm real."

"And I'm falling in love with your real, Harley," he said, the words a confession and a promise. "You've shown me a different way of living, a different way of creating. You've reminded me of the importance of the whisper." He paused, a flicker of determination in his eyes. "I don't want to lose that. I don't want to lose you."

"And I don't want to lose you either," she replied, her voice laced with vulnerability. "But we have to be honest. It won't be easy. There will be miles between us, and different demands on your time."

"We'll figure it out," Sage insisted, his voice firm with conviction. "Maybe... maybe I can find a way to incorporate more of this. More of the quiet. Maybe I can find a way to create music that speaks to both the roar and the whisper."

He imagined it—writing songs inspired by the stillness of Deadwood, by the authenticity he'd found here, and then sharing that with the world. It was a daunting prospect, a delicate balancing act, but the thought of it filled him with a renewed sense of purpose.

"It would have to be a partnership," Harley said, her gaze unwavering. "We'd both have to be willing to meet in the middle. To understand each other's worlds, even if we can't always inhabit them together."

"I'm willing to do whatever it takes," Sage vowed, his heart swelling with a love that was both exhilarating and terrifying.

Sage stood at the edge of something new—a life more complex yet richer than before. Unplugging from fame's noise had been a beginning, not an end. His new compositions carried a depth they'd lacked before, like the Dakota sky stretching endlessly above them.

Deadwood's rhythm, Harley's laughter, the slow unfurling of quiet days—all had bewitched him. He'd started to believe he could stay, leaving behind the roar of crowds and stage lights. In this harbor town, he could hear himself think and feel his heartbeat sync with something authentic. The peace was so complete that breaking it felt physically painful.

Then his cell rang. The chirp cut through the quiet, yanking him back to the life he'd fled. Harley read, curled up on the couch, brow furrowed, unaware. He reached for the phone with a knot in his stomach. His manager's name lit the screen, and Sage felt a chill. Mark never called without purpose—only deadlines, logistics, career.

"Hey, Mark," Sage said, keeping his voice as even as possible, a stark contrast to the sudden turbulence in his chest.

"Sage! Finally. Good, you picked up. I've been trying you on your usual burner, but nothing." Mark's voice was a rapid-fire delivery of news, laced with his usual, efficient urgency. "Listen, the tour bus is almost good to go. We're looking at a Tuesday turnaround. Means you need to be back in Denver by Monday night, latest. We're pushing the Chicago dates up to get back on track."

The words struck Sage like a physical blow. Tuesday turnaround. Denver by Monday. Chicago dates pushed up. It was a sudden, jarring return to the relentless momentum of his life. The quiet harbor he'd found seemed to shrink, its protective walls dissolving under the force of Mark's practicality. He felt a pang of regret so sharp it stole his breath. He looked at Harley, who had stopped reading and was now watching him, her expression a mixture of concern and understanding. She knew this was coming, of course. She'd always known. But knowing and experiencing were two vastly different things.

"Mark," Sage began, his voice tighter than he intended, "I... I'm not sure I can make it by Monday. Things are... a bit complicated here." He chose his words carefully, unwilling to articulate the full extent of what "here" meant to him now.

Mark, bless his efficient, business-minded heart, was not one for ambiguity. "Complicated? What's complicated, Sage? The bus is fixed. The crew's ready. We've got a schedule to keep. The fans are expecting you. You can't just... disappear for an extended vacation and expect everything to pause, my friend." There was no accusation in his tone, only a statement of irrefutable fact. Sage's career was a complex, self-sustaining entity, and it didn't do pauses.

"It's not a vacation, Mark. I've been... I've been working on new material. Finding inspiration." He tried to inject a hint of his artistic pursuit into the conversation, hoping it would soften the blow.

Mark's sigh was audible. "Inspiration is great, Sage, and we all love the new stuff, believe me. But inspiration doesn't pay the bills, and it certainly doesn't fill stadiums. We're talking about millions of dollars and a global brand here. I need you focused. Back in the saddle. The tour is a machine, and it needs its engine. And right now, you're the engine."

Sage closed his eyes for a brief moment, the weight of his responsibilities pressing down on him. The engine. He'd always been the engine, pushing, driving, creating the momentum. But here, in Deadwood, he'd begun to feel like something more than just an engine. He'd felt like a heart, beating with a different rhythm, a more resonant cadence. The thought of returning to the relentless hum of that machine, of becoming just the engine again, felt like a betrayal of the man he was discovering himself to be.

"I understand, Mark," Sage said, his voice now resigned. "I'll... I'll make arrangements. I'll be there."

"Good man," Mark boomed, a hint of relief in his voice. "Monday night. Denver. I'll have someone meet you at the airport. We'll debrief, get you settled. We'll be back on track before you know it. Just... try not to lose too much of that road weariness, all right? We need the full Sage experience."

Sage hung up the phone, the silence that followed feeling deafening. He looked at Harley, his heart heavy. The spell was broken. The gentle hum of Deadwood was now overlaid with the discordant clang of his impending departure. The future, which had seemed so bright and promising just moments before, now felt clouded with the familiar anxieties of his old life.

Harley's gaze was soft, her eyes reflecting in the dim light. She didn't need him to say the words. She could see it in the slump of his shoulders, the faraway look in his eyes. "Tour bus?" she asked, her voice barely a whisper.

Sage nodded, the lump in his throat making it difficult to speak. "Yeah. They're fixing it up. I have to be in Denver by Monday." He watched her closely, searching for any sign of disappointment, of anger, but found only a quiet acceptance that somehow made the ache in his chest even worse.

"I knew it wouldn't be forever," she said, her voice steady, though a hint of sadness laced her tone. "This quiet life... it's not the life you're built for, Sage. Not entirely."

"It feels like the life I want to be built for," he confessed, the words raw and honest. "Harley, you have no idea how much I've... how much I've come to fall for you." He reached out, his hand finding hers across the space between them. Her fingers interlaced with his, a silent confirmation of their connection, a fragile tether in the face of his impending departure.

"I know," she said softly, her thumb stroking the back of his hand. "And I've fallen for you too. These weeks with you... they've been... everything." She paused, her gaze meeting his, and for a moment, the vastness of his world and the intimacy of theirs seemed to converge. "But your music, Sage. It's a part of you. It's what you do. It's who you are."

"But is it all I am?" he countered, the question hanging in the air, heavy with unspoken longing. "Because I've spent so long being 'Sage the singer-songwriter' that I've almost forgotten how to be just... Sage. And I think I found him here. With you." He squeezed her hand, his gaze earnest. "I don't want to go back to being just the engine, Harley. I want to be more."

"And you are," she insisted gently. "You are more. You've just... rediscovered parts of yourself that the noise had drowned out. But the noise is still there, Sage. It's your life. It's your calling." She sighed, a small, almost imperceptible sound. "It's just... hard. Knowing that the time we have now is limited. That soon, the miles will be between us again. That the roar will come back between us."

Sage's mind raced. "I've been thinking about that," he said. "Leaving you feels impossible, but so does abandoning the person I'm becoming. What if I don't have to choose? What if I bring the whisper into the roar?"

He scanned the room—the stacked books, Harley's face with its quiet strength. This was his inspiration. He imagined writing in hotel rooms, being in Deadwood with Harley, channeling this authenticity into songs about connection rather than just fame's fleeting highs.

"It won't be easy," Harley said with a realism he both appreciated and dreaded. "Your world is demanding. Mine is different. We'll need intention. And honesty. Always honesty."

"I'm willing," Sage promised. He stood and walked over to her, kneeling beside the armchair. He took her hands in his, his gaze locked with hers. "This tour... it's a deadline, yes. It's a force pulling me back. But it's also an opportunity. An opportunity to prove that I can be both. That I can still create the music the world expects, but with a new depth, a new soul. A soul that was awakened here, with you." He paused, searching her face. "I want to try to write music that has both the roar and the whisper. I want to write about this, the small things that are taken for granted. I want to bring feeling to my words through you."

Harley's eyes softened, a faint smile gracing her lips. "That's a beautiful thought, Sage. A daunting one, but beautiful." She reached out, her fingers tracing the line of his jaw. "It will take work. A lot of work. From both of us. You'll be on the road, and I'll be here. We'll have to build new bridges across that distance."

"We will," Sage vowed, his voice filled with a renewed sense of purpose. The regret hadn't disappeared entirely, but it was now mingled with a flicker of determination. The looming deadline wasn't an end; it was a challenge. A test of his resolve, of their connection. He knew he couldn't abandon his career, not entirely. But he also knew he couldn't abandon the man he was becoming, the man Harley had helped him find. "This... this unplugging from the noise, it wasn't just about finding peace. It was about finding a new way to create. A more authentic way. And I'm not ready to go back to the old way, not entirely."

He stood, pulling her gently to her feet. He held her close, breathing in the scent of her hair, the comforting aroma of her home. The thought of leaving this embrace, of trading it for a sterile hotel room, was almost unbearable. But he knew he had to. He had to face the roar, but this time, he would carry the whisper with him, a silent, steady melody in his heart.

"So," he said, a hesitant smile playing on his lips, "Denver by Monday. And then... Chicago... and I will be back here. But the music I write on the road... it's going to be different. It's going to be for us, Harley. A bridge. A promise. A testament to the fact that even in the midst of the loudest crowds, the quietest whispers can still be heard."

He kissed her then, a kiss that spoke of both farewell and a commitment to return, a tender exchange that acknowledged the looming deadline but held fast to the enduring strength of their connection. The roar was calling, but the whisper, he now knew, was just as powerful, and far more enduring. He would carry it with him, a secret symphony playing beneath the noise.

The weight of the approaching departure settled over Sage like a shroud, a stark contrast to the light, airy feeling that had permeated his days in Deadwood. The phone call from Mark, once a distant hum of his former life, had become a blaring siren, shattering the fragile peace he'd cultivated with Harley. He looked at her now; her silhouetted form outlined against the dying embers of the fire, and a profound ache settled in his chest. This was the choice, wasn't it? The stark dichotomy between the roaring applause of a thousand adoring fans and the quiet, resonant beat of a single heart that truly saw him.

He'd spent years chasing a definition of success that was inextricably linked to sold-out stadiums, platinum records, and the deafening roar of adoration. It was a gilded cage, beautiful and impressive, but a cage nonetheless. Here, in the unassuming embrace of Harley's home, surrounded by the scent of pine and old books, he'd begun to question the very foundation of that pursuit. The melodies that had once flowed from a place of ambition and external validation now felt hollow compared to the raw, honest compositions that had emerged from his time here. They were born not of a need to impress, but of a deep, unarticulated longing for something real.

Harley, ever perceptive, had watched his internal struggle with a quiet understanding that both soothed and unnerved him. She didn't push, didn't demand explanations. She simply was, a steady presence that anchored him in a way no amount of critical acclaim ever had. He'd confessed his doubts, his burgeoning desire to redefine his own path, and she had met his vulnerability not with fear or doubt, but with a measured hope that mirrored his own nascent optimism.

He looked at Harley, his heart brimming with a love that felt both ancient and brand new. "You've given me so much more than just a place to hide from the noise, Harley. You've given me a new way to hear. A new way to be. And I won't let that go, and I won't let you go either. I can't."

Harley's smile widened, a genuine, radiant thing that chased away the last vestiges of his doubt. "Then you'll have to learn to play that new song, Sage. You'll have to find its rhythm on the road. And I'll be here, listening, cheering you on, waiting for you to come home and play it for me."

The promise in her words, the unwavering faith in her eyes, was the anchor he needed. The departure was inevitable; the roar was calling, but it no longer sounded like a threat. It sounded like an opportunity. An opportunity to prove that the quiet moments weren't a retreat from his life, but an essential part of it. An opportunity to weave the whispers of Deadwood into the grand symphony of his career, creating a melody that was richer, more resonant, and undeniably more authentic. He would carry his love for Harley with him, a reminder of the true cadence of his heart, all the way home so he could build the life he had promised her.

The End

Subscribe to A.L. Long's newsletter and get the inside scoop on new releases and upcoming events. https://bit.ly/3jo8VZo.

ABOUT A.L. LONG

Multi-award-winning author of the Book Excellence, Independent Press Award and NYC Big Book Award, A.L. Long is also the National Indie Excellence Award recipient.

Some would call me a little naughty, but I see myself writing spicy thoughts. Being a romance writer is something that I never imagined I would be doing. There is nothing more rewarding than to put your thoughts down in words and share them. I began writing in 2013 and have enjoyed every minute. When I first started writing, I wasn't sure what I would write. It didn't take me long to realize that romance would be my niche. I believe that every life deserves a little bit of romance; a little spice doesn't hurt either. When I am not writing, I enjoy the company of good friends and relaxing with a delicious glass of red wine.

Visit me at www.allongbooks.com for all of my new releases and book signing events.

Keep up with all A.L. Long's latest releases:

THE HOUSE ALWAYS WINS

A NOVELLA BY ANN SCHREIBER

PROLOGUE

The sun had felt absolutely glorious the day my life changed forever. I could remember it like it was yesterday. Hell, I could remember it like it was just five minutes ago.

I was stretched out on a soft plaid blanket, wearing the Lilly Pulitzer shift dress I had bought just for this trip. Mitch was lying next to me. He was on his side, propped up on his elbow. He kept grazing the exposed portion of my bare leg with his finger, his expression a bit suggestive, a bit drunk.

I had a glass of Chardonnay in my hand. In front of us sat a charcuterie tray spilling over with Brie, Camembert, Havarti, strawberries and grapes, and a small container of Spanish olives. They were the fancy ones with the pits still inside.

It was the last afternoon of our trip before flying home. Our "pre-moon," he had called it when he had surprised me with the plane tickets and boutique hotel reservation just a few weeks back. It was a chance to steal one more week together before the chaos of the wedding swallowed us whole. In weeks from now, I'd be Mrs. Mitchell Raines.

He'd even practiced the name out loud once, grinning as he said it. "Brooke Raines," he'd declared, as though the name had been meant for me and me alone.

Now, lying on that blanket beneath a sprawling oak, I'd laughed and told him to stop tempting fate. "You're going to jinx it," I'd teased, tossing a grape at him.

"Please," Mitch had said, catching it easily. "Nothing could jinx us."

I could still hear his voice. That gravelly, easy tone that had made me say yes after five years of dating and one long Minnesota winter spent wondering if he'd ever get around to a proposal. He finally had, on my thirtieth birthday, right after I'd finished a night shift at the medical center in International Falls. I'd come home exhausted to find candles, lasagna, and a tiny wooden jewelry box perched between two stemmed wine glasses and plates.

He'd built the ring box himself, using leftover walnut from a recent job at the shop. He'd never been one for grand gestures, so I had been swept away with the thought he had put into the proposal, the ring, the box, and the getaway.

That afternoon, the vineyard stretched wide and endless around us, vines curling in even rows under the soft hum of bees. A few other couples picnicked nearby, but it had felt like the world had drawn a circle around the two of us. It was like we were in our own world. Mitch and I. Me and Mitch.

I plucked an olive from the bowl and moved it toward his mouth. "Open up, big boy," I chided playfully.

He grinned, leaned forward, and let me feed it to him. He leaned forward to kiss me. I could taste the saltiness of the olive that was still in his mouth. I moaned subtly as his tongue swept over my lips. Then I pulled away, laughing, and thought: *This is it. This is happiness in its simplest form.*

Then he'd coughed.

At first, it was small. There wasn't much to it. It wasn't anything that had me alarmed in any way. I'd been about to make a joke about the olive going down the wrong hole, but then the sound of his cough changed. His eyes grew wide, and his hands reached up to his throat. Seconds later, he was starting to turn blue.

"Mitch?" I said, sitting up fast, wine sloshing over the blanket.

When he didn't answer, and his eyes simply grew wider, my instinct took over. I scrambled behind him, my heart hammering, wrapping my arms around his chest. I'd taught the Heimlich maneuver to other nurses, practiced it hundreds of times on training dummies. My hands were sure, and my movements were precise. I knew just what to do. Thrust in and up. Again, again.

"Mitch, come on. Come on," I'd begged. His body convulsed, once, twice. Nothing. The olive didn't seem to budge.

My mind screamed the steps, but my body had already betrayed me, muscles burning as I tried again, harder, desperate. His eyes rolled back into his head, and his arms fell to his sides.

We were no longer alone. Someone had shouted for help. Another voice said an ambulance was coming. I barely heard them.

I'd kept trying, my arms locked around him until strangers pulled me away, my dress scooting up too high, but I didn't care. I'd fought them, screaming Mitch's name, clawing to reach him again. The world had gone blurry. The sunlight was too bright, my breath too short.

But when the paramedics arrived, I already knew. His skin had taken on a pallor. It was the color of death. And when they took his pulse and confirmed he was gone, I simply nodded my head. Someone had covered him with a blanket. The medical examiner came an hour later. His body was loaded into the back of an ambulance and taken away.

Two days later, I boarded a plane home to Minnesota.

Mitch had splurged on first-class tickets for the trip. But now, the seat beside me remained empty, still ticketed in his name. Somewhere below, in the storage hold, Mitch was enclosed in a polished oak casket. I didn't cry until we touched down.

I knew that Mitch choking on an olive wasn't my fault. But it was I who had fed him the olive that had caused his death. I had killed the love of my life. Even though I had replayed every movement in my head in slow motion, it didn't matter. Mitch was dead. And I was alone.

I spent the days after returning home with Mitch's mom and dad, planning his funeral. My parents took on the process of canceling all of the wedding plans. It was a terrible juxtaposition of things, telling people there would be no wedding, but there would be a funeral instead.

A week later, I returned to work, even though my boss told me I would take more time. But more time for what? When someone dies, there's not much more to do, is there? I felt like I was simply going through the motions. My colleagues didn't know what to say. So they chose silence, and that spoke to me more than their sympathy cards or flowers ever did.

I started skipping my lunch breaks. I took on extra shifts to stay busy. Yet it wasn't enough.

At home, alone in our queen-sized bed, the same memory always found me: the way the sunlight had hit the wineglass, scattering speckles of gold across his face. I remembered the way he'd laughed when I'd told him he'd eaten all the brie.

I kept my engagement ring in a small jewelry box on our dresser. I couldn't bring myself to wear it, but I couldn't bear to put it away either. And his family hadn't asked for its return. Mitch's parents and sister, and my own parents and two brothers, had all tried to support me, asking what they could do. But how do you respond when the only thing you want is for them to give you your fiancé back? As the weeks went by, they all stepped back, getting back to their own lives.

Mitch and I were still relatively young. Well, I was still relatively young. Mitch would never celebrate another birthday. In any case, our parents are still young, not yet retired. They had their own careers to go back to. And before I knew it, everyone was back doing what they did, except me.

Over the next two years, I moved through life like a ghost. Polite, efficient, invisible. And at one point, I realized I couldn't take it anymore. Almost two years to the date that Mitch left me forever, I walked into my boss's office, a flyer in my hand. It was for a traveling nurse position. "I want to do this," I said to Rebecca. She looked at the flyer, then at me. There was that look of pity. It was the only look I seemed to get from people these days.

But after a moment, she nodded her head. "You're one of the best we have, Brooke. Are you sure?"

"I just..." She paused, searching for the right phrase. "I need to be somewhere else for a while."

When the email came a week later, confirming my first assignment at Lead-Deadwood Regional Hospital for three months for emergency department coverage, I felt something I hadn't felt in years. It wasn't joy. And it wasn't excitement. Not really. If anything, it was relief. As though the old song was calling to me, it was the chance to go somewhere where nobody knew my name.

And so, I cleared out the refrigerator and cupboards of food. I covered the furniture with white sheets. I turned off the water to prevent any leaks. And I locked up my house. Shortly after, I made the five-hour drive from International Falls to the airport in Minneapolis.

As the plane taxied toward takeoff, I looked out the window at the fading skyline of the Twin Cities and thought about the one thing Mitch used to say whenever we played poker with our group of friends.

"Doesn't matter how many times you fold, babe," he'd tease, tossing chips into the pot. "Sooner or later, everyone gets dealt a good hand." And maybe Deadwood, South Dakota, was the good hand that I needed.

1

It was a short flight to Rapid City, South Dakota, barely enough time for a snack and a few pages of reading, but I didn't mind. I probably could have made the drive, but my car was one that Mitch and I had bought together. Every time I sat behind the wheel, I could see the day it had been delivered to the local dealer. The memory was too sharp, too heavy. So before leaving Minnesota, I'd sold it.

The dealership in the Cities paid me cash, which padded my pocketbook more than I'd expected. Not that I needed the money. Unbeknownst to me, Mitch had updated the life insurance policy through his job, naming me the sole beneficiary. The payout, one and a half times his annual salary, wasn't a fortune, but it had covered his funeral expenses and left enough to tuck away for a rainy day.

That rainy day fund had come in handy for the tiny rental house I'd found in Deadwood. It also meant I could pay cash for the used SUV I'd already picked out online from a local dealer. The salesman was expecting me tomorrow to finalize the paperwork.

Though the flight was short, I had enough time to thumb through a few books I'd ordered from the bookstore back home in International Falls. I'd never been to South Dakota before. The idea of turning over a new leaf in a place with that kind of history felt right.

Just over an hour later, the plane touched down in Rapid City. I made my way through the small airport to baggage claim, where I retrieved my single suitcase. The rest of my belongings, including boxes of household items and clothes, would be delivered to my new house later in the week.

After grabbing my suitcase off the carousel, I found the rental car desk and signed the paperwork for a compact sedan that looked like it had seen its share of tourists.

Rapid City Regional wasn't large, not compared to MSP or the other airports I'd been through. Within forty-five minutes of landing, I was on the highway, headed toward the Black Hills. Another forty-five minutes later, I turned down the narrow gravel driveway of the small house on Williams Street that would be home for the next three months.

The key was exactly where the real estate agent said it would be, tucked beneath a ceramic planter on the back deck. The house itself was tidy and fully furnished, except for the bedroom. My new bedroom set was scheduled for delivery later in the week. Making arrangements to ship boxes, buy furniture, and shop for a car online had been oddly therapeutic. It gave me something to focus on besides the silence of my empty house back home.

Inside, the place smelled faintly of lemon cleaner and old pine floors. I spent the next couple of hours wandering from room to room, opening cupboards and drawers, unpacking what I could. By the time I hung the last few clothes in the closet, evening shadows were starting to stretch across the deck, and my stomach reminded me I hadn't eaten since morning, and the chips I had devoured on the plane.

I drove into town, following the narrow, winding roads that cut through Deadwood's historic district. It was clear why tourists loved it. The old brick buildings with ornate facades, wooden boardwalks, and saloon signs glowed against the twilight. I found a small grocery store tucked between a coffee shop and an antique store.

Despite it being peak tourist season, I still caught a few curious looks from locals as I filled my cart with staples. Eggs, milk, cheese, bread, salad fixings, a case of Diet Coke, and some lunch meats from the deli. Nothing fancy. I wasn't interested in cooking elaborate meals for one. Besides, when I was working, the hospital cafeteria would be good enough. I'd long gotten over the stigma of "hospital food."

After paying for my groceries, I loaded them into the trunk and drove back to the house. The sky was dark by the time I pulled in. I made a quick sandwich, turned on the TV for background noise, and grabbed one of the books from my bag.

As I flipped through the pages, I stopped on an old photo of Deadwood's main street. Men in wide-brimmed hats, women in long skirts, the dirt road bustling with wagons and horses. The caption read: *Rebuilt after the fire of 1879.*

Rebuilt. The word lingered in my mind.

I took another bite of my sandwich and leaned back in the chair. Maybe that was why I'd come here. Not to start over, exactly, but to rebuild. Brick by brick. Theoretically speaking, of course.

I didn't report to the hospital until the day after tomorrow, which meant I had tomorrow free to explore. To get my bearings. To see what kind of town Deadwood really was.

I closed the book, stacked my dishes in the sink, realizing just now that the house did not have a dishwasher. I sighed and glanced out the window. The mountains were barely visible now, just faint silhouettes against a deepening sky. Somewhere out there, a new chapter was waiting for me. And for the first time in a long time, I was ready to see where it led.

2

The sun woke me before my alarm did. It cut straight through the half-drawn blinds, a golden line across the couch where I'd spent the night. Without a bed yet, the couch had been my only option. My back protested immediately when I sat up, stiff and sore from the lumpy cushions.

I stretched, arms overhead, and muttered something unladylike before padding into the kitchen. The silence was thick. No traffic, no voices, not even birds yet. I opened the cupboard, spotted the empty coffee maker, and realized what I'd forgotten.

"Damn it," I said aloud. No coffee pods. Of course.

Defeated, I grabbed a Diet Coke from the fridge, cracked it open, and took a long drink. The carbonation burned my throat in the best way. Caffeine was caffeine, after all.

Breakfast came next. I cracked two eggs into the frying pan. I nearly burned them, just the way I liked them. A sprinkle of shredded cheese over the top, a splash of milk for fluff. When they were done, I slid them onto a plate and sat at the kitchen table, planning out my day while I ate.

The night before, I'd jotted down a few ideas after flipping through the Deadwood history books. I'd start with a guided walking tour using an app I'd downloaded. It promised to keep me away from the heavy tourist crowds and share stories about Calamity Jane, old saloons, and even something called Deadwood's Chinatown. Who knew? Deadwood once had a Chinatown.

Next, I'd stop by the Historic Adams House, built in 1892 by pioneers

Harris and Anna Franklin. I'd read that it was preserved just as they left it. Furniture, décor, even the dishes still set on the dining table, like the family might walk back in any minute.

From there, I wanted to see the Broken Boot Gold Mine and try my hand at panning for gold. For dinner, I'd already made up my mind. The Silver Spur Casino was on my list. Maybe I'd drop a few quarters into a slot machine while I was there. Do slot machines even take quarters anymore? I had no idea. I'd never been to a casino.

But first? I needed a shower. And actual coffee.

After freshening up, I drove into town and stopped at the same coffee shop I'd seen next to the grocery store the night before. It was early, but the place was already busy serving locals. I found myself surrounded by construction workers in reflective vests, women in scrubs, and a few retirees reading the morning paper. I ordered a large latte and a blueberry muffin, enjoying the smell of roasted beans and warm pastry before heading out.

Following the walking tour app's directions, I parked near the spot once known as Deadwood's Chinatown. The narration in my earbuds guided me through narrow streets, pointing out historic plaques and preserved foundations. The app explained that during the late 1800s, Chinese immigrants had come to work in the mines and laundries, carving out a small but prosperous community before much of it was lost to fire and time.

From there, the route wound past old saloons with names like The Gem and Number Ten, where Wild Bill Hickok had been shot in the back of the head while holding what would later be called the *dead man's hand*: aces and eights.

The tour ended at the Wild Bill statue, carved by Korczak Ziolkowski, the same artist who'd begun work on the Crazy Horse Memorial. Curious, I looked it up on my phone. It was over an hour away. Maybe another day, I told myself.

I walked over to the Adams Museum next and spent the next hour wandering its exhibits. I browsed the Victorian furniture, sepia photographs, gold nuggets behind glass, and artifacts from the devastating fire. Deadwood had burned, rebuilt, and burned again. And yet here it stood, restored and resilient. Once again, the thought came to mind that maybe that was what I wanted, too. To rebuild.

When my stomach growled, I decided it was time for lunch. I found a small café a few blocks away and realized, as I walked, that my rental house was only a few minutes from downtown. The whole area was smaller than I'd pictured, charming and self-contained.

As I passed storefronts, I counted at least six casinos, each one tucked between souvenir shops and restaurants. The Silver Spur Casino caught my eye again, this time because of the dinner special posted in the window: *Steak and Potatoes – $18.99*. That sounded perfect.

After lunch, I drove out to the Broken Boot Gold Mine, about five minutes outside of town. It wasn't far, but far enough that I didn't want to walk. The road curved around the hillside, offering glimpses of the Black Hills through the trees.

The mine tour was short and kitschy, but I didn't mind. I panned for gold alongside a few families with kids, swirling the pan in the cool water until I spotted a few glittering flecks at the bottom. "Gold dust," the guide said cheerfully. "Worth about five cents."

I laughed, pocketed the tiny vial they gave me, and decided that was enough mining for one lifetime. It was for kids, really. Still, I could check it off my list, not that it had ever been on my list to begin with.

From there, I drove to Spearfish for my 4 p.m. meeting at the car dealership. The process was painless. Ninety minutes later, I slid behind the wheel of my new-to-me 2020 Cadillac XT4, inhaling that faint leather scent that never quite goes away.

It felt good. Different, of course, but good to have something that was wholly mine again.

By the time I got back to Deadwood, the sun was dipping low behind the hills, washing the town in amber light. My stomach growled again, reminding me I hadn't eaten since lunch. The steak dinner at the Silver Spur was calling my name.

As I parked and turned off the ignition, I sat for a moment, taking in the neon glow of the casino sign. The air smelled faintly of pine and fried food.

I thought of Mitch then. How he would have teased me for spending the day on a "history binge," as he used to call it. How he'd reach for my hand in a crowd, his thumb tracing lazy circles on my skin. How we'd snuggle under a blanket on nights like this, legs tangled, his breath warm against my neck.

I missed those small, ordinary intimacies. The way a man's touch could quiet the noise in my mind. It had been so long since I'd felt that kind of closeness. Two years. Too long.

I took a deep breath and climbed out of the car, smoothing the wrinkles from my shirt. "Okay, Brooke," I whispered to myself. "New town. New start."

The lights from the Silver Spur glowed brighter as I stepped inside.

Tomorrow, I'd meet my new colleagues at the hospital. But tonight, I'd let myself enjoy a meal, maybe a drink, and a little company.

3

I'd always wanted to visit a casino, and Minnesota had them, but they were never exactly close by. Plus, it had never been something Mitch was interested in. Sure, he liked to gamble, but his idea of gambling was a poker game with our friends around the kitchen table.

It was a small group of friends, too. Most of them had moved away years ago after high school, chasing bigger and better things in cities like St. Paul, Denver, New York, and Los Angeles. One of our friends had even relocated to Paris and sent the cutest postcards every Christmas.

But Mitch and I had always been hometown people. I went to nursing school in Bemidji and moved back to International Falls after graduation. Mitch entered an apprenticeship program right after high school. We hadn't been high-school sweethearts; he was two years older than me, which struck me now because he had died at the same age I was today. That was a bit morbid, I thought to myself.

Anyway, we'd known *of* each other, but didn't really get to know each other until about seven years ago. And, as is typical of small towns, we'd been set up by family members. My older brother and Mitch's older sister had dated for a while. It hadn't worked out for them, but somehow, it had worked out for us, until it didn't. Obviously.

I tried to keep these thoughts out of my head as I walked through the sea of poker tables at the center of the casino. Mitch's poker setup at home had been a fold-out contraption he'd spread across the kitchen table. These tables, though, were the real deal. Green felt, shiny chips, and dealers in crisp shirts.

A few tables caught my attention that I didn't recognize. One had a giant spinning wheel in front, and I assumed it was a roulette table. That was about the extent of my limited gambling knowledge.

Of course, I knew how to work a slot machine. I'd played those on phone apps off and on for years, but never with real money. I walked over to one and was surprised to see that coins weren't even required anymore. I was reaching into my purse for a twenty-dollar bill when I noticed that all the players around me had little plastic cards inserted into their machines.

I turned to the elderly woman next to me. "Excuse me, what's that card for?"

"Oh, that's the *Players Club card,*" she said, giving me a look that made it clear I was absolutely clueless. I was. "You can get one over at Guest Services." I must have looked confused because she pointed behind me to a large sign that said exactly that.

"Thank you," I said, and made my way to the counter.

There were two people ahead of me, and then it was my turn. "I'm curious about the Players Club card," I told the man behind the plexiglass.

He was dressed in what I assumed was standard casino attire. Black vest, white shirt, a little too much hair gel. He handed me a pen and a small form. I filled out my information, dug out my Minnesota driver's license, and slid it through the cutout.

Five minutes later, I had my very own card. *Brooke Cassidy,* it read in bold print. Seeing my maiden name on yet another document hit me in the gut. By now, it would have been *Brooke Raines.* But now, it would never be.

I worked my way back to the quarter slots I'd been eyeing earlier. It was a Triple 7 machine. I slipped in a twenty and pressed the button, only to realize too late that the bet cost five dollars. I won nothing.

"What?" I muttered, leaning closer to check the screen. That's when I noticed I could change the betting amount.

The woman from earlier was still at her machine. She glanced over, rolled her eyes in dramatic exasperation, and said, "Never played slots before?"

"Never even been in a casino before," I admitted.

Her expression softened. She stood and pointed to a section of machines about twenty feet away. "Those are better for beginners. Max bet is $1.25, and you've got higher odds of winning."

I thanked her, cashed out my remaining fifteen dollars, printed on a slip that looked like a receipt, not cash, and removed my card. Then I walked over to the machines she'd pointed out. I inserted my Players Club card and fed in the voucher for fifteen bucks.

I pressed the button for *Max Bet* and was relieved to see it only cost $1.25 this time. Nothing.

Pressed again. Nothing.

"Third time's the charm," I muttered, hitting the button one more time. Three little farmers holding pitchforks appeared in a perfect row across the center. Lights flashed. Music blared. The machine erupted in a flurry of digital confetti, and a bright "BIG WIN!" banner filled the screen.

Two hundred dollars. I'd just won two hundred dollars.

Not wanting to test my luck, I cashed out immediately. At the cashier window, a young man scanned my ticket and handed me $211.15 in crisp bills and shiny coins. "Congratulations," he said with a smile.

"Thanks," I replied, tucking the money into my wallet and heading toward the restaurant.

By now, I was starving. I followed the scent of grilled meat until I reached the Silver Spur Restaurant, attached to the casino's main floor. A man who looked like the host was speaking with another man wearing a black suit over a black T-shirt.

The host was good-looking, sure, but my eyes kept drifting to the man in the suit. He was everything Mitch wasn't, except for the height. Mitch had been six feet even, but this man was easily six-two, maybe six-three. Where Mitch's hair had been light blond, his was a deep, satiny black. Mitch had worn a goatee; this man was clean-shaven. Mitch had been lean and toned, but this guy filled out his suit in a way that left little doubt he spent time in the gym.

After a few seconds, he met my gaze. He didn't bother to hide the way his eyes traveled over me, my turquoise sundress, my light sweater, lingering just a bit too long on my chest. I felt self-conscious but also...aware. Mitch used to tell me I had "perfect handfuls." I blushed, both at the memory and at the way this stranger was looking at me.

He leaned in to whisper something to the host, who nodded. The man in the suit turned back to me. "Miss, are you waiting on another?"

"No, just me," I said. His eyebrows lifted, surprised.

"Very well then," he said. "Desmond, will you please seat our guest?"

Desmond, the host, nodded, grabbed a menu, and gestured for me to follow. The man in the suit went back to the computer screen, though I could still feel his gaze on me as I walked away.

Once seated, I ordered a cosmopolitan because it sounded fancy. When it came time to order dinner, I went with the special. The steak and potatoes I'd seen advertised earlier. The waitress smiled knowingly and jotted it down.

When the food arrived, I realized I was hungrier than I'd thought. The steak looked perfect, and the baked potato steamed invitingly. As I buttered it, I noticed the older woman from the slot machines walk by with an older man who was clearly her husband, simple gold bands glinting on their left hands.

The steak was delicious. I'd ordered it medium-well, and the waitress had raised an eyebrow, as if silently judging me, but I didn't care. I wasn't interested in pink meat. Not that I'd ever tried it that way.

While I ate, I pulled my Deadwood history book from my purse and flipped to a chapter on gambling in the Old West. Apparently, by the 1870s, Deadwood had been filled with saloons and card games, some legal, some not. Gold miners had lost fortunes overnight, and shootouts weren't uncommon when luck turned sour.

I smiled at the irony. Here I was, sitting in a modern-day version of the same thing, eating steak in a room where people still tested their luck.

When I finished, I reached into my purse for cash. Two twenties. The meal had been wonderful, and the place was upscale enough to warrant a decent tip. I was just scooting out of my chair when a commotion behind me made me freeze.

A familiar voice gasped, followed by frantic coughing. I turned.

The woman from the slot machine.

"Oh my God," I whispered. "This cannot be happening."

She was choking. The host was already beside her, slapping her on the back. He was doing it wrong. Completely wrong.

"Crap on a cracker," I muttered under my breath, hurrying over.

"Move," I said firmly, pushing the host aside. He stepped back, startled. My mind went instantly into clinical mode. I wrapped my arms around the woman's chest and pulled hard, up and in. Nothing. Again.

The second thrust did it. A piece of chewed steak shot out of her mouth and landed squarely on the table.

The woman sagged with relief, coughing and wiping her mouth. Her husband clutched her arm, eyes wide. Around us, people who had stood up to watch began to relax, murmuring their own relief.

"Thank you," she managed, voice raspy. I grabbed a napkin from the table and handed it to her.

"Are you okay?" I asked, even though I could already tell she was breathing fine.

"Yes, it just went down the wrong hole, is all," she said weakly, dabbing her mouth. Then she smiled. "Thank you. And I hope those $1.25 machines were good to you."

I couldn't help but laugh. "They were, thank you."

Satisfied she could sip water without trouble, I turned to leave, only to collide hard with something solid. Someone solid.

I looked up. The man in the black suit. His hands caught my shoulders before I stumbled. Up close, I could see a faint shadow of stubble along his jaw, smell the clean scent of soap and something faintly woody.

For a heartbeat, neither of us spoke. Then his mouth curved into a slow, knowing smile. And just like that, I had the distinct feeling my luck in Deadwood, rather in life, was about to change.

4

My heart skipped a beat at the solidity of him. Up close, literally pressed against him, he was even more handsome than I'd noticed at the host stand. And solid. His chest felt like a wall, his arms firm. Those biceps had to be bigger than my thighs, not that that was saying much. I'd always been told I had chicken legs. Curvy with chicken legs, that was me. A size 4 on a good day, a 6 around Christmas when there were too many homemade caramels and cookies to resist.

But next to this man? I felt small. Tiny. Almost delicate.

"Miss, please allow me to introduce myself," he said, stepping back only when he was sure I had my balance again. His voice was smooth, with the faintest rasp, like whiskey after dark. His gaze flicked down, and I realized with horror that the neckline of my sundress had slipped in our collision.

Of course it had.

"My name is Dane Walker," he continued, meeting my eyes again. "I'm the owner of the Silver Spur Casino."

My face flushed as I adjusted the fabric back into place. "Nice to meet you," I said quickly, extending my hand.

His mouth curved into a faint smile as he took it. His handshake was firm but careful, confident without crushing. I'd always hated those over-compensating squeezes some men used to prove they were powerful. Dane clearly didn't need to prove anything. Or he was trained to know better.

"I have to thank you for what you did for our guest," he said. "She's a Deadwood native, one of our regulars."

"Oh, her?" I began. "She actually helped me earlier. She taught me how to use the slot machines. I've never been in a casino before, so ..." I stopped myself, realizing I was rambling. "Anyway, I was happy to help."

He studied me, the corner of his mouth lifting as though he found my nervous chatter amusing. "You knew exactly what you were doing. My staff is trained in the Heimlich, but clearly Desmond may need a refresher course."

"He reacted naturally," I said. "In a stressful situation, most people panic first and think later."

That seemed to surprise him. His eyes narrowed slightly, curious.

"I'm a nurse," I added, with a shrug.

Understanding dawned. "Ah. That explains it." His voice softened, the hint of admiration unmistakable. "Are you visiting? Or—" He glanced at the empty seat behind me. "Dining alone seems an odd choice for a tourist."

"I'm not visiting," I said. "I just moved here. Yesterday, actually."

His brows rose. "Moved here? To Deadwood?"

"Yes," I said, a small laugh slipping out at his disbelief. "I'm here on a short-term assignment. I'm covering for the charge nurse at Lead-Deadwood Regional Hospital. She's going on maternity leave later this week."

"Short-term," he repeated, testing the words as though he didn't like the sound of them.

"Three months," I clarified. "Maybe longer if they need me."

Something unreadable flickered in his eyes before he nodded. "Well, Deadwood is lucky to have you, even for a short while."

He turned briefly toward the dining area, where Desmond was still hovering near the woman who had choked. "If you'll excuse me," he said, "I should check on our guest. You've already done the hard part."

"Of course," I said, brushing imaginary crumbs from my dress. "It's late anyway. First day on the job tomorrow and all that."

He hesitated, eyes locking on mine again. "Good luck to you, Ms.—"

"Cassidy," I supplied. "Brooke Cassidy."

He repeated my name, slowly, as though tasting it. "Ms. Cassidy. Thank you again."

And just like that, he was gone, moving toward the other end of the restaurant, the black fabric of his suit jacket stretching across broad shoulders as he walked. I should have looked away, but I didn't.

I stood there for a moment, my pulse still hammering in my throat. Around me, the restaurant buzzed with quiet chatter again, forks clinking, glasses refilling, the clatter of normal life resuming after chaos. But I couldn't shake the heaviness in my chest.

I'd saved a woman's life.

The thought should have made me proud. Grateful, even. Instead, it made my stomach twist. Because for all my training and experience, for all the times I'd saved strangers in emergency rooms and trauma bays, I hadn't been able to save Mitch.

He'd choked, too.

My mind flashed back. His face blue, my arms locked around him, the helpless sound that came from deep in my chest when I realized he wasn't going to breathe again. It was the same motion tonight. The same panic in the air. The same desperate rhythm of thrust and pray. But this time, it had worked.

Why now? Why her? Why not then?

I blinked hard, forcing the tears back. The dining room suddenly felt too bright, too crowded, too alive.

I sank into the nearest empty chair, exhaling shakily. My palms still tingled, the adrenaline refusing to fade. It was strange how quickly old instincts took over. I hadn't thought. I hadn't even hesitated. My body just *knew*.

And then there was Dane.

The way he'd looked at me, not just with gratitude or curiosity, but with something deeper, something that made me want to both hide and step closer. It had been years since a man's touch had sent a rush of heat to my skin, but one accidental collision with him had done just that. I couldn't remember the last time I'd reacted to anyone like that.

When Mitch died, I'd buried every part of myself that wanted to be touched, wanted to be seen. Grief had left no room for anything physical. But now, here I was in a casino in South Dakota, heart racing because a stranger had smiled at me. A stranger who owned the place, no less.

I laughed softly to myself, shaking my head. "Get a grip, Brooke," I whispered.

But when I finally stood to leave, I couldn't help glancing toward the far end of the restaurant. Dane was talking with Desmond and the older couple, his posture relaxed but commanding. The woman who had choked gave him a grateful smile, and he nodded before turning his gaze straight back to me.

Our eyes met again. He smiled, small but knowing.

I smiled back, then turned and headed for the exit before I did something stupid, like linger.

Outside, the night air was crisp against my flushed skin. The lights from the casino marquee blinked overhead, reflecting off the hood of my car. I drew in a deep breath, letting it out slowly.

Deadwood had been meant as a temporary stop, a place to work, to rest, to reset my life. Yet somehow, within forty-eight hours, it was already stirring something inside me I hadn't felt in years.

Hope. Attraction. Maybe even a flicker of something deliciously sensual, something I thought I'd buried with Mitch.

I slid into my car and started the engine. The steering wheel felt cool beneath my palms. In the rearview mirror, I could still see the casino lights, flashing in rhythmic pulses of red and gold.

Somewhere behind those walls was Dane Walker. Handsome, confident, mysterious, Dane Walker.

I wasn't sure whether meeting him had been luck or trouble. Maybe both. But for now, I needed to put him out of my mind. I have a big day tomorrow. The first day of my future.

5

The next morning came early.

I woke before sunrise, my stomach tied in anxious knots that only a first day in a new hospital could bring. The house was quiet except for the sound of the refrigerator and the faint chirp of morning birds outside. After a quick shower and a breakfast bar, I slipped into a pair of navy-blue scrubs and a lightweight jacket, double-checking the hospital's address in my phone before heading out.

By seven-thirty, I was in the staff parking lot of Lead-Deadwood Regional Hospital, clutching a to-go coffee. I had taken a liking to that little coffee shop on Main Street. The hospital was modest, far smaller than what I was used to, even in International Falls, but the building looked well-maintained, modern, and surprisingly busy for a weekday morning.

Inside, the air smelled of disinfectant, as most medical buildings do. I was glad, however, that I did not notice a lingering smell of urine, which also seems to creep into hospitals, despite the best efforts of the cleaning crews. I checked in with the front desk, who directed me toward the nurses' station where I'd be meeting Amber, the charge nurse I'd be replacing.

Amber was impossible to miss. Heavily pregnant, she moved down the hall in a determined waddle, one hand bracing her lower back while the other balanced an electronic tablet. Despite her obvious discomfort, she was cheerful and full of energy.

"Brooke!" she said as soon as she saw me. "Thank goodness you're here. I'm not sure how much longer I'll be walking upright, so I'm thrilled to have someone ready to step in."

Her smile was genuine, and I liked her immediately. She began introducing me to the rest of the team as we made our way through the ward. I said hello to the nurses, a couple of techs, and several physicians who were in and out of rooms. Everyone seemed friendly enough, though it was clear the hospital ran at a brisk pace.

"And this," Amber said, motioning to a tall man at the nurses' station, "is Dr. Ford Adams, our hospitalist. He's one of the best. Just don't let him know that."

Dr. Adams turned toward us with a smile that didn't quite reach his eyes. His white coat was immaculate, and his ID badge hung perfectly straight from the pocket. His gaze swept over me quickly, taking in my blonde hair, blue eyes, and everything in between. The heat of his stare made my skin prickle.

There was something about him. Something faintly familiar that I couldn't place. A tilt of his head, maybe, or the sharpness in his eyes. I doubted we'd ever crossed paths before, yet for a moment, I felt as though I should know him.

"Welcome to Deadwood, Ms. Cassidy," he said smoothly. "We don't get many new faces around here. Especially not ones from Minnesota, despite the proximity."

I shifted my weight, uncomfortable under his gaze. I couldn't quite place his expression, and I was pretty sure I didn't like it. "Thank you. I'm looking forward to working with the team."

"Likewise," he said, his smile tightening a fraction before turning back to the electronic chart that he had been studying.

Amber nudged me gently. "He's harmless," she whispered. "Mostly."

I wasn't so sure.

By mid-afternoon, I'd fallen into the familiar rhythm of patient care. Updating charts, checking meds, and working on discharge paperwork for a handful of patients eager to get home. My feet ached, but it was a good ache. It was the kind that reminded me I was back in my element.

I was standing at the counter, reviewing a file, when I heard a low, unmistakable voice behind me.

"Ms. Cassidy."

I turned, startled. Dane Walker stood just inside the double doors of the emergency department, looking wildly out of place among the scrubs and stethoscopes.

He wore jeans, a button-down shirt rolled to his elbows, the fabric pulled tight across his shoulders, and yes, cowboy boots. His dark hair was slightly tousled, as if he'd run his hands through it a few times. I blinked, trying to make sense of it.

"What are you doing here?" I asked before I could stop myself.

He smiled, a slow, confident curve of his lips that sent a flicker of heat up my neck. "Checking in on someone."

Before I could respond, I noticed Dr. Adams approaching from down the hall. His jaw clenched when he saw Dane.

"Hello, Dane," Ford said, his tone polite but cold. "Are you in need of medical treatment? I'm sure one of our nurses can assist you."

It wasn't what he said. It was how he said it. The air between them crackled with tension.

Dane's gaze flicked to him, then back to me. I could practically feel the standoff forming. But why? What was the history between these two?

"Dr. Adams," I said quickly, stepping forward, "I can help Mr. Walker with whatever he needs."

"You know each other?" Ford asked, frowning.

"We met at my restaurant last evening," Dane said before I could answer, his tone oddly formal. "Ms. Cassidy saved one of our guests from choking. I just came to thank her again."

Ford's frown deepened. "Ah. Of course." He glanced at me, something sour in his expression. "Well then, Ms. Cassidy, when you're done playing hero, I'll need those discharge forms prepared."

"Of course, Doctor," I said evenly.

Dane's jaw tightened, but he didn't rise to the bait. I gave him a small nod toward the nurses' station, guiding him away before the tension could escalate.

Once we were out of earshot, I crossed my arms. "All right," I said. "How did you even get back here? You need a badge to get through those doors."

He grinned, clearly amused. "The Silver Spur contributes a fair amount to the hospital's annual fund. I suppose that comes with... certain privileges."

"I see," I said, arching an eyebrow. "So you really came all the way here just to thank me again?"

"Yes, well," he began, hesitating.

I tilted my head, waiting.

"I wanted to see you," he said simply. "To thank you in person, of course, but also to ask if you might allow me to take you to dinner tonight."

My eyebrows shot up. "Dinner? With you?"

"Unless you're otherwise engaged," he said, his tone teasing but his eyes sincere.

"I—well, I have patients to discharge. And a shift that ends at seven," I said, flustered.

"Perfect," he said without missing a beat. "I'll pick you up then."

"Mr. Walker—"

"Dane," he corrected, that lopsided grin returning. "Call me Dane."

"Dane," I said, lowering my voice. "I don't usually mix work and..."

"Dinner?" he offered.

"Exactly."

"Well, you're not working *then,* are you? And, we don't work together," he said, his gaze holding mine with quiet challenge. "And besides, I'd like to get to know you better, Brooke. You said yourself. You're only in Deadwood for a short time. No reason to wait."

I exhaled, torn between common sense and curiosity. "All right," I said finally. "Dinner."

His smile widened. "I'll pick you up at half past seven. At your house."

And just like that, he turned and walked out, leaving me standing in the middle of the emergency ward with my heart pounding like I'd just sprinted a marathon.

By the time 7:30 rolled around, I'd convinced myself at least three times that agreeing to dinner was a mistake. But curiosity, and maybe a flicker of something stronger, won out.

Dane picked me up outside the house, and as I was walking out to his car, a fancy, shiny BMW, I realized I had never given him my address. Shaking it off, I figured it was probably not difficult for a wealthy business owner in a small town to figure out which house the newcomer had rented.

Instead of taking me somewhere fancy, he drove us to a saloon-style restaurant just off Main Street. The place looked like it had been pulled straight from a western movie with wooden swinging doors, tin ceilings, antique photographs on the walls, and servers dressed in old-timey outfits.

Inside, the scent of grilled meat and whiskey hung in the air. A live band played soft country rock in the corner, and the chatter of locals filled the space.

"This is Deadwood," Dane said as he pulled out my chair. "Loud, a little ridiculous, and proud of it."

I laughed, relaxing for the first time all day. "It's perfect."

Dinner was surprisingly easy. We talked about where we'd grown up, he in Rapid City with his mother and half-brother. His father had passed away when he was young. I shared how I had grown up in Walker, MN, and had relocated with my family to International Falls when my father had received a job opportunity working the United States-Canadian border. I'd lived there ever since, aside from my time away at college.

We went on to discuss our favorite small-town quirks and the kind of people who ended up in a place like this. He told me stories about the Silver Spur and the challenges of running a casino in a historic district.

At one point, though, my curiosity got the better of me. "So," I said, setting down my fork, "what's the deal between you and Dr. Adams?"

He paused, a flicker of annoyance crossing his face. "That's a story best left for another day."

I was surprised by his response, but chose to let it go.

He leaned back in his chair. "I'd rather not spoil a good meal." There was something in his tone, a warning, maybe, but it only intrigued me more.

The rest of dinner flowed easily, full of laughter, teasing, and a few lingering glances that said more than either of us dared to put into words. When the check arrived, Dane slipped his card to the server before I even had a chance to reach for my purse.

"Don't even think about it," he said when I started to protest. "You saved one of my regulars. Dinner's the least I can do."

Outside, his shiny black BMW gleamed under the saloon's neon sign, its polished surface reflecting the gold and red lights of Deadwood's nightlife. He opened the passenger door for me with an old-fashioned courtesy that caught me off guard.

The short drive back to my house was quiet, but not awkward. Every so often, I caught him looking at me out of the corner of his eye. When he pulled into the narrow driveway, he turned off the ignition but didn't move right away. The soft instrumental track still playing through the car speakers seemed to thrum in the silence.

"I enjoyed your company this evening," he said finally.

"Me too," I admitted.

He smiled and got out, circling the car to open my door before I could even reach for the handle. "Let me walk you to the door," he said.

The porch light cast a soft halo around the front steps as we climbed them. The night had deepened into that kind of quiet that only small towns know. Crickets in the grass and the occasional rustle of leaves from a squirrel or other critter.

"I really do appreciate the invitation," I said, fishing my keys from my purse. "It's been a long time since I've... well, since I've had a night like this."

"I'm glad," he said, his voice low. "You deserved it."

I smiled, but as I reached the door, I instinctively pressed a hand to my lower back, stretching slightly.

He noticed immediately. "You all right?"

"Fine," I said quickly, laughing it off. "Just sore. I've been sleeping on the couch while I wait for my bed to be delivered."

He raised an eyebrow, his lips curving into something halfway between a smirk and a grin. "Ah. A good bed can make all the difference," he said, his tone warm and unmistakably suggestive.

I felt the heat rise to my cheeks. "I'll, uh, keep that in mind," I said, forcing a small laugh as I turned the key in the lock.

He stepped a little closer. Not uncomfortably so, but close enough that I could feel the warmth radiating from his body and the faint scent of his cologne.

"Well," I began, my voice catching slightly. "I should probably—"

Before I could finish, he leaned in, his body brushing lightly against mine, one hand braced on the railing behind me. The world seemed to narrow to the space between us, the pulse in my throat pounding like a drum. When he tilted his head toward mine, instinct took over. I pulled back, my shoulders pressing against the porch railing.

He froze immediately, eyes searching mine.

"I don't kiss on the first date," I said, my attempt at a smile coming out softer than I intended.

"Ah," he said, a slow grin spreading across his face. "So this *was* a first date?"

"I didn't say that," I countered, though the words came out breathier than I'd hoped.

He chuckled, the sound deep and low. "I think you just did."

Then, instead of leaning in again, he took my hand gently in his. His touch was warm, deliberate. He turned my palm slightly, brought it to his lips, and pressed a light kiss to the back of it.

My breath hitched.

"Well then," he said softly, still holding my gaze. "We'll have to do this again."

He released my hand, stepped back, and nodded once before heading down the steps toward his car. I stayed there on the porch for a long moment, my pulse still racing, my fingers tingling where his lips had been.

When his taillights disappeared down the road, I finally let out the breath I'd been holding. Something was happening here, and it was something I wasn't sure I was ready for. Yet, as I stood in the quiet night, the echo of his kiss still ghosting over the skin of my hand, I couldn't deny it.

6

The next two weeks came and went in a blur.

Amber was now the proud mother of a baby boy. She'd sent photos to several of the staff, and the nurses had passed their phones around so everyone could see. I was happy for her, genuinely, but I couldn't help wondering if things had turned out differently, if I might have been a mother by now, too.

Work kept me busy. I was on a rotation of four twelve-hour shifts followed by three days off, then rinse and repeat. My new furniture had finally been delivered, which meant my back no longer ached from sleeping on the couch. Having a dresser and bedside tables again felt strangely comforting, like reclaiming small pieces of normalcy. My moving boxes had arrived as well, and it felt good to unpack a few familiar things: photos, books, clothes. I finally had drawers for my underwear instead of plastic bags in the closet.

The days were long but satisfying. I'd handled everything from broken bones to dehydration to a tourist who had drunk too much on Main Street and mistaken a stairwell for an elevator.

But it wasn't the patients who wore me down. It was Dr. Ford Adams.

Every time I ran into him, he left me feeling unsettled. He was a good doctor; that much was clear. Sharp, competent, and confident. But there was something behind those dark eyes of his, a kind of watchfulness that made my skin crawl. His hair was neatly styled, his smile perfectly measured. But was it really a smile, or a sneer disguised as one?

He'd stand too close sometimes, lowering his voice when he spoke to me, his tone a little too smooth. And though he was polite, there was an edge beneath it. It was something possessive, almost predatory.

One afternoon, I bent over a patient's bed to adjust an IV line, and when I straightened, I caught him staring at my ass, and then, as I turned, my breasts. Not subtly. His gaze was fixed, dark, and unapologetic. I wanted to say something, but the words froze in my throat.

Another time, I was charting alone in one of the smaller exam rooms when he appeared in the doorway, leaning casually against the frame.

"Everything all right in here?" he asked.

"Fine," I said quickly.

He lingered longer than necessary before finally walking away, and when he did, I let out a breath I hadn't realized I was holding.

I couldn't explain why, but I was glad I'd never been alone with him behind a locked door.

I hadn't seen Dane since our dinner at the saloon.

Not for lack of trying. I'd even stopped by the Silver Spur one evening for dinner, hoping to run into him. But he wasn't there. I told myself it was for the best, that my focus should be on work, not some charming casino owner who made my pulse race.

Then, one night, after a particularly grueling shift, my phone lit up with a text from an unfamiliar number.

I'm sorry I've been away. Business in Rapid City. Would you do me the honor of joining me for a late dinner this evening?

My heart gave a small, traitorous flutter. I typed back, *Who is this?*

A moment later came the reply:

My apologies for my ignorance. This is Dane Walker. How about it? Dinner tonight? Surely you must be hungry after a long day. I've asked the chef to make some Deadwood favorites for us.

The invitation was tempting. I was tired, hungry, and, if I was honest with myself, a little lonely. I glanced at my watch, the one every nurse relied on, and realized it had been at least six hours since I'd last eaten.

In the mirror above the small bathroom sink, I barely recognized myself. My hair was slightly mussed, dark circles were forming under my eyes, and my scrub top wrinkled from the day. Still, a little mascara and a change of clothes could fix that.

That actually sounds nice, I typed back. *Can I meet you at the casino in twenty minutes?*

I'll be waiting.

. . .

I dug through my closet and pulled out a pair of dark skinny jeans and a red-and-white button-down blouse with flowy sleeves. At first, I buttoned it all the way up, then paused. *What the hell,* I thought, leaving the top two buttons open. In the mirror, I caught a glimpse of the curve of my breasts. Just enough, but not too much.

Since it wasn't quite dark yet, I decided to walk. The casino was only ten minutes away, and I'd recently found a shortcut: a small walking path that connected Williams Street to Main. The evening air was cool and fragrant with pine.

When I reached the entrance, Dane was waiting just outside.

He looked devastatingly handsome in faded blue jeans and a plaid button-down shirt, the sleeves rolled to his elbows. It wasn't the polished businessman I'd met before in his tailored suit. This was something else. He appeared more rugged, more real. His shirt was unbuttoned just enough to reveal a smooth, hairless chest beneath.

"Brooke," he said with that easy smile. "You made it."

"I said I would," I replied, though my voice came out softer than I intended.

He gestured toward a side entrance. "I thought we'd eat somewhere a little quieter tonight."

He led me through a hallway to a private dining room just off the main restaurant. A small round table sat in the center, set for two, with a single candle flickering between us.

"Forgive me for being presumptuous," he said. "It's just that this town gets a bit lonely, seeing the same faces every day. So, I'm grateful for your company."

I blushed. What was it about this man that made me blush like a schoolgirl?

The dinner was everything he promised. His chef had prepared a mix of regional favorites, including crispy chislic, something I'd never tried before, Indian tacos, and tiny bison sliders. By the time I was done, I was full and happy, my earlier exhaustion replaced by a warm, pleasant buzz from the wine.

"This music is beautiful," I said, noticing the soft, melodic tune playing in the background.

"It's my own playlist," he said, standing and rounding the table toward me. "I get tired of the music in the main dining room. Too loud. Too predictable."

He extended his hand, his eyes catching the candlelight.

I hesitated. "What are you—"

"Dance with me, Brooke," he said quietly. "Indulge a lonely man."

I hesitated for only a second before taking his hand. His fingers wrapped around mine. They were warm, confident, unhurried. He pulled me gently to my feet and placed one hand at the small of my back. The touch sent a spark through me.

We swayed slowly to the rhythm, our bodies moving together in an easy rhythm. He asked me about the hospital, and I found myself telling him more than I'd intended.

"It's a good place," I said. "Busy, but the team's solid. Though..." I paused, my cheeks heating. "There's one doctor I could do without."

"Dr. Adams?" Dane asked, his tone casual but his eyes sharp.

I looked up, surprised. "How did you—"

He smiled faintly. "Small town."

"He's a very good doctor," I said carefully. "But he makes me uncomfortable. I don't know why. There's just something about him..."

I felt Dane's body tense slightly, though his expression didn't change.

"I'd keep your distance," he said after a moment. "He's not one of my favorite people in Deadwood."

There it was again. That quiet warning, the one he'd hinted at before. I wanted to ask why, but something in his tone told me not to press. Instead, I changed the subject, asking about his casino and how he'd gotten into the business.

He smiled, the tension easing from his shoulders. "It was my family's. My grandfather started it when gambling was first legalized in Deadwood, and my dad eventually took it over. My mother ran it after he passed, until I came of age. I've been at the helm ever since I turned eighteen."

"It must have been a lot of responsibility at that age," I said.

He chuckled softly. "It was. But it taught me everything I know."

The song changed, and something in the tempo shifted to one that was slower, deeper. Dane's arm tightened around my waist, pulling me closer. I felt his breath warm against my temple. I could feel the strength of his body pressed against mine. His strong arms and his tight abs.

Then his lips brushed the curve of my neck, lightly at first, then again, lower. My breath caught. It had been so long since a man had touched me like that. Mitch had been the only one. My first. My only.

I tilted my head back, a quiet sigh escaping as his lips traced the line of my jaw. Then, suddenly, his mouth was on mine. Hot, insistent, his tongue sliding against mine, tasting, teasing.

The kiss deepened, and before I realized it, we were moving, his body guiding mine until my back pressed against the wall. His hands roamed over my hips, up my sides, cupping the curve of my breast through the thin fabric of my blouse. His lips found the top of my chest, and I heard myself moan softly.

Oh God, what was I doing? Did I want this? Yes. Every nerve in my body screamed yes. But somewhere deep inside, another voice whispered *too soon.* I placed my hands on his chest and gently pushed. "No," I said softly. "You feel amazing, and this was... amazing. But it's too soon, right?"

He stepped back immediately, his hands raised. "Perhaps it is too soon," he said quietly. "Forgive me for getting ahead of myself."

The air between us was heavy, charged, and a little sad.

"Shall I take you home?" he asked.

I nodded. It was late anyway, and I had to be at the hospital by seven.

The drive was quiet but comfortable, for all of five minutes it took. When we reached my house, he walked me to the door. He took my hand, pressed a soft kiss to it, and said, "Goodnight, Brooke. Until next time."

Once inside, I stripped off my clothes and slid naked beneath the covers, the cool sheets against my warm skin. My body still hummed with the memory of his touch. As I stared at the ceiling, one question circled my mind again and again. Where could this night have gone, if I had let it?

7

When I woke the next morning, it felt as though I hadn't slept at all. I'd drifted in and out through the night, half-dreaming, half-remembering the heat of Dane's hands on my body. Each time I closed my eyes, I felt him again. His breath on my neck, the press of his lips, the strength of his body.

And each time, I jolted awake, guilt settling over me like a heavy blanket.

For so long, I had reserved every part of myself, including my touch and my heart, for Mitch. But the feel of Dane against me had been intoxicating, electric. Even though I was the one who had stopped things, it had left me aching, wanting, and confused about what that meant.

By the time I dragged myself out of bed and into the shower, I felt like I'd been run over. The hot water beat against my skin as I leaned my head against the cool tile, trying to rinse away both exhaustion and temptation. It didn't help much.

I worked mousse through my damp hair, twisted it into a ponytail, brushed my teeth, and slipped into a fresh pair of scrubs. My reflection in the mirror looked as tired as I felt.

Ten minutes later, I was on my way to The Daily Grind. The little coffee shop had become a morning ritual. It was one indulgence I refused to give up.

The bell chimed as I stepped inside, the warm scent of espresso and cinnamon pastries wrapping around me. I joined the line, pulling out my phone to scroll mindlessly through texts from family and friends at home when I felt someone step up behind me.

"Nurse Cassidy."

I turned, startled. "Dr. Adams! I—uh—didn't expect to see you here."

"Good morning," he said, his voice low and overly formal. "A pleasure to run into you." He smiled, though as always, it didn't quite reach his eyes.

There was something unsettling about how he looked at me. It felt like he was taking an inventory. His gaze trailed down my body before returning to my face, unbothered by being caught. I tugged lightly at the hem of my scrub top, wishing for a lab coat.

"What brings you here?" I asked, trying to sound casual.

"I could ask the same of you," he said, his tone almost teasing. "The Daily Grind makes the best coffee in the Black Hills. I thought I'd make a pit stop before my rounds."

"Yes, they do," I replied politely, glancing toward the counter, hoping the line would move faster.

He leaned closer, just slightly. "How are you settling into Deadwood so far?"

"Oh, it's been good," I said, forcing a smile. "Between the long shifts and unpacking, I haven't had much time to explore. But I'm enjoying what I've seen so far."

"It sounds like you could use a proper tour guide," he said, his voice dropping a register. His height suddenly felt imposing, the air between us too close.

"That's very kind of you, Dr. Adams," I began carefully, "but that's not necessary."

He stepped closer still, the faint scent of aftershave clinging to him. "You don't know what you're missing."

I opened my mouth to protest, but before I could, another voice cut through the space between us. I knew his voice before I saw him.

"Ford, I believe Ms. Cassidy has already said no."

I turned to see Dane standing just behind me, his broad shoulders filling the doorway. He wasn't in a suit this time, just jeans, cowboy boots, and a dark Henley that fit him far too well. His tone was polite but sharp, the warning clear beneath it.

"Perhaps," Dane continued, "you should take her at her word and let her get on with her day."

The two men faced each other in silence for a moment. They were nearly the same height, and the resemblance between them was startling. Both dark-haired, broad-shouldered, commanding. But where Ford's eyes were cold and assessing, Dane's held warmth. Fire, even.

For a fleeting second, I wondered if they were related. But then I remembered their names. Walker and Adams. No connection there. Only hostility.

"Thank you, Dane," I said, breaking the tension. "I appreciate that. And Dr. Adams, I'll pass on the offer. Again."

I stepped forward as the barista called me up. "Vanilla latte, extra shot of espresso," I said quickly.

When I turned back, Ford was gone. Dane, however, remained, arms folded across his chest, watching me with an unreadable expression.

"Would you like a coffee?" I asked, gesturing toward the counter.

He gave a faint smile. "Americano, please." Before I could protest, he handed his credit card to the barista.

"Dane, that wasn't necessary," I said as we stepped toward the door, steaming cups in hand.

He shrugged. "I wanted to."

Outside, the morning sun was climbing over the hills. I glanced at my watch. Fifteen minutes until my shift. Not enough time to linger, but enough that I didn't want to rush off just yet.

"About last night," I began.

He reached for my free hand, gently guiding me to the edge of the sidewalk as a small group of hikers passed by. "No," he said softly. "Let me speak first."

I swallowed, suddenly aware of how close he was.

"I'm sorry if I was too forward," he said, his eyes searching mine. "But I don't regret it. Not the kiss. Not the way you felt in my arms. I find myself thinking about you more than I should."

The honesty in his voice stole my breath. "I... find you attractive, too," I admitted, my cheeks warming. "But what are you doing here, really? Don't you have coffee at the casino?"

He looked briefly irritated, then sighed. "I saw Ford in here with you. I don't like him, Brooke. I don't trust him." His tone left no room for doubt.

"I can handle myself," I said, though a part of me appreciated his protectiveness.

"I believe you," he said, a faint smile tugging at his mouth. "But that doesn't mean I want you anywhere near him."

Before I could respond, he lifted my hand to his lips. "Now," he murmured, brushing a kiss over my knuckles, "allow me to redeem myself. Dinner again? Or perhaps something different tomorrow? I believe you're off."

He remembered my schedule. That small detail sent a thrill through me.

"I'll think about it," I said, trying to hide my smile.

"I'll text you," he promised. And then he was gone, striding down the street toward his casino as if nothing had just happened.

. . .

By the time I reached the hospital, I had just enough time to clock in before shift change. The night nurses were bleary-eyed, passing off notes and updates while I scanned the charts on my tablet. A dozen patients, two new admits, and a stack of discharge paperwork waiting for signatures.

Once the chaos of the morning had settled, I started assigning nurses to rooms and making rounds. The rhythm of the hospital was its own kind of comfort. I appreciated that it was predictable, structured, and full of purpose, even if it was an emergency department.

About an hour later, I was hunting down one of the doctors to sign discharge papers for an elderly patient who'd taken a tumble down some stairs the night before. I turned the corner and nearly walked straight into Dr. Ford Adams.

"Nurse Cassidy," he said, that smug half-smile curling his mouth. "What a pleasure to see you twice in one morning. I'm only sorry our earlier conversation was so rudely interrupted."

"I don't think Dane meant anything by it," I said carefully.

"Oh, *Brooke*, Dane Walker and I go back a long way," he said, placing a strange emphasis on my name. "He meant every word of it."

He stepped closer, lowering his voice. "But let's not dwell on that. I'd rather encourage you to revisit my offer. A private tour of Deadwood to some of the less touristy spots, maybe a local favorite or two. Tomorrow?"

I resisted the urge to roll my eyes. "That's kind of you, Dr. Adams, but I'll have to pass. I already have plans tomorrow."

He studied me for a beat, and I knew he caught the flicker of a smile I couldn't quite hide.

"With Mr. Walker, I presume?"

I said nothing, stepping to the side to move past him. But as I did, he reached out and grabbed my arm. The touch was light, but it stopped me cold. "I said," I repeated evenly, pulling my arm free, "no thank you."

He held my gaze for a moment longer, something unreadable flashing in his dark eyes. Then he nodded slowly, a thin smile crossing his face.

"Of course," he said softly. "No harm in asking."

I turned and walked away, my pulse hammering. Behind me, I could still feel his eyes on my back long after I disappeared around the corner.

8

I was saddened not to hear from Dane by the end of my shift. And I didn't hear from him by the time I got home, or by the time I slipped beneath the sheets. I was nearly asleep the second my head hit the pillow, so I missed the text he sent shortly before midnight.

I am afraid that the day got away from me. However, Brooke, I would very much like to spend the day with you. If you would be so kind as to accept my invitation, I believe we can get to know each other better, and you can also explore the Black Hills and see why I love this area so much.

It was a rather long text, and I was sad I didn't see it until I woke up the next morning after nine. Clearly, I'd needed the sleep. I grabbed my reading glasses off the bedside table to make sure I'd read it correctly, then typed my response.

I am so sorry I missed your text. I was exhausted when I got home last night.

Almost immediately, three dots appeared, bouncing. The man must have had his phone in his hand.

I hope you received the rest your body needs for a fun day. Please don't hold out on me, Brooke. Please say yes.

I smiled in spite of my blurry eyes. I set my head back on the pillow and closed my eyes for just a moment, weighing my options. Was there any rule about how long you're supposed to wait before moving on from grief? It had been two years. And I was lonely. Plus, there was something about Dane that pulled me in, and it wasn't just his looks. Though that was definitely a bonus.

I sat up, grabbed my phone again, and looked at his message, knowing he was waiting.

Why not. Where should I meet you?

I will pick you up. Be ready in thirty.

Thirty minutes? That wasn't nearly enough time to shower, dry my hair, and put on makeup. I flew out of bed, tossing clothes behind me on the way to the bathroom. This little house didn't have an ensuite, which I sorely missed, but it was just me here. I prayed no one was peeking through the windows at my stark-naked sprint down the hall to pop a pod in the coffee maker. No time to run to the coffee shop.

As the coffee brewed, I raced through the shower, washed and conditioned my hair, then ran a razor quickly up and down my legs. Not perfect, but good enough. Out of the shower, I wrapped my hair in a microfiber towel to soak up the water while I brushed my teeth. Then I plugged in the dryer and got my hair as dry as possible before the doorbell rang.

He was early. I looked at my watch. Five minutes early. Clearly, he didn't understand how much a woman could tackle in five minutes.

"Be right there!" I called, grabbing my silk robe from the hook on the back of the bathroom door. There was no way I'd wriggle into jeans and a top fast enough. I cinched the robe tighter and opened the door.

Dane stood there with a bouquet of daisies. Bright white and sunny yellow. I couldn't remember the last time Mitch had brought me flowers. He saved that for my birthday or Valentine's Day, never just because.

Dane's jaw dropped when he saw me, clearly not expecting the robe. "I was still in bed when I responded to your text," I said, tugging the robe closer. Not because I was afraid of him seeing anything, but manners. And I wasn't precocious.

"I'm sorry," he said, a hint of color touching his cheeks. "Would you like me to wait in the car?"

"Umm..." I started, unsure. Then, "No, please, have a seat in the living room. I just need five minutes."

"These are for you," he said, thrusting out the bouquet. If I didn't know better, I'd say Dane Walker was a little off his game.

"Thank you. They're beautiful and unexpected," I said. I took them into the kitchen, one hand on the flowers and my other holding the robe closed. I set the flowers on the counter and reached up to the high cabinet where I'd seen a vase while unpacking. It was just out of reach.

Dane moved up behind me as if to grab it, then stopped short. "Uh—" he started, then fell silent.

I turned, confused by the look on his face. Was that pain? "Are you—" I began, but he lifted a hand.

"I'll take care of the flowers," he said, clearing his throat. "Why don't you finish getting ready? We have a big day ahead."

Still unsure what had gotten into him, I nodded and hurried back to the bathroom. It wasn't until I caught a glimpse of myself in the mirror that I understood. The front of my robe had hitched high on my thigh, and in the back, it barely covered me at all.

Well. That explained the throat-clearing.

I dressed fast: a soft cream tee under a denim jacket, a pair of black and cream plaid shorts, and sandals. I tossed socks and tennis shoes into my backpack in case we ended up hiking. A quick swipe of mascara and tinted balm, a light brush through my hair, and I was presentable.

I found Dane in the living room, placing the daisies in the vase he'd located, water already added. He glanced up when I entered. His gaze warmed, resting on my face.

"Ready?" he asked.

"As I'll ever be," I said, grabbing my bag.

I decided not to mention the bare-all moment at the door, or whatever he'd seen in the kitchen. Instead, once we were in the car, I opened the conversation.

"So, what's the plan for the day?"

Dane cleared his throat again. He'd been doing that a lot this morning. He shifted in his seat as he pulled away from the curb, as if to reposition something. I tried to keep my mind from just what he needed to reposition, but couldn't help myself.

"I thought we'd start with breakfast. There's a great café in Hill City. The chef is the brother of our head chef. The food is excellent."

My stomach rumbled. I hadn't realized how hungry I was. "Sold."

"And then?"

"Impatient, Ms. Cassidy?" His mouth tipped in amusement, the tension easing out of his shoulders.

"Just curious."

"I thought Mount Rushmore, then Crazy Horse. We'll end the day with a drive through Custer State Park. If we're lucky, we'll spot bison. And donkeys."

I laughed. "Donkeys?"

"They're a tourist highlight," he said, then added, deadpan, "Hopefully they'll show and not make an ass out of me."

It took a second to land. I blinked. "Did Dane Walker just make a joke?"

"Do you think I can't be funny?" He looked wounded.

"No, I just—"

"Brooke, I'm kidding," he said, chuckling. "That joke's older than half this town. Anyway, people come here for work and never get the time to see anything. Today, you get to play tourist. And I'll be your guide."

I felt a little like a schoolgirl, giddy at the prospect. I knew myself well enough to know that if left to my own plans, I'd spend the next three months working and maybe peeking at a few attractions, if that.

"If we have time," he added, "I want to take you on a short hike. Two miles. Think you can handle it?"

I laughed, relieved I'd packed shoes. "Challenge accepted."

Breakfast in Hill City was exactly what I needed: hot coffee, fluffy pancakes with a ribbon of lemon curd, and eggs that tasted like they'd come from a farm down the road. Dane ordered a skillet, then insisted we split a side of their famous cinnamon roll "just so you know what you've been missing."

"I'm going to need that hike," I said, licking frosting off my thumb.

"I planned accordingly," he said, smugly, and I kicked him lightly under the table.

The drive to Mount Rushmore wound through hills thick with pine. The presidents rose into view all at once. They were unexpected and massive, pale against a razor-blue sky. We lingered at the overlooks, shoulder to shoulder, while a breeze lifted the ends of my hair. He kept up a running commentary, providing bits of history and a few stories he'd heard growing up, just enough to make me feel like I was seeing it through local eyes.

From there, we headed to the Crazy Horse Memorial. The scale of it humbled me. We stood quietly for a while, the two of us facing that unfinished face and outstretched arm. Dane slid his hand against the small of my back, just a light touch, and I felt it everywhere.

"Hungry?" he asked when we finally headed back to the car.

"Always."

We stopped at a roadside café for burgers and fries. I ordered a bison burger and found myself liking it more than I expected. I'd now tried two bison burgers during my time in South Dakota, and wondered if I could ever eat a regular hamburger again. "Probably not the best pre-hike meal," I said, wiping my fingers, "but delicious."

"We'll walk it off," he said, eyes lingering just a second too long on my mouth.

. . .

He turned onto Needles Highway, and I pressed a hand to the window like a kid. I'd never heard of it, but the name fit. The road curled and climbed through narrow stone tunnels, rock spires stabbing the sky like church steeples. It felt like driving through some ancient cathedral carved by wind.

We parked near a sign: Cathedral Spires Trailhead. In front of us rose the spires themselves, taller and stranger up close, their fluted sides catching light and shadow.

"How's your shoe situation?" he asked.

I lifted my bag. "Prepared."

We traded sandals for sneakers and headed up the trail. The path wound through granite boulders, switchbacked across sloping pine, then opened into bright clearings where the spires crowded close like sentries. A hawk circled overhead. Somewhere below, water moved, hidden.

Dane kept pace beside me, letting me set the speed. When the trail narrowed, he dropped a half step behind, hand hovering near my elbow as we navigated loose gravel. Every so often, his palm settled at my back as I stepped over a crack in the rock. It wasn't much, just that warm point of contact, and still it stirred something low in my belly.

"You all right?" he asked when I paused to catch my breath.

"I'm good," I said, a little breathless for reasons that had nothing to do with the climb.

He smiled. "You're tougher than you look."

"I'll take that as a compliment."

"It is."

We hiked in companionable quiet for a while, our footsteps crunching in unison. When the trail crested a ridge, the view opened. Spires crowded the horizon, and the valley spilled wide below. Wind skated across my skin; I shivered.

"Here," he said, shrugging off his windbreaker. Before I could protest, he draped it over my shoulders. It held his clean, woodsy scent, and for a second, I had to close my eyes.

"Thank you," I said, voice soft.

He tipped his head, studying me. "I like this," he said. "Being out here with you."

"Me too."

We followed a side path that tunneled through a seam in the granite and opened into a sheltered alcove the size of a small room. There was stone on three sides, the fourth framing a slice of sky and the far line of spires. The rock held the day's heat. It felt private. Quiet. A place where voices wouldn't carry.

I turned to say something, maybe a joke about his donkey line, anything to cut the thrum under my skin, but the words tangled. He stepped closer, close enough that I could see the faint sun-lines at the corners of his eyes and the dark sweep of his lashes.

"Brooke," he said, barely above a whisper.

My name in his voice did something to me. My pulse leaped. His fingers touched the edge of the jacket he'd given me, trailing lightly down my arm until they found my hand. He laced our fingers together, palm to palm, then lifted our joined hands to his chest. His heartbeat thudded steadily against my knuckles.

"I don't want to rush you," he said.

"I know," I whispered.

"And I don't want to stop wanting you," he added, honest in a way that felt like stepping off a cliff.

I swallowed, the world narrowing to the warmth of his hand and the quiet around us, the hush of pines, the wind threading through rock.

"Then don't," I said.

He exhaled with relief, or maybe hunger, and eased closer, his free hand skimming my waist, settling at the small of my back. The jacket slipped a little, and his fingers brushed bare skin. My breath hitched.

"Tell me to stop," he said, voice rough.

I didn't.

He bent his head. His mouth hovered over mine, close enough for me to feel the heat of it, the faint tease of his breath. He waited, letting me meet him halfway.

I rose onto my toes.

His lips brushed mine. They were soft at first, then firmer, deeper, the kind of kiss that unraveled time. I curled my fingers in his shirt, drawing him closer. He pressed me gently against the warm rock, our bodies aligning, the heat between us spiking. His mouth trailed to my jaw, then lower, tasting the salt at my throat. I heard my own sigh. It was needy and unguarded, and I didn't recognize myself, didn't want to.

His hand slid up, slow and sure, palm fitting the curve of my side, then higher. My pulse thundered. The world beyond the stone room fell away until there was only his breath, his hands, the yes unfurling through me.

I tipped my head back, the sky a thin blue ribbon above the stone.

"Dane," I breathed.

He lifted his head, eyes searching mine. "Tell me what you want."

I wet my lips, heart racing, the answer right there on my tongue, but no words would form. I slipped off his windbreaker and my jacket underneath. They fell to the ground, and Dane moved closer, a questioning look in his eyes.

"Dane," I breathed again.

Clearly tired of my waiting to give him further instruction, he took matters into his own hands. And when I say matters, he took me into his own hands. As though I weighed nothing more than a feather, he placed his hands under me, hoisting me up and against one of the tall rocks. I wrapped my legs around him and let my head fall back against the flat stone.

Using the rock as leverage to keep me in position, he moved one of his hands along my body to my breast. Feeling me through my shirt, he met my gaze, and when I didn't stop him, he slid his hand down and under my shirt, thumbing my nipple through the lace of my bra. I was glad I had had the foresight to grab a cute, matching bra and panties set, rather than the sensible underwear I typically wear on work days.

I gasped at the feeling of his hand against my skin. Carefully, he let my body drop just a bit, so that I could feel his erection against my center. Good God, what was this man doing to me? What was I *letting* him do to me? Whatever it was, I did not want him to stop.

"Brooke, you are absolutely divine," he breathed, finding my mouth was his. Whereas his kisses at the casino had been more gentle in nature, he was more rough this time. And it was blissful and agonizing all at once.

"We—" I began, not sure how to tell him we couldn't possibly continue here, with the risk of someone coming around the corner and finding us in a precarious position. But as much as I knew I did not want to be discovered, I did not want him to stop.

He hoisted me up again, higher this time, so that my breasts were now even with his mouth. "Oh God," I moaned as he shoved the material up and out of the way, and took my nipple and the lace of my bra in his mouth. His tongue was heavenly as it circled and sucked. I wished that the material would simply disintegrate from the heat of his mouth, but it did not.

The heat between my legs was intense, and I was practically dripping with my juices. I wanted him. Here and now, and I no longer cared that anyone might see.

But as though he sensed exactly what I was thinking, he released my breast and returned my shirt to its position. He suckled on my neck for a moment before putting me down.

"Not here, Brooke," he said. "I will not defile you and make you a spectacle."

"But—" I pouted, missing the heat from his touch.

"Brooke, trust me, I will defile you." He said, leaning his left hand against the stone wall that remained behind me. With his right hand, he ran it down my shirt, circling my breasts once again before running his index finger down to my belly, stopping at the top of my shorts.

I bucked my hips forward, unable to stop myself. "I want you," I said.

He flattened his hand against my belly and slid it down between my shorts and skin, underneath the hem of my panties, and crooked his finger into my heat, just enough to make me cry out with pleasure. "Oh," I exclaimed as his lips took mine, silencing me. And with just a mild flick to the one spot that needed his touch most, he removed his hand. He stepped back and took my hand in his.

"Not now," he said. "Not yet."

And with that, he led me down the rest of the path and back to the car.

9

Neither of us said anything when we got back to the car, which was probably for the best. I needed a minute, maybe an hour, to come down. He likely did, too. Those twenty minutes, however long they were, pressed against warm stone had been the hottest, most sensual experience of my life.

I wanted more.

I opened my mouth to say something honest and reckless when we rounded a curve and nearly ran into a small drove of donkeys blocking the road.

"Oh my," I said, laughing. Dane laughed too.

"They love this stretch," he said. "Wildlife Loop Road. Some days they're friendlier than others. Today looks like a good day." He tipped his chin toward the cars ahead. Windows down, people handing out snacks like Halloween.

"Are they dangerous?"

"No." He reached back and pulled a bag from the rear floorboard. "They'll eat almost anything, but they're partial to apples and carrots."

He handed me the bag with two oversized zipper bags inside, one with sliced apples, the other with baby carrots.

"Let me guess," I said. "Your chef prepped these."

Dane gave me a wounded look. "You don't think I can slice some fruit and vegetables?"

I grinned, and the car ahead rolled forward. Three donkeys shuffled toward us, velvety noses already working the air.

"What do I do?"

"Flat palm," he said. "Offer a piece. They'll do the rest."

They did. Two came to my window, lips gentle on my skin as they took apple and carrot, one by one. The third drifted to the next car when Dane kept his window closed, clearly content to let me have the moment. In minutes, both bags were empty, and our new friends moseyed along in search of the next generous stranger.

Dane eased the car through the cluster and back onto the open road. I dug out hand sanitizer and rubbed away donkey slobber, smiling like a kid.

"Now what?" I asked, settling back.

He was quiet for a beat. "What would you like from me, Brooke?"

The phrasing tripped me. "What do I want from you?"

"I'll give you what you want," he said, eyes on the road. "You just have to tell me."

My throat went dry. Wanting in the heat of a moment was one thing. Saying it out loud was another. "I want you," I finally said.

His mouth curved. "Then you'll have me. But first, we eat."

We drove back to Deadwood and stopped at the Silver Spur's casino buffet. It had been ages since I'd eaten at a buffet; I never knew where to start. I was grateful for a fast metabolism and the fact that twelve-hour shifts burn through just about anything. I built a plate consisting of a crisp salad, fried chicken, and a scoop of okra, and slid into a corner booth. Dane excused himself to "check on a few things," and was back ten minutes later. Desmond, the host, appeared with a plate already arranged for him, then returned with a tray of desserts. Perks of being the owner: everyone knows your favorites.

We ate in comfortable silence for a few minutes.

"What was your favorite part of the day?" he asked.

I looked at him, knowing the real answer and deciding to tease. "Mount Rushmore. The donkeys. And that bison we saw on the way out."

He held my gaze. "Is that all, Brooke?"

There it was, my ridiculous blush. "I enjoyed our hike," I said.

"Oh, you did?" His tone warmed, eyes narrowing with an intensity that didn't match the casual clink of plates around us.

Suddenly, I wasn't hungry. Not for food.

"I did," I said.

"What was your favorite part?" He slid his plate away and leaned in. "The spires?"

"They were lovely."

"Or when I lifted you and set you against the rock?"

A shiver ran through me. "That was... good. The rock was smooth."

"Yes," he said, voice lower. "Very smooth. Was that all you liked?"

"No." My voice had gone breathy.

"Was it when I took your breast in my mouth?" His eyes had gone darker, hunger threaded through them.

Heat flooded my face. Not embarrassment, exactly. More like memory, rushing back in color.

"Or when I slid my finger inside you?" he asked, voice barely above a whisper.

I nearly choked on a sip of wine.

"Would you like more of that, Ms. Cassidy?"

I nodded.

He stood and held out his hand. "Come with me."

Later that night, I shifted in Dane's bed and realized that somehow, without ever letting go, Dane had pulled the covers up and over us. The air in the room was warm and faintly scented with cedar and soap.

I tilted my head back to look at him in the dark, the faint orange glow from the streetlights tracing the lines of his face. His breathing was deep and even, a quiet rhythm against my shoulder.

For the first time in a long while, my body felt both spent and weightless. My heart, though, was another story. It thudded softly, calm but uncertain all at once.

I wanted to memorize this moment. The hush of the room, the heat of his skin, the ache that felt equal parts longing and relief. But beneath it all lingered a quiet question: what happens when morning comes?

10

A week later, I was wrapping up my first month in Deadwood. The hospital felt familiar now, including the squeak of the supply-room door, the hum of the monitoring stations at the nurses' bay, and the way the elevator always paused too long on two. Amber stopped by that morning with her baby boy, Wyatt Paul, bundled in a blue blanket. She kept him in the main lobby to spare him the parade of germs that greeted us in the emergency department. We took turns sneaking out to say hello. He was tiny and perfect, with a little knit hat and a yawn that made everyone soften around the eyes.

"Sleep?" I asked her, and we both laughed at the unfairness of the question.

"Some," she said, and her smile said it was worth it.

By late afternoon, I was closing out day four of my twelve-hour run. Tomorrow should have been my start to three days off, but I'd picked up an extra shift to cover bereavement on another floor. I didn't mind. The work steadied me. It also kept my brain from spiraling to the place it went when the floor went quiet, and the hall lights dimmed.

Of course, even work couldn't erase the memory of Dane.

I'd told myself not to expect anything after that night in his penthouse. Part of me had even worried he wouldn't be there when I woke. And he wasn't in the bed, anyway. He was in the chair beside it, in a dark suit, watching me with a softness that startled me.

"I didn't want to leave you," he said.

Sitting up, I pulled the sheet closer and squinted at the light edging around the curtains. "How long have you been there?"

"It doesn't matter," he said, and then raked a hand through his hair. "But I need to go downstairs to meet security. We've got a tour group coming later this morning."

"Do you want me to leave?" I slid toward the edge of the bed, then stopped when I realized I was still naked and tugged the sheet back to my chest.

"No. Brooke—no." He crossed the space in two steps and knelt in front of me. "I don't want you to leave, now or ever. But I have to work. They're a good group, and they bring real money into the casino and the town."

The only words that stuck were *I don't want you to leave.* Everything after that was a blur.

"I'll be gone awhile," he said. "I don't expect you to wait. But I'd like to see you tonight. Or tomorrow."

"You want to have sex with me again," I said before I could stop myself. It came out flat and suspicious, as if I'd tripped over a wire in my own head.

He flinched. "Brooke, no. Yes. I would love to make love to you again." The phrasing hit something inside me and set it glowing. "But if you think that's all I want, I've said this wrong. That was never my intention."

"What is your intention?" I asked, still holding the sheet like a shield.

He stood, and the suit didn't hide the muscle under it. "To keep knowing you," he said. "I'm drawn to you. Not just your beauty, though God, you are." He reached for the sheet, and I let him pull it away. His gaze traced my skin as if he were memorizing it. "I hope you know that."

I stood, bare in the morning light, and faced him. "If you want to see me, then yes. But I should go home. Text me later. We'll figure it out."

I stepped toward the bathroom, but he followed, catching my arm with a gentleness that tugged at me. He wrapped his arms around me, mouth near my hair. "Dinner tonight," he murmured.

We did have dinner that night. And the next. Over the following week, we found a rhythm without meaning to. Some nights we stayed in Deadwood, other nights he drove us to Spearfish or Hill City on a whim. Once, he said he had to go home to Rapid City and asked if I wanted to see the house. It wasn't sprawling or flashy, not for a man who owned a casino. But the Black Hills framed it like a painting, and the quiet there felt deep and good. He explained that the penthouse was a seasonal perch. It was close enough to sleep a few nights a week during the rush, but never meant to be a forever home.

I told him about Mitch. Not all at once. I didn't have it in me to hand over the whole story like a file folder laid wide on a desk. It came out in pieces over wine on his porch, the afternoon sun sliding along the fence, our feet up on the railing. The vineyard. The olive. How I'd tried. How the world kept turning anyway. I said it without tears, but he touched my hand like he could feel the ache threaded through my voice.

That night, he made love to me as if he understood. No pressure, no performance. Just warmth and patience and a care that settled something I hadn't known could settle. It felt like grief and comfort had locked hands and agreed to share the space for a while.

He offered his past in fragments, like puzzle pieces without edges. His father. Cancer, gone too soon. His mother had been tired, exacting, and made of iron. And a half-brother who never stayed out of trouble for long.

The brother was older, and their mother had always seemed to wrap him in a layer of protection that Dane never quite understood. Whenever his brother got himself into trouble, and it happened more than once, she handled it quietly, firmly, and without explanation. Checks were written. Meetings were held behind closed doors. Questions were waved off with a tired "It's nothing you need to worry about, sweetheart."

As Dane told it, he'd learned early not to push. His mother had carried enough weight on her shoulders without him adding to it. All he really knew was that Ford had a habit of landing himself in "hot water," as she put it, and she made sure it disappeared before the steam could rise.

And then there was the other part, the only part she'd ever shared with him outright. A portion of the casino's profits, every year without fail, was to be directed into a hospital fund. No explanation. No context. Just a firmly held promise she expected him to honor.

Dane had shrugged as he told me this, his expression a mix of resignation and old confusion. "She was always protecting him," he'd said quietly. "I just never knew from what."

"Where is he now?" I asked.

"Around," he said, and that one word carried a weight I didn't poke at. We sat with that for a while, side by side, not needing to fill the silence with anything else.

At the hospital, the week tilted toward being busy again. I floated up to med-surg one afternoon to help discharge a gentleman who wanted to argue with the monitor that said he needed his meds. I found myself back in the ED by evening, triaging two sprains and a kid with a fishhook stuck in his thumb. My life was a braid consisting of work and sleep and an unexpected thread of Dane braided through both. It startled me how natural it felt to text him *off at seven* and have a plan waiting before I'd peeled off my surgical gloves.

We never spoke about labels. We didn't need to. He showed up, and so did I. We learned the small things: he took his coffee black; I ordered lattes with an extra shot and a sprinkle of cinnamon. He hated green bell peppers. I would never understand people who put raisins in coleslaw. He liked classic rock in the car; I could sing along to nineties ballads without looking up the words. He drove with one hand and drummed the other on the steering wheel. I curled my feet under me in every chair like I was afraid someone would take the seat if I didn't claim it fully.

We learned the bigger things, too. He kept promises. He also kept his distance from Ford Adams, and when Ford appeared in a hallway or at The Daily Grind, Dane's shoulders sharpened. I noticed it. I tucked it away. The story would come out when it needed to.

On my one day off that week, he drove us to his Rapid City place again. We walked the property line and watched a deer step out from the brush. We ate sandwiches on the back steps and argued amiably about the right amount of mustard. When a breeze rolled down from the hills, he reached back without looking and found my hand. It felt simple, and the simplicity felt rare.

That night, back in Deadwood, he moved like a man who knew my map. My body answered before my head had anything to say about it. After, we lay there with the window cracked to the night, the scent of pine and dust and summer seeping in. It wasn't the same as the first time or the second; it had lost the edge of wonder and gained something else. I hadn't known that I could feel even better.

At work, the pace kept up. And in small moments, grief still stood up. It didn't knock me flat like it once had. It just tapped me on the shoulder. Wyatt's tiny fist, the sweetness of his smell, the way Amber leaned into her husband's side in the lobby, those things opened a door in my chest. I looked through it without stepping inside. I wasn't ready for the room beyond. Maybe I never would be. But I could stand at the threshold and breathe.

By the end of the week, I was counting hours in a way that surprised me, not to be done with work, but to see Dane. And then, standing at the nurses' station with my tablet, I realized what the calendar was saying out loud: four weeks down. One-third of my assignment is already gone.

I finished documenting vitals, signed off on a discharge, and leaned my elbows on the counter. Across the hall, one of the techs coaxed a toddler into a hospital gown shaped like a pirate shirt. The kid scowled, then grinned. The overhead lights hummed. A monitor beeped. The world was ordinary and relentless.

Three months had sounded long when I applied. It didn't feel long now.

When my shift ended, I stepped into the evening and waited a beat before walking to the car, letting the air cool my cheeks. My phone buzzed. It was Dane.

Off soon? Dinner at seven?

I smiled at the screen, thumb hovering over the keyboard.

Off now. Seven works.

As I slid behind the wheel, I let myself admit the simple truth: I wanted more time. More dinners that stretched late. More drives through the hills. More quiet mornings that didn't need apologies or explanations. And I had to admit, I wanted more great sex.

I put the car in gear and pulled out, the hospital shrinking in the rearview. A month ago, Deadwood had been a place to hide in plain sight. Tonight, it felt like a place I didn't want to leave. As long as Dane was a part of it.

11

It was near the end of another long day when I found myself crouched on the floor of the medical supply room, clipboard in hand, double-checking the end-of-month inventory. One of the orderlies had already done it, but I'd always believed in double-checking. The last thing any hospital needed was to run out of gauze or IV tubing in the middle of a crisis.

The room was narrow, the kind of place that smelled faintly of antiseptic and latex gloves. I was halfway through counting packaged gowns when I heard the door open behind me. I didn't look up. People were in and out all the time, but when the door didn't close again, I paused.

A minute passed. Two. Maybe I'd imagined it.

Satisfied that the numbers matched, I stood, brushing off my scrubs, ready to move to the next shelf. As I rounded the corner, I nearly collided with someone standing in the aisle.

"Dr. Adams," I said, startled. "You scared me."

"Well, hello, Nurse Cassidy." His tone carried a lazy amusement that didn't fit the sterile air of the supply room.

"I didn't realize you were back. I heard you'd been on holiday," I said, forcing a polite smile. "Can I help you find something?"

"Oh, I think I've found what I was looking for." He didn't move.

"Good," I said, trying to step around him. But he shifted to block my path. "Excuse me, Dr. Adams," I said, keeping my voice even.

He reached out and laid a hand on my arm, turning it so that the back of his fingers brushed slowly down from my shoulder to my elbow. My stomach tightened. I stepped back instinctively, straight into the metal shelving unit.

"Dr. Adams, please," I said. "I need to finish the inventory and enter it before shift change. Don't want to run out of supplies and all that." My voice cracked on the attempt at humor.

He lifted his other hand, catching both of my arms now, not hard, but enough to make it clear I wasn't free to leave.

"You still owe me that tour," he murmured. "I'm an excellent guide."

"Dr. Adams," I said louder, hoping the sound might reach the hallway. "I already told you I'd have to pass."

"And why is that, Ms. Cassidy?" His lips twisted into something that looked like a sneer. "You think I wouldn't make good company? I could show you the real Deadwood. The places the tourists never find. Calamity Jane's old haunts, for one. You'd appreciate that, wouldn't you? Nurse to nurse."

I forced a tight smile. "I've read plenty about her, thank you. I don't need a personal tour."

He leaned closer, and the air between us grew thin. "Is that all you're focused on, your work?" he hissed. His fingers dug into my arms. "Because I hear you've been... otherwise occupied."

My pulse kicked up. "Excuse me?"

He smiled without humor. "Dane Walker," he said, voice low and venomous. "He's not someone you want to associate with."

I froze. How did he know? And why would he say that? "My personal life is none of your concern," I said, my tone sharp now.

"Oh, but it is," he said, stepping forward until the edge of the shelving pressed against my back. His breath hit my face, hot and sour. "I make it my business to know who newcomers get tangled up with. Dane Walker's one of the ones you should stay far away from."

"And why is that?" I asked, my voice calm despite the fear crawling up my throat.

"He's a womanizer," Ford said flatly. "Likes the fresh ones. Plays the gentleman until he gets what he wants." His mouth curved upward, but it wasn't a smile. "You know all about that, don't you?"

"I don't know what you're talking about," I said, pushing at his chest. It didn't budge him.

He dropped one hand from my arm and let it trace the line of my hair, then down the side of my neck. When his knuckles brushed the top of my breast, I jerked back, but there was nowhere to go.

"He's had his way with you, hasn't he?" Ford seethed, spittle flecking my cheek. "I can see it in your face. He's fucked you."

"Dr. Adams!" I snapped, my voice breaking. "This is completely inappropriate. I'm asking you to step back."

"Not until you give me what I want." His voice was a rasp now, and when he dipped his head toward my neck, I acted on instinct.

I slammed my heel down on his foot. Hard. At the same time, I snapped my head forward, the crown of it colliding squarely with his nose. The sound was a dull crack followed by a sharp curse.

Blood spattered across the front of his white coat. He stumbled backward, clutching his face.

I didn't wait. I darted for the door, yanked it open, and nearly collided with a solid chest.

"Brooke?" Dane's voice was rough, his hands immediately on my arms. "What's wrong?"

"Dr. Adams—he—"

Dane's expression shifted in an instant. Whatever warmth had been there drained away, replaced by something I hadn't seen before. His jaw locked, his eyes darkened. He moved me gently aside and stepped through the doorway.

"Fo-ord!" The name came out like a growl.

Ford barely had time to lift his head before Dane grabbed him by the collar and slammed him against the wall. The shelves rattled from the force.

"Dane, stop!" I said, stepping in after him, but it was too late. Dane's fist connected once, clean and hard, sending Ford's head snapping to the side.

"Dane!" I repeated, pulling at his arm. "You'll get yourself arrested!"

Ford slumped slightly, one hand pressed to his bleeding nose. "Mother would be disappointed in you, little brother," he spat.

The words hit like a gunshot. I froze, looking from one man to the other. The same jawline, the same dark eyes, the same coiled rage. Little brother. And in that moment, the pieces clicked together. Ford Adams was Dane Walker's older half-brother.

12

The next few hours passed in a blur. Security had been called. Then the police. Questions came fast, one after another, until they all blurred together in my head.

Was I hurt? Did I want to press charges? Did I need a nurse?

Sexual harassment or assault was the choice I was given. And not knowing the right answer, or maybe too afraid to pick the wrong one, I said no.

What kind of mess had I gotten myself into?

All I'd wanted when I came to Deadwood was a clean slate. A chance to outrun Mitch's ghost, figuratively, at least. But now, the very man I was growing to love, dare I even think that word, turned out to be the younger half-brother of the man who had just tried to force himself on me in the hospital supply closet.

Confused didn't begin to cover it. I was shaken, ashamed, and more than a little lost.

Both Dane and Ford had been taken into custody. The hospital administrator had been called in, too. Even though I had declined to press charges, it seemed that this new administrator wasn't one of the ones who could be bought by Walker's money.

And suddenly, all the little things I'd noticed started falling into place. Dane mentioning that The Silver Spur contributed generously to the hospital's annual fund. The way Amber had offhandedly said on my first day that Dr. Adams was "harmless, mostly."

And what Dane had told me about his brother: older, reckless, quick to find the line and cross it. Fights. Debts. Accusations. Women who spoke up and others who didn't. All those stories that money made disappear.

It all fits now. But what didn't fit was why Dane hadn't told me. Why hadn't he just said that Ford Adams, the man who'd assaulted me, was his brother? What else hadn't he told me?

And as the thought sank in, I couldn't help but think about the irony of it all. The Silver Spur had donated thousands to this hospital over the years, patching up its cracks, funding new equipment, new walls, a better image. But in Deadwood, as in the casinos, the house always wins. And in this case, "the house" looked a lot like the Walkers. Had Dane simply been paying off the hospital to cover up Ford's transgressions? I didn't want to believe that was possible, but I began to wonder.

A knock at the door startled me.

"Nurse Cassidy," a man said, stepping into the room. I recognized him from orientation. Paul Jackson, head of Human Resources. "While I understand that you've chosen not to press charges against Mr. Adams, I'll need you to provide a written statement for our records. The legal department will require it."

His choice of words caught me. *Mr.* Adams, not *Dr.*

"Yes, of course," I said quietly, staring at the wall, keeping the corner of my eye on him. Now, I wondered just who I could trust.

He nodded once and gestured for me to follow. "Sooner would be best."

I rose and followed him down the corridor, into the elevator, and up to the administrative floor. I'd never been here for anything but first-day paperwork. Sitting in HR made me feel like I'd done something wrong, even though, logically, I knew I hadn't.

Jackson's office smelled faintly of stale coffee. A brass nameplate sat on the corner of his desk. He motioned to a chair, then handed me a clipboard thick with papers. It felt outdated, this paper process, in a hospital that prided itself on being digital.

The questions were blunt:

Where did the altercation take place?

Did you report it to the police?

What is the current state of your employment?

Your mental health?

Did you seek medical attention?

And then, the one I dreaded most:

Please detail the altercation to the best of your ability.

My hand shook as I began to write. I described the supply room. The way Ford had blocked my exit. The sound of his breath when he leaned in. The way his hand had brushed over my breast before I'd fought back. My head throbbed just remembering the impact from when I'd rammed him in the nose.

For a moment, I froze. Was it harassment? Assault? I wasn't even sure anymore. I unlocked my phone and typed a quick search, reading the answer right there, in black and white. Sexual assault refers to any physical sexual act that occurs without someone's consent, while sexual harassment refers to non-physical sexual conduct such as gestures or comments. By that definition, I was a victim of sexual assault.

The realization hit hard. Tears blurred the words on the page, and I pressed my fingertips to the small bump forming on my forehead. There'd be a bruise later. A mark to remind me that this wasn't some fever dream.

"Nurse Cassidy?" Mr. Jackson's voice was gentle but tentative. He stood, then hesitated, uncertain whether to come closer. Maybe this was what it felt like to be *that woman*, the one others didn't know how to approach, unsure whether comfort might hurt more than silence.

"Can I call someone for you?" he asked.

I swallowed hard. "No. There's no one."

My family was hours away. My friends were scattered. The only person I'd truly connected with in this town was Dane.

As though the thought had conjured him, the office door burst open. Dane stood in the doorway, his expression torn between fury and guilt. A fresh bruise darkened his left eye socket; a cut split his lip. His suit was rumpled, and his knuckles were scraped raw.

"Brooke," he said, stepping toward me.

I held up my hand before he could get any closer. He froze.

He was the only person I knew here, the one I'd trusted. The one who could have prevented all this, if only he'd been honest.

I turned to Mr. Jackson, my voice steady despite the tremor in my chest. "Could you please ask Mr. Walker to leave?"

13

Two weeks had passed, and I'd spent every minute of them wondering how everything had gone so wrong so fast.

The hospital had placed me on paid administrative leave while the administrators and legal team determined "next steps." Their wording. It sounded so formal. So detached.

When the call came that morning, it was short and to the point: *The investigation has concluded. You are cleared of any wrongdoing.*

No wrongdoing on my part. The words felt clinical, like they belonged in someone else's story. But I was relieved all the same.

I'd kept myself busy, or at least tried to. I cleaned. I reorganized the kitchen twice. I caught up on laundry I didn't even remember having. I'd even painted my fingernails and toenails. A deep red. But mostly, I sat with my own thoughts.

And Dane hadn't called. He hadn't texted. He hadn't even sent one of his formal, polite messages like before.

I'd asked Mr. Jackson to have him leave that day, and I knew that probably stung. But if he truly cared, wouldn't he have tried? Wouldn't he have at least *knocked*? He knew where I lived. And I hadn't blocked his number. The silence was its own kind of answer.

I'd only left the house a handful of times in the past two weeks, mostly for groceries or air. I'd avoided my usual haunts: no coffee at the local coffee shop, no local market. Instead, I drove into Lead, where nobody knew my name. I stocked up on food, bought a couple of cheap paperback novels, and filled my pantry as if I were settling in for a long winter, despite the heat of late July.

One day, out of sheer boredom, I drove to Sturgis just to see what all the fuss was about. Thankfully, the rally was still two weeks away, so the streets were mostly quiet, just a few early riders and souvenir shops prepping for the chaos to come. Even back in International Falls, we'd heard stories about what went down during rally week, all the wild stories that made Vegas blush. Seeing the empty streets now, I couldn't help but wonder what the town would look like in full swing.

Amber had been my only visitor. Her text had surprised me, coming just a few days after *the incident*, which is what I'd started calling it in my head. I couldn't bring myself to use the word *altercation* as the legal forms did. That word felt too sterile.

She'd brought baby Wyatt with her, his tiny fingers wrapped in a blue blanket. She let me hold him, and I'd forgotten how light a baby could be. The smell of baby powder and milk clung to him, and something inside me ached. My maternal clock, silenced over the last two years, began to tick again. If Mitch had lived, would I have been a mother by now? Would our baby have had his eyes? His laugh?

Amber must have caught whatever flashed across my face, because she gently shifted the conversation. She told me that more nurses had begun whispering about Dr. Adams. Not formal complaints, not accusations, just confusing stories about women who'd been there one day and gone the next. No one ever explained why. At the time, Amber had chalked it up to burnout, better job offers, or personal issues. But now, after hearing what Ford had done to me, she couldn't help wondering if there had been a pattern all along. If those disappearances hadn't been coincidences at all.

Her words left an unsettling hollow space inside me, a quiet echo where all my anger had been. And now, with confirmation that I could return to work the next morning, I told myself I was ready. Ready to walk back in. Ready to settle into my role again. Ready to start fresh, whatever *fresh* looked like now.

My life, I thought. *Just me. Alone.* And I was fine with that. At least that's what I kept telling myself.

The next morning came early.

I arrived at the hospital just after six thirty. When I checked in with Mr. Jackson, he greeted me with a small nod. I was surprised to see him there, actually. But it was a small hospital, and I supposed someone had to be there to welcome me back.

"Welcome back, Nurse Cassidy," he said, sliding my ID badge across the desk.

"Thank you," I said.

He hesitated, then added, "You should know that Mr. Adams has been relieved of his post as hospitalist. Dr. Nelson will be taking over his duties for now."

There it was again, that pointed use of *Mr.* instead of *Dr.* I gave a small nod. "That's probably for the best."

The rest of the day passed in a haze of patient charts, rounds, and catching up on everything I'd missed. It felt strange to be back, but also grounding. The rhythm of the hospital was familiar. Predictable. And after two weeks of isolation, predictable felt good.

By the end of my shift, exhaustion had settled deep into my bones. I was ready to head home, shower, and eat something that didn't come out of a vending machine. But when I reached the parking lot, I stopped short. Parked beside my Cadillac SUV was a black BMW sedan. Sleek. Polished. Familiar. Dane.

He stepped out of the car, looking just as devastatingly composed as ever. Dark jeans, black button-down, sleeves rolled to his forearms. A light wind tousled his hair. He held up a hand as I opened my mouth to speak.

"Brooke," he began, his voice calm. "I know you have a lot of questions. And I understand why you wouldn't want to talk to me. But I came here to apologize for what happened, and for what I didn't tell you. I want the chance to explain everything."

For a moment, I couldn't move. Couldn't breathe. My heart was hammering, but not just from anger. Because the truth was, I'd missed him.

I wanted to be mad. I wanted to tell him to leave, to let me be. But there was that same tug in my chest, the one I'd felt the first time he'd looked at me across the Silver Spur dining room.

Maybe it was the loneliness talking. Or maybe it was something deeper. With six weeks left on my contract, what did I have to lose? Ford was gone. I was safe. At least, I believed I was.

I nodded once, taking a slow breath. "Fine," I said. "I'll listen. But we'll do it on my terms, somewhere neutral. Not at your casino, not at the restaurant. And not tonight. I need time, Dane."

He looked down at the asphalt, his jaw tightening, and for a second, I thought I saw something raw in his expression. Regret, maybe. Or sorrow.

"Wherever you want, Brooke," he said quietly. "Just give me the chance to tell you why I didn't tell you about Ford."

I nodded again and took a step back toward my car. "I'll text you after my shift tomorrow. We'll figure something out then."

He didn't argue. Didn't push. Just stood there, hands in his pockets, watching me.

As I drove away, I checked my rearview mirror. He was still there, standing in the same spot, the summer breeze tugging at his shirt, the shadows of the parking lot stretching long around him.

And for the first time in the last two weeks, I wasn't sure whether driving away was the right thing to do.

14

I'd let another few days pass before finally deciding it was time to talk to Dane. I'd done a lot of reflecting, and I still believed everyone deserved a chance to explain themselves. Besides, I missed him, truly missed him. Not just the sex, though I'd be lying if I said I hadn't caught myself replaying the feel of his hands, his mouth, the way he looked at me like I was the only woman in the room. But it went deeper than that. It wasn't about missing someone to touch me; it was about missing *him*. His quiet humor. The way his voice softened when he said my name. The calm I felt just being near him.

So, I texted him. Told him I wanted a *proper* date. Not at The Silver Spur. Not in his world, where he always seemed to hold the upper hand. I wanted neutral ground, somewhere he couldn't hide behind charm or control. I told him to take me to dinner at another casino in town, one of his competitors. Let him play by someone else's rules for once.

By Saturday night, I was ready. Dane pulled up in his BMW at exactly seven, ever punctual, ever composed. I stepped out of my house wearing a short black strapless cocktail dress that hugged my curves and ended just high enough to make him swallow hard when I approached. My hair was down, soft waves brushing my shoulders, and I'd swiped on red lipstick that matched my heels and the paint on my toes and fingernails. For the first time in weeks, I felt like *me* again.

He smiled when he saw me, that slow, deliberate smile that always made my pulse trip. "You look... incredible," he said, opening the passenger door.

I slid in and smoothed my dress over my thighs. "Remember," I said, teasingly. "Best behavior tonight."

His grin widened. "I'll do my best, Ms. Cassidy. Though I make no promises if you keep looking like that."

We drove to the Gold Mine Casino, one of Deadwood's newer establishments. It was a little glitzier, a little less steeped in the town's old charm. Inside, the air smelled faintly of perfume, whiskey, and money. The restaurant was upscale but cozy, tucked away from the noise of the gaming floor. Over flickering candlelight and the low hum of conversation, I looked at Dane and decided it was time to lay everything out.

"Tell me," I said, setting my napkin down. "All of it. No half-truths, no skimming past the ugly parts. I want to know why you never told me Ford was your brother."

Dane leaned back, shoulders tightening as though bracing himself. His gaze drifted toward the window before returning to me. "When my mother was dying," he began, voice low, "she made me promise I'd look after him. Give him a place to live. A job. Some kind of foundation. She always believed he could turn things around if someone kept him steady."

He rubbed a hand along his jaw. "I thought she meant the usual trouble—late nights, bad decisions, stupid fights. But these last two weeks... I've learned a lot more than she ever told me. I've had people digging. Looking through old hospital records, settlements, and HR reports that never saw daylight. And yes," he exhaled, slow and heavy, "I threw some money around to get answers."

My stomach tightened. "What did you find?"

Dane hesitated only a moment. "My mom paid off women. Multiple women." His expression twisted, disgusted, not at them, but at the truth. "Accusations of sexual harassment, going back years. She kept it all quiet. Checks were filed under 'miscellaneous hospital donations.' Lawyers handled the rest. No one ever used the word 'assault,' not officially. But Brooke..." His eyes met mine. "After what happened to you, I don't believe for a second that harassment was the worst of it."

A chill worked its way down my spine. "Your mother actually paid women to keep silent?"

He nodded, shame pulling at the edges of his expression. "She thought she was protecting him. Protecting our family. I don't think she ever understood what she was covering. Or maybe she did, and she just couldn't face it."

I sat back, stunned. "That's horrifying. Women came forward about a powerful doctor and were paid to disappear. And she let that continue?"

His jaw tightened. "Ford never stopped when he wanted something. Never. And I think when he realized you and I were... involved, he pushed even further. He always had a competitive streak, but this—" He shook his head. "This was him crossing a line he never should have been anywhere near."

I swallowed hard, anger rising in my chest, not at Dane, but at the years of women who had tried to speak and been told their voices didn't matter.

Dane reached for my hand, more cautious than I'd ever seen him. "I've spent the last two weeks working with my attorneys and some people in law enforcement. Ford is gone. He agreed to leave Deadwood permanently."

"Where?" I asked.

"Montana. A ranch." He paused. "And before you worry, he won't be without supervision. Let's just say the men checking in on him are the kind of people you don't want to irritate. His brow lifted slightly. "Nothing illegal. Just... persuasive."

I blew out a breath, interpreting exactly what he meant. These men were likely of the break-your-kneecap-to-get-the-point-across type. And somehow, I was fine with that. Ford wouldn't be hurting anyone else anytime soon.

"And you think that fixes this?" I finally asked, voice quieter than I intended.

"No." Dane shook his head. "It won't undo what happened. But it keeps him away from you. And away from anyone else he might hurt."

The sincerity on his face, the raw apology behind his eyes, was something I hadn't expected to see. Not from a man so controlled, so careful.

"I'm asking for your forgiveness," he continued. "For not telling you sooner. For not protecting you sooner. For not knowing what he really was."

I watched him for a long moment, letting silence settle between us like a third presence at the table.

"I don't know if I can forgive all of it," I said finally. "But I can forgive you for trying."

Relief flickered across his features, softening the tension in his shoulders.

"But listen to me, Dane," I added, leaning in. "If you ever hide something like this again, something that matters, I won't be this understanding next time."

He nodded, solemn enough to make it feel like an oath. "Understood."

For a moment, neither of us spoke. Then another thought pulled at me. "What happens now," I asked quietly, "with the money? The funds your casino has been sending to the hospital every year?"

His expression shifted, the tension returning, but different this time. Calculated. Resolved. "I've already stopped all transfers," he said. "Every cent. An investigation is underway to see who at the hospital knew... who helped keep things quiet." His voice darkened. "When it all comes to light, those people won't be working in Deadwood again. Not in healthcare. Not anywhere close to women who depend on them."

My stomach twisted with a mix of anger and something like relief. "Good." Then, after a beat, "But maybe those funds shouldn't disappear."

His eyes narrowed slightly, curious.

"What if," I said, choosing my words carefully, "instead of sending the money back into the same account, we redirect it somewhere that actually helps women? Programs for survivors of sexual assault or domestic violence. Places that don't rely on silence."

Dane watched me, really watched me, and something shifted behind his eyes. I would say it was something like pride. "That's a damn good idea," he said. Then he paused, shook his head once. "But I've got a better one."

I lifted a brow. "Better than supporting organizations that already do the work?"

A slow smile spread across his face, edged with possibility. "We start something here," he said. "In South Dakota. A resource center. Counseling, legal help, emergency housing... whatever women in crisis need." His jaw tightened. "Somewhere real. Somewhere safe. A place that doesn't hide predators. One that stops them."

My chest warmed at the conviction in his voice. "You'd fund all of that?"

"I'd fund it with my last dollar," he said simply. "But I'd want you to help shape it. You'd understand what victims actually need far better than I ever could."

For a moment, I just let his words settle. Then another thought surfaced, practical, but still important. "And what about the hospital?" I asked. "Some of that money did help. The problem wasn't the hospital. It was the people who allowed Ford to keep working there. And they're being dealt with. But the ED..." I hesitated, remembering Amber's wish list, including updated monitors, new trauma carts, and better family rooms for loved ones waiting through emergencies. "There's a lot that could use support."

He nodded slowly. "I'll ask for a full review. Department by department. Once we know what's needed, I'll funnel money where it does the most good. I'm not pulling support from the community, Brooke. I'm pulling support from the people who abused it."

The distinction landed with surprising clarity. "Good," I murmured. "Then maybe we can do both. Help the hospital do better... and help women who need it."

Dane's fingers brushed mine, warm and certain. "We will," he said. "All of it."

The idea hung between us. It was bigger than both of us, but suddenly, I felt that I had a new purpose in life. Something to help me continue to move forward from all that I had lost back in Minnesota. "You have the resources to do that?" I asked.

He leaned in, threading his fingers through mine. "I have the resources to do just about anything, Brooke. But this... this I would want to do with you."

My breath caught, because it wasn't a romantic declaration, not exactly. It was something deeper. A commitment. A path forward.

And for the first time in weeks, the tension in my chest eased. Just a little.

And for the first time since everything happened, I felt like we were finally standing on something real. Messy, complicated, but real.

Dinner carried on, lighter now, both of us testing the edges of peace. When we finished, I pushed back from the table and smiled. "Show me the tables."

He blinked. "The poker tables?"

"Yes," I said. "You told me all about them earlier. Let's see if your rival runs a tighter ship than you do."

He laughed, and soon we were weaving through the casino floor, the sound of chips and laughter surrounding us. Dane pointed out the blackjack and roulette tables, explaining odds and strategies, his voice smooth. But just as we reached the high-limit poker room, his phone buzzed. He frowned when he saw the caller ID.

"I need to take this," he muttered, stepping aside. His tone shifted immediately. It was low, sharp, authoritative. "Handle it quietly," I heard him say. "I'm on my way."

He hung up and looked at me, jaw tight. "I'm sorry. There's been an altercation at The Silver Spur. A bachelor party got out of hand. I need to go. Please come with me?"

Something in his eyes told me this wasn't a request. And truth be told, I didn't want the night to end. I nodded.

Back at The Silver Spur, Dane led me through a side corridor I hadn't noticed before and into a private suite off the private dining room we had dined in a few weeks earlier. "We use this for special events," he said.

The room was dimly lit, elegant but intimate. A long mahogany table sat in the center, surrounded by plush chairs. A polished bar lined one wall, and a smaller poker table gleamed in the corner beneath a hanging chandelier.

"Will you wait for me here?" he asked softly.

I nodded, and he disappeared through the door.

Donavan appeared a few minutes later with a chilled glass of Chardonnay and a reassuring smile. "Mr. Walker asked me to bring you this to keep you company."

"Thank you," I said, settling into one of the chairs around the large table. I watched as Donavan left the room.

By the time Dane returned half an hour later, the wine was gone, my nerves beginning to soothe. His shirt was unbuttoned at the collar, his hair slightly mussed.

"The men have been escorted out," he said, exhaling. "Bachelor party gone sideways. Nothing serious."

I stood up from the chair at the end of the table and leaned my weight against it. I held out my empty wine glass. "It's empty," I said.

Dane walked toward me and removed the glass from my hand. He walked over to the bar and set it down, his back to me. "I know you told me to behave. But how can you expect me to when you wear a dress like that? You're a beautiful woman, Brooke."

I looked down at my dress, then held up my hands and admired the red nail polish. As a nurse, it wasn't an indulgence I often enjoyed. "You're not so bad-looking yourself, Dane," I said, watching him as he turned to me. I wondered where the night would go. And thankfully, he didn't leave me guessing.

If I could say anything about my sex life with Dane, it would be that it left nothing to mystery. That night in the private gaming room of his casino, on the long mahogany table and yes, on the poker table, I realized something I had been trying not to admit to myself:

I was absolutely in love with Dane Walker.

And though the sex was incredible, that wasn't the whole story. I kept replaying the moments after my *fourth* orgasm of the night, when he had helped me down from the poker table, careful with my body, holding me as though I were something precious. He'd wrapped his suit jacket around my naked skin, the fabric warm from his own heat. I watched him pull on his underwear and pants with quick, practiced movements, then he lifted me into his arms and carried me to the oversized couch tucked into the corner of the room.

We curled there together, tangled and breathless. We talked. Kissed. Traced each other's skin like we were trying to memorize the shape of something we weren't ready to lose. And yes, maybe we made love once or twice more. The man was incorrigible.

But what struck me wasn't only the demanding, scorching sex on the tables. It was how the night shifted afterward into something softer, quieter, threaded with a kind of tenderness I hadn't expected. A tenderness that made me realize I wasn't just falling for Dane... I was finding my footing again. Finding purpose. Somehow, in the chaos of being hurt and then choosing to rise anyway, I'd uncovered a strength I didn't know I had, one I could use to help others who'd been through their own terrifying moments. And beneath all of that, steady and undeniable, was something that felt suspiciously, terrifyingly like love.

CHAPTER 16

After that night at The Gold Mine and then at the Silver Spur, I'd done a lot of thinking. More, I think, than I had allowed myself to do since Mitch died. When I first arrived in Deadwood, I'd seen the next twelve weeks as a pause button for my life. A place to hide, to gather myself, and maybe, if I was lucky, to start feeling like a whole person again.

I'd believed grief had a set shape. That healing had to look a certain way, full of quiet reflection, long walks, sleeping alone, staying busy. I'd told myself that time and distance would eventually mend a broken heart if I just followed the "right" pattern.

But, as it turns out, grief isn't tidy. It isn't predictable. And it isn't something you must shoulder in isolation. It changes alongside you. It softens corners you never planned to revisit. And sometimes, if you're open to it, compassion slips in when you least expect it, wrapped in the arms of a man you weren't looking for.

In the weeks that followed, Dane and I spent long stretches of time together, talking through our pasts, slowly revealing the pieces we kept tucked away. He'd been gentle with my memories of Mitch, never once making me feel wrong for still loving someone who was no longer here. He told me more than once that he didn't expect me to be "finished" with my grief. "How could you be?" he had said one night as we lay tangled in his bed. "He was your first love. You don't lose someone like that and just close the door behind you."

And because he was honest, I felt safe enough to ask about his first love. He told me her name. Margie. The girl who had gotten away when her family moved after high school. They'd kept in touch for a while, but life has a habit of shifting people in different directions. Eventually, they both moved on.

We talked about other things too. More intimate things. Our sex lives, the choices we'd made, the people we'd been with. Dane didn't shy away. When I asked bluntly about the rumors of him being a womanizer, he didn't deny them. He told me he'd had a full dating life for years, but somewhere along the way, about two years ago, he said, something shifted. It hadn't been one moment, but a gradual realization that casual connections weren't fulfilling him anymore. He didn't want nights that ended as quickly as they began. He wanted something that stayed. Something that mattered.

Ironically, that shift happened around the time Mitch died. I wasn't sure what to do with that coincidence, but it sat with me. And then came the question I had been avoiding: what was *I* going to do once Amber returned from maternity leave?

That answer hit a snag when Paul Jackson informed me that Amber had resigned. She wanted to stay home with her baby. And she'd recommended that the hospital offer her position to me. I'd been floored. I'd also been terrified.

I spent two full days turning the offer over in my mind. Accepting it meant real, permanent change. It meant choosing Deadwood not just as a temporary escape, but as a place to plant myself. It also meant something else... something I hadn't been able to shake since my dinner with Dane.

If I stayed, building the organization we'd talked about would be easier. More possible. South Dakota wasn't just where I'd ended up; it was turning into the place where I could actually *do* something.

Still, I didn't want Dane to think I was choosing any of this *because* of him. What we had was still new. Intense, yes, but still settling into shape. I'd expected him to be cautious, maybe even hesitant.

Instead, when I told him, he lit up like someone had handed him an unexpected gift.

"I'd love for you to stay," he told me, voice low and grounded. "Not for me. For *you*. You're brilliant at what you do. They'd be lucky to have you. But we, together, could do so much."

His reaction spilled warmth through me that I wasn't prepared for.

I spent time on the phone with my mom, my oldest brother's wife, and even Mitch's mother. I told them about the offer, about the town, and, without getting into details, about Dane and my plans to help women who needed it. To my surprise, every one of them encouraged me. They told me I deserved happiness. That I deserved a fresh start. That Mitch would have wanted me to keep living, not stay stuck out of loyalty to a future we never got to have. And that Mitch would have been proud of me.

So the choice became clear.

At the end of my tenth week, I walked into Paul Jackson's office and asked if the offer still stood. When he said yes, I accepted without hesitation. Later that afternoon, after signing the contract, I walked out of that office as the new lead charge nurse of the emergency department.

It felt surreal. Thrilling. A little terrifying. But right.

That left only one major question: where would I live?

Commuting from Rapid City wasn't practical. Forty-five minutes each way after twelve-hour shifts would wear on anyone, especially in winter. The small house I'd been renting in Deadwood was no longer an option; the owner had already booked another tenant to move in as soon as I moved out.

So Dane and I made a plan.

When I worked, I'd stay in the penthouse apartment at the casino. On my off days, I'd be wherever Dane happened to be. That means sometimes Deadwood and sometimes Rapid City. He spent more time at the Rapid City home in the off-season, when the casino slowed down.

It wasn't a perfect arrangement, but it felt manageable. And natural. And, if I were being honest, comforting.

Still, there was one more decision to make. The house Mitch and I had shared in International Falls. The place is full of memories. The place I had clung to, unsure if letting it go meant letting go of him.

But standing in my small rental kitchen one afternoon, phone pressed to my ear as I talked to my realtor in Minnesota, I realized that sometimes moving forward requires releasing the weight that holds you in place.

I loved Mitch. I would always love Mitch. But selling the house didn't erase him. It didn't erase who we had been. It simply made space for who I was becoming.

And I was becoming someone new.

Someone who could build a life in a historic town in the Black Hills. Someone who could fall deeply, feverishly in love with a man like Dane Walker. Someone who could stand on her own two feet, no matter whose arms she fell asleep in.

Deadwood had changed me. It had surprised me. It had pushed me in ways I didn't foresee. But as I signed the final paperwork for my new position, arranged the sale of my house, and packed up the last of my things, one thought stayed with me. I wasn't losing myself. I was finding a new version of my life.

A life built in a town where grit and beauty coexist. A life with a man who challenged me, comforted me, and frustrated me, sometimes in the same breath. A life shaped not by fear of the past, but by hope for what came next.

And in this life, my life, my house always wins.

ABOUT ANN SCREIBER

Ann Schreiber writes contemporary romance with heart, heat, and heroines who refuse to settle. Her spicy novella The House Always Wins takes readers to Deadwood, where risk, temptation, and unexpected love collide. Known for bringing emotional depth and sizzling chemistry together, Ann crafts stories about second chances and bold new beginnings. When she's not writing, she's likely plotting her next love story set somewhere unforgettable.

RETURN TO DEADWOOD

CHARLES BROWN

1

"Step into the light, or I'll shoot," Violet Daniels stared into the darkness, a Colt .45 revolver held ready in her hand.

"And what if I shoot first?" a man's voice asked from the darkness to her right.

"Then my husband will see the muzzle flash and kill you," Violet replied calmly.

The night air was crisp. Violet stared past the campfire into the darkness, looking for any movement that might give away the man's position, and praying Jack would return soon.

"I think you're bluffin'," the man spoke again, this time further to her right.

Violet stood perfectly still. Her heartbeat quickened, and she could feel beads of sweat forming on her forehead despite the chill in the air. A log burning in the fire weakened and snapped in half, causing the log above it to fall into the embers. Sparks shot skyward, momentarily flooding the area with light.

In her peripheral, Violet caught the glint of metal. Instantly, she turned and shot. The big gun kicked hard, forcing her hand skyward. As she began to lower it, something struck her arm just below the wrist. She lost her grip on the gun, and it slipped from her hand. Panic and pain filled her lungs, and she screamed.

Without her gun, she was vulnerable. The logical part of her brain begged her to find it, but before she could move, something hit her hard on the side of the head and blackness closed in around her.

~

A blood curdling scream followed by the sound of three shots split the night air as Jack pulled his second boot on. Grabbing one of the walnut-handled Colt .45 revolvers from his gun belt, he sprinted toward camp. The trail ran uphill, then curved slightly before rounding a large tree. Legs churning and all caution gone, he ran. He had left Violet smiling by the fire when he slipped off to bathe himself in the creek. Fear filled his mind and fueled each step.

Breathing hard, he rounded the large tree and scanned the campsite. Violet's crumpled body lay beside the tree where he had left her. The unnatural position she was in told him something was very wrong. Gun ready, he crossed to her.

"Violet," he whispered, "Violet, honey."

When she did not respond, he used his free hand to roll her from her stomach onto her back. Light from the campfire flooded across her bloodied face, and Jack nearly dropped his gun. His eyes searched for movement in the darkness as he placed his free hand over her heart. It was still beating.

Knowing he would do her no good, dead or shot himself, he stepped away from her long enough to throw more wood on the fire. Before the new wood caught fire, he retraced his steps and moved Violet further into the night shadows.

There he waited. That she had been shot, he had no doubt. The extent of her wounds worried him. That she was a fighter, he knew. Seconds turned into minutes. Five minutes passed. He squatted beside her, gun in his right hand, his left on her chest above her heart.

The new wood caught, and the fire blazed. To his right, at the far edge of the campfire's light, he spotted the soles of a worn pair of boots. For the next few minutes, he watched to make sure they did not move. Then, keeping to the edge of the darkness, he made his way to them.

They belonged to a man. In the darkness, he looked tall and thin. Jack pressed the barrel of his pistol into the man's side. Nothing. The man did not stir. Grabbing one booted leg, Jack dragged him into the campfire light. Only then did he see the hole where his right eye had been. Turning him over, he found that a good portion of his skull was gone.

Satisfied that there was no immediate danger, Jack left the dead man and returned to Violet. Hoisting her in his arms, he carried her to the edge of the campfire and laid her down gently. There he began to examine her more thoroughly. She had been shot twice. One of the bullets had shattered her right arm a couple of inches below the wrist. The jagged end of a bone was visibly jutting out of the skin. The other bullet had struck her in the head. Carefully, Jack turned her head in an effort to see the damage better.

Blood matted her long red hair, but a nasty welt was all he could find. No entry wound and no exit wound. He searched for some comfort in the knowledge that the bullet had only grazed her but found none. She was unconscious, and they were two days from Deadwood, and that was the closest place a doctor could be found.

Jack had learned early in life that some decisions had to be mulled over while others needed to be made immediately. This was one of the latter. First, Violet's wounds needed to be taken care of, so he grabbed a pot from one of the mule's saddle packs and started for the creek. His mind had worked out the sequence of steps he would take before he reached the water's edge.

Quickly, he retrieved the rest of his clothes and his gun belt. Once dressed, he filled the pot with water and started back. He searched his memory for all information that would help him care for Violet's wounds. By the time he arrived back at the camp, he had a plan.

While the pot of water heated in the center of the fire, he retrieved both of his spare shirts and tore them into strips. As soon as the water was warm enough, he cleaned Violet's head wound, placed a bandage on it, and tied it in place with one of the strips. He knew the bone in her arm needed to be reset, but he had no previous experience to draw on, so he cleaned the arm as best as he could, then wrapped it well before splinting it.

Saddling the horses came next. The mules and supplies, he decided would have to be left behind. He considered the gold they had with them and decided one of the mules would be needed after all. Once, he had both horses and a mule ready, he doused the fire with what was left of the water in the pot.

Picking up Violet, he cradled her in his arms and hoisted himself into the saddle. Leading Violet's horse and the pack mule, he started into the dark. He did not like the idea of riding at night but knew that if he did not get Violet to a doctor, he might lose her, and that was not an option.

A horse neighed off to his left moments minutes after they left the campsite. He veered toward the sound. It neighed again, and he saw its silhouette in what little moonlight filtered through the trees. He decided a third horse might come in handy as he made his way toward it.

He found it saddled and tied to a small tree. Loosening its reins from the tree, he tossed them across its saddle, and clicked at it, hopeful that it would follow on its own accord. To his surprise, it did.

~

The gentle roll of the carousel horse was not nearly exciting enough for Violet. She glared at her father each time she passed the place where he stood waving at her. In her mind, she knew that he was trying to protect her, trying to appease her, by taking her to Cremorne Gardens in Chelsea instead of buying her the horse she wanted. But in her heart, she despised him.

The wooden horse beneath her bucked hard, and she felt herself falling. Something was wrong. She searched through her memories and could not find one in which she had fallen from a carousel horse, or any other horse, for that matter. Pain exploded in her head as her body struck the ground. Confusion set in, and as she tried to make sense of it all, and then everything faded to black.

~

The first hue of orange showed on the eastern horizon before Jack allowed himself to stop. After crossing a shallow stream that had deep cuts on both sides, leaving its banks steep, they descended into the bed of the waterway. The climb down had been precarious. Getting the horses up the far bank and out had been even more difficult. Twice he had almost lost his hold on Violet. Once across, the trail had turned south and followed the flow of the creek.

Now, the water glistened in the fading moonlight, and the gentle gurgling of the stream threatened to lull him to sleep as he watered the horses and the mule, in a spot he had found downstream from the crossing. He had dismounted and gently laid Victoria on the ground before leading the livestock to the water's edge. The stream here was wider, and he thought the water was possibly a little deeper. Across the stream, the far bank rose nearly twenty feet high.

Somewhere in the night, the adrenaline rush had worn off. As exhausted as he was, Jack knew there would be no rest for him until he reached Deadwood. Violet needed a doctor more than he needed sleep. Throughout the night, she had moaned a few times, but mostly her body had simply rested against his as they rode slowly along.

By the time he had the livestock watered and was ready to continue, the sun had found its way into the sky. He switched horses, mounting Victoria's and putting his own on a lead. The dead man's horse had stayed with them throughout the night, and Jack, having little doubt that it would continue to do so, decided not to take the time to put a lead on it.

The dull throb of a headache gnawed at his temple as he started the horses moving once again. It had only been two days since he and Violet had left Deadwood. That he was not welcome there was of little concern to him now. Violet needed the doctor, so Sheriff Bullock would just have to deal with it.

~

The carriage ride home from the Gardens took them through the streets of London. Victoria's father sat stoic across from her, staring out at the city through a small opening in the curtain. She was curled up in the corner, pouting.

"Alright, fine," he broke the silence finally. "If you are so damn determined to have one, I'll buy you a horse, but I don't want to see one single tear if you get thrown. Do you understand me?"

Victoria shook her head.

"How a ten-year-old girl can be so exasperating is beyond me," her father's eyes narrowed as he spoke. "And now, there you are. You've always gotten whatever you wanted. Always done whatever you wanted to do. Gone wherever you decided to go with whoever you decided to go with. Oh, yes, I suppose in a manner, I am partially responsible, but don't you think for one second you don't have to shoulder at least a portion of the blame, young lady. It was not I who fell for that no account gambler, nor I who left England and never returned. It was not I..."

Victoria looked from her father to herself. She was no longer ten. She was a grown woman, and every part of her body ached. That she was dreaming, she was almost certain. She tried to force herself awake and could not. Why she did not know, but she did not like the way her dreams kept changing memories from her past. She tried harder to force herself awake, but instead of waking, she felt herself slipping back into the darkness.

2

Deadwood's main thoroughfare was bustling with activity as Jack navigated through its muddy center. Along the way, folks stopped and stared as he made his way to the far end of the town and down the street where the doctor hung his shingle. The building itself was not much to look at, but Doctor Babcock was a talented physician.

Jack dismounted with Violet in his arms, stepped up to the door, and tapped it twice with the toe of his boot. Exhausted and barely able to stand himself, it was pure willpower that kept him upright.

"Come on in," Jack heard the doctor shout from the other side of the door.

Irritated, Jack kicked the door twice more, harder this time. The doctor loudly muttered something Jack did not understand, and then Jack heard footsteps moving toward the door. Seconds later, the door opened to the doctor saying, "I said come on in."

Jack watched as the doctor's demeanor changed from annoyance to concern. Jack stepped past the doctor and, without being told to, placed Violet on the table in the middle of the room.

"What happened?" Doc Babcock asked as he stepped around Jack.

"She was shot twice," Jack replied. "Once in the head. Once in the arm. The bone was sticking out of her skin, and I didn't know what I should do, so I just wrapped it and headed here. I'm not sure how bad the head injury is. I found her unconscious, and she's been like this ever since. Sometimes she groans a bit, and once she screamed out, but she hasn't woken."

The doctor was already removing the bandage from Violet's head. "Who shot her?"

"I don't know who the man was," Jack told him, "but he's dead. She killed him."

Too exhausted to stand any longer, Jack sat down on one of the two chairs located against the wall next to the table. He could feel the last bit of energy seeping from his body, and he fought to stay awake.

"Is she gonna make it, Doc?" he asked.

Doc Babcock looked up from examining Violet long enough to say, "Only time will tell. Her pulse is weak, but from what I know of her, she's a strong-willed young lady."

"What can I do to help?" Jack asked, knowing he was in no shape to be of any real assistance.

The look the doctor gave Jack told him that Babcock was aware of Jack's state. With a shake of his head, he said, "Best thing you can do for me right now is get your horses to the livery, then go find Jane and get some rest."

"Calamity?" Jack asked.

"Yes," Doc Babcock confirmed. "And let's pray she's past last night's bottle."

Jack stood, stumbled as he walked to the door, opened it, then asked, "Any idea where I might find her?"

"First place I'd look is Utter's Freight," Doc replied. "You know where that is?"

"I do." Jack answered as he pulled the door shut.

Tennessee William T. Jones sat directly across the table from Violet's father. She was nearly seventeen, and he was handsome, exciting, and forbidden. All the attributes a wealthy young lady desired. Four other men sat at the table, all of them closer to her father's age than her own.

Violet had sat in on enough of her father's weekly games to know the rules and had learned to figure the odds fairly well most of the time. Tonight, many of the larger pots had gone to Tennessee Williams, perhaps too many.

"Mr. Jones, I was wondering," Violet's father studied his cards as he spoke. "Why is it you Americans feel it necessary to precede your names with your place of origin?"

William, Bill to his friends, Violet would find out later, smiled as he replied. "Well, kind sir, not all Americans feel the need to do so, but as for me, there is a fellow known on my side of the pond as Canada Bill, whose actual name is William Jones. Mr. Canada Bill is, well let's just say, a confidence artist – a swindler – in addition to being a gambler, and to alleviate any misunderstandings, I felt it necessary to separate my good name from his by including, as you say, my place of origin prior to my name." As he finished speaking, he tossed several chips into the pot and added, "I call."

Violet, who had been leaning against the wall, smiled as her father laid his cards on the table. If she had figured the odds correctly, the handsome Mr. Jones had lost this hand to her father. She looked from her father's cards to Mr. Jones, only to find him staring at her. Their eyes met, and he gave her a quick wink before turning his attention back to the table and laying his cards out.

"Sometimes the odds, no matter how well figured, are incorrect," Violet heard Bill say, and once again confusion set in. Yes, he had told her that many times, but it was not part of this memory. She looked from him to her father, who was now staring at her, and the anger in his eyes was clearly visible.

"That's right, daughter," he hissed, "Sometimes the odds, no matter how well figured, are incorrect. But then sometimes, wisdom trumps youth, and a father knows exactly what will happen if his daughter falls for a no-account American gambler. Sometimes..."

Violet did not want to hear anymore, and so let the memory slip away.

Jack found Jane exactly where Doc Babcock had said she would be. She was nursing a cup of coffee and a hangover. A man wearing a beaded buckskin shirt and matching pants was standing beside her, giving her what for. "Knowin' when to stop, Jane, that's where you're lackin'. I ain't sayin' a drink or two is bad for ya, but you just don't seem to know when enough is enough."

"Piss off, Charlie," Jane snarled as Jack stepped up onto the boardwalk.

"Jane," Jack spoke her name, drawing her attention away from Charlie.

"What the hell are you doin' back in Deadwood, Jack?" Jane's eyes widened as she stood. Tall and lanky, she was also dressed head to toe in buckskin apparel, but unlike Charlie's, hers was tattered and stained.

"Voilet's been shot. She's in a bad way," Jack explained. "Doc sent me to get you. He needs your help if you're sober enough."

"Damn right, I'm sober enough," she was already stepping off the boardwalk and into the street as she spoke.

"Hey, that's my cup," Charlie shouted.

"Piss off, Charlie," Jane hollered back over her shoulder as she trudged through the mud headed for the far side of the thoroughfare. "Ain't like ya ain't got other cups."

Jack started to follow Jane, but as he reached the edge of the boardwalk, Charlie spoke, "Jack, now that wouldn't be the famous Jack Abbott I've been hearin' about since I got back from Cheyenne yesterday."

Irritated, exhausted, and worried about Violet, Jack turned. "And if it is?"

"Wow, now friend," Charlie smiled. "I was just askin' a question. I didn't mean to rile ya. I'm Charlie Utter, by the way."

"Then, yes, I'm Jack Abbott," Jack nodded as he spoke. The man in front of him was at least a head shorter than Jack, who stood six foot two inches in his socked feet. With long wavy hair and a matching set of pearl-handled pistols strapped to his waist, Charlie Utter looked more like a pistolero from a traveling show than the owner of a freight and mail company.

Charlie stuck out his hand. "Nice to meet ya, Jack."

"Likewise," Jack shook his hand. "I've got to get back to Doc's."

As he turned to go, Charlie said, "I hope your girl is okay. If there's anything I can do to help, let me know."

By the time Jack made it back to Doc Babcock's, the doctor and Jane had already removed all the bandages from Violet. Babcock directed Jack to a cot in the back corner of the building. When Jack refused to listen, Jane stepped in, "Doc here can either argue with you or fix Violet, Jack. He cain't do both, and you look like hell. So, what's it gonna be?"

Knowing his odds of winning an argument with Jane, Jack decided to stretch out on the cot but refused to allow himself to sleep. Instead, he listened as Jane and the doctor went about preparing to set Violet's arm.

"It's her ulna that's shattered," he heard the doctor say. "I know she's unconscious, but I think it best if we still use ether just in case. Do you remember how to administer it?"

"I do," Jane replied.

"Good," Doc Babcock said. "Once the ether has taken effect..."

"How will we know?" Jane asked.

"If I start moving this arm around and she shows a pain response, then the ether hasn't taken effect," he told her.

For the next several minutes, neither of them spoke. Jack listened as they moved between the table Violet lay on and the various shelves and counters that held supplies. The clinks and clatters of metal and glass nearly lulled him to sleep.

"I think it's time," Doc's voice brought him fully awake once again.

Jack could no longer force himself to lay still. He sat up and watched from his place across the room as the doctor secured Violet's arm to the table in two places below her elbow. Once he had her arm secure, he picked up a scalpel and a pair of forceps. Jack was glad he could not see over Violet's body as the doctor began to work. If Violet felt any pain, it did not show.

Slowly, meticulously the doctor probed while Jane stood by with additional ether. After what seemed like hours to Jack, he watched the doctor place the scalpel and forceps aside, take Violet's hand, and gently pull it while working the bone back into place. Doc Babcock gave a nod when he was satisfied and began to stitch the open wound. When he was done stitching, he wrapped several clean strips of cloth around the wound itself, then slowly covered Violet's arm from her hand to just below her shoulder with linen. Next, he began to apply wet strips of cloth, he pulled from a large bowl. After several minutes, Violet's arm was covered to her elbow. With care, Doc Babcock bent her arm to ninety degrees and then continued. When he was finished, Violet's arm was completely encased. Jack had never seen anything like it before.

"That was the easy part," the doctor said to Jane as he stepped back. "Now we have to deal with the head wound."

"I thought that the bullet only grazed her," Jane lifted the ether-covered sponge away from Violet's face as she spoke.

Doc Babcock stepped forward and gently lifted one of Violet's eyelids, then stood studying it for several seconds before lowering it and doing the same with her other eyelid. Shaking his head, he looked at Jane. "On the outside, the bullet only grazed her, but the shock to the skull has caused her brain to swell."

"How do you fix that?" Jack asked as he rose from the cot.

"A procedure called trepanning," the doctor answered. Jack gave him a confused look, and Babcock explained, "I'll have to drill a hole through her skull to relieve the pressure."

3

Violet stood beside Tennessee Bill on the deck of a steamship bound for New Orleans. Bill had promised her the world if she would run away with him. She had insisted they be married first, and the two had taken a train to Scotland and eloped. Now with him by her side and the whole world in front of her, Violet could not wait to see America.

The memory shifted. She still stood beside her husband, but now she was on a Mississippi steamboat. They were arguing. She wanted a seat at the card game he had organized, and he had told her no. Violet had stormed off to their cabin.

Much later that evening, there was a knock on the cabin door. Then, still angry, she had answered it. Now, as the memory played in her mind, she refused. If she did not open the door, then she did not have to deal with the news that was on the other side of it. The knock came again, and she chose the darkness.

~

"And if you don't drill?" Jack could feel his stomach turn as he asked.

"The swelling will kill her," Doc Babcock replied firmly.

Jack stood looking down at the woman he had fallen for and could not imagine a future without her. He had faced many problems in his life. Most of them he had handled with his fists or with his guns, but neither would be of help now. He looked from Doc Babcock to Jane, hoping for some kind of guidance. At no point in his life had he felt so helpless.

"When I've finished the procedure," Doc Babcock's tone had softened, "we will need to move her. I am not set up to house patients."

Jack looked around the room as he tried to comprehend what the doctor was saying. Whether it was the lack of sleep or the news he had just heard, Jack found it hard to think. He felt frozen, like time had stopped and he was trapped.

"Jack," he heard Jane's voice say his name and turned toward her.

The motion seemed unnatural, almost like the air around him was thick and his movement slowed by it. He had heard people talk about the weird effects grief and worry had on a person's body and mind, but this was a whole new experience for him. Violet will be okay, he told himself, then repeated it over and over.

"Jack!" Jane screamed his name.

Reality registered, and he spoke, "What?"

"Do you understand what the doctor is tryin' to tell ya?" she asked.

"No," he answered.

"You need to find lodgin'. Some place to make Violet comfortable when we're done here. Can you do that?"

"Lodgin'," he repeated the word. "Yes, I can do that."

"Good," Jane pointed toward the door as she spoke. "Then go. I'll come find you when we're done."

~

The knocking was back. Violet tried to ignore it, tried to force it from her mind. It continued. Frustration set in as she opened the door.

"Ma'am, your husband has been shot," the ship's captain informed her. "I'm sorry to have to be the one to inform you that he is dead."

The memory of the moment did not break her like it had the night it happened. It did not bring her to her knees in agony. She still felt saddened by her loss, but strangely, she no longer felt devastated. Why, she wondered. What had changed? She searched for an answer, but the darkness refused to allow her in. She fought against it. Pounded her fist against it. Each time she struck it, the edge of the darkness vibrated but refused to give. Her fist grew heavy, and still she swung. Frustration turned to anger, anger to fury, then the darkness exploded, and as it covered her like a huge gray blanket, a calmness filled her, and she drifted away on its nothingness.

~

Jack leaned against the counter of the Star & Bullock Hardware store, waiting for Sheriff Bullock to return. Sol Star, co-owner of the hardware store, busied himself behind the counter. When Jack had walked in and told Sol he needed to see the sheriff, Sol had simply shaken his head and said, "This should be good."

"Where can I find him?" Jack had asked.

"I'm not rightly sure," Sol replied. "He said he had some errands to run and would be back shortly when he left. Might be best to wait here."

Jack had taken Sol's suggestion, and now, as he waited, he tried to decide the best approach to take with the sheriff. That Bullock did not want him in town was clear. The sheriff had made that evident the day Jack and Violet had left for the Wyoming Territory.

The front door swung open, and Jack turned in time to see the sheriff walk through it. Their eyes locked, and Bullock broke stride, then continued to the counter. "What's he doin' here?" the sheriff asked Sol.

"Says he needs to talk to you," Sol replied.

"That so?" Bullock mumbled.

"That's so," Jack pushed himself away from the counter and squared his shoulders to the sheriff.

"Can't be," Bullock responded but did not turn toward Jack. Instead, it seemed to Jack like the sheriff was still talking to Sol.

"Why not?" Sol asked.

"Because," Bullock replied, "Jack Abbott promised to leave town, and I kinda took him for a man of his word."

Jack could feel himself reddening. "I am a man of my word, Bullock. Violet has been shot and is in a bad way. Doc Babcock was the closest doctor, so I brought her back. I have no more desire to be in your stinkin' town than you have for me to be here, but until she is well and we can travel again, I'm here. If that's gonna be a problem, it might be best if we work it out now."

Bullock turned slowly to face Jack. Sol's hands dropped below the counter.

"Mr. Star, I got no quarrel with you, but if the good sheriff here draws and your hand clears that counter with a weapon in it, my second shot will be aimed at your heart," Jack warned.

"Sol, hands on the counter," Bullock ordered, then to Jack, "You know I don't like gunplay, and you don't look like you're in shape for fisticuffs, so how 'bout you walk with me over to Doc's so I can see how bad this situation really is?"

Sol's hands moved from beneath the counter, and Jack relaxed slightly. "Doc Babcock is drillin' a hole in her head right now. That's how bad the situation is," Jack told him. "I've come to ask whether or not you still own the house she sold you when we left?"

"I do," Bullock nodded.

"I need to buy," Jack's eyes narrowed. He was not in the mood to be denied. "Violet will need a place to mend once the doctor is done."

"Why not just keep your word and move along when he's done?" Bullock asked.

"You are one cold-hearted son of a bitch," Jack responded.

"Perhaps," Bullock remained calm. "But I intend for this town to have peace, and in my opinion, your being here threatens that intent."

"Right now, Bullock, I could give an outhouse rat's shit about your opinion or your intent," the frustration in Jack's tone was clear. "Are you or are you not gonna sell me the house?"

Instead of answering Jack's question, the sheriff turned to Sol. "I'm gonna mosey over to Doc's. I'll be back shortly."

Sol nodded, and Bullock turned and started for the door. Jack looked at Sol, who shrugged. Irritation that he was not given an answer mixed with relief that there had not been gunplay filled Jack as he shook his head and started after Bullock.

Jack caught up to Bullock as the sheriff pushed Doc Babcock's door open. Jack followed him in to find the doctor wrapping a white cloth around Violet's head. Jane was wiping blood from the table into a bucket.

"Doc, Jack here tells me Miz Violet has been shot and can't travel. Is that so?" Bullock got straight to the point.

Doc Babcock gave the sheriff a look of disgust. "Bullock your bedside manner sucks."

The sheriff shrugged. "Maybe so, but that doesn't answer my question, Doc.

"No," Doc Babcock tucked the end of the cloth into a fold of the bandage. "No, she cannot travel. I'm not even sure when she will wake up or, sorry Jack, if she will wake up. I did the best I could, but the odds are not with someone with this kind of injury."

"If she should wake," Bullock ignored the doctor's belligerent tone and asked, "how long before she can travel?"

"Good Lord, Bullock," Doc Babcock glared at the sheriff. "You might as well be asking me if President Hayes suffers from piles."

"So, you don't know?" Bullock pushed.

"No, dammit, I don't know," Doc Babcock replied.

Bullock turned to Jack. "Three months, I'll rent you the house for three months. Money up front, and if she's able to travel earlier than that, I'll have your word the two of you will leave."

"Deal," Jack agreed, offering Bullock his hand.

Bullock shook it and added, "And you'll leave without refund."

Jack nodded agreement with the additional term. Doc Babcock swore aloud. "Heartless son of a bitch and proof that not all jackasses have tails."

The sheriff ignored the doctor's rant. "You can pick up the key to the house at the hardware store. If I'm not there, Sol knows where it is."

"How much?" Jack asked.

"Three hundred dollars," Bullock answered.

Doc Babcock let loose with another string of obscenities.

"Gold?" Jack asked ignoring the doctor.

"Sol can weigh it out at the store when you pick up the key," Bullock replied.

Jack nodded acknowledgment, and the sheriff turned and left. Doc Babcock continued to curse as he began to drop various medical devices covered in blood into a pot of water.

"When can we move her, doc?" Jack asked as soon as the sheriff was gone.

"As soon as you pay that damn charlatan and get the key," Doc Babcock replied.

"You go get the key," Jane ordered as she dropped the rag she had been using in the bucket beside her, "and I'll go get Charlie to help us carry her."

Instead of immediately following her order, Jack stepped up to the table and took Violet's left hand in his. Her eyes were closed, and she looked as if she were merely sleeping. If it had not been for the cast on her arm, the blood on her clothing, and the bandage on her head, he might have been able to convince himself she was only napping. His heart hurt, and he wished for nothing more than for her to open her eyes and say, "Well, hello there, darlin'."

"She'll make it," Jane reassured him.

Jack forced a smile. He told himself that as soon as she was able after she woke up, he was going to marry her – if she would have him.

4

Violet barely opened her eyes when the light from the window to her left caused her to shut them. It was as if she had looked directly into the sun, if the sun were five feet away. Even with her eyes tightly closed, the light was more than she could handle. She moaned.

"Well, look who decided to grace our presence," she heard a woman's voice say. The voice was gruff but familiar. She refused to open her eyes but searched through her memory for the person's identity.

Violet tried to raise her right hand, but it felt heavy. Instead, she raised her left hand and motioned toward the window in hopes whoever was in the room with her would pull the curtains shut.

"Oh, my," the voice exclaimed, "you really are back."

Violet attempted to speak as she motioned at the window again. In her mind, she had formed the words, but when she tried to verbalize them, they came out as a series of jumbled grunts. Confused, she tried again.

"The curtains?" the woman said. "Oh, Violet, I'm so sorry. I didn't think 'bout the light hurtin' your eyes after all this time."

Jane? The voice sounded like Calamity Jane's voice, but Jane was back in Deadwood, so that was impossible. The sound of fabric moving was followed by the bright light fading. Violet slowly opened her eyes. Without the light, it was easier, but even the filtered light caused her to blink and turn her head away from the window.

"How's that?" Jane's face came into view as she asked the question. Everything, including Jane's face, was blurry, as if Violet were looking through a piece of chiffon material.

"Better," Violet formed the word, but again the sound that came out of her mouth was far from the one she had mentally fashioned.

"I better get Doc Babcock," Jane's face disappeared as she spoke. "Oh, and Jack, I'd better get Jack."

Jack?

Jack was at the creek taking a bath. Violet's mind tried to reconcile the memory of Jack walking away from the camp and the appearance of Jane. It was more than she was capable of at the moment. She closed her eyes and allowed sleep to come.

~

Jack rushed from the livery where he had been checking on the livestock. The boardwalk was crowded with folks going about their daily business. As quickly as possible, he wove his way around them. Violet was awake. He could think of nothing else as he moved along.

"Violet opened her eyes and tried to speak," Jane told him when she arrived at the livery.

Jack did not need to hear anything more. He left Jane standing in the doorway and started for home. "I'm goin' for the doc," he heard her say somewhere behind him.

It had been nearly three weeks since he rode back into Deadwood. Three weeks of pure torture waiting for some sign, any sign, that Violet was going to return to him. Doc Babcock came daily, always with the same message, "These things take time."

Now as Jack opened the front door and made his way through the house and up the stairs to the bedroom where Violet lay, he struggled with what to say to her. During their first day on the trip out of Deadwood, he had suggested marriage. Violet had laughed and told him they should give it a little time. That night they had cuddled by the fire, and he had given her a long goodnight kiss before they bedded down in separate bedrolls. The second day they had discussed whether or not they should do more than cuddle. Violet had smiled and told him that when it was time, there would be no need for discussion, it would happen as nature intended it.

When they had made camp that evening, Violet had arranged their bedrolls into a single bed. Then she had informed him that she was going to the creek to bathe and that he was not to follow her. She had returned as the sun dropped from the sky and suggested he should make a trip to the creek himself.

He pushed the bedroom door open and stepped inside, still not sure what to say. The room was half-lit. Violet lay as she had for weeks, and for an instant, Jack thought that perhaps Jane had been mistaken.

As he turned to go, Violet made a noise. Not a moan, as he was used to hearing, but not words either. It was something between a low growl and an 'mmm' sound.

Stepping to the side of the bed, Jack looked down into eyes filled with confusion. Violet lifted her left arm and again made the noise. Carefully, Jack knelt at the side of the bed and took her hand in his.

"I'm here, darlin'," he assured her, "I'm right here."

~

Violet looked up into Jack's eyes as he knelt and took her hand. Questions raced through her mind as she squeezed his hand. Why were they back in Deadwood? Had they found land for their cattle ranch? What was wrong with her arm?

She decided to start with her arm, "What happened to my arm?" She formed the words, spoke the question, and grimaced at the sound that she heard. Something was wrong. Why did her words sound like that?

Jack looked as confused as she felt. In desperation, she pulled her hand from Jack's and pointed to the cast on her right arm.

"It's a cast," Jack explained as he took her hand in his once more. "You were shot, and the bullet broke one of the bones in your arm. Doc Babcock set the bone and put the cast on your arm to keep it in place."

Violet heard a door open and close, followed by footsteps drawing closer. Jack turned but did not let go of her hand as first Jane and then Doc Babcock stepped through the bedroom door.

"See, I told ya, she was awake," Jane smiled gleefully.

Doc Babcock made his way around the bed and reached for the curtains.

"Wouldn't do that if I was you," Jane warned.

The doctor's hand paused in midair. "And why might that be?"

"Cause it hurts her eyes," Jane shrugged.

"Okay, then," Doc Babcock said as he looked around the room. "In that case, Jane, why don't you find some candles, and we'll see how that works."

Violet watched Jane disappear and then turned toward the doctor. He pulled a chair from the corner of the room, moved it to Violet's side, and sat down in it.

"How do you feel, young lady?" he asked.

Again, she formed the words. "I've been better." Again, the sentence did not sound anything like it had in her mind.

"Well, I was afraid of this," Doc Babcock nodded, then explained. "Violet, you were shot twice. Once in the arm. Once in the head. The bullet that struck your head did not penetrate the skull, but the shockwave from it caused swelling in your brain. To relieve the swelling and save your life, I had to drill a small hole in your head. Because of where the bullet struck you, I was afraid you might have trouble with speech."

"So, this is normal?" Jack asked.

"It is," Doc Babcock answered.

"Is it permanent?" Jack asked the question that Violet desperately wanted answered.

"Only time will tell," the doctor replied. "I don't have a lot of experience with this type of injury. To tell you the truth, I have no experience, only cases I've read in journals, but from what I know, she has a better-than-average chance at full recovery."

Violet felt tears slip over the edge of her eyelids. Jack leaned forward and wiped them away. "It'll be okay, Violet, it'll be okay."

She wanted to scream, "How will it be okay? I can't speak. You can't understand me. I can barely see. How will it be okay?"

"I brought a candlestick and two candles, but there is more, if you need them," Jane said as she stepped back into the room.

Doc Babcock took one of the candles and lit it. The light from it stung Violet's eyes but not nearly as bad as the sunlight from the window. She watched as the doctor examined her. He began by passing the candle in front of her eyes.

"Good, good," he half-whispered as he stared intently. "Violet, I'm going to ask you some yes or no questions. Instead of trying to answer with words, answer by shaking your head. Do you understand?"

Violet nodded yes.

"Is everything blurry?"

Yes.

"That's what I thought," he smiled at her. "It will get better with time."

He pushed the candle onto the spike of the brass candlestick Jane had brought and placed it on the table beside Violet's bed. Violet looked from the doctor to Jane to Jack. The doctor looked serious, Jane looked elated, and Jack looked worried.

"Are you in pain?" Doc Babcock asked.

Violet considered the question. Was she? She did not think so. She shook her head no.

"Good," Doc Babcock said as he stood up. "That means the laudanum is working."

Violet shook her head no.

"It's okay. Right now, it's necessary," the doctor explained. "When you're better, we'll slowly wean you off it."

Again, Violet shook her head no. She could feel her mind growing heavy. With her last bit of consciousness, she pointed at the doctor's chair. Confused, the doctor looked from her to Jack.

"I think she wants to sit up," Jack said.

Violet squeezed his hand and shook her head yes as the darkness closed in around her once again.

~

"What do you think, Doc?" Jack asked.

Doc Babcock moved to the window and eased it open a crack. "I think she's got a long journey ahead of her. She's going to come and go, but if things progress as I suspect they will, she will stay with us a little longer each time she comes around."

"I meant what do you think about sittin' her up?" Jack inquired.

The doctor stepped away from the window and began to examine Violet. "I think it would be okay, but she's going to be awful weak, so she will need to be braced well. And I believe it would be best to wait to move her until she's conscious again."

Jack nodded that he understood, as Jane said, "I'll gather up as many pillows as I can find around the house."

"What else can we do for her?" Jack asked.

Doc Babcock smiled. "Have patience, son, have patience. That will be the absolute best thing you can do for her. I did not get to know her well during the time she was in town, but she seemed to me a very strong, very independent woman who had very little patience of her own. I figure her patience is going to run out long before she can speak or stand or walk, so it's going to be very important that she can draw on yours."

"That I can do," Jack assured the doctor as he stood up, then repeated, "that I can do."

5

Violet opened her eyes to see Jack sitting near the window with a book in his hands and realized how little she knew about him. A memory of her father lounging in the parlour with a copy of the latest penny dreadful tucked inside Charles Dickens's *A Tale of Two Cities* emerged. She had once snuck up on him and asked him why he had the little book inside the big book.

"Proper gentlemen do not read such literary swill," he had told her, "but I do find the stories fascinating."

For some reason, Violet felt a sense of pride watching the man she loved reading. The thought came innocently enough, and then the reality of it surfaced. It was the first time she had allowed herself to use the word love. She had admitted that she had feelings for him – the kind of feelings that should and would one day turn to love, but now was not the time. Uncomfortable with her thoughts, she shifted slightly.

"Oh, wonderful, you're awake," Jack closed the book, stood, and crossed to her side.

Violet started to respond, then remembered how badly it sounded when she tried to talk. So instead, she forced a smile and nodded her head. Jack set the book he had been reading on the table beside her bed, leaned over, and kissed her lightly on the cheek.

She wanted badly to talk to him. She had so many questions that needed to be answered. He must have seen something in her expression when he stood up because a concerned look furrowed his brow, and he asked, "Are you in pain?"

She shook her head no.

"Can I get you anything?"

Frustrated, she lay there looking up at him. How could she communicate with him? An idea took form. She nodded yes and pointed at the book he had just set down. With a confused look, he picked up the book and handed it to her. The cover had an illustration of a boy sitting on a barrel watching a second young man as he painted a fence. Above the image was the title – *The Adventures of Tom Sawyer*. She laid it in the crook of her cast arm and flipped the pages until she came to the first chapter. Slowly, she began to scan the text line by line. The words were blurry, but if she concentrated hard enough, she could make them out.

On the first page, she spotted one of the words she was looking for and pointed to it. Jack leaned forward and looked at where she was pointing.

The word Violet was pointing at was "up." The sentence it was in read, "The old lady pulled her spectacles down and looked over them about the room; then she put them up and looked out under them."

"Ah," Jack smiled at her. "You want a pair of spectacles?"

Violet shook her head in frustration and continued to scan. Two pages later, she found three words enclosed in parentheses – "picking up chips". Again, she pointed at the word up. Jack shook his head in confusion and said, "Up?"

Violet nodded yes.

"Oh, I think I understand," Jack's eyes widened with excitement. "Do you want to sit up?"

Yes.

Jack turned and left the room. His footsteps grew fainter as he moved down the stairs and through the house. The front door opened, and she heard Jack yell, "Hey, you, I've got a half dollar if you'll fetch Doc Babcock and Calamity Jane to this house."

A muffled voice shouted something Violet could not make out, then she heard Jack respond, "No, sir. You get nothin' until they arrive here."

She listened as he moved through the house again. Shortly, his frame filled the doorway. In his arms he carried several pillows. With a huge smile, he crossed to her side and carefully began to place them along the headboard of the bed.

Once he had positioned them, he took the last three and placed them at the foot of the bed. Then he took the book from the crook in her arm and set it on the bedside table before saying, "I'm not sure how to do this from here. I think it is best if I move you away from the headboard briefly, then situate the pillows before setting you up. Is that okay with you?"

Violet nodded yes.

Jack leaned down and tenderly placed one arm under her torso and his other behind her knees. She felt like a rag doll as he picked her up and moved her toward the foot of the bed. Her body ached, more from stiffness than injury, she thought.

As soon as Jack laid her down, he grabbed the remaining pillows and placed them with the others. After fluffing them a bit, he lifted her once again and placed her gently in a seated position against the pillows.

It felt good to view the world from the new vantage point.

Jack pulled the chair he had been sitting in by the window across the room and was about to sit down in it when there was a knock at the front door. He smiled at Violet and winked. "That'll be Jane and Doc Babcock," he told her as he stepped around the bed and started for the steps.

Before he made it to the door, it opened and Jane stuck her head in. "Jack, we're comin' in, and there's a fella out her says ya owe him a half dollar."

"Indeed, I do," Jack responded as he dug a coin from his pocket.

At the doorway, he flipped the half dollar to man who had retrieved Jane and the doctor. "For your trouble, friend, and thank you," he said then closed the door and led the new arrivals to Violet's room.

"Oh my, Violet," Jane was nearly giddy as she began to fuss over her friend. "Look at you sittin' up in bed."

Violet smiled, and Jack, for a second, thought his heart might melt. It was the first time he had seen her really smile since the shooting. Hope welled in his chest and he could not help but smile.

"Good afternoon, Miz Violet," Doc Babcock said as he sat down in the chair Jack had pulled to the bedside. "How are you feeling today?"

Violet's smile faded. Her brow scrunched, and her eyes narrowed. It was clear to Jack that the doctor's question had irritated her.

"I don't think she likes to talk," Jack told Babcock. Then he pointed at the copy of *The Adventures of Tom Sawyer*, and said, "She used that book to communicate with me this mornin'. She pointed at the word up until I understood she wanted to sit up."

Doc Babcock raised an eyebrow. "That's good. I wouldn't have thought of that myself. It shows that her ability to reason out a problem is intact."

"What's the next step?" Jane asked as she pushed a strand of hair away from Violet's face.

"I'm glad you asked," the doctor replied. "I sent a message to a good friend of mine back east, and he has promised to send all the literature he can find on helping Violet her learn to talk again. In the meantime, though, he did say in his response that it was important for her to continue to try to talk every day. Even if the sound she makes is unintelligible, he said in his return telegram that using her vocal cords would strengthen them."

Violet shook her head no.

"What if we get a piece of slate and some chalk from Mrs. Smith?" Jane asked.

Both Jack and Doc Babcock turned to her, looks of confusion on their faces. Jane shook her head as if the two men's inability to understand had somehow disgusted her.

"You know, Mrs. Dottie Smith," Jane explained, "She runs the select school at the far end of town. Got pupils and everything. If she'll loan or sell us some chalk and a slate, then Violet could communicate with us by writing on it."

Jack looked from Jane to Doc Babcock. "That's not a bad idea," the doctor said, "but it is still important that she try to talk."

Again, Violet shook her head.

"Alright then," Doc Babcock stood as he spoke. "It's up to you, Violet. I'm not going to argue with you. I think now's a good time to take the bandage off your head and see how the wound is healing."

Violet shook her head no again and pointed at Jack.

The doctor chuckled, "Violet, I've changed your bandages twice a week for nearly four weeks now. Jack has helped on more than one occasion."

She shook her head no once more and pointed at Jack and then at the door.

"So be it," Doc Babcock shrugged. "Jack, this might be a good time for you to see if Mrs. Smith has that chalk and slate Jane was talking about."

Jack tried to hide the hurt in his heart behind a smile as he bowed and backed out of the room.

~

Once Violet heard the front door close and knew Jack was gone, she nodded to the doctor to let him know he could begin. Using her hands to imitate using a mirror, she communicated to Jane what she wanted. Jane brought it to her, and Violet watched in the mirror as Doc Babcock slowly removed the bandage from her head.

When he was done, a steady stream of tears ran down her cheeks as she handed the mirror back to Jane. On the left side of her head, from the ridge down, her hair was less than a half an inch long. The area that had been shaved wrapped around the back of her head and stopped just shy of the midline.

"It'll grow back," Jane said, attempting to comfort her as the doctor examined the place where he had drilled.

Violet sat still. How could Jack love her looking like this? How could anyone love her? She willed herself to stop crying, but the tears refused to cease. *You are stronger than this*, she told herself, but doubt filled her mind and her heart sank.

Jane took her by the hand as Doc Babcock finished his examination, took fresh bandages from his bag, and began to wrap Violet's head once again. Violet looked at the hand mirror propped against her casted arm. She wondered how long it would be before the cast came off.

She gave Jane's hand a squeeze, then pulled hers away and tapped the cast with her finger. Doc Babcock seemed to understand immediately. "Another four weeks at least," he answered her unspoken question. "It's been almost four weeks now. At eight weeks, I'll remove the cast and see how it looks. If it looks okay, we'll leave it off. If not, I'll recast it."

Four weeks seemed like an eternity to Violet. There was no doubt in her mind that she would go stir crazy if she had to lay in bed for four weeks. She needed to get up and move around. With two fingers, she used the cast as a platform and made a walking motion.

Doc Babcock smiled. "I told Jack you were not a patient person," he chuckled. "Let's take it a day at a time. You rest today and tomorrow, I'll come by and show Jane how to help you get around. Deal?"

Violet wiped the tears from her eyes and shook her head yes.

6

Jack started up the boardwalk feeling surly and mean. It was not in his nature to coddle himself, but Violet had hurt him. He knew it was not intentional and reminded himself of what Doc Babcock had told him about needing to be patient. For Violet, and in Violet's presence, he would be patient, but out here on the street, he wanted to hit something or someone.

He passed the Banner Grocery Store and was almost to the Bella Union when he saw Bullock standing in the middle of the street. Jack took several more steps before realizing what the scene before him meant. People on the boardwalk on both sides of the throroughfare had stopped, and most were standing like statues with their backs to whatever building they were near.

Further along the muddy street, some twenty to thirty yards past Bullock, a man stood facing the sheriff. The right hand of each of man hovered near the guns on their hips. Jack stepped to the nearest post and stopped. From somewhere down the street, a dog yelped. Time seemed to stand still.

"You let me ride, and I'll let ya live," the man facing Bullock hollered.

Bullock shook his head and raised his voice loud enough for the other man to hear. "Tolbert, you know I can't do that."

"I ain't hangin' for no whore," Tolbert shouted back.

"She's dead by your hand," Bullock responded. "You'll get a fair trial."

Tolbert stood firm. Jack scanned the far side of the street. Jane and Charlie Utter had stepped away from the building and were poised to assist Bullock. A young mother hustled her son and daughter through the door of one of the shops. Between that storefront and the one next to it was a three-foot opening. Jack's eyes scanned past it to the people on the porch of the next establishment before his eyes registered movement. Quickly he looked back. From the corner of his eye, he saw Tolbert move for his gun as a man stepped from the opening and leveled a pistol at Bullock's back.

Jack never saw Bullock draw because as the second gunman's gun came up, Jack drew both of his revolvers and fired. Both of his bullets found their mark, and the would-be ambusher's body disappeared back into the opening.

As Jack turned to see what had happened in the street, he found himself facing Bullock. Bullock's gun was aimed at him, and for a brief instant, Jack was not sure if he should fire again or holster his weapons. He decided the latter was the right move.

Guns back in their holsters, Jack raised both hands. Bullock glared at him, "That's a good way to get dead, Abbott."

"Might want to check between those two buildings before you shoot me," Jack smiled as he spoke.

Bullock holstered his weapon and started for the opening. Jack stepped off the boardwalk, crossed the street, and met him there. They stared down at the man's body lying in the dirt.

"Know him?" Jack asked.

"Yeah," Bullock replied. "That's Tolbert's kid brother, Zane."

"You mean that was his kid brother," Jack corrected, then turned and looked up the street to where a group of people were standing over the body of Tolbert. "Looks like Tolbert didn't make it either."

"He made the first move," Bullock's tone was more than a little defensive.

"If that helps ya sleep at night," Jack responded.

"What's that supposed to mean?" Bullock turned toward him.

Jack shrugged, "It means you're fast. Maybe as fast as me. And that would put you in the same category as me...let's see if I remember it right...I shot two men that braced me, and because of that, you told me I needed to leave town."

"I told you to leave town because gunslingers draw more gunslingers who think they're faster on the draw," Bullock returned, "and we're tryin' to bring some law and order to this town."

"Well, sheriff, the way I see it is if I'm a gunslinger then you are too, and the only difference between us, is that one of us just saved the other one's ass," Jack stepped back, took a mock bow, and started up the street to Mrs. Smith's.

~

Violet laid the writing slate Jack had brought her against her cast-right arm, and using the chalk that came with it, she began to write. It was not the hand she was used to writing with, and so it took her longer. When she was finished, she looked at what was on the slate. It looked like a young child had written it, but it was legible. The slate contained but a single word – How? Laying the chalk aside, she pointed at her arm and head.

"How did you get shot?" Jack asked her, verifying it was the question she wanted him to answer.

Violet nodded yes.

"You don't remember?" he asked.

No.

Not sure where to start, he asked, "Do you remember us leavin' Deadwood together?"

Yes.

"Do you remember why we had to leave?" he asked.

Yes.

"Do you remember camping the second night not far from a creek?"

Violet smiled and nodded yes.

"Do you remember me goin' to the creek to bathe?

Yes.

"But you don't remember anything after that?"

No.

Jack paused and considered how detailed he should be. Finally, unsure about it, he asked, "How much do you want to know?"

Violet used the edge of the bedsheet to clean the slate and then wrote – Everything.

Jack took a deep breath and began. He started from the time he heard her scream and the three gunshots then walked her through what he had found when he got back to the camp. Explaining that because of her condition, he had not taken the time to do a lot of scouting, he then gave her a brief summary of what he thought might have happened.

He did not go into great detail about the trip back to Deadwood, only telling her that after getting her cleaned up, he had held her in the saddle with him and rode straight through the night and half the next day. To finish, he told her how he had laid her down on the table at Doc Babcock's and gone to get Jane.

Violet closed her eyes for a long time, letting all Jack had told her sink in. She remembered nothing from the moment he walked away down the trail until she opened her eyes in the room in her old house. When she opened her eyes again, she cleaned the slate, and wrote – House?

"This house?" Jack asked.

Yes.

"What about this house?

Again, she erased and wrote – How?

"How did we get it?" Jack asked.

Yes.

Jack smiled. "When Doc Babcock told me you would need to stay here until you were well, it was the first place I thought of. I knew you had sold it to Bullock, and I went to see him."

Violet wondered how that exchange had gone. Something in her expression must have registered the question because Jack laughed.

"Oh, he was not happy to see me at all," he continued. "So when I told him you had been shot and what Doc Babcock had said, he marched off to the doctors to see for himself. To make a long story short, me and Bullock exchanged a few more words but, in the end, he agreed to rent the house to us for three months."

The slate was erased again, then – After that?

"After that, we leave again," Jack responded.

Violet shook her head as she erased, then – If I can't?

Jack smiled, "If you can't, I'll renegotiate the terms. I think Bullock might be a bit more understanding now."

Violet was growing tired, but decided she needed to know the answer to one last question – Why more understanding?

"I think that's a story for another day," Jack told her. "Let's just say he owes me."

Violet smiled and wrote along the edge of the slate – Tired.

Jack took the slate and chalk from her, leaned forward, and kissed her full on the mouth, then gave her a wink. At the door of the room, he turned back and said, "I love you."

Violet held back the tears until he was gone and then let them flow. In her mind, one word formed – Why?

Jack was in the sitting room reading his book by the light of a kerosene lamp when someone knocked on the door. Not expecting visitors and knowing that the nights in Deadwood could be wild, he pulled one of the revolvers from his gun belt hanging from the back of his chair. Crossing to the door, he flattened himself against the wall and cocked the gun before asking, "Who's there?"

"Bullock," came the answer.

Lowering the hammer on his pistol, he opened the door, "What can I do for you, sheriff?"

"I was hopin' it wasn't too late for a conversation," Bullock replied.

"Been thinkin' I needed to visit with you myself," Jack told him as he stepped back and motioned him inside.

Bullock stepped inside and looked around. Jack pointed him toward a chair and was about to return to his seat when a thought crossed his mind. "Violet's asleep, and I'd like her to stay that way, so if'n there's a chance this exchange is gonna get loud, maybe we better take it outside."

"Unless what you've got to say causes a ruckus, then I see no need to," Bullock told him. "My conversation is of a civil nature."

Jack seated himself before saying, "Go ahead then."

Bullock sat quietly staring at the window behind Jack for several seconds before beginning, "It is not in my nature to express remorse. My wife, Martha, says it is one of my worse vices."

Bullock paused, and Jack, not sure as to where the sheriff was heading, kept quiet. Again, Bullock stared at the window for several seconds before continuing, "What I am attempting to say, and doing a mighty poor job of it, is that after considerable deliberation, I realized that what you said to me on the boardwalk today was true."

Bullock paused again, and after several more seconds, Jack realized that the sheriff was expecting him to say something in return. "Well, Bullock, I'd say your wife is a mighty smart woman 'cause that was about the most pitiful apology I've ever received."

Jack watched and waited and prayed his response did not cause a ruckus that would wake Violet. Slowly, a smile spread across the sheriff's face. "As pitiful as it might have been, you recognized it for what it was, and therefore, nothing further needs to be said on that account, so on to the next item for discussion."

"And what might that be?" Jack asked.

"As you saw today on the street," Bullock replied, "I did not have anyone to back my play. At least not anyone who I knew would," he clarified before continuing, "I am hoping to rectify that problem here tonight."

"How so?" Jack asked.

Bullock pulled a deputy's badge from his pocket. "I'd like to offer you a job as my deputy."

Shocked, Jack stared across the room at Bullock. When he finally spoke, he asked, "Why me?"

"You've been a lawman before. You're quick, you're not inclined to go looking for a fight," Bullock replied, "but mostly because when trouble does show up, you know how to handle yourself."

Jack stared at the badge in Bullock's hand and mulled the offer over in his mind. He was not sure what he should do. If it was only himself, he had to think of, he would have accepted, but there was Violet to consider.

"The job pays a hundred dollars a month, plus additional fees for arrests and serving papers," Bullock said.

Jack chuckled. "Well, considering rent here is a hundred dollars a month, I'm not sure if it's the right job for me."

Bullock grinned. "I know your landlord, and I think I can talk him into giving you a much better deal on your rent."

Jack sighed. "Bullock, I'd really like to help you out, but I think I should run it by Violet first."

"You do that," Bullock said, "then come find me tomorrow."

7

Violet woke to the smell of breakfast. Someone, she figured it must have been Jack, had laid her flat in the bed after she had fallen asleep. She started to call for help, then remembered how she sounded. The thought of knocking on the headboard of her bed crossed her mind, but instead, she decided it was time she learned to do things for herself.

Except for the pillow beneath her head, all the others Jack had brought in were still in place. She raised her head enough to pull the pillow from beneath it, then, rolling to her left side, she used her good arm and her legs to ease herself up in the bed until she was seated amongst the pillows that rested against the headboard. It took every ounce of strength she had to perform the simple task.

When she had rested for several minutes, she tapped on the headboard twice and waited. No one came, so she tapped again, louder this time. Almost immediately, she heard the sound of footsteps climbing the steps toward her room.

"Did I wake you?" Jack asked as he stepped through the doorway.

Violet shrugged and pointed at her nose.

"Breakfast," Jack chuckled. "I guess it was me. Are you hungry?"

Violet nodded yes.

"Wonderful," Jack said as he turned to go.

Quickly, Violet tapped twice on the headboard, causing Jack to turn back. Motioning with her left hand, she asked Jack to retrieve her slate and chalk. He made his way around the bed to the bureau that sat against the far wall, picked up the slate and chalk, and handed it to her.

On it she wrote – Why? Then pointed at Jack and then herself.

A look of confusion on Jack's face told her he did not understand. Frustrated with her inability to verbalize her question, she put chalk to slate again and under the – Why? – she wrote – You and me.

Jack looked at it before asking, "Why are me and you still together?"

Violet nodded yes.

Jack smiled, "That one's easy darlin'. The answer is love."

Violet erased the slate, pointed to her head, then made a circular motion around her whole body, and wrote – Broken.

Jack chuckled. Violet glared at him. Her message was clear, and she saw the humor fade from his features before he spoke, "Darlin', you are not broken. You are injured, and in time you will heal. I reckon you've heard the phrase 'in sickness and in health.'

Violet erased the slate and began to write as Jack continued, "You know it comes after 'to have and to hold, for better or for worse' and before 'until death do us part.' Of course, I think there's something about you obeyin' me in there too."

Once again, she glared at him. This time he only chuckled as she turned the slate to show him what she had written. The slate read – We're not married.

Jack smiled and started to drop to a knee. Mixed emotion filled Violet as she felt her face redden. This was not the way things should happen. Even if he asked, she could not answer him properly. She shook her head and tried to say no, but the sound that came from her was only a long 'oooh'. Frustration filled her, and tears welled in her eyes.

Jack rose quickly, "I'm sorry. I did not mean to upset you. I love you."

Through her tears, Violet erased the slate and wrote – Why?

After she showed it to Jack, he stood for a long time. She could tell he was trying to form an answer. Finally, he said, "Tis not ours to reason why, as the months and years go flying by. Ours is but to hold and love each other, until the day we both shall die."

Violet shook her head, erased, and wrote – Really, Tennyson?

Jack gave her a weak smile. "I may have borrowed that first bit, but the rest is all mine, and I think it answers your question quite well. Violet, I knew the day I woke up on your floor after you shot me that I was in love with you. Nothing will ever change that or my love for you. Not your injuries, not your stubborn nature, nothing."

Once more, Violet erased and wrote, then motioned to her mouth as she showed him the slate. It read – What if?

"What if you can never talk again?" Jack asked.

Yes, she nodded.

The smile on his face told her she was not going to like his answer before he ever opened his mouth. He reached over and gently took the slate and chalk from her before saying, "Well, darlin', I will miss hearin' your lovely voice, but if you decide to never speak again, I'll simply hide your slate and chalk when I'm not in the mood to hear you nag at me."

It was all Violet could do not to scream at him. She knew it was his way of challenging her to speak, and in that instant, a single thought ran through her mind – Challenge accepted.

~

Jack laid the slate on the kitchen table along with the chalk. A plate of bacon sat at the far end of the table. Jack opened the door to the oven and checked the biscuits. They were close to being done but not quite. He thought about frying some eggs and decided against it. Bacon stuffed inside of fresh biscuits was easier for Violet to handle, and after his exiting comment, he figured she would not want him feeding her.

Jack picked up a piece of bacon, folded it two, and bit half of it off. He allowed the flavor of it to flood his mouth and then began to chew. Life's little pleasures, he thought to himself as he swallowed and put the remainder of the bacon in his mouth.

Wiping the grease from his fingers, he checked the biscuits again. They were ready. Using a rag to move the biscuits from the oven to the top of the stove, Jack thoughts turned to Bullock's offer and how he should present it to Violet.

~

Jack's return was heralded by the smell of fresh biscuits and bacon. Violet was hungry, but as hungry as she was, she found herself praying this morning's breakfast was something she could handle herself. She had already made up her mind that if it was something Jack had to feed her, she was going to refuse it, or at the very least, try to eat left-handed.

Jack entered the room with a smile on his face as if nothing had happened. As he set a plate of biscuits filled with bacon on the bed beside her, Violet felt the flush of annoyance darken her cheeks. Eyes narrowed, she made a motion as if she were writing and pointed at the doorway.

"As you wish, my love," Jack bowed and left. When he returned, he held out her slate and chalk.

She took it from him and wrote. When she was done, she turned it around for him to see. It read – You are an ASS!

To her surprise, Jack doubled over laughing. When he had composed himself again, he pointed at the slate. "You're getting much better with that left hand, darlin'. Even managin' whole sentences now."

Violet glared at him. This was not supposed to be funny. He was supposed to fight back, not laugh at her. She thought about throwing chalk at his head but figured if she did, he would refuse to give it back, and without it, she could not write any further hateful messages to him. Her next thought was to throw one of the biscuits, but she was not sure how accurate she was with her left hand and imagined him ducking the biscuit and laughing at her once again.

While she continued to glare at him, Jack made his way to the other side of the bed, pulled the chair up beside her, and pointed at the biscuits. "Might as well eat. You may be unhappy with me, but that ain't no reason to go hungry. Plus, I need to discuss something with you."

She started to refuse just to spite him, then decided he was not worth it, laid the chalk down, and picked up a biscuit. After taking a bite from it, she put it back on the plate, erased the slate, and wrote – What is it?

Jack's disposition changed. She recognized immediately that what he wished to discuss was of a serious nature. Their relationship had not been a long one, but she had learned early on to spot when his natural playful demeanor became somber.

"Sheriff Bullock came by to visit last night," Jack began, and her first thought was they would have to find new lodging. She held her breath as Jack continued, "He offered me a job as his deputy."

Picking up her slate,she erase it, and wrote – Why?

Jack smiled. "Well, I kind of saved his bacon yesterday afternoon."

She started to erase the slate again, but Jack reached over and touched the back of her hand. "How? No need to write it."

He spent the next several minutes walking her through the actions that led to him shooting Zane Tolbert before he put a bullet in the sheriff's back. By the time he finished, Violet had finished one of the bacon biscuits and was halfway through with a second.

"Anyway, as I said before, he came for a visit last night and offered me the job," Jack paused, looking a bit sheepish, then continued. "I know you said that we aren't married, and I ain't gonna push you on the issue, but I feel like because of our relationship, the decision merits your input."

Violet nearly dropped the biscuit she was holding. Her input? Had she heard Jack correctly? She tried to recall the last time a man wanted her input in a decision, important or otherwise. Her father had always doubted her ability to make decisions, perhaps for good reasons. She had not been married long to Tennessee Bill, but never once had he asked her to weigh in on anything.

Her mind ran through a series of different thoughts as she reached for her slate. If he was off doing deputy work, it would give her more time to work on her vocal cords. That was not the thought that pressed furthest forward in her mind as she erased and wrote – Dangerous?

"Yes, it could be dangerous," Jack replied, "I'm accustomed to the dangers of being a lawman. What worries me more than the danger of the job is leaving you here alone."

Violet tapped the chalk against the slate, reiterating that she thought it was dangerous. She was not sure what the future held for her or him or them, but she could not live with the thought of him hurt again.

"Yes, it's dangerous, darlin'," Jack smiled. "I'm glad to see you love me enough to worry about the dangers of me takin' the job."

Love him!? Love him! She was not sure if it was the word love or the smile that had infuriated her, but it took all the willpower she could muster to not test the accuracy of her left arm. Instead, she erased and wrote – Jane!

Jack looked at the slate and asked, "What if Jane is too busy?"

Again, she erased and in much bigger letters wrote – JANE!!

Jack raised his hands in surrender, "Okay, I'll let Bullock know he's got a deputy, and I'll see if Jane will help out around here."

Violet dropped her slate in her lap, turned away from Jack, picked up the half-eaten biscuit, and pretended to ignore him while she ate it. From the corner of her eye, she watched as he stood and moved the chair back against the wall. He made his way around the bed and was almost out the door when she realized she had not gotten the last word in.

Quickly, she tapped the headboard twice. When Jack stopped and turned, she grabbed her slate, wrote on it, and turned it around for him to read. On it, she had written – I'm still mad at you.

Jack walked back to her bedside, and Violet, afraid he was going to take her slate and chalk, quickly shoved it under the bed coverings and held it tight against her legs. Defiant, she glared at him. Before she could react, he leaned down and kissed her soundly on the mouth, then turned and left the room.

Half of her wanted to throw the slate, what was left of the plate of biscuits, and the chalk at him. The other half wanted him to come back and kiss her again. Frustrated and emotionally confused, she took the slate from under the covers and slowly wrote – ASS!!

8

True to his word, Doc Babcock returned in the middle of the afternoon with Jane in tow. Violet was setting up in her bed when they arrived. In addition to his bag, the doctor carried a wide leather belt of sorts. Attached to it were three large metal rings. Jane carried a pair of wooden crutches.

"Good afternoon, Miz Violet," Doc Babcock spoke as he entered the room smiling. "I see you're sitting up. That's good."

Violet picked up her slate and began to write as Jane leaned the crutches against the headboard. "You look so much better," she said. "There's even a bit of color back in your cheeks."

Violet found herself wondering if she were able to talk, if she would have told Jane the reason for the color was her irritation with Jack. As she finished writing on the slate, she decided she probably would have kept it to herself. No sense airing a couple's differences with a gossip like Jane. She turned the slate so the doctor could see that on it she had written – How to learn to talk?

"Funny you should ask," Doc Babcock said. "Just this afternoon, I received a telegram from the doctor I told you about out east. He wanted me to know he had sent a package with the literature we had talked about. In the message, he also mentioned that one common method was singing words and humming songs."

Violet considered this and decided humming was something she could do. Singing, on the other hand, was not something she had been comfortable with even before she had been shot.

"I ain't got much of a singin' voice," Jane announced, "but if'n it'll help, I'll sing with ya."

Violet could not help but smile. She could imagine what Jane's coarse voice would sound like in song. Not willing to attempt song or speech in front of the doctor, Violet remained quiet.

Doc Babcock stepped forward and without speaking, began to unwrap the bandage from Violet's head. When the last of the linen was removed, he gently examined the area around where he had drilled. Violet sat patiently, waiting while his fingers pressed first here and then there. When he finished, he stepped back, "Your head is healing beautifully, Miz Violet. Bone formation where I drilled may take a year or two to complete, but I'm satisfied that you are well on your way to recovery. You are a very lucky young lady."

Violet nodded that she understood. As to feeling lucky, she was not so sure she agreed with the doctor. A voice in her head that sounded a lot like Jack reminded her that she was alive. Her response to the voice was that alive and lucky were two very different concepts.

"Are you ready to get out of that bed for a bit?" Doc Babcock's question interrupted the argument that was going on in Violet's mind.

She nodded yes, and the doctor picked up the strange belt he had arrived with, "Jane if you will help me wrap this around her waist, we'll get the process started."

It took only a couple of minutes to get Violet ready, but the actual process of standing her up took much longer. Easing her to the side of the bed so that her legs hung off it took almost all the energy she had. Doc Babcock held two of the rings in the belt tightly while Jane held the crutches stable. After a short rest, Violet was able, with the assistance of Jane and the doctor, to rise and use the crutches for support to stand upright. In mere seconds, her legs began to shake and without the aid of the crutches she had no doubt she would have toppled.

After several seconds, Doc Babcock and Jane eased her back to a sitting position. In her mind, she had believed that she was going to walk around the house once they got her to her feet. Realizing that even one step on her own was not going to be possible brought tears to her eyes.

Doc Babcock took a handkerchief from his pocket and wiped her tears, "It's a process, Miz Violet, but believe it or not, it will go much faster than you think. Today, we'll work on standing up. Maybe tomorrow or the next day, we'll help you walk around the room, and by next week you'll be crutching up and down the stairs and all around the house by yourself."

His encouragement did little for Violet's mood. Over the next half hour, with their assistance, she stood four more times. By the time they helped her back into bed, she was exhausted.

Doc Babcock offered her laudanum. She refused it. The physical pain she could and would endure. The mental strain and the injury to her pride were a different matter. When she had regained her energy, she picked up her slate and wrote – Head?

Doc Babcock gave her a confused look. Jane understood and explained, "She wants her head wrapped."

"There's no need for that anymore," he responded.

"Dull brained, dimwitted excuse for a human," Jane's tone was anything but friendly. "Just like a man. Single track runnin' all the way to the horizon. Cook, clean, toss your legs in the air, but God forbid a woman have feelin's."

Violet watched as Doc Babcock's confusion turned to embarrassment as Jane continued to let him have it. She could not help but feel a bit sorry for him as he turned and began to apologize, "I'm so sorry, Miz Violet...I didn't realize...I just didn't..."

"No, you didn't because you're a man," Jane continued her tirade, "and men don't..."

Violet waved her hand, interrupting Jane's rant.

After a few seconds of silence, the still red Doc Babcock spoke, "I can rewrap your head if you really want me to, but maybe a scarf would be nicer."

Violet nodded and the doctor continued, "If Jane here is finished with her criticism of the male species, perhaps she might see what is available at millinery store or Ed Whitehead's Dry Goods. Now, if you two ladies have no further need of me, I think I'll bid you both good day."

Violet nodded. Jane held her tongue but continued to glare at the doctor until he was out of sight. Then she turned to Violet, "Might have been a bit hard on him, huh?"

Violet nodded again, then erased her tablet and wrote – You help me talk?

Jane smiled, "I sure will, but first I'm gonna go find you the purdiest scarf in Deadwood."

~

Jack found Bullock at the hardware store going over a ledger with Sol. As he approached the two, Bullock looked up and asked, "What's the verdict?"

Jack decided he liked the man's straightforward, get-to-the-point attitude, as he answered, "I reckon I'll be needin' that piece of tin you were flashin' at me last night."

"That's wonderful news," Sol stated, "I've been telling my partner he needed help for weeks now."

Bullock ignored the comment, pulled a badge from his pocket, and tossed it to Jack. Jack caught it, and as he pinned it to his shirt, Sol continued, "God be with you, Jack. Seth here is so particular about who he pins one of those tin stars on that it may be weeks before he finds anyone else."

"So, you think there's a need for more deputies?" Jack asked.

"Of a certain," Sol replied. "This isn't just a mining camp anymore. It's a full-blown town, complete with all the lawless riffraff a sheriff and his deputies can handle."

"Law takes time and consistency," Bullock responded. "We've got the start of it. Now it's just a matter of following through."

"Guess I should warn you now, your boss has a tendency to get philosophical every now and again," Sol chuckled.

Again, Bullock ignored his partner as he closed the ledger, stepped around the counter, and said, "Might as well get you acquainted with your duties. Come along. Let's take a walk."

As Jack followed Bullock out the door and along the boardwalk, he thought about what Sol had said. He had spent little time in the town of Deadwood when he first arrived, instead using his time to find a claim and work on it. His occasional trips to town had been only to register his claim at the Gem, pick up needed supplies, and send the sporadic letter to his folks back in Texas. Now, as he trailed behind Bullock he began to wonder exactly what he had gotten himself into.

Bullock stopped to let a woman with a small child pass, and Jack took the opportunity to ask, "Is it really just you and me?"

Bullock grinned, "It really is."

"Was what Mr. Star was sayin' back there true?" Jack asked. "Do we really need more help?"

Bullock's grin faded, "I'd be lying to you if I said no, Jack. But here's the sticky of it. There's talk of an election soon. I'll throw my name in the hat, but voters are fickle creatures, so there's no guarantee, and I'd rather not hire a bunch of deputies when I can't assure them a job going forward."

Jack took a second to consider what Bullock had said before asking, "Then why hire me?"

"Several reasons, but mostly because if you're gonna stay in town, I want you where I can keep an eye on you," Bullock chuckled, "and I figure you'll be gone once Violet is healthy anyway."

"Maybe, maybe not," Jack replied. "Ya never know, we might just settle down here and raise us a brood."

"I'll believe it when I see it," Bullock chuckled again as he turned and continued down the boardwalk.

9

Doc Babcock's timeline was a bit off. Even with pushing herself hard and daily help from Jane, it was a solid week and a half before Violet was secure enough in her ability to move around the upstairs portion of the house when no one else was there. It took her even longer to brave the steps. Doc Babcock's trip to the house had become less frequent, and on his last visit, he had assured her that in two more weeks, he would remove the cast.

Now, as she made her way from the bedroom down the stairs and into the kitchen using only one crutch for support, she found herself thinking about the strange dreams she had been having lately. She had not thought of her father or England in a long time, but for some reason both had haunted her sleeping hours since she awakened in Deadwood. Her inability to communicate through speech was of little help with the matter. She was not comfortable enough with her progress to try to have a conversation with Jane about it, and as far as Jack knew, she was not talking at all, or if he suspected, he had said nothing about it.

As Violet pulled a chair out from beneath the kitchen table, someone knocked on the front door. Before she could move to answer it, Jane's voice rang through the house as she sang, "Oh, Miz Violet, I have arrived."

Violet smiled. Most people would have found Jane's singing voice atrocious, but to Violet it was as if one of Heaven's angels had come to Earth. Had it not been for Jane, Violet might never have had the courage to try singing herself. Now, when Violet knew they were alone, she was perfectly comfortable singing right back.

"I'm in the kitchen," Violet sang back.

Seconds later, Jane appeared. "How are you today?" she sang.

"I'm doing well," Violet sang her response.

"Really?" Jane sang holding the y-sound much longer than necessary.

Violet laughed. "Yes," she replied, this time in her normal voice.

"Oh, my, that was very good," Jane praised her. Violet felt herself blush. She had struggled with the 'y' in yes during the first few days after she and Jane began working on her speech. Now, Jane's simple compliment made her heart soar.

Violet recalled the first day Jane had sat down to work with her. Jane had asked her what words she wanted to learn first. After giving it some thought, she had made a short list on her slate. The list of words included – no, yes, why, how, and ass.

Jane had looked at the list, pointed at the last word, and laughingly asked, "Still mad at Jack?"

Violet pointed at the word yes, and they both giggled. She was no longer angry with Jack, but their relationship had been a bit strained since he went to work with Bullock. His work kept him busy most of the day and sometimes late into the night. He stopped in to check on her as often as he could throughout the day, but he had not kissed her or told her he loved her since she had called him an ass.

~

Bullock turned the key and locked the door of the makeshift cell, then tossed it to Jack, who hung it on a peg on the wall behind the table that served as his desk. The night had already been a fiasco. Besides the drunk Bullock had just tossed into the cell, a stabbing at Gem had led to a miner being carried to Doc Babcock's, and a shooting over a poker game in front of the Forty-Hundred had left two men dead.

"I suppose you heard about the upcoming election," Bullock said as he eased into a chair.

"I did," Jack replied.

"Any thoughts on my opposition?" Bullock asked.

Jack shrugged. "None come to mind. I'm not much on politics, and quite honestly, I've been too busy helpin' you bring law to this hellhole to worry much about an election."

"On that note, I'd like to commend you," Bullock leaned back in his chair as he spoke. "It's been nearly three weeks since you pinned on that star, and you haven't killed a single person."

Jack smiled. "Week ain't over yet, boss."

Both men sat lost in their own thoughts for several minutes before Bullock lowered his chair to the floor and said, "Abbott, it's late. I think things have calmed down. Why don't you go ahead and start home? If anything happens I can't handle myself, I'll send for you."

"Fair enough," Jack replied as he stood up and headed for the door.

~

Sleep eluded Violet. It was well after dark, and Jack had not made it home. She had spent an hour lying in bed before frustration had driven her from it. Pulling a robe on over her nightgown, she had made her way through the house to the kitchen. Now, as she sat at the kitchen table, she found herself contemplating the future. Once the cast came off, she would have a better idea of what she was capable of, but something told her the life of gambling she had made her living at before Jack arrived in her life was over.

She recalled the night she had thought Jack was a burglar and shot him through her back door. It seemed so long ago, but in reality, it had been just over two months. Had the spark she felt for him been real? Had she been foolish to run off with him after such a short time? Was the spark he claimed to have for her still there?

The front door opened amd interrupted her thoughts. Where was her gun? This was not the first night she had been alone in the house, so why was she just now realizing she was without a weapon?

Jack stepped into the kitchen, looking exhausted, and came to a sudden stop as soon as he saw her. "I wasn't expecting you to be awake," in his voice was a touch of worry, "Are you okay?"

Violet nodded yes.

An awkward silence followed. Violet wanted to talk, but her slate and chalk were in the bedroom, and she still was not sure if she was comfortable trying to communicate with Jack. What if he laughed?

"Did you need something?" Jack asked.

Again, she nodded yes.

He turned and started for her room as he said, "I'll grab your slate."

"No," she said, and Jack stopped in his tracks.

When he turned around, Violet could see the surprise in his expression. Heart pounding, she took a chance and sang, "We can talk if I sing."

For several seconds, he stood staring at her. She felt her cheeks flush and had begun to think she had made a mistake when Jack asked, "Do you want me to sing, too?"

"No," she replied.

Jack put a hand against his chest, an expression of relief on his face, as he said, "That's good because my singin' would start every dog in Deadwood howlin'."

Violet pointed at the chair across the table from where she sat. Jack pulled it out and seated himself, before asking, "What was it you wanted to talk about?"

It took Violet a minute to collect her thoughts before she sang, "I want to talk about us and the future."

"Okay,"

"What are your plans?" she sang, paused, then continued, "And I need to know where I stand."

Jack stood up, moved around the table, and took a seat in the chair next to her. Before she realized what he was doing, he took her hand in his and kissed it gently. When he looked up into her eyes, he said, "I have no plans past gettin' you well. As to where you stand, nothing has changed there. You stole my heart in the parlor of this very house, and I will never ask for it back. It is yours to keep. Before you, I did not really know what love felt like and I'm just as surprised as you at how fast I fell for you. The only regret I have is that I did not tell you from the beginning how much I felt for you and that I told you I wouldn't take you with me when I left Deadwood."

Violet remembered how mad she had been when he had refused her. Now she understood that he had been trying to protect her from a dangerous life.

"I will never make such a mistake again," he continued, "When I leave Deadwood again, it will be with you by my side if you will still have me."

Violet squeezed his hand, smiled, and nodded.

"Is that a yes?" Jack asked.

"Yes." Violet answered before pulling her hand from his, then touching her finger to his mouth and then to hers.

As Jack leaned toward her, she met him halfway. The kiss that followed melted her heart. When Jack finally pulled away, Violet was breathless.

"I love you, darlin'," Jack whispered.

Violet looked deep into his eyes and sang, "And I love you."

Jack pushed his chair back and stood up. Violet still had questions and was about to say so when he pulled something from his pocket and got down on one knee. This time, she did not have time to refuse before Jack spoke. "Violet Daniels, will you do the me the honor of being my wife?"

Violet looked down at the ring Jack held between the thumb and index finger of his right hand. It was gold with a single diamond, and it was beautiful. As tears of joy filled her eyes, she said, "Yes."

Jack smiled, carefully slipped the ring onto her finger, wiped the tears from her cheeks, and kissed her again. When he tried to pull away, Violet wrapped her left arm around his neck and refused to let the kiss end. She still had questions, but they seemed far less important now than they had an hour ago.

Breathless and happy, she finally ended the kiss. Once she could breathe again, she sang, "I love you."

"And I love you," Jack responded. "And I really like it when you sing that to me."

Violet smacked him on the arm. "Don't get used to it. It won't last forever," she sang. "Now take me to bed."

Jack looked surprised. "Before our vows?"

Violet laughed. "I'm too weak and you're too tired, but it would be really nice if you would hold me while we sleep."

Jack stood, and Violet started to stand, but before she could, he picked her up in his arms and carried her upstairs to the bedroom. He laid her in the bed, and as she worked herself out of her robe and under the covers, Jack stripped to his linen drawers. Violet could feel her heart beating in her chest, as he slid under the covers and pulled her up against his body.

10

"I need a favor," Violet told Jane in her usual singing voice.

"What kinda favor?" Jane sang back.

"I need you to help me learn to say two words," Violet sang, "but I need to say them not sing them."

"Okay," Jane said, then sang, "What two words?"

Violet smiled and sang, "I do."

Jane looked confused, then as understanding set in, she began to grin, "Oh my goodness. Are you serious? There's gonna be a wedding?"

Violet could only nod and smile.

~

"Looks like the election's been set for week after next," Bullock told Jack as he sat at his table in the sheriff's makeshift office.

"You don't say," Jack responded, not really listening.

After several seconds of silence, Jack looked up to see the sheriff studying him. Bullock continued to stare at him, until finally Jack said, "What?"

Bullock raised an eyebrow. "Something's different about you. I can't put my finger on it."

Jack shrugged. Bullock refused to let it go. "You look less solemn... happier..."

"Who've you been talkin' to?" Jack interrupted, giving a sideways look.

"About what?" Bullock asked.

"Fine," aggravated Jack said, "Don't tell me who told you I'm gettin' married."

"Seriously," Bullock stood as he spoke.

"Like you didn't know," Jack shook his head.

"Actually, I didn't," Bullock countered as he crossed the room and offered his hand to Jack. "Congratulations, Abbott."

Jack stood and took the sheriff's hand. As the two men shook hands, Bullock asked, "And just when is the special occasion supposed to take place?"

"Well, to be honest," Jack said, "We haven't gotten around to discussin' that, yet."

~

The week following Jack's proposal proved to be a turning point for Violet. Even though her voice did not sound like it had before she was shot, she had become comfortable enough with it that she began to speak more and sing less.

By the end of that week, she had tossed her crutch into the corner. She still tired easily and had to take breaks more often than she would have liked, but overall, she was happy with the progress she was making.

Jane still came daily to check on her, but more often than not, they sat and visited about town gossip instead of working on Doc Babcock's speech exercises. The town was buzzing with the coming election, and Jane, who was always in the thick of everything, kept her apprised of shifts in the town's moods.

Most days, Jack stopped by for lunch unless his job kept him from it. Violet had made a habit of waiting up for him at night. She loved watching him get undressed before he got into bed with her. The fact that it was dark and he was little more than a shadow did not diminish her joy. She had nursed him back to health after she had shot him. She had seen every inch of him, and while the darkness could hide his body from her, it could not hide the images from her memories.

The first night after his proposal, he had eased into the bed, pulled her close, and said, "Bullock asked me today when we planned to be married. I had to tell him I didn't know exactly when. Do you have any thoughts on the subject?"

Violet had taken his hand, placed it on her cast, and spoken a single word, "After."

~

Two days before the election, Jack arrived home in the middle of the day to find every door and window in the house thrown open and Violet stirring a pot of stew. When he stepped into the kitchen, she turned and gave him a nervous smile.

"I didn't know you could cook," he smiled back at her.

"A lot you do not know about me," she told him, pointing at a chair, "sit down, we need to talk."

The seriousness of her tone let Jack know this was not a suggestion. Not sure what was coming, he pulled out the chair and sat down in it. Violet turned back to the stove, stirred the stew once more, then, using a spoon, scooped up a bit of the juice and did a taste test. Jack watched her nod as if satisfied, then she took a bowl from the shelf above the stove and filled it. She placed it on the table in front of him, returned to the stove, took fresh rolls from the oven, and placed them on the stovetop.

Not sure if Violet planned to eat with him, he waited and watched while she put two of the steaming hot rolls on a plate and brought them to him.

"Go ahead and eat," she told him, "I'll talk."

Jack picked up his spoon and began to eat. Violet pulled out the chair across from him, sat down, and after a few seconds, said, "I know some about you and want to know more. I know you are from Texas. I know you were a sheriff there. I know why you came to Deadwood. But before I know more about you, I want you to know about me."

Violet paused as if she was waiting for some sign from him to continue. Jack picked up a roll, tore it in half, and nodded.

"First, I want you to know, I was married once before," Violet's tone and expression told him she was worried about his response, "is that a problem for you?"

Jack laid what was left of the roll back on the plate and, as he picked up his spoon, answered, "Darlin', most folks I've met have a past. You know a bit about mine, and I'm willing to share anything you need to know to make you happy. As for what I know about you, if you want to tell me about your past, so be it, but as long as you're not wanted by the law or still married, then I don't see how our future changes."

Several seconds passed before Violet spoke again, "I was born in London, England. My father was...still is, I suppose...a wealthy man, a banker. I wanted for nothing except his affection and attention. My father wanted a son, so after I was born, he and my mother tried again. By the time I was three, she had miscarried twice. Shortly after my third birthday, she died in childbirth. It was a boy. He was stillborn. My father never got over it."

Again, Violet paused. This time, Jack got the impression she was forming her next thought, so he continued to eat.

"When I was seventeen, father invited a gambler from America to one of his weekly card games. His name was Tennessee William Jones. I called him Bill. When it was time for him to return to America, he asked me to come with him. I told him only if he married me. My father would have had to agree to the marriage before we could obtain a marriage license, and he did not like Bill, so we took a train to Scotland and eloped. From there, we took a steamship to New Orleans. We spent the next eighteen months on riverboats on the Mississippi River. It was all very exciting until one night, after Bill and I had a fight, he left me in our room and went to gamble. He was shot and killed that night playing poker. They claimed he was cheating."

Jack had finished his stew and was listening intently to Violet's story. His thoughts turned inward. At eighteen, he had still been punching cows with his father on Mr. Goodnight's ranch. He could not imagine what he would have done at that age if he had found himself alone on a different continent.

"I was too proud and too afraid of my father's anger to go back to England. I knew my marrying an American gambler without his permission would have caused an awful scandal, and even if I had not been so prideful, I'm not sure father would have allowed me to return. So, I took what I had learned watching father's card games and the little Bill had taught me, and I gambled."

Violet stopped talking, and Jack sat quietly contemplating all she had told him. When it became clear to him that she was not going to continue, he asked, "How long ago was it that your first husband was shot?"

"Thirteen years ago," Violet answered.

Before Jack could do the arithmetic in his head, Violet said, "I'm thirty-one, Jack."

Jack smiled, "Already reading my mind. When's your birthday?"

Violet smirked, "July the fourth."

Jack was not sure if she was serious, but when he gave her a "really" look, she shrugged, "July the fourth. Bill used to tell people, "I was born to come to America." Do you have any more questions?"

"Two," Jack said, "You said your first husband's name was Jones, but you introduce yourself as Violet Daniels."

"Daniels is my maiden name," Violet told him. "I was afraid that people might associate me with Bill, and since they accused him of cheating, I did not want to answer the questions that might arise. That's one question. What is the other?"

"You said you supposed your father was still a banker. Does that mean you haven't been in touch with him since you left England?" Jack asked.

"It does," Violet replied as she rose from her seat, took his dishes, and placed them on the counter. "That is one of the things I wanted to talk to you about, but I did not see the point if anything about my past was going to ruin our chances of a future together."

"Nothing you've said makes me want you any less than I did before I sat down here," Jack reassured her.

"Only if I had been wanted by the law, then you would, as they say, have run for the hills," Violet gave him a stern look as she spoke, then, unable to maintain it, giggled.

"As usual, you don't listen," Jack drew his brow down hard. "I said if you were wanted by the law, our future would change. I didn't say anything at all about us not being together." A grin spread across his face as he continued, "That's not to say we wouldn't have had to run for the hills to save your hide, but even then, we'd have been together." He finished with a wink.

Violet came around the table and motioned for him to scoot his chair out. When he did, she sat down in his lap, put her good arm around his neck, and pulled him in for a kiss. It ended too soon to suit him, and he started to pull her back when she put her finger to his lip and said, "We're not through talking."

Jack pouted, then smiled, "In that case, you better get up 'cause I don't think I can concentrate on what you're sayin' with you sittin' in my lap."

Violet laughed, gave a little wiggle, and then asked, "Are your mother and father alive?"

"They are," Jack responded.

"Where are they?" Violet asked.

"On a ranch in Texas," Jack told her.

"Do you keep in touch with them?"

"I do," Jack answered.

"Do they know about me?" Violet asked.

"They do."

"Will I ever meet them?"

Jack smiled. "That's something I've been meaning to talk to you about."

Someone knocked on the front door, interrupting their conversation. Violet stood up, and Jack started for the living room. Before he made it to the door, Jane opened it and stuck her head in, "It's Jane. Oh, I'm sorry Jack, I didn't know you were home. Just stoppin' by to visit with Violet."

"It's okay. Come on in," Jack told her. "I've got to get back to work anyway."

He turned to find Violet had come up behind him. To his surprise, she tiptoed and kissed right in front of Jane. He felt himself reddening as he turned to go.

"We'll finish our talk when you get home," he heard Violet say as he pulled the door shut.

11

The day before the election, Doc Babcock arrived to see Violet, with Jane in tow. He checked Violet's head injury first and told her everything was healing as expected. While she tied her scarf back in place, he pulled a strange-looking instrument from his bag. It looked like someone had crossed a pair of scissors with gardening shears. He laid the contraption on the table, then took a strange knife with a long handle and a rather short blade from his bag.

"Are you ready to see how that arm looks?" he asked Violet.

"I am," Violet replied.

On Doc Babcock's orders, Violet shifted in her chair so that she could lay the casted arm on the table. With Jane's help, he slowly cut the cast away, exposing her arm. The first thing Violet noticed was the smell. As careful as she had been, somehow dirt and grime had managed to find their way beneath the cast and mingled with her sweat it was a terribly rank odor.

Jane left and returned with a bucket of water and some rags. Doc Babcock carefully wiped away the grime, but even after washing the odor remained. Violet found herself praying the arm had healed enough that another cast would not be necessary.

Doc Babcock delicately felt along her arm from her pinky finger to her elbow. When he finished, he looked at Violet and said, "It has healed well. There is a very slight twist in the bone, but considering the break, you are very lucky. Now, I need you to carefully lift your arm, move it slowly around, and tell me if it hurts at all."

As the doctor had directed, Violet picked her arm up carefully. She felt no pain. As she began to slowly rotate her hand, she realized how weak the muscles in the arm were. When she turned her thumb toward the ceiling, she was shocked at just how skinny her arm looked.

"Nothing hurts," she told the doctor. "It feels weak, though."

"That's muscle atrophy from not using it," Doc Babcock explained. "It'll come back pretty quickly, but I want you to promise me you won't overdo it."

"Yeah, right," Jane chimed in. "Tellin' her to take it easy is like tellin' wind which way to blow and expectin' it to listen.'

Violet gave Jane a "shut up" look that caused Doc Babcock to chuckle. "Well then, promise me if it starts to hurt, you'll rest it."

"I will," Violet promised.

"Any questions?" he asked.

"Would it be okay for me to take a bath?" Violet asked.

Doc Babcock chuckled again. "Absolutely."

"Then if we're done, I think I'll have Jane help me heat up some water," Violet told him. "I may soak until noon."

"Well before you do that," Doc Babcock held up a hand as he spoke, "you better let me take those stitches out. I'm a bit surprised they look as good as they do. I was afraid of infection."

Violet laid her arm back on the table as he took a small pair of scissors out of his bag. "I'm afraid this may hurt a bit. They've been in too long but if our luck holds, you won't scar."

Violet grimaced each time the doctor removed a stitch. When he was through, he gathered his instruments, put them in his bag, and said, "I'll show myself out."

As he disappeared toward the front door, Jane said, "Let's get that bath goin', shall we?"

Jack arrived home to a house filled with the aroma of a woman's perfume. Unsure of what to expect, he made his way through the living room and started down the short hallway past the stairs. He took a quick look into what he called the reading room and Violet called the parlor and found it empty. The door to Violet's bathing room was slightly ajar, and he could hear humming coming from it.

"Violet, you in there?" he asked from the hall.

The humming stopped. He heard the splashing of water and the patter of feet.

"Everything, okay?" he asked.

"Everything's fine," Violet shouted from the other side of the door, "Just give me a minute."

Jack retraced his steps. In the living room, he settled into one of two chairs found there. As he stared at the sofa across the room from where he sat, he wondered how Violet had drawn a bath with her arm in a cast. He was still mulling the question over in his mind when she stepped into the living room wearing a robe with a towel wrapped atop her head.

"I did not hear you come in," she told him as she took a seat on the sofa and pulled her legs up beneath her.

His eyes moved over her body as she said something. The cast was gone, but its absence was not what was causing the distraction. It took his mind an instant to register that she was speaking. He looked into her eyes and stammering interrupted her. "My God, you are, huh... so beautiful." He could see Violet beginning to redden as he continued, "And your cast is off...and, huh, damn you smell so good."

He started to rise from his seat, but Violet held up a hand for him to stop. "I think it best if you stay where you are," she suggested.

"Why?" Jack pouted, his heart racing.

"Because we need to finish the conversation you were too tired to finish last night," Violet told him, "And because I don't want you starting something we can't finish since you will most certainly have to return to work soon."

Reluctantly, he returned to his chair. Once seated, he asked, "What was it we needed to talk about? I think I'm gonna need remindin'."

"Our parents," Violet said, "and our future."

"Right," Jack nodded. "Why don't you go first?"

As she began to speak, Jack tried to focus on her words but the sight of her was more than he could handle. At some point, Violet must have realized he was not actually listening to her because, in a raised voice, she chided, "Jack Abbott, you are not listening to me!"

Jack shook his head. "I am tryin'. It ain't easy."

"You better try harder," she warned, "or you'll be spending tonight on this sofa."

Jack laughed. "You would do that to yourself?"

"Jack, I'm serious," she glared at him, her tone half-begging.

"Alright," Jack replied. "I'm sorry. I'll listen."

He watched as she composed herself and began again. "I'm ashamed to say I have not thought much about my father in a long time. I guess I figured if I was dead to him, then he was dead to me, but since this," she pointed to her head before continuing, "I've been dreaming about my life with him in London. I don't know if he would even want to hear from me, but a part of me wants to contact him. What do you think?"

Jack considered her question for a short time. Violet seemed to understand he was pondering the pros and cons of it because she sat quietly, waiting until finally, he responded, "I can see no reason why you should not contact him. If he does not wish to be a part of your life, then he can simply do nothing. If he does not respond, you will have your answer. If he does, well then, I guess we'll cross that bridge when it happens."

When Jack finished speaking, he watched as Violet took some time before responding. "I think you are right. How do you think I should contact him?"

"I'd suggest a letter," Jack replied, "or maybe two, in case the first gets lost in transit. It would be sad if after all this time you reached out and he did not even know it."

Violet nodded, then asked, "What about your parents?"

"What about my parents?" Jack repeated the question a bit confused.

"I asked you if you thought I would ever meet them," she reminded him, "and you said that was something you wanted to talk to me about."

Jack looked from Violet to the floor as he collected his thoughts. When he looked up again, he said, "To answer your question first, let me say, it is my hope that you will meet my parents, but before we get too far along that line of conversation, I think we should talk about our future. What did Babcock say about your arm? Is it okay?"

"It is a little weak, but otherwise okay," Violet answered. "Doc Babcock seems to think everything is fine."

"That's wonderful," Jack smiled. "I don't know if you've given much thought to our future, but it's been on my mind for the last few weeks. First, I want you to know that whatever we decide, we decide together, okay?"

Violet nodded, and Jack continued, "I still have most of the gold from my claim. Minus what we spent on supplies when we left Deadwood, rent on this house, and the few things we've needed to survive since we got back. I haven't settled up with Doc Babcock yet, but I will. There are things I still want for us, children, a ranch, cattle, but I think our luck has run out in this part of the country. I got shot four times. You got shot twice. Both of us are lucky to be alive. Now I'm not sayin' it's all Deadwood's fault...I'm just sayin'," Jack paused not sure how to finish his thought.

"Sometimes you need to know when to fold'em," Violet finished it for him. "At least that's what a gambler would say."

"Yes," Jack agreed. "So, I was contemplatin', and if you are in agreement, I think we should take our gold, return to Texas, buy land and cattle, and start our lives there. What do you think?"

"I think I love the idea," Violet smiled. "But darlin', that was a very long answer to my question."

"What question would that be?" Jack asked.

"Do you think I'll ever get to meet your parents?"

Jack laughed.

Violet smiled, then said, "I think we should wait and have our wedding in Texas. What do you think?"

"If that is what you want darlin' then it will be so," Jack replied, then pouted, "but I'll sure hate waitin' to..."

Violet interrupted him, "The wedding can wait, but the consummation does not have to. Now you get on back to work. I'm going to take a nap. And Jack, I strongly suggest you get home early tonight."

12

On the morning of the election, Bullock handed Jack papers to be served to Grasshopper Jim. When Jack asked which salon he should check first, Bullock informed him that Jim had returned home. It turned out his home was a half-day ride to the east, so Jack made a visit to the Montana Carroll Livery.

"What can I do ya for today?" Tom Carroll asked Jack when he arrived at the livery.

"I'm gonna need one of my horses," Jack told him.

"They're in the back corral," Tom rubbed his chin as he spoke, then asked, "Particular as to which one?"

"Not really," Jack replied.

Tom hollered over his shoulder at a stable worker passing by and then turned back to Jack. "You gonna be back in time to vote in the election?"

"Depends on how fast I find Grasshopper Jim, I reckon," Jack responded.

"This about that shooting over at the Swearingen's place last week?" Tom asked.

"Might be," Jack shrugged, bored with Tom's questions, "I didn't read the summons so I can't rightly say."

Either Jack's subtle hint did not register, or Tom opted to ignore it. "You gonna read it before you deliver it?"

Before Jack could answer, the liveryman approached the two men leading a horse. The horse was that of the dead man Violet had shot and killed. Jack would have preferred his own horse, but since he had not specified, he took the reins.

Five minutes later, he was riding out of town.

~

Violet sat in the parlour listening to Jane regale her with the day's election process. The fact that women were allowed to vote in Wyoming and Utah Territories but not in the Dakota Territory had been the subject of a conversation Jane had overheard between two women outside Charlie Utter's freight store. She relayed the information to Violet between rants about how Al Swearinger was attempting to fix the whole damn election.

"I didn't know you were so interested in politics," Violet interjected when Jane paused for a breath.

"Politics? Humph," Jane reacted. "I got about as much use for politics as a pimple on my muff."

Violet shook her head in amusement before asking, "So, why do you care what Swearinger is doing?"

"Cause I cain't tolerate a cheat," Jane responded, venom in her tone.

For the next ten minutes, Violet sat quietly while Jane poured out her thoughts and feelings about many of the prominent males in town. Violet decided that for someone who did not care about politics, Jane sure was privy to a lot of information about the town's civic structure.

Seemingly out of nowhere, Jane, in her very Jane-like way, switched topics and asked, "So, have y'all settled on a wedding day?"

It took Violet, who had been thinking about Jack and only half-listening to Jane, a second to realize Jane had asked a question. Once she did, Violet blushed, "I'm sorry, Jane. What?"

"When are you and Jack gonna get married?" Jane rephrased her question.

Violet smiled as she answered, "We're not sure, yet. It might be a little while. We're not sure where the future is going to take us."

Jane's brow furrowed, "You mean y'all might be leavin' Deadwood again?"

"There is a good possibility," Violet told her.

"Why?" Jane asked.

Violet could tell by her surly expression and the set of her jaw that her news had not pleased Jane. She considered the best way to explain how she felt to her friend. Finally, after giving it some thought, she said, "Everything in life is a gamble, Jane. Me coming to Deadwood to try to make a living at the card tables was a gamble. Shooting Jack, now that was an accident that turned into a blessing, but leaving Deadwood after Jack got in the shootout with those fellas from Texas was a gamble. If I have learned anything in my years of playing cards, it is that sometimes the cards are hot and other times they are as cold as ice. My ability to know when the cards were growing cold is what kept me afloat when others would have gone under. Me and Jack have discussed it, and we're of a mind that our stake in Deadwood is growing cold, and it's time for us to fold our cards, leave the table, and find a new game."

Jane shook her head as if she understood, then still pouting, asked, "So, when are y'all leavin'?"

"I'm not sure," Violet told her. "I think it will depend on the outcome of the election for one thing and how soon we can make travel plans for another, but I hope sooner than later."

"Why?" Jane asked.

"Because," Violet replied, "I've got a bad feeling that if we wait too long something horrible is going to happen."

Jack had been in a sour mood most of the day. Even though he understood Bullock's need to stay in town for the election, the ride east to find Grasshopper Jim had not been something he had wanted to do. Riding hard, he had made it to Grasshopper Jim's station well before noon, only to find that he had taken supplies to repair a wheel on a stagecoach. An hour later, he and the stagecoach arrived, and Jack served him with the summons. Now, as the lights of Deadwood came into view and the longing to hold Violet again crept into his thoughts, his mood began to lighten.

Half an hour later, with the sun starting to make its evening run for the western horizon, Jack dismounted in front of the livery and stretched. Tom was nowhere to be seen, but the stable worker who had brought Jack his horse stepped out and asked, "Done with him for the day?"

"I am," Jack responded and handed him the horse's reins.

A man's voice shouted from somewhere behind Jack, "Hey mister, that's my brother's horse."

As the liveryman led the horse away, Jack eased the leather thong from both of his pistols, turned, and scanned the street. Thirty yards down the street a man stepped off the far boardwalk into the street. He was tall and lanky, with a pistol worn in a cross-draw position.

"That's my brother's horse," he repeated.

Jack shifted so the man was sure to see his badge and said, "That's far enough. State your business from there."

"My business," the man stopped, "is that's my brother's horse you just stepped off of."

"Is that what brings you to Deadwood?" Jack asked.

"What?"

"I asked you if you came to Deadwood lookin' for your brother's horse," Jack explained.

"No," the man replied. "I came to vote."

"Did you vote?" Jack asked.

"Yes."

"Then, I reckon your business here is done," Jack stated calmly. "Maybe it's best you move along."

The man's eyes narrowed, and he positioned his hand above his pistol. "Mister, I don't really much care for your attitude and that badge don't scare me none, so how's 'bout you tell me how you came to be ridin' my brother's horse."

"First, maybe you should tell me your brother's name," Jack countered.

"My brother is Daniel, Daniel Collins. Now why do you have his horse?"

"And you would be?" Jack asked.

"Listen, mister, I've 'bout reached the end of my patience."

"Your name, sir," Jack's calm tone had yet to waver.

"Joel Collins."

"Well, Mr. Joel Collins, if the man who rode that horse was indeed your brother..."

"What do you mean was?" Collins interrupted.

"Was, as in past tense," the pitch of Jack's voice changed to a harsher, more calloused tone, "as in the worthless son-of-a-bitch who owned this horse before me was a no-good scoundrel who shot at my wife from the dark."

Collins tensed. "So you killed him?"

"No," Jack replied with a smile that was as dark as his mood. "It was my wife who killed him. Shot him right through the eye and sent his useless soul to hell."

The slight twitch of Collins's eye told Jack there would be no more conversation. He readied himself and waited. In the periphery of his vision, he could see people scrambling for cover. Mentally, he blocked it and concentrated on the task in the street before him. In Jack's experience, most gunfighters, like most gamblers, had a tell. A sudden clenching of the jaw, an eye twitch, some small indications that they were about to draw. It turned out that Joel Collins did not.

Collins's pistol was half-drawn before Jack mind registered movement. Already a split second behind, Jack felt the walnut grips of his matching .45 Colts as he drew the guns. In Jack's mind, motion slowed, and he watched the muzzle of Collins's pistol as it swung away from the leather cross-draw holster and toward him. Jack thumbed the hammers of both guns as they cleared their holsters. A flash of smoke and fire erupted from Collins's pistol as Jack brought both Colts to bear on Collins's chest. The sting of a bullet tearing at his right shoulder told Jack that Collins had shot too soon as he pulled the trigger of both guns. The impact of Jack's shots knocked Collins backward and caused his second shot to careen into the evening sky.

As the life faded from Collins's eyes, he managed to right himself and make one final attempt to bring his pistol level. Instinctively, Jack thumbed both hammers and fired. Again, both shots found their mark, and Collins staggered back and dropped to his knees as his gun fired harmlessly into the muddy street. As he toppled forward, Jack holstered one of his pistols, ejected the spent cartridges from the second, and was in the process of reloading the chambers when he saw Bullock coming down the street with a shotgun in his hands.

By the time the sheriff reached him, Jack had reloaded both Colts and returned them to their holsters. Jack listened as bystanders yelled contradictory verdicts. Most claimed that Jack was in the right and that Collins had braced him. Others argued that Jack had pushed him.

"You're hit," Bullock pointed at Jack's shoulder as he spoke.

"It's just a scratch," Jack told him, then nodded at Collins. "He drew first."

"Charlie Utter," Bullock hollered and Jack turned to see the freighter standing across the street on the now crowded boardwalk.

Charlie stepped down into the street and approached. When he was close enough, Bullock asked, "Did you see what happened here?"

"I did," Charlie replied. He pointed at Collins's body. "This man asked Jack why he was riding his brother's horse. They had some words, and then he drew on Jack. He got a pretty good jump on your deputy, sir. To be honest, I thought Jack here was a goner. I don't think I've ever seen a faster draw."

"Thanks, Charlie," Bullock said. "Mind doing me one more favor?"

"What's that, Sheriff?" Charlie asked.

"Would you let Doc Pierce know he's got another customer?"

Charlie nodded and started off up the street. The crowd seemed to sense the excitement was over and began to disperse. Bullock looked at Jack and shook his head. "Maybe it's best I lost the election. Nothing personal, Jack, but I think my first opinion may have been accurate."

"And what opinion would that be?" Jack asked.

"The one I had about Deadwood being a better place without you in it," Bullock smiled and patted him on the back.

"Can't say as I disagree with ya," Jack said. "Reckon it's about time to think about movin' on."

13

Violet finished the second letter she was writing and signed it. With care, she folded it, placed it in an envelope addressed to her father at his address in London, England, and set it near the first letter she had written to him. Now that she had them ready, she found herself second guessing whether she should send them or not. What if he did not write back? Or even worse, what if he did and told her he never wanted to hear from her again?

"I'm leavin' for town," Jack announced as he stuck his head into the parlour. "You need anything while I'm out?"

Violet pushed her fears aside, held up the two letters, and said, "Could you post these letters for me?"

"I can," Jack answered as he crossed the room and took them from her. She tilted her head as he leaned down for a quick kiss.

"Anything else?" he asked as he started for the door.

"If you see Jane, please ask her to stop by this afternoon," Violet told him before turning back to her writing table.

Tomorrow the stage would come to town, and when it left, she and Jack would be on it. It was not the first time she had traveled by stagecoach, but it was the first time her plans had extended past the next poker game. From banker's daughter to professional gambler to rancher's wife, nothing about her life had been dull. She thought about her future with Jack and smiled.

~

Bullock stared down at the star Jack had handed him and said, "You're a good man, Jack. A dangerous one, but a good one, and I'm glad we always saw eye to eye."

"Me, too," Jack told him. "With help from men like you, I think one day this could be a real nice town."

"Men like me?" Bullock chuckled. "Next month, Manning will take over as sheriff, and I'll return to the hardware store with Sol."

Jack considered what he had heard briefly, then responded, "I haven't been in Deadwood all that long, but one thing I know is you've got an iron in damn near every legitimate fire that's burnin' in this town. I'm not a bettin' man, but if I was, I'd put money on the fact that when they write this town's history yours will be among the names of those who helped form it into a place worth living in."

~

Violet looked down at the package in her lap. It was wrapped in brown paper and had been secured with twine.

"You shouldn't have," Violet looked up at Jane and smiled as she spoke.

Jane shrugged, "Ain't much. Figured it could be an early wedding present."

"Or you could come to Texas and be my maid of honor," Violet suggested.

Jane shook her head, "Gotta stay 'round here and keep Charlie out of trouble."

Violet pulled the twine from the package, then unwrapped it. Inside, she found a bright red scarf. Wrapped in the scarf was a set of playing cards.

"Figured you could use a new scarf for the trip," Jane explained, "And them cards are to remind you of Deadwood."

"Of Deadwood or you?" Violet asked.

Jane reddened. "Could be a bit of both."

"I did not get you anything," Violet frowned.

"Ain't necessary."

Violet rose from her seat, set the scarf and cards down, and spoke as she walked across the living room. "It is necessary to me. I'll be right back."

Quickly she made her way upstairs. Two carpet bags and a small steamer trunk sat at the foot of the bed. Violet opened one of the bags and retrieved her hand mirror. With it in hand, she returned to the living room.

"I want you to have this," she told Jane as she handed it to her friend.

"I ain't much on lookin' at this ugly mug in such as this," Jane said as she took the mirror from Violet.

Violet laughed, "Jane, to the rest of the world, you may be grime and dirt mixed with the smell of booze, but to me, you are beautiful. To me, you are my friend." Violet picked up the scarf and cards, and continued, "When I wear this, and when I look at these, I will remember the woman who helped me nurse Jack back from the dead, and I will remember the woman who did the same for me." Pointing at the mirror, she smiled, "And I hope, even if you never once look at yourself in that mirror, that when you see it, you will remember how you helped me when I was broken and bloodied. How you helped me find the will to live and the strength to continue when my body and my mind and my soul wanted to quit. And when you remember those things, I hope you know what a beautiful, wonderful person you are."

Violet watched as Jane turned the mirror slowly in her hands. She had not realized how close the two of them had become and the realization brought a lump to her throat. As she returned to her seat, she tried to lighten the mood, "Hey, if nothing else, we can write to each other, right?"

Jane looked up and shook her head, "Wouldn't do no good."

Violet started to ask why, then the answer registered, and she refrained. Her friend could not read. Changing the subject quickly, Violet asked, "Will you be there to see us off tomorrow?"

Jane shook her head. "Ain't no good at goodbyes, I reckon. Besides, I told Charlie, I'd make a mail and supply run to Cheyenne for him. I was fixin' to leave when Jack stopped me and said you wanted me to stop by."

"I'm glad you did," Violet found herself not wanting the visit to end.

Jane stood quickly, and spoke while staring down at the floor, "Well, Miz Violet, I guess I better get on now. Thanks for the mirror. You take care of yourself."

Before Violet could respond, Jane crossed to the front door and left. Violet picked up the scarf and cards and held them in her hands as tears slowly began to flow.

Jack helped the driver secure the streamer trunk and the carpet bags on top of the stage. Violet stood on the boardwalk, looking up the street. At her feet were his war bag and a set of saddlebags. These would ride inside the coach with them. Each bag held gold – half in the war bag beneath his extra clothes, the other half in the saddlebags.

Climbing down from the stagecoach, Jack stepped to the edge of the boardwalk and offered Violet his hand. She took it, and he helped her into the street. As the driver held the door open for her, Jack picked up the bags. When he turned around, Violet was already stepping up into the stage. He crossed the short distance to where the driver was waiting, stopped, and looked up and down the street of Deadwood one last time before stepping up into the stage himself.

Violet had been quiet all morning, and he was a bit worried about her. After stowing the bags beneath their seat, he took her hand in his. She turned to look at him and smiled.

"Are you okay?" he asked.

"I'm fine, dear," she assured him. "I'm excited about the future but also a bit sad about leaving friends behind, that's all."

"I understand," he said thinking about Bullock and Sol.

With a jerk, the stage started forward. Violet laid her head on Jack's shoulder, squeezed his hand, and whispered, "You got to know when to fold'em."

ABOUT THE AUTHOR

One Pen – Endless Possibilities. I cannot think of a better way to describe my writing. Born and raised in Southern Oklahoma by a high school English teacher and a newspaper columnist, there was little doubt that at some point I would turn to words for comfort. Surrounded on all sides of my family by spinners of yarns and tellers of tales, there was little hope that I myself would not become a storyteller.

DRAWN INTO DANGER

INK, JUSTICE, AND COURAGE

LYNN DONOVAN

Editing by Cyndi Rule

INTRODUCTION

Deadwood, South Dakota—1882.

A frontier town where law and lawlessness share the same dusty street.

Brynn Ellison came west chasing hope—a mail-order promise that crumbled the moment she arrived. Alone and deceived, she finds shelter in a small church, scrubbing floors by day and sketching faces by lamplight, her charcoal drawings the only place she dares to dream.

Gideon Carver, a printer's apprentice haunted by guilt and secrets, spends his days pressing wanted handbills for the sheriff—until he discovers Brynn's lifelike sketches. Her art gives his craft new purpose, and together their talents bring long-awaited justice to the Black Hills.

But when one likeness sends an outlaw to the gallows, vengeance inked in blood turns its sights on the unknown artist. As danger closes in, Gideon and Brynn must stand against both sin and circumstance—and find, amid the smudged lines of ink and courage, the chance to print a new beginning.

1

A PROPER LADY IN A ROUGH TOWN

Kneeling between the empty pews, Brynn Ellison bowed her head—not in prayer, but to reach the scarred wood before her. The wax stung the raw places on her fingers as she worked the threadbare rag in slow, aching circles, its scent clinging like remorse. If only polishing oak smooth could erase more than scratches—if only it could wipe clean the mistake that had brought her here.

The reverend's wife, Evelyn Doubtmire, had shown her how to properly polish the sanctuary—its seating and wooden floors. Respect swelled in Brynn's heart for Millie, Father's housemaid back home in Albany, New York. She always kept their red-brick townhouse with beautiful oak banisters and tall lace curtains spotless and polished like these pews. Brynn had no idea how much work had been involved in keeping things that way.

The stinging scent of turpentine made her eyes water, but the beeswax's honeyed scent softened the bite. Leaning back to ease the ache from her neck to her waist, she glanced toward the rafters and whispered a small prayer of thanks that Reverend Thomas Doubtmire didn't expect her to polish those, too.

Although she'd gladly scrub every nook and cranny of this church, rather than spend another hour where the wagon had first deposited her in Deadwood. Each polished plank felt like a welcome escape from a fate she had never sought. Each breath was a whispered apology to her grandmama —for trusting the wrong man, for nearly losing everything a proper lady should hold dear.

This pew, at the back of the sanctuary, was permanently reserved for the women from the brothels—where she herself had sat last Sunday, trembling and praying for mercy. The memory pricked like a splinter under her skin. Fooled by a mail-order bride scheme, she'd come terribly close to a life she'd never wanted.

The reverend had spoken to her after service, his voice gentle and full of grace. Mrs. Doubtmire made an offer that she live in the back room and clean the church for room and board until she found her bearings. The kindness had felt like salvation.

A spark of color on the pew caught her eye. A hair pin. Its owner was likely fretting over where she'd lost it. Placing it in the lost-and-found was not enough. A tightness gripped her chest at the thought of going back there. Still, the idea of one of the girls fretting over what she'd lost tugged harder than fear.

Brynn would take it to the girls she had traveled with. Believing the lies told to them in New York, they had become fast friends. Expecting to be brides and mothers soon, they had giggled and exchanged hopes and dreams, and planned tea parties together. But all that squelched silent the minute their wagon arrived in Deadwood and they were hustled past the Green Door. It took no time to figure out they were not mail-order brides.

Her friends would know who it belonged to and see that she received it right away. Gathering the hair accessory and slipping it into her pocket, she finished the last wooden row of pews.

"I'm finished cleaning," she told the reverend.

He looked up from his studies in his quaint office.

"I need to run an errand," she said.

He frowned. "It's not safe for you to walk through the streets alone."

Brynn lifted her chin a notch, exhibiting her determination.

He sighed. "However, if you will be careful, and stay away from the main street, I will pray you safe until you return." Glancing at his desktop, he added, "Oh, since you are out, could you drop this by the printer?" Reverend Thomas added.

"Of course," she said. He handed her a sheet of folded paper. "Is this Sunday's service announcement?" she asked.

"Yes. Mister Shumacher wants it by Friday. I'm afraid I don't have time to deliver it." He chuckled. "Not unless I mean to deliver His word unprepared come Sunday."

She dipped her head politely before leaving his office. Drawing her shawl from the hook outside the small room behind the sanctuary, she patted her skirt pocket as she stepped out into the cool afternoon sunlight.

First to drop off the trinket, then to the *Deadwood Pioneer*.

Summer in Deadwood was as changeable as its people—heat one hour, chill the next. A wagon rattled by, throwing dust that caught in the sunlight like smoke. Piano music drifted faintly from a saloon two streets over, tangled with the curses of a teamster and the jingle of harness chains—Deadwood's own roughhewn hymn.

Dodging the main street where saloon doors dominated the boardwalk, she slipped down a back alley. Climbing a set of narrow stairs, she tapped on the green door. An oversized grizzly man opened it.

"Who're you?" he growled.

"Brynn Ellison," she stated.

"You wised up and come back where you belong?" he guffawed.

"No," she murmured. "I came to see Lily."

"Is she the brunette?" he asked.

"Don't you even know who lives here?" Brynn frowned.

A shrug was his only answer. He stepped back to allow her entrance, but grabbed her arm violently, halting her progress. "What kinda name is Brynn anyway?"

A shiver rippled down her spine. Trying to pull out of his painful grasp, she murmured, "Welch." She blinked. "I-it was my mother's family name."

He released her arm as if he were tossing it away in disgust. "Don't take long. She got work, don't you know."

Brynn rubbed her arm as she hurried away from him, meandering through the long corridor that smelled of rose powder and whiskey. She searched for Lily's room.

Tapping on a doorframe, she hoped was the right one, she glanced over her shoulder and waited.

The door opened slowly. Lily peeked through the narrow gap.

"Oh," she exclaimed, opening it wider. "What do you want?"

Brynn's heart ached. Letting her eyes fall on Lily's skimpy underthings—such bright, fragile colors in this dim place—she whispered, "I found this in the church pew." She held out the hairpin.

Lily stared at the bobble in Brynn's palm. "So?"

Did Lily hate her for escaping their fate at the first opportunity she found? "Lily, please. I know someone is missing this. See that she gets it back."

Her friend's brow lifted dismissively. She took the trinket without a word and closed the door.

Brynn stood for a moment in the heavy air. Tobacco and cheap perfume clung to the velvet drapes. Her stomach turned—she had slept one night beneath that same gilt ceiling. Somewhere behind another door, a girl laughed, high-pitched and hollow. It made Brynn's heart quake.

She turned and found her way back down the narrow staircase. Outside, the street noise crashed over her like cold water. She pressed a hand to her chest and tried to breathe.

Not all the women in those upstairs rooms were prisoners; some had chosen the life because it paid when nothing else did. But others—the ones with eyes dulled like her own reflection that day—had been fooled, just as she had. Was there any way to free them?

Struggling for composure, she made her way to the printer's shop.

Standing before the glass doors of the *Deadwood Pioneer*, the local newspaper, Brynn stiffened. *A lady never revealed her troubles to strangers,* Grandmama's voice echoed in her thoughts. She drew in a deep breath and entered.

A young blond man looked up from carving a wooden block. "May I help y—"

"Brynn?" He gasped, dropping the block with a thud. "Brynn Ellison?"

She froze. Recognition unfolded slowly, like a memory coming into focus. *Gideon Carver!* She hadn't seen him in years—not since his parents sent him away to boarding school. How could he be here, in Deadwood, in a print shop?

"Is it really you?" he said.

She nodded. What else could she do? She was indeed Brynn Ellison.

"Gideon Carver?" she murmured.

"Well, I'll be hornswoggled. It is you." He grinned, then his glee faltered into something like worry. "What are you doing here?"

The paper rattled in her trembling hand, reminding her why she'd come. "I... I've been sent to bring the church's announcements to Mister Shumacher—for the newspaper."

"No, I mean what are you doing in Deadwood?"

She stared at him. An explanation, the truth, impossible to articulate.

Gideon wiped his hands on a thick apron, though ink still etched his fingertips. "Mister Shumacher just stepped out. I can take it." He started toward her, a dirty hand extended.

Her feet slid backward.

"I'll just lay it here," she said quickly, placing the paper on the sales counter. "I assume the reverend has a tab?"

"Yes, we bill him at the end of the month."

"Well, then, I'll be going. It was nice to see you, Mister Carver."

"Likewise," he answered, puzzlement in his eyes. "May I ask a question?"

Her spine stiffened. "Of course." She lifted her chin.

"How long have you been in Deadwood?"

Brynn swallowed hard. "Not long."

Silence hovered between them.

"Well, I need to get back," she choked.

"Back where?" he asked. "To the church?"

"Yes." She turned on her heels and rushed out the door.

Almost running, she hurried down the boardwalk. Tears blurred the dust and sunlight into one shimmering haze. *Gideon Carver. In Deadwood. What were the odds?*

Her heart pounded a rhythm to match her footsteps. *He'd known her as a girl of polish and promise—what would he see now? A woman lost in Deadwood?*

Slipping inside the back door of the church, she went straight to her small room and collapsed onto the narrow bed. Breath tore ragged from her throat as tears escaped into her hair.

Gideon Carver.

The boy she had loved since she was nine years old. Did he still have feelings for her? Not likely. If she could find a respectable job, earn enough to leave this town, she could build a quiet life out west. Somewhere not built on a reputation of lawlessness and ill-gotten gains.

Outside, evening bells rang. Her next breath steadied. She sat up. Perhaps if she proved herself capable, the reverend could pay her. Just enough to board a train for anywhere but here.

x x x

Gideon rubbed his fingertips together. Dried from the ink he massaged into the plates, his fingers looked gray as spent ash. No wonder she'd backed away when he reached for her paper. He bent to pick up the dropped wooden block. His eyes remained on the shop door she had slipped through.

Brynn Ellison. Here. In Deadwood.

The one person he'd admired most for being fearless, now flinching like a frightened sparrow at the sight of him. Did she know?

The whispers in Albany had surely spread the news.

He rubbed his thumb along the edge of the wooden block he'd been carving—a border for an ad on page five—and tried to stop the tremor in his hand. Deadwood had been his salvation. A town where everyone overlooked one's past. No matter how dark.

He found work using his skill in wood carving. An apprentice to the printer. Not college, but education, just the same. He knew everything going on around town. Simply because he had learned how to set the print and pressed the ink to the page.

Brynn. His childhood first love. How he had missed her chatty, devil-may-care, headstrong and fearless approach to everything. There wasn't a tree she couldn't climb higher than he. Or a horse she couldn't stay seated on. There was nothing that scared her outdoors. Yet, among the gentlefolk, she acted disciplined and well mannered. Her grandmother's pride and joy. Maybe he had been the only person to whom she could be true-to-herself?

She looked worn, thinner, yet the same mix of gentleness and stubbornness he remembered. What had brought her here of all places? Church? Was she here on a mission trip? Many people sought to save the savage souls out west. Lord only knows they didn't come any more savage than those in Deadwood.

A gust from the open back door scattered paper proofs across the floor. He bent to gather them, his mind already turning over the certainty that he'd see her again.

"Got anything for delivery?" Elias Hart, the nephew of the general store owner, and possibly his only true friend, blustered in through the back.

"Yeah, I did, but that tail wind you let in scattered 'em all over. Help me bundle these back together and you can take them"

Together they piled the announcement flyers and tied them with twine. Another wedding... here in Deadwood. Even men as ruthless as these found love. Could Gideon ever hope for the same?

Tomorrow, the newspaper would be delivered before sun up. A bundle at the general store and other public filled places. Perhaps he'd deliver one to the reverend, just for proofreading purposes. Although it'd be too late if there were any errors. Still, it sounded like a legitimate excuse, and perhaps he'd run into Miss Ellison.

Then he could ask her to join him for a cup of coffee or tea. Maybe he could decipher what she knew about him and why she landed in such a God-forsaken town as Deadwood.

2

INK, CHARCOAL, AND SECRETS

Bone-weary from cleaning until darkness settled like a blanket over the town, Brynn collapsed onto her bed. Grateful for the down-filled pillow and mattress, she folded her hands and gave God the glory for all she had—despite all the things she had left behind. Her trunk full of promises—a sacrifice for her freedom.

She'd carried her carpet bag like a purse after the other girls mentioned they attended church Sunday mornings. She had escaped with a day-dress and a change of small clothes, her drawing pad, and a box of charcoal sticks.

Had it been God's nudging that prompted her to take it with her? At least she could still draw and release her feelings. She yawned and pushed herself upright. Sketching still offered a release for everything bottled up in her heart.

She touched the page with the charcoal stick and began to capture the one face that had lingered in her mind after she'd dropped off the church's advertisement to the *Deadwood Pioneer*. The boy she remembered so clearly had haunted her all day.

As a man, he hadn't lost his boyish good looks she remembered. The stutter he once struggled with was gone, and so was the innocence in his eyes. Life did that to a person. How well she knew.

Losing his father the same day he returned home from boarding school must have been hard. She could only imagine. The townsfolk gossiped that his father's blood had been on Gideon's hands, but that couldn't be true. She knew him too well to believe such a heinous accusation.

He had left Albany without stopping to see her. With no one to defend him, the rumors had taken root. Still, she trusted only what her heart told her.

She hadn't heard from him since. Not until today. How strange to find him again when she felt so lost.

Her fingers swept across the pad, leaving behind the shape of Gideon's jaw, the lift of his cheekbones, and the spark she remembered so well in his eyes. It wasn't there today, but she took creative liberty to put it back in—it was her sketch, after all.

Exhaustion forgotten, she drew the lines, smudging where shadows were needed, and lifting with the erasing pencil where highlights should be. Soon, she let her arm flop down beside her and stared at the likeness. Gideon Carver.

Now, perhaps she could sleep. With his face hidden among others she'd drawn since leaving New York, she closed the flap and slid it under her bed. Tomorrow—a day of rest. Mrs. Doubtmire had told her a reverend's family gathered their strength on Saturday before they gave every bit of their mind and soul to the congregants on Sunday.

She'd never thought about what it took to be a reverend or his wife, but it made sense that it would be as labor-intensive as cleaning the sanctuary—or Millie cleaning her father's home—or any number of things she'd taken for granted most of her life.

With a satisfied sigh, Brynn let her eyes close. Blissful sleep washed over her almost immediately.

The next morning, she rose with the sunlight streaming into the one window in her little room. She brushed her dress clean, twisted her hair into a neat chignon at the back of her neck, and grabbed her pad and charcoal sticks. Today, she would spend her time committing to memory every interesting person who crossed her path. And to ensure she was safe while observing the citizens, she would go to the top of the bell tower and watch from there. Climbing the circular stairs, she carried also a three-legged stool —suited more for milking a cow—and ventured to the highest point in Deadwood.

Adjusting herself on the stool, pad on her knees, charcoal in hand, she flipped the pages to a fresh sheet. Scurrying feet echoed below, drawing her attention. She stared back the way she'd come for a moment. Probably a rat. Ridding the church of rodents was not her job. She continued with her task at hand.

Lost in her drawing, Brynn sat against the wall, out of the way of the large brass bell, where she could see down below. Four hours had slipped away. Hunger gnawed at her middle. Taking the stool and her supplies, she made her way down into the tiny kitchen, also at the back of the church. A loaf of bread, smoked meat, and raw vegetables filled a basket. Thanks to Mrs. Doubtmire, it never went empty—like a cornucopia.

Brynn sliced the meat, a portion of the bread, cleaned and cut up a parsnip, and piled it on a small plate before carrying it to her room to eat.

"Hello?" a voice echoed from the sanctuary. A voice that sounded very familiar.

Gideon Carver.

The reverend and his wife were in their parsonage. Brynn would quickly tell him and return to her midday meal. Stepping to the door of the sanctuary, plate in hand, sketch pad and sticks under her other arm, she stared at the man she'd known since childhood.

"Good day," she said. "Do you need the reverend?"

"No." He fidgeted with his hat. "I, well, that is, I came to see you."

"Me?" Her heart sped up. "Why?"

"Isn't it obvious?" he asked. "I was hoping we could... talk."

"About what?"

"About how it is you showed up at the print shop yesterday." He glanced at her plate, then the pad under her arm. "You still sketch?"

Nodding her head, she adjusted her bundle. "You hungry?"

"I could eat," he said.

"Don't have much to offer." She shrugged and held out her plate to demonstrate. "But I have enough to share."

"That would be kind of you," he said.

Turning on her heel, she led him to the small kitchen, set her things aside, and prepared the same modest meal.

"We'll have to go to the basement—" She lifted her eyes from the food.

He had her sketchpad. Flipping the pages slowly, he examined each drawing.

Heat filled her cheeks. "Don't."

"Alright." He closed the book, just before he saw the sketch of him.

Her heart hammered in her chest, making her breath more labored than she'd like.

Grabbing several matches with trembling fingers from the box nailed to the door frame, she snatched her pad and lifted her plate to continue through the back hall to a set of stairs leading to the servants' entrance of the basement.

"You always drew with such precision," he said behind her in the stairwell.

Glancing over her shoulder, she said, "It's nothing."

Putting her plate down, she struck a match and lit an oil lantern. Even though it had been dark as pitch, she knew the room well from cleaning yesterday. Now he could see as well. She pulled out a wooden chair at a fellowship table. He rushed up behind her and took hold of the chair. She nodded her thanks and sat. He sat across from her. An odd smile quivered on his lips.

"You've hardly changed since I saw you last," he said.

"Hardly, indeed." She glided her fingers through imaginary loose strands and tucked them behind her ear.

"No—I mean you've grown lovelier," he paused.

He hadn't meant to use the word *lovelier*, but it had already leapt out.

"You still see the world in clean lines. It shows in your sketches," he forged ahead.

Heat colored her cheeks. "It's truly nothing."

"It is... something," he said softly. "The way you capture a man's likeness in charcoal. It's uncanny."

He bit into the bread wrapped around the slice of meat and chewed, all the while watching her.

Why was he so interested in her sketching?

"Eat," she said at last. "Let's talk about something else."

"Yes." He smiled. "I want to know everything about you."

Oh Lord. She didn't want to tell him anything about how she'd been fooled into coming here or how she was desperately trying to figure out how to go anywhere else.

"I'm certain your story is much more interesting than mine." She lowered her eyelashes.

His Adam's apple bobbed hard against a gulp. "Maybe we should leave all those stories for another time."

Relief washed over her. "Yes. Another time."

His eyes landed on her sketchpad. "Listen, I've got an idea. I-I don't know what the reverend is paying you to clean—"

She laughed softly. "Room and board is all I get. But it's better than—" she ducked her chin close to her chest. "I mean, I'm grateful for a roof and food, but I'm looking for respectable work that pays."

"Have I got an offer for you?" He grinned. "And you'd be helping me and the lawmen around here to boot."

Her brow slammed together as she cocked her head back on her shoulders. "What are you going on about?"

"As the printer's apprentice, I carve wooden blocks so we can print some sort of a illustration of outlaws. The better the poster's likeness, the more likely they will be found. There are two ways we could manage it. One, you might see them around Deadwood, and two, the lawmen could give you a description for you to reproduce. You draw one of your sketches, I can use that to whittle the block, and print the wanted poster."

Shaking her head vehemently before he finished speaking, she scooted back away from him. "No. I can't."

"Why not?" he slid his chair toward her. "You've certainly got the talent."

"I told you—it's nothing."

"And I'm telling you… it's not nothing. You're very talented. This could make a huge difference to Sheriff Seth Bullock."

He studied her a moment. "Look, I'll make you a promise. I'll never leave you alone when spotting the outlaw, and I will see to it that you are paid well for each likeness you produce."

She gaped at him. "How well?"

A smile curled across his lips. "Better pay than most any respectable position a lady might find in a place like this."

"And…" she considered her words carefully. "No one will know it's one of my sketches?"

"If that's how you want it." He nodded.

Chewing her bottom lip, she angled her chin away from him. "I'll give it some thought."

3
POSTERS ON THE WIND

Brynn's skirts swooshed over her boots as she and Gideon walked along the boardwalk. It had been three weeks since he made her the offer she could not refuse. Carrying her sketch pad under one arm, the locals became accustomed to their stroll through town, and didn't realize she gave him her latest drawing when they reached the print shop.

It had been a miracle—her running into him in Deadwood, South Dakota. The feelings she'd tried to stamp down when he vanished from Albany all those years ago were fluttering to the surface of her heart like migrating monarchs.

Did he feel the same for her?

A cool breeze tugged at the corners of each paper nailed to every post and storefront. Sheriff Bullock and his men made sure every eye could see the faces of the criminals he searched for daily. These morning walks carried the scent of pine smoke and coffee; secrets and truths. Only Brynn and Gideon knew how the likenesses printed on the wanted posters came to be. She did not allow herself to peruse a single one for fear she'd give away her secret.

Like a hand in cards, they kept the truth close to their vests. Only Mr. Shumacher knew how Gideon had improved his carvings. For this, she received a generous salary.

She had neither opened a bank account nor mentioned the income to Reverend and Mrs. Doubtmire—or anyone else for that matter. She continued to clean the church for room and board and hid the money at the bottom of the four-drawer dresser the Doubtmires provided in her small bedroom.

Her longing to continue west faded with each passing day. Deadwood wasn't as terrifying as it had been.

Outside a saloon, a pair of lawmen stood appraising a poster.

"Best likeness we've had yet," one said.

"Nobody's gonna hide in Deadwood with posters this good," said the other.

Gideon tipped his hat, and Brynn tucked her chin in greeting. The touch of her charcoal stick had set justice in motion.

Sheriff Bullock smiled a lot more these days.

For all anyone knew, Brynn and Gideon were simply a young couple courting. Every day without incident gave Brynn a sense of confidence that their secret would not lead to her demise, as Gideon had first feared.

Gideon held the door for her, and she entered the print shop at noon. The familiar scent of ink and turpentine wafted out to meet them.

"Mr. Shumacher?" Gideon called to his boss. "Mr. Shumacher, we have good news."

Silence greeted them. "Hmm." Gideon pursed a smile at Brynn and walked toward his boss's office. "Hey, we heard James Leighton Gilmore got caught last night. Another poster did the job—" Gideon gasped.

"What is it?" Brynn hurried toward him.

"No! Don't." Gideon held up his hands to stop her. "Go get the sheriff."

"Why?" she tiptoed and swayed to see over or around him. "What's wrong?"

"Brynn, please, stay back. Mr. Shumacher has been assaulted."

She gasped. "Oh no." Shoving past Gideon, she entered the office. The man slumped forward onto his desk. A hole in the back of his head, and blood pooled beneath his face indicated he was more than just assaulted.

He'd been shot.

Her stomach turned, and she slapped her hand over her mouth to stay the nausea. "Lord help us," she whispered.

Gideon grabbed her shoulders and guided her into the front of the print shop.

"Go. Get. The. Sheriff," he said through gritted teeth.

She staggered back, turned, and ran. Her corset cinched too tightly for her to run as fast as she'd have liked, but she did her best. It was four blocks to the sheriff's office.

Wheezing for air, she shoved through the front door. "Sheriff!" she panted.

Two deputies looked up from under their hats. Had they been sleeping?

"Where's the sheriff?" Brynn heaved.

"Locking up a prisoner," one said.

"Shumacher," Brynn struggled to breathe. "Shot. Dead."

The deputies scrambled to their feet. "What? How?"

"Don't. Know," she stammered.

Metal clanked in the room behind them. The sheriff pushed through the door. "That's all taken ca—"

He stared at Brynn. "What's wrong?"

Her breathing leveled out enough for her to speak plainly, but her mind was still a tangle. "Shumacher. Shot. Gideon. Found him. He's dead."

The sheriff grabbed his hat from the nail behind his head and hurried out the door. He took such long strides that she could not keep up. The deputies ran past her, following the sheriff.

She walked quickly, but could not run to catch up.

When she entered the print shop, Gideon sat at his desk, his head in his hands. "I told you, he was like this when we walked in. I didn't see who shot him."

xxx

That evening Gideon found her in the bell tower. The sun, sinking behind Bald Mountain, turned the rooftops copper. "Bullock wanted you to know our work makes a difference."

She didn't look up from the pad in her lap. "Unless we have no idea who committed the crime."

"No, but your drawings have made their jobs easier."

"Does anyone else know?" she asked.

"Only him. And Shumacher and me."

She exhaled, shoulders easing, then tightening again. "I only wish I could make a difference in Mr. Shumacher's murder."

Gideon's eyes softened. "The sheriff will have to solve his murder the old fashioned way."

xxx

Two days later, the town gathered by the gallows.

Brynn stayed near the back, bonnet brim casting a heavy shadow across her eyes. James Gilmore stood straight, defiant. Even from a distance she could see the similarity—the jawline, the narrowing eyes she herself had darkened on paper. Her throat seized as he turned, scanning the crowd.

"Curse the artist who damned me!" he shouted, voice rough as gravel. "Name him, so I can know the hand that betrayed me!"

Gasps rippled through the onlookers. Brynn felt Gideon's hand close gently around her wrist.

"Don't move," he murmured.

The rope snapped taut. A ragged cheer burst from some, solemn silence from others. In the midst of it, a bearded stranger near the livery spat into the dust and muttered something low before disappearing into the milling crowd. Brynn caught the gleam of malice in his eyes.

Those eyes hunted her mind.

Dusk settled thick by the time Gideon walked her back to the church. Lantern light swung between them, painting the boards in gold arcs. For once, words seemed too fragile to bridge the weight of what they'd witnessed.

At the steps, he paused. "You did what you were meant to do," he said finally.

"Did I?" Tears filled her eyes. She sniffed. "It didn't protect your boss."

He met her gaze. "I'll see you safe, Brynn. Whatever comes next."

She wanted to tell him she trusted him, that fear and gratitude often wore the same face. But instead, she only nodded.

He walked her to the small room. "Lock the door," he said.

"I will."

With the reverend and his wife next door in the parsonage, she no longer felt safe even though she lived in a church. Evil knew no boundaries.

Lifting her sketchpad, she settled on her bed and drew the face of the bearded man near the livery. First just his eyes, then his whole face.

A gust lifted another loose poster. It fluttered past her little window—a ghost of paper tumbling into the dark.

4
LANGLEY'S WARNING

"Brynn?" A familiar voice called through the quiet morning. She peeked out of her bedroom door.

"Yes?"

"Brynn—"

The voice dissolved into sobs. Brynn ran for the sanctuary.

Lily lay crumpled on the hardwood floor Brynn had scrubbed clean just hours before. "Lily?" She dropped to her knees beside her friend. "What is it?"

Brynn caught the weight of Lily's shoulders and gently helped her sit up. When Lily's face tilted toward the light, the breath left Brynn's chest. Her lower lip was swollen and torn. The blood dried dark along its edge. One eye had swollen shut beneath a bruise that bloomed purple and blue; the other glimmered red-rimmed and frightened. A blackened patch shadowed her cheek where a small cut gaped open—shallow but deliberate, as if struck by a ringed hand.

"Who did this to you?" Brynn whispered. She pulled Lily to her feet, wrapping an arm around her waist and draping her friend's arm over her shoulder. She guided her to the small bedroom. Easing her onto the bed, she assessed the damage to her face. "Are you hurt anywhere else?"

Lily shook her head.

"I'll be right back." Brynn dashed to the kitchen and gathered supplies to tend to Lily's wounds.

"Who did this?" Brynn said, kneeling beside the bed. She lifted a rag from a bowl of cool water and gently wiped the crusted blood patches.

"I don't know his name." Lily stammered. "He wanted... information. I told him nothing."

Brynn tsked her tongue. "I don't want you going back to that place."

"I don't have a choice."

"I'm giving you one. Stay here—with me."

Lily gave a weary laugh. "And clean the church for supper, sharing your only bed? I think not."

"No." Brynn's mind raced. "I'll buy a house. We'll live together."

"With what?"

Brynn crossed the small room, tugged open the bottom drawer, and drew out the hidden envelope of bills. Lily's one good eye widened. "Good Lord, Brynn, where—"

"Never mind that," Brynn said quickly. "Just say yes."

She rinsed the rag—the clear water turned pink. When she pressed it once more to Lily's cheek, her friend sucked a sharp breath between her teeth.

"Maybe," Lily murmured.

Brynn shifted the basin closer. Her elbow brushed her sketchbook, knocking it to the floor. The pages spilled open.

Lily's gaze fell to the drawing. Her body went rigid. "How do you know that man?" she whispered.

Brynn glanced down. "I don't. I saw him at Gilmore's hanging."

Lily trembled.

"Is that the man who did this to you?"

"I—I have to go."

Before Brynn could stop her, Lily staggered to her feet. She stumbled into the doorjamb, then fled down the hall.

"Lily! Don't—please!" Brynn called, but her friend was already gone.

Sobs echoed through the church.

x x x

The shop bell jingled on its iron ribbon. Gideon looked up from his carving bench.

A bearded man stepped through the door, his eyes sharp with fury.

"Can I help you, sir?" Gideon asked, keeping his voice even.

The man's gaze swept the room, settling on the presses. "This where you been making them posters? The ones that got my brother killed?"

"Your brother?" Gideon's chest tightened. The likeness was there—the jaw, the eyes. "And who might your brother be?"

"James Gilmore," the man growled. "My name's Langley. Silas Langley."

Gideon forced a calm he didn't feel. "Ah. Then he was your brother, but not full blood?"

Langley's lip curled. "You're a real wise a—"

"Careful," Gideon cut in, cool but firm. "No foul language in the print shop."

Langley's snarl deepened. "I'll use whatever language I please."

He lunged.

Gideon snatched the wooden block in his hand and flung it. It struck Langley squarely between the eyes. Blood welled and ran down his nose.

For an instant, the man wavered.

Gideon leapt from his stool. But Langley charged him. Fists balled, he cocked his right arm back and hit Gideon in the jaw.

Gideon fell back with the momentum, spitting out a tooth. The man stood over him. A fury of fists, punching him in the ribs, the stomach. Gideon rolled into a ball. A boot landed hard on his back. Air whooshed from his lungs. He curled up tighter, but the blows kept coming.

Gideon crawled to his knees. He yanked open the desk drawer and drew a pistol. Swirling on Langley, he leveled the gun. "Stop!"

Langley froze, grinning through the blood. "You ain't got the guts."

He charged toward Gideon.

Gideon squeezed the trigger.

The blast shattered the silence, and the gun's recoil slammed against his palm. It slipped from his grasp and clattered to the floor.

Langley staggered back, clutching his arm as blood seeped between his fingers. "You'll be sorry you done that."

Gideon steadied his breath. "That was a warning shot," he said, lifting his chin. "Next time I'll aim to kill."

"I'll be back," Langley rasped. "Next time, I'll break your hands—that'll stop them posters from gettin' made."

He stumbled from the doorway, leaving droplets of dark blood on the threshold.

Gideon exhaled, slow and shaky, then retrieved the pistol and set it back in the drawer.

Thank God Shumacher had told him about the weapon. Why hadn't he used it the night he was killed? A hollow ache opened in Gideon's chest at the thought.

Then fear replaced it. Langley wanted revenge—and he'd start with the poster maker.

Would he find out who drew those likenesses?

Was Brynn safe?

5
THE PRINTER'S PRICE

Brynn dressed quickly in a new, refitted walking gown and waited for Gideon to arrive for their morning constitution. She had intentionally avoided the tailor's shop. Keeping her secret required caution. She didn't want to make it obvious that she had a steady stream of income. Instead, she rummaged through the church's goodwill barrel, choosing garments suitable for refitting.

As far as Reverend and Mrs. Doubtmire knew, Mrs. Sinclair, a local seamstress, altered the items out of charity. Brynn had even requested that she blend in end-of-bolt fabric scraps that locals would recognize from their own tailored dresses to maintain the façade.

What passed between a woman's purse and her seamstress was nobody's business.

Her heart fluttered as she waited. But Gideon didn't come. Frustration mounting, she huffed, rose, and started toward the print shop unescorted.

What could be keeping him so long?

She shoved through the print shop door. The bell rang overhead. Gideon jerked his head up from the shadows, moaning as he stood and backed against the wall.

"Brynn, what are you—?" His breath came in shallow pulls. Bruises marbled his face. He looked as battered as Lily had.

"Gideon!" she rushed to him, tossing her sketchpad onto his worktable.

He flinched, palms lifted. "Don't—please."

"You need a doctor."

"No. I'm fine."

"No. You're. Not." Her tone cut through his bravado. "How did this happen?"

"A printing press bites back when cleaned careless." A wry smile tugged at his mouth, splitting open a cut. Fresh blood ran down his chin. The attempted chuckle turned into a wince.

"Hog wash." She slipped an arm under his to steady him. "Lock the door."

Slowly, painfully, he turned the key. They started toward the clinic. "Who did this?" she asked as they walked.

"Silas Langley," he breathed.

"Who?"

"A *comrade* of Gilmore's."

"Why?"

"He wants to stop the wanted posters," he said.

Brynn's step faltered.

"He's looking for me," she whispered. "A bearded man beat the girls at the brothel. Lily came to me bruised and bleeding, but she wouldn't say who had hurt her. She recognized his face from a sketch."

"Langley's got a beard," Gideon said softly. "No one knows you have anything to do with the posters."

"And yet people that I... care for are getting hurt protecting my secret," she murmured.

"Does Lily know?" he asked.

"No. I don't think so... 'though she saw my sketch of the bearded man. It terrified her. She ran from the church."

He frowned, studying her. "Brynn." He blinked slowly. Swallowing seemed painful. "You can't help her or anyone by giving yourself away."

She met his eyes, fierce with resolve. "Then tell me how else to stop this."

"You'd stand on the corner and announce you're the artist? Darling, you'd paint a target on your back?"

She wasn't swayed.

At the clinic, she pushed open the door. "In with you."

The doctor looked up, startled. "Goodness, me—looks like you lost a fight with a bobcat."

Brynn stepped back, letting the door close between them. She could hear Gideon grunt and moan.

She bowed her head and prayed—unsure if the words sought healing or mercy.

6

FRIENDS SPEAK

Brynn tapped on the green door. The behemoth of a man peeked through the crack, then opened it wide. "Come in. Miss Lily said you'd be here 'fore long."

She frowned at the man as she walked under his arm, which held the door. Glancing into the parlor, where some *gentlemen* waited, she made her way to the last hall where Lily lived. Gently rapping on the doorframe, Brynn swallowed hard. She hated coming here, even to see that her friend was alright, but today's visit was necessary.

"So, it's you," Lily said, stepping back from the open door. "Come in, then."

Brynn handed Lily a carpetbag. "Here. I brought you these."

Lily looked inside, then pulled out a day dress, two sets of small clothes, a cotton sleeping gown, and two cotton petticoats. "Where'd you get these?"

"People donate to the church." Brynn shrugged. "I thought you might need something new."

Looking around Lily's room, Brynn listed in her mind other items to bring her friend as well. She'd never reveal that Mrs. Sinclair had made these for Lily, upon Brynn's request, and she had paid her well not to tell.

"I don't need charity." Lily snapped.

Brynn shrugged again. "Throw them away, then. Somebody else had, why not you?"

Lily ran her finger over the robin-egg blue embroidery on the nightdress, admiring the delicate stitching. "Well, I don't suppose it would hurt to hang on to these." She cleared her throat. "Thank you."

Brynn nodded. "How are you?"

Looking directly at Lily's face for the first time, she studied the fading bruises and healing cuts. "You look better."

"I'm fine."

Brynn nodded again. An awkward silence settled between them.

"How do you know Silas Langley?" Brynn asked, breaking the stillness.

Lily lifted widened eyes. "Who?"

"Don't," Brynn said. "I know you know the man with the beard is Silas Langley. And I know he's the one who hurt you."

"How would you know?" Lily lifted her chin.

"Because, he hurt Gideon Carver too."

Lily gasped. "Why?"

"Same reason he hurt you," Brynn said.

Lily gawked at Brynn for a long moment. "He's hunting the artist who makes the wanted posters so exact."

Once again, Brynn nodded. "And you protected me, by not telling him it was me."

Lily shrugged.

"Oh, Lily." Brynn wrapped her in a sisterly embrace. "I love you, dear friend. Please let me help you move out of here."

Lily shoved Brynn's arms down, as if to shrug off a too-warm shawl. "You don't owe me anything."

"Yes, I do." Brynn's eyes filled with tears. "Please let me help."

"The way I hear things," Lily's eyes narrowed, "you'll be a married woman soon."

Brynn's mouth dropped open. "What? Where'd you hear that? He-he's just a friend."

"Um-hum." Lily grinned. "That's not the word around town."

Heat filled Brynn's cheeks. "Gossip. That's all it is."

"That's why," Lily continued. "You've gotta be careful. This town doesn't cotton to folks helping Bullock, no how." She lowered her voice to a whisper. "You need to stop giving Mr. Carver your sketches."

Brynn shoved her chin out defiantly. "I have no idea what you're talking about."

Lily chuckled. "Right."

Scurrying down the stairwell, Brynn couldn't outrun the scent of cheap perfume that clung to her clothes. She turned toward the print shop.

Gideon needed to know what she had learned. She pushed on the printer's door. It was locked. She glanced toward the clinic.

Was Gideon still with the doc?

Her heart sank to her knees. How severely had Langley hurt him?

"Brynn?" Gideon's muffled voice called her name. She looked up. Gideon slowly approached the door and unlocked it. "Come in."

He shuffled back.

"You've closed the print shop?"

"Doc recommended I get some rest."

"But the newspaper..." She glanced at the silent press.The partially filled frame. "Gideon, can I help?"

"It takes... skill," he said.

"I can learn," she tilted her head. "This town's not gonna appreciate no newspaper tomorrow."

Gideon braced his arm against his ribs. "I-I could use some help."

He demonstrated how to set the type. "It's all backward. Takes some getting used to."

She watched attentively, then gathered the handwritten articles to be printed.

"I'm gonna go lie down. Call me if you need anything," Gideon said.

Her eyes drifted to his chest. "Do you need your bandages changed?"

"No. Doc said he'd be by tomorrow to do that."

"Suit yourself," she said, turning back to the task at hand. She bit her lip, wondering what lay beneath his starched shirt.

The clock chimed with each passing hour.

"All done," she announced when all the little letters were set in a frame and stacked, ready to print. She had proofread each one for mistakes. He was right. It was challenging to read backward, but she'd adjusted quickly.

Slowly returning to her side, he said. "I don't want you sketching any more likenesses for the posters."

"Why not? It has made a big difference for Sheriff Bullock."

"You know good and well why not."

"I'm not going to stop helping."

"But—"

"Gideon, we both know for me to stop giving you sketches, is not going to stop the wheels that have been set in motion. Langley knows somebody is the artist and he's not gonna stop seeking revenge until somebody is dead."

He closed his eyes, drawing in a shallow breath. "You're probably right."

"Of course I am," she chuckled.

"Now show me how to print these." She gestured to the frames.

He showed her how to roll the ink and press the paper. "Maybe we can talk to Bullock. In the morning. Perhaps there'd be a way to set a trap, for Langley."

"Good idea," she said.

By midnight, they had the newspapers printed and hanging on the drying racks.

She yawned. "Now, we fold them together and deliver in the morning?" she asked.

He nodded. "I'll deliver them. You need your rest."

"Why?" she cocked her head back. "You think I need my beauty rest or something? I'll be back... what time do you deliver the bundles?"

"Four o'clock." He sighed. The breath cost him a painful grimace. "But I can do it."

"As can I," she insisted. "I'll be back at three-forty-five."

He shook his head. "I'll walk you to the church, but you don't have to be up so early."

"And neither do you, but I know you will," she chastised.

He frowned. "Let's get you home safely."

"And who's gonna protect you on your way back to the print shop?" she asked.

7
INTO THE HILLS

Rising before the sun, Brynn dressed quickly, wrapped a shawl around her shoulders, and dodged between back-ways to the print shop. Walking in the dark without an escort was frightening. Especially with Langley hunting for *the artist*. Would rushing to the printer's at such an early hour give away her secret?

Tapping on the back door, she shifted her weight anxiously. Gideon opened the door, tucking his shirt into his pants. A cot sat along the wall, rumpled as if he'd just risen from it to answer the door. He pulled her inside, glancing behind her. "I told you—"

"And I told you, I'd be here to help."

A sigh slipped from his mouth. "You're the most stubborn—"

She crossed her arms over her bodice and smiled at him. "Yeah, tell me something we both don't know."

A thud resounded at the front door. They both turned toward it. "Wait here." Gideon pushed her back gently.

He hurried to the entrance, looking right and left. But seeing no one. He opened the door and jerked when Brynn gasped behind him.

"I told you to wait!" he growled.

"What is that?" Her trembling finger pointed at a knife holding a piece of paper against the wooden siding.

He reached out and removed the knife, bringing the paper into the shop.

A wanted poster. Scrawled with what looked like blood, "The artist dies!"

"That's it. We've gotta talk to the sheriff." Gideon crumpled the poster in his fist.

"But what about delivering the newspapers?"

"You think I care about the newspapers now?" he barked. Staring down at the wad of paper, he pressed it out, smoothing it flat. "We need to give this to Bullock."

"Then what?" she asked.

"I have an idea." Gideon nearly smiled. "We'll wait until daylight. Delivering the bundles will disguise our true intent."

"What are you thinking?" she tilted her head to one side.

"To devise a plan to trap Langley without putting your life at risk."

She tilted her head, eyebrows furrowed.

He continued, "There's a cabin in the hills. It's where Shumacher put surplus news bundles for those folk who live way out. They pick up a paper and drop a coin in a tin can. Shumacher empties the can next time he's there.

"Only the hill folk know about it, so you know all the outlaws know too. We can hide you out there. I'll be with you, though," he added quickly. "Word will get out and Langley will come looking for you."

"I see. So, Bullock will watch for Langley and when he comes, they'll stop him before he can... kill me."

"I know it sounds dangerous. But I think this will work. Besides, I'll be there the whole time. You won't be by yourself."

"I need to let the reverend know."

"The less that know the better," Gideon said.

"Then, I need to make up a story. I don't want the reverend or his wife to worry about my absence."

Gideon rolled his eyes up, thinking. "Tell them I need your help in the print shop and you will be staying here for a few days."

Brynn gasped. "They'll think that's most improper. I'll never be allowed to stay at the church again... it's my home."

"Once Langley is captured, we'll tell them the truth."

She stared at him. At last, she nodded. "Alright."

They delivered the bundles as the sun's golden-pink rays stretched across the sky. The shop owners began opening doors and sweeping the boardwalk. The clatter of wagon wheels and the clank of a milkman's cart broke the quiet. At the sheriff's office, Bullock looked up from his desk as the pair entered. His eyes narrowed when he saw the crumpled, blood-streaked poster Gideon laid before him.

"Found it nailed to the siding outside the printer's shop," Gideon said. "I'm certain it's a warning from Langley."

Bullock smoothed the paper. "He's crossed the line from threats to promises."

Brynn swallowed hard. "Can you catch him before he kills me?"

"That's the aim," Bullock said. He leaned back in his chair, considering. "You two vanish for a spell. I'll spread word you left town. My men'll keep watch on the ridge road."

"That was my idea, as well, Sheriff. But you'll have to make it look convincing," Gideon added. "We'll hole up at the old Schumacher cabin. If Langley's watchin', he'll follow the trail."

"There's no doubt he'll be watchin'." Bullock nodded. "Leave by afternoon, when folks can see you heading north. He won't resist the chase." His gaze softened toward Brynn. "Miss Ellison, I promise you—we'll not let him get close."

She managed a nod. Her throat tightened. "Thank you, Sheriff."

x x x

By midday, they'd packed a small crate of food, blankets, and Gideon's medical salves, hauling them into the borrowed wagon. The hills swallowed the last traces of Deadwood as they climbed the rutted road, sunlight flickering through the pines. When the wagon jolted to a stop at a lonely cabin, Brynn shivered despite the warm wind.

Inside, dust motes drifted in narrow beams of light. Gideon found the tin coin box on the floor next to the door. He gave it a little shake, smiling faintly. "Even hill folk keep their word."

"Then we're safe enough here," she said, brushing cobwebs from the hearth.

He nodded. "Safe as we can be."

Evening settled like a quilt across the peaks. Gideon built a small fire while Brynn set a kettle on the hook.

They spoke little, save for the whisper of the flame and the creak of settling timbers. Brynn mended one of his torn sleeves while he whittled kindling down to toothpicks, lost in the rhythm of knife against wood.

After supper, she sketched quietly by the firelight—his profile caught in amber glow.

"You shouldn't draw me," he said, glancing up, embarrassed.

"It calms me," she whispered. "And you sit still better than anyone I know."

His lips twitched. "That's not sayin' much."

For a long while they listened to the owls calling their mates.

"You remind me there's still something pure in this world," he said finally. "After all I've been through, I'd near forgotten."

She lowered her pencil. "You think me pure?"

"Of course. I know you too well, Brynn Ellison."

"Gideon Carver, you've surely not been paying attention. I'm here with you, without a chaperone. I sneak around town, unescorted. I draw things that get men killed."

He shook his head slowly. "You draw truth. You can't fault a lantern for the shadows it casts."

"And you," Brynn said softly. "I never believed the rumors."

He stared at her, long and hard. "I didn't kill my father."

She nodded.

"Everyone thought I did, didn't they?"

She nodded again. "But I didn't."

"Thank you." He looked into the fire. "When I walked in, after boarding school, he was in his study." Tears reflected the flames in Gideon's eyes. "I knew something was wrong the instant I saw that wild look in his eyes. He told me we were broke. I asked why he'd spent all the money on my schooling, and he just said it wasn't his choice." Gideon swallowed hard. "He was sipping whiskey—or so I thought. Then he started choking, and froth, like whipped egg whites, oozed from his mouth. I... I just stood there. Stunned. I didn't know what to do."

He wiped a hand down his face. "Franklin Holmes, Father's solicitor, walked in behind me. Told me I shouldn't be there—that I should run. Run as far away as I could. So I did. But I should have run straight to the sheriff. Instead, I left town and never went back. I worked where I could, kept moving until I got to Deadwood. Mr. Shumacher offered me an apprenticeship, and I accepted. The rest you know."

"Was it suicide or murder?" Brynn breathed.

"I never knew." Gideon shrugged.

The wind outside shifted. Somewhere down the slope, a branch snapped—too heavy for a fox. Both froze.

Gideon slid to the window and pushed aside the curtain with two fingers. A flicker of light moved among the trees. Then another.

"Lanterns," he whispered.

Brynn's heart seized. "Is it Langley?"

"Could be. Could be Bullock's men." His tone was tight, unreadable.

Another hoofbeat in the dark, nearer this time.

Gideon turned from the window, crossed to her, and took her hand. "Go to the back room—keep low."

She shook her head. "Not without you."

His thumb brushed across her knuckles. "I won't let anything happen to you, Brynn. You have my word."

Outside, a lantern flare caught the cabin wall. The world narrowed to firelight and shadows.

She held his gaze, whispering, "Then we wait."

And in that strained silence, each heartbeat sounded louder than the last.

8

THE SIEGE

Gideon rushed to the bucket of water he'd drawn from the well while it was still light outside. He tossed its contents onto the fire in the hearth, plunging them into darkness. Putting his finger to his lips, he quelled Brynn's protest.

Moving quietly to the window next to the front door, he peeked out without moving the fabric nailed to the frame. Hooves snapped twigs as horses moved among the trees. The lanterns outside had gone dark as well. It had to be Langley and his men.

"Lord in Heaven," Gideon prayed. "Protect Brynn from these venomous men."

He gripped the press lever he'd tucked under his vest before they left town. Were Bullock and his men out there too? Did they see the outlaws creeping toward the cabin?

The night held its breath. Even the crickets fell silent. The only sound was the drenched ashes hissing like a snake.

Through the thin wall came the scrape of a boot on the stoop and the whisper of a low curse. Gideon's pulse pounded in his ears. The door burst wide, splintering wood against the frame. Two shadows lunged inside, steel glinting in the spill of moonlight.

"Get her!" one growled.

Brynn screamed, stumbling back against the hearth. Her hand found the bucket—reflex, not thought—she hurled it toward the men. It hit its mark. One man stumbled backward, cursing.

Gideon swung the iron lever, striking the other man hard across the forearm. The weapon clattered to the floor. A flash—gunfire split the dark—the smell of gunpowder and smoke burned their throats.

Brynn opened her mouth, working her jaw, as if to open her ears from the deafening gunfire. She dropped behind the overturned table, clutching a jagged chair leg as if it could save her. Shadows thrashed; feet thundered; the room pulsed with shouts and breaking wood.

The sound of something heavy whooshed through the air, and someone grunted, hitting the floor hard.

"Brynn!" Gideon yelled.

She didn't answer. A man's outline loomed above her—then toppled when Gideon's lever struck home again.

Another body lunged toward Gideon. He grappled with him, both hitting the floorboards hard. The outlaw's fist caught Gideon's shoulder, jolting his still-sore ribs. Pain flared white. He rolled, gasping, but heard Brynn cry out, "Behind you!"

She was alive. He twisted, swinging again. The lever struck bone. The man went down.

For a heartbeat, there was only the rasp of breathing and the smell of blood and smoke. Then—hoofbeats, nearer now. A single gunshot cracked outside.

A sharp whistle cut through the chaos—Bullock's signal. More hooves, more voices. The cabin filled with shouts from every side.

"Langley! Drop it!" Bullock's voice thundered.

But Langley ignored the command. A match flared near the doorway, revealing his sneer. He lit a lantern and held it high, casting a beam across the wrecked room. The sheen of his pistol caught the glow—aimed squarely at Brynn.

"Artist, is she? Let's see her draw her way outta this."

He lunged toward her.

Gideon threw himself between them. The shot echoed, ear-splitting. He staggered, his arm numb from the impact. The lever fell from his grasp. Brynn screamed his name, clutching at him as he fell against her.

Langley raised his pistol again—but the door filled with bodies. Pistol fire blazed from the threshold. Splinters rained like sparks. Bullock and his deputies flooded the room, shouting commands lost in the din. Langley fired wildly. Bullock's return shot found its mark. The outlaw slammed back against the wall and slid down, the sneer still frozen on his mouth.

Smoke hung heavy in the dark. Gideon slumped beside the hearth, breathing raggedly.

Brynn knelt, pressing a scrap of his torn sleeve against the bleeding arm. He caught her trembling hand.

"You're safe," he rasped.

She shook her head fiercely. "I just mended this shirt."

"I'm sorry," Gideon whispered.

"Well." Her tears caught the gleam of a lantern that one deputy held. "You did save me. I know a seamstress who can make you a new one." A smile quivered on her lips.

She leaned over him and kissed his cheek. His eyes closed—half from pain, half from joy.

Bullock crouched beside them, voice low but steady. "It's done. Y'all can go home now." He looked toward the door, half-smiling in weary relief. "I'll assign my deputies to clean up the mess out here."

As Bullock spoke, Gideon glimpsed a pale light edging the trees and the thin note of a meadowlark calling the first sign of morning—the sound of a town, and a love, still breathing.

9
A NEW EDITION

A year later...

The sticky kiss of ink as Gideon slid the roller over the form. A faint, tacky peel followed. Brynn lifted her chin, inhaling the scent and sound of her husband's work. His muscles bulged tight against his shirt sleeve as he drew the iron lever forward. A dry *click-clack* like teeth counting off beats as the platen met the form with a muffled *thock*. Paper pressed breathless against the inked letters. A moment later, the lever returned. Springs snapped and metal sighed. The sheet came free with a whisper, air sucking softly between two damp surfaces.

Brynn lifted the page with two fingers and set it aside on a drying rack, careful not to allow her round belly to brush against the oozing excess ink. The smell of linseed oil, warm metal and drying ink filled the room as the rhythm began again—clack, sigh, thock, release—steady as a heartbeat in iron skin. She moved in perfect synchronization with her husband. Gideon worked in perfect harmony with the machine—a perfect concert with the iron heart that fed their living and their own hearts that still beat wildly in each other's presence.

A bundle of wanted posters sat on the front desk, ready for Elias to come deliver them to all the businesses and finally the sheriff's office. In the smallest font available in Gideon's letter box was the print shop's name, Carver & Ellison, Printers and Stationers.

Brynn stretched her back between impressions, lifting her eyes to the framed wedding invitation.

"Mr. Gideon Carver and Miss Brynn Ellison request your prayers as they pursue a shared calling in print and purpose."

She had thought it quite clever from the usual dull *you are cordially invited* wording of the other announcements they printed. Reverend Doubtmire officiated, and Mrs. Doubtmire played lovely music on the piano while Lily stood with Brynn and Elias Hart stood beside Gideon.

The nightmare of Langley's revenge fell back into the shadows of their lives. Although in a town like Deadwood, another could easily rise to stifle the creation of such excellent likenesses on the wanted posters. Bullock and his men appreciated the added help when searching the countryside for those who thought they were above the law.

Her sketching skills reached far and wide. Wealthy people and printers wrote to her requesting illustrations for books, flyers, cards, and portraits. Between helping Gideon in the print shop and sketching for private entreaties, she stayed quite busy. So busy she had little time for the typical wife's housework. The added income allowed her to hire Lily and other girls to cook and clean their home—fulfilling her promise to help her friend stay away from the Green Door. When the girls married, her source for new hires were readily available, much to the chagrin of the madams who owned the brothels.

Brynn smoothed the ruffled feathers by providing a free and flattering portrait in a gilded frame. Their vanity overrode their concern about losing a worker. Brynn couldn't save all the girls who were delivered to Deadwood to work behind the Green Door, but she could save one at a time.

The baby inside her kicked and moved, seemingly in rhythm with the machine his father skillfully ran. Would he enjoy creating print for the public, or would he be the one writing the newsworthy articles to be printed by his father? Perhaps he'd inherit her talent for sketching and would draw the illustrations his father would carve into wood.

Outside, the town was alive—the clop of hooves, the shout of a newsboy, the slow rise of another Deadwood morning. Inside, ink rolled and pressed and whispered, leaving its dark signature on each waiting page. Gideon leaned close to inspect the print, his sleeve brushing Brynn's hand as she steadied the sheet. For a heartbeat neither moved, listening to the rhythm they had made together—iron, paper, breath, and love.

In a town built on rough hands and rougher hearts, two gentle souls found each other and became one.

Somewhere beyond the shop's open door, a meadowlark sang.

The End

Love the Story?
Leave a review, please.

ABOUT THE AUTHOR

Lynn Donovan is an author, playwright, and director who spends her days chasing after her muses trying to get them to behave long enough to write their stories. The results are numerous novels, multi-author series, anthologies, dramatizations, and short stories.

Lynn enjoys reading and writing all kinds of fiction, paranormal, speculative, contemporary romance, and time travel. But you never know what her muses will come up with for a story, so you could see a novel under any given genre. All that can be said is keep your eyes open, because these muses are not sitting still for long!

Oops, there they go again...

Want more?

You can learn more about Lynn when you follow her on her Facebook Author Page at https://www.facebook.com/LynnDonovanAuthor, join her reading group on FB at Books by Author Lynn Donovan @ https://www.facebook.com/groups/BooksbyAuthorLynnDonovan/, her website LynnDonovanAuthor.com and Twitter @MLynnDonovan,

For more publications by Lynn Donovan go to: Amazon.com/author/ldonovan

Appreciation

Thank you to everybody in my life who has contributed in one way or another to the writing of this book. My husband, my children, my children-in-law, and my grandchildren. You all are my unconditional fans. My BETA reader and grammar guru who make me look gooder than I am. [Bad grammar intended.] My fellow author friends who chat with me daily to exchange ideas, encourage, maintain sanity, and keep me from being a total recluse/hermit.

Mostly I thank God for the talent he has given me. I hope to hear you say, "Well done, my good and faithful servant," when I cross the Jordan and run into your arms—Many, many years from now. :).

NEWSLETTER AND A FREE GIFT FOR YOU

Hey! Thank you for purchasing and reading this book. I'd like to give you a parting gift to show my appreciation. Sign up for my newsletter at https://lynndonovanauthor.com/newsletter. I will send you an e-copy of a collection of short stories I wrote purely for your entertainment. I will

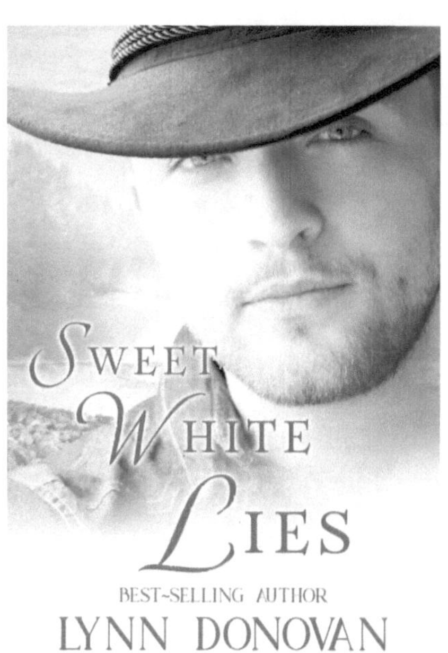

happily send you this e-copy for FREE, if you ask. I will also add you to my NEWSLETTER list and you will receive up-to-date information on new release before anyone else.

This book will **not** be sold anywhere, at any time. I am keeping it exclusively for you, my readers, and only if you ask for it.

Thank you again, and God Bless.

~Lynn Donovan

A REAL TROOPER

REBEL VIPERS MC

JESSA AARONS

A Real Trooper

WARNING

This content is intended for mature audiences only. It may contain material that could be viewed as offensive to some readers, including graphic language, dangerous and sexual situations, murder, abuse, and extreme violence.

1
TROOPER

"Anyone else have something to add? Or any news to share before we adjourn?"

Looking around the table, everyone is giving various responses all boiling down to the same answer—no. Whiskey, the Rebel Vipers MC President, slams his gavel down on the repurposed bowling lane turned Church meeting table, and our weekly Friday evening meeting is done.

"It's been a long day. I need a beer and a blowjob," our club funny man, Haze, says with a chuckle as we all head toward the door out into the clubhouse main room. "And not necessarily in that order."

"Let me help you with that." Smoke, one third of the polyamorous throuple, throws his arm over his male partner's shoulder. "Let's go find our lady Raven and get this party started."

"Not that I don't like the club girls we have, but we need some fresh meat around here." Gunner, the resident pain in the ass grumbles as he grabs his phone from the lock box we all put our devices in before going into Church. "Am I right?"

My eyes roam around the room filled with all my Brothers, Old Ladies, and club girls, and I count the female to male ratio. There are several more women here than there was five years ago when I joined the club, but they are still significantly outnumbered by the XY chromosome.

"Some new ladies would be okay by me." I turn my phone on and it immediately starts dinging with notifications. "Maybe one is looking for me now."

"Lucky fucker." Gunner strolls toward the bar, leaving me standing by my lonesome.

Four missed calls and three text messages.

> Warren Gates: Call me.
>
> Warren Gates: I need a favor.
>
> Warren Gates: Seriously Luke. CALL ME NOW!

Warren was one of my supervisory agents back when I was in the FBI. I met him the day I graduated from the training academy in Quantico when he walked up and introduced himself as my new boss. He became not only the man who dished out the orders, and my mentor, but also one of my best friends. When I left the bureau eight years later and planned to join the club, he was supportive of my decision and threw me one hell of a going away party. We don't talk as much as we used to, one of the downsides of living half the country away and being busy doing different things on opposite sides of the law, but I still consider him a friend. Whatever it is that's going on, whatever favor he needs, if I can do it, I will do it in a heartbeat.

I play the voicemails to see what is so important.

> *"Luke, Warren here. I don't know why your phone is off, but you need to call me back ASAP. I need your help with something. Call my cell. Five five five. . ."*

My eyes roll listening to him rattle off his phone number. He called me. What other number would I call back? Crazy old fart.

> *"Dammit, Luke. Where the hell are you? Call me back. I need some back up with a case."*

Not bothering to listen to any more of his increasingly grumpier voicemails, I hit the red circle on my phone screen and have a call back to him ringing in seconds. I don't even think a full ring jingles over the line before he picks up and barks my name.

"LUKE! Did you fall off the Earth? What the hell, son?"

I can feel the anxiety and anger coming through the speaker, so I head down the hall toward the back door and step outside for some privacy. Whatever he is about to dump on me, I have a feeling it's not meant for the ears of people he doesn't know.

"What the hell is right, Warren?" I bark back. "I was in a club meeting and turned my phone back on to see your barrage of calls and texts. What's so damn urgent that you're sniping at me the second I call you back?"

"You never turned your phone off when you were in the bureau." And here comes the guilt trip. He may have initially been supportive of my life changes, but as time goes on, he randomly likes to drop little digs on how much I've changed. They didn't bother me in the beginning, but for some reason, this time the burr stings a bit.

"Warren," I close my eyes and roll my neck as I lean against one of the porch posts. I can feel a tension headache coming on. "You're not my boss anymore. I don't have to scream *'how high'* every time you tell me to jump. We've had this talk before."

"Whatever," his dismissal wiggles that digging burr a little deeper. "But anyways, if you're not doing anything super important for the next couple weeks, I need your help with a WITSEC case."

"Isn't it the Marshalls job to deal with people in witness protection?" In my time as an agent, I only dealt directly with one person who went into the program, but from the day their deal was signed with the lawyers and the Department of Justice, the FBI was off the case. "Why do you need me?"

"Are you somewhere private?" he asks as if this is my first day on the job. "I don't need your club getting involved. This is too important of a case to just be telling anybody."

"Yes, Warren. I'm outside by myself." The headache is here.

"Okay, good."

"Now tell me what's going on."

Warren starts telling me about a woman who is currently at a ranch in Deadwood, South Dakota that is owned by a former Secret Service agent named Bill Hinders. The ranch is used as a safe place for people who are on their way into the witness protection program but haven't received their new identities yet. She is a witness in an upcoming case who needs protection until the trials start. She's been there for a while, but since the judicial system is so backed up, and there is no set trial date yet, she needs to be in protection until she is picked up to be brought in for pretrial interviews.

He goes on to tell me that her father was an accountant who worked for a very bad southern mob family and he had turned himself in to provide evidence against his soon-to-be former employer. Racketeering, human trafficking, drugs, you name it. If it is illegal according to the United States government, this family had their fingers in it and this man helped move money around to hide it. This woman, his daughter, is his only living relative, so the bureau wants her off everyone's radar until she testifies and is then given a new identity.

"The agents who are watching her now say they think her location has been compromised. On a run into town yesterday, they say they spotted someone who looks like a mob assassin from the family, so I need another person to go and keep a closer eye on her until I can get there myself."

"Why do you need to go there? Or me for that matter? What can I do that the agents there aren't already doing?" I get that every case is different, and different cases and different witnesses have different needs, but wanting to send me when other agents are already doing the job seems a little weird. "Or why not just have her brought back in? If she's that important, she shouldn't be so far from D.C. anyway."

"I am currently in the middle of a different trial and can't leave town until it's over. I know this is an inconvenience, but to be honest, I don't know who I can trust right now. The case is too sensitive and important to just let any Joe Schmo agent do what needs to be done. If this case goes like I hope it does, it very well be my golden ticket to retirement. I am ready for sunshine and sandy beaches and need everything to go right. I need someone there I can trust. Can you help me? I will owe you so fucking big."

Maybe the stress I am hearing in his voice is really about his need for retirement. I totally understand the feeling of being overworked and fed up with the bureaucracy and needing to get away from it all, so I can't fault him for wanting everything to go off without a hitch. I don't miss the days of having to juggle multiple cases at the same time, flipping back and forth from one to another.

As crazy as it sounds, I lose a lot less sleep being an outlaw biker than when I was a federal agent. While I still have things I need to do every day, my schedule is a lot more flexible and there is a fuck ton less paperwork. Being in charge of maintenance for all the properties and businesses owned by the MC is a walk in the park compared to the bureau. I'll mow the grass, fix a leaky pipe, or blacktop a parking lot any day before I'd go back to the marble walls in our nation's capital.

"How much time do I have to think about it?"

"I need an answer now, Luke. Like, right now."

That's another thing I don't miss. My legal name. Luke.

When I was given my road name by the club, Trooper, it was like I shed the itchy skin of my past and was starting over. And I was. But no matter how many times I have told Warren to call me by my new name, he never listened, so I gave up and deal with it. Sometimes I need to remind myself there are battles that can't be won, so they aren't worth the hassle of even starting.

"Give me a half hour and I'll call you back."

"But, Luke—"

"No." I snap a bit harshly. "I have a life here, responsibilities and a job. I can't just hop on my bike and ride out when you snap your fingers."

"Fine. Oh, but before you go."

"What?"

"Leave the bike and drive your truck."

"Warren—" Now he cuts me off.

"When you get to Deadwood," Warren says like me saying yes is a given, ignoring the possibility of me being unable to leave at the drop of a hat. "don't introduce yourself to Hailey as a former agent. I need you to pretend to be just another person in pre-WITSEC so she doesn't spook."

Hailey. Pretty name.

I don't know if he meant to say her name yet, but he did. Now to hunt down Whiskey and try to see about heading to South Dakota.

2

HAILEY

"Come on, Bandit." I call out to the approximately four year old, all black, Murgese gelding male horse at the end of the lead rope in my hand. "Why are you being so stubborn today?"

He has been restless and unresponsive to every order I have given since I fed him his breakfast this morning. Then after my other chores, when I brought him out of his stall and attempted to put his saddle on, he bucked against the ropes until I gave up. I had already managed to get his bridle on, and attach a long lead to that, so I called that a win and we moved on. I am currently trying to get him to walk in circles around the outdoor corral, but he keeps zigzagging across the sand and gravel.

Bandit isn't the only one who is feeling something off today. It's been a weird day for me too.

I slept through my alarm and was woken up by Brenda, the ranch owner's wife, knocking on my bedroom door. Most mornings I am in the kitchen and have breakfast started before the others wake up, but today the kitchen was dark and empty when she came down to help.

Next, I went to pour the scrambled eggs onto the flat top, I lost my grip on the bowl and half of the uncooked eggs spilled down the front of the oven door and all over the front of my jeans.

And the straw that broke the camel's back, was when I went back to my room to change into a new pants, I ripped a hole in the crotch as I was pulling them up and had to throw away my favorite, most comfortable jeans. Apparently, that worn in denim had seen its final day and decided to give up the fight.

It's days like this, when everything that can go wrong does but somehow still keeps trucking, which bring back memories of my favorite person that ever lived. My grandma. Mabel Kellerman was a force to be reckoned with, but I knew she loved me more than anything or anyone else.

After my mother died in childbirth, grandma took me home and raised me like I was supposed to be hers all along. As she got older, and her body decided it wasn't strong enough anymore, I cared for her. Being there for her, until the day the cancer took her from me, was my time to repay her. It was me giving back for every day she gave for me. I miss her smile, her laugh, her spunk . . . she was my everything.

If she was here right now, she would be laughing up a storm at Bandit's antics. She would cheer him on and encourage every unacknowledged order he was given. Every time he turns left when I tell him to go right, I imagine it is her whispering in his ear, telling him to do the opposite of what I say.

Thinking about her toady also makes me wonder what she would think about the situation that I'm currently in. Not only is South Dakota so far from our home in Arizona, the reason why I am here is one that neither of us could have ever seen coming from a mile away. As someone who thought their biological father had died in a car wreck before she was born, and having a totally different name, I never expected to be hiding from the mob while waiting to be put in witness protection.

I am very grateful that Grandma isn't having to go through this with me though. I miss her every day, but she wasn't made for living her life in the unknown. She had her routines and she stuck to them like a drill sergeant in the military.

Just as I decide that it is time to take this rebellious renegade horse back into the barn, I see Bill headed my way with a tall dark haired man I have yet to have the pleasure of meeting.

In contrast to Bill's chubbier, mid-five foot stature, this man is easily an inch or two over six feet tall. He has shaggy black hair that is a bit longer on the top. It looks messy, but not in a bad way. Instead like he just rolled out of bed, ran his hands through it, and called it good. He has a short beard and mustache that look more like a few days of stubble that he was too lazy to shave, but instead decided to sleep in a few extra minutes instead.

Wowza . . . I'm sensing a pattern here, and it all has to do with him and a bed. He's damn good looking and who would blame a woman who hasn't had a roll in the hay in well over a year for daydreaming?

Continuing in my probably not so secretive perusal of this new creature, I see a peak of tattoo sneaking out of the right sleeve of his forest green t-shirt. Yellow, green, and black swirls run down his arm, ending just above his elbow. I wonder what the full picture is like and how far up it goes above the dark fabric.

As the men step up to the paddock fence, I can finally see his eyes. Slate blue. A little gray, but with some brightness sneaking through, his eyes look like a blue sky fighting to break through dark clouds as they slowly melt away after a daytime thunderstorm.

Wrapping up my inspection of the new mystery guest, I take in his medium blue denim jeans, black work boots, a knife clipped to the left side of his belt, and finish with a black metal ring hanging from the right.

"Is Bandit giving you trouble today?" Bill asks with a smile as I stop in front of them on my side of the fence.

"He sure is," I reply as a pat the flank of the stubborn horse. "It's just been one of those days."

"We all have those every once and a while." The attractive enigma chuckles and his smile brightens my mood instantly.

"Don't I know it." I can't help but say back with a small laugh of my own.

"Hailey, meet Luke. He's going to be staying with us for a while and I was hoping you wouldn't mind giving him a tour of the different barns and buildings." Bill hitches his thumb over his shoulder, pointing at the house. "I have phone meeting in a few minutes and need to get inside so I don't miss it."

"I don't mind at all." I spin around in a circle as Bandit pulls on his lead and I need to move or else he'll pull me off my feet. "Why don't you head inside the barn through the side door? I'll meet you in there and walk you through getting this rascal brushed and back in his stall. Then I can give you the grand tour."

"Sounds like a plan to me."

"You two kids have fun now," Bill calls out as he walks back toward the house.

"Don't worry, Bill. I'll keep her out of trouble." Luke winks and I can feel my cheeks burning instantly.

"Behave now, sir." I say with some sass as I turn to lead my stubborn steed into the barn. "Maybe it's you who needs to behave."

"Be careful there, tiger. I just might like taming you yet."

"Promises, promises."

~

As the day progresses, and I walk Luke between the bunkhouse, various storage buildings, and animal barns, he asks a million questions about how the ranch works. He wants to know everything—about the hours we all work, the animals names, and how it is decided that who does what. I feel like every answer I give him, he is absorbing it all like a sponge.

The sweet and fun flirting doesn't stop either. Luke compliments about how I know so much about the ins and outs of the ranch, and how I seem to have an answer to every question. He holds open every door, closes every gate behind us, and even gently grabbed my arm to steer me out of the way of a few fresh piles of horse poop that I definitely would have stomped through because I wasn't paying attention to where I was going. I can't help it that I occasionally was getting lost in his blue eyes and not watching my feet.

And it's not just me he is friendly too, although he doesn't wink or smile quite the same to the other men we come across. He is polite and shakes the hand of every other person here that's in the program. I think Luke even has the memory of an elephant, because he seems to be picking up and remembering everyone's name as soon as they introduce themselves.

"Are you the only woman here?" Luke asks me as we round the last barn and head back in the direction of where we started.

"I am right now," I reply with a nod as I tuck my hands in my back pockets. "There was another woman here when I first arrived, but she left about three months ago."

"You must have your moments being stuck here with all these goofballs." And there is that part smile part smirk again. The right side of his mouth quirks up just a smidgen higher than the left when he smiles, and it makes a small dimple pop on his cheek.

"I don't mind it too much," I smile back. "Even before coming here, I preferred working with men over women. They are less catty and spread less gossip."

"If you think men don't gossip like a bunch of old biddies, you haven't been around the right men." That really makes Luke laugh. He lets out a deep belly rolling, full from-the-gut, guffaw and I can't help but join him. "My friends back home, they will keep a true secret locked up tighter than the vault at Fort Knox, but give them some juicy gossip and it will fly through the group like a piece of paper in a tornado."

"They sound like a fun bunch."

"They sure are."

"I had friends like that back home. I miss them." And leave it to me to grab hold of the wheel of the happy, fun mood and drive it straight into dumpster.

"I obviously haven't been here as long as you, but I get it." Luke wraps his arm around my shoulder and pulls me into his side, squeezing me tight. "If you ever need an ear to chatter off, I'm here."

"Thanks, Luke."

"No problem." One more small squish and he lets me go as we stop behind the main house. "Now where do we go next?"

"Did Bill give you your room assignment yet?"

"He did."

"Bunkhouse or main house?"

"Main house," he replies as he steps up onto the back porch. "Room four."

Oh, crap on a cracker. I am never going to sleep again. If he is in four, and I'm in three, that means we share a wall. Our headboards are on the opposite sides on the same wall. The devil on my shoulder is dancing a jig, while the angel tries to cover her blushing cheeks with her wings.

I try to hide my own giddiness by rushing inside. Of course Luke follows. "Very cool. Well, I think the tour ends here." I beeline straight for the kitchen and separate myself from the sexy temptation as much as the large island allows me. "I need to get started on dinner, so if you want to head back outside and see if any of the others need help, feel free. Since the workday is almost over, I doubt that Bill will give you any formal tasks until tomorrow."

Luke steps around the side of the island, erasing about half of the space I put between us. I don't know if he's doing it on purpose, making my cheeks inflame and my lower lady bits perk up, wanting attention too, but whatever he is doing is chiseling at my defenses.

"Do you need help with dinner?"

And another brick falls.

"You don't have to." I try to wave him off as I grab a few long rolls of hamburger meat from the refrigerator.

"But if I want to?" His smile and wink should come with a warning label.

"Careful there, stranger." I decide to let the wall halfway down and embrace the flirtiness for now. What can it hurt? He could be gone tomorrow for all I know. "You offer to help now, you just might be roped into being my sidekick for breakfast and dinner every day."

"Don't threaten me with a good time."

That makes me laugh. "Alrighty then," I clap my hands, "grab that big bag of potatoes from the bottom shelf in the pantry and start washing. We've got work to do."

"What's on the menu, chef?"

3
HAILEY

Saturday nights are my favorite nights of the week. Since Sunday breakfasts are a self-serve, fend for yourself meal, I don't have to wake up early to feed whatever crowd is around. More often than not, my brain doesn't know how to sleep on the days the alarm clock is shut off, but my mission for tomorrow is for it not to be one of those days.

Before I take a shower and get ready for a long night of watching useless television, I grab a sweatshirt, slip on my tennis shoes, and head outside for a short walk in the cool night. Mid-June nights in South Dakota, when the sun goes down, so does the temperature. The humidity during the day is starting to ramp up, by July and August we will all be miserable and sweaty all day, but right now the nights are heavenly. It's probably in the mid-fifties right now, so I will enjoy the cooler weather while I can.

As I round the corner on the gravel path between two barns, intending to walk along the paddocks towards the tree line, I freeze in my tracks when I see what I can only describe as a mythical triton named Luke. Wet muscles glisten under a combination of moonlight and the small light above the side barn door he is standing next to. Rinsing himself off with the garden hose, shirtless, is the object of my dreams for the last five nights.

I get my feet to move and step to the side, into the shadows, hoping he doesn't see me and stop what he's doing now. Since I missed the start of the strip tease, I stand back and watch as the show continues. In an instant, Luke toes off his boots, has his jeans pushed down and off, and is climbing up and into the horse's outdoor water trough.

I saw Luke's naked butt cheeks and my oh my are they a sight to see. I could tell that his backside doesn't get much sun, but that's not different from the rest of us. He has very light toned skin, so his twin globes were shining bright until they disappeared underneath the water.

"Are you gonna hide in the shadows all night?" Luke's voice breaking the silence around us sends a jolt of electricity and I stumble forward a step and fully into the barn door's light beam. "Or do you wanna come join me in the water? It's not too cold."

"I, uh, um," I hesitate and hem and haw a bit while my brain reboots, then decide to give into the temptation. "Why not?"

With the grace of an ice skater on wet concrete, I fumble and kick my shoes and jeans off, then wrestle with my sweatshirt and t-shirt next. Once I'm down to my panties and bra, I pause for a second to debate if I should leave them on or go the full nine yards and strip down to my birthday suit.

"I vote for the birthday suit."

My head snaps up and my jaw drops. "Did I say that out loud?"

"You sure did." Luke has his forearms propped up on the rolled metal edge of the trough, biceps bulging, holding the top half of his torso out of the water. "I showed you mine, so it's only fair that you show me yours."

"Fuck it." The words come out fast as I flip the front clasp of my bra open, then shimmy my boy cut panties down and drop everything on top of my pants. As I hoist myself over the slide of the trough, I send a small splash toward Luke. "I didn't get to see everything, sassy pants."

"Oh yeah?" he says with a smile as he flicks a hand full of water at me. "What did you not see?"

Sinking as low as I can go, my butt comes to a stop on the bottom and the water line laps just below my shoulders. Using the hair tie on my wrist, I tie my long inky back hair up into a messy bun to keep it from sticking to me as the water shifts around us.

"I only got to see your full moon as you climbed in, but I missed the twig and berries." I trail my eyes down, imagining what is hiding below the water's surface, and pout my bottom lip. I don't toot my own horn often, but my over exaggerated pout is one of my crowning achievements. It's even gotten me out of a speeding ticket or two.

And in a flash, Luke pushes off and seems to float toward me on a wave and is kneeling between my now bent knees.

How did he do that? He moved himself, and readjusted my legs, all in one smooth movement. He really is like a merman.

"Oh, woman." He growls as he readjusts us again so he is sitting to my left and my legs are straight with his right leg pressed up against my left, hip to heel. "I'm bigger than a twig, that I can promise you. Wanna see?"

"Maybe later, big boy," I replay with a smile as I rest my head against his arm. "Let's just chat for a bit first."

"We can do that."

Working together on the ranch this week has been the most fun I've had since I got here. Luke is always awake and dressed, ready and waiting for me in the kitchen every morning. Our daytime chores don't have us in the same areas, but we cross paths a few times before we meet up in the late afternoon to start prepping dinner.

But the flirting . . . that has ramped up tenfold. Just like he is now, holding my hand clasped in his bigger one, Luke is always sneaking touches when no one is looking. A hand glide across my lower back, a soft elbow bump as we circle around each other in the kitchen, a boot pressed to the side of mine underneath the dining room table as we eat meals with the others, Luke is a sneaky flirt and I am quickly becoming addicted to it. But I am starting to crave more. I want to know more about who he is outside of this ranch. I want to know what he's like out there in the real world, because here in our bubble, life feels like someone pressed the pause button and all we do is sit around and wait.

Other than the fun flirting, or asking what the next step is in preparing a meal, Luke doesn't talk much unless there is something important to say. He's not nosey, and doesn't talk to hear himself speak, yet he listens to everyone equally and chimes in when necessary.

I want to see if I can get him to crack his shell without it snapping shut and pinching my fingers.

"How old are you?"

"Thirty-five. You?"

"Twenty-nine." One question and no snap back. Let's try another.

"Any siblings?"

"Nope. You?"

"No." Two questions and still safe.

"Did you go to college?" Three.

"Yup."

"Where?" Four.

"What about you?"

"I did a two month hybrid course to get my certified nursing assistant certification. Any pets?" Five.

"Kinda. You?"

"I had fish when I was a kid. Your parents still alive?"

"As far as I know. Yours?"

And that's where I stop asking and answering. All he is doing is giving vague one word answers, followed by tossing the same questions back at me. I'm doing all the asking, trying to crack the shell and it isn't opening more than a millimeter.

I know I have no right to be annoyed by his non-answers but I have no choice but to let it go because when you break it down, we are still strangers. We will remain strangers who will both be sent to who knows where, who knows when, never to see each other again. And since I don't want to ruffle any feathers in the fun, flirty, laidback situation that we have going on, I drop it for now.

A bit more time passes as we stay in our water cocoon, but soon the lateness starts to make my eyelids heavy. And I'm not the only one who notices.

"Alright, sleepyhead. Your yawns are making me tired." Luke stretches his arms above his head, then stands up, giving me a few second flash view of his twig and berries before getting out of the trough and hiding them behind the towel he wraps around his waist. "It's time to get you inside to bed."

He wasn't lying about being bigger than a twig. I'd say he's more like a very thick branch, one of the main supportive ones with girth and strength. And he definitely is not lacking in the length department either. I have no doubt he could please a woman and still have some to spare.

"But I don't want to." There is no hiding the yawn that accompanies my words.

"Up you go." Holding out a hand, Luke helps me balance as I step out too.

I have a two second thought of trying to be less bold in showing my nudity as water trickles in rivulets down my body, but it's gone just as quick. It's unavoidable and irrelevant at this point. He's seen it all already.

Luke wraps the over-large towel around me and I pull it tight around my chest, leaving my arms free. As I tuck the end in the front, he steps in as close as we can without touching and leans his head down to whisper in my ear.

"Can I?"

"Can you what?"

"Kiss you." His whispered words slide across my neck and send a shiver down my spine. A good shiver.

"I'd be mad if you didn't," I whisper back as I look up and find his eyes almost glowing in the dark.

And Luke kisses me. Starting out slow, our lips are just pressed together, but then things amp up when he takes a small nip at my lower lip. Instinctively I let out a small gasp and he dives in for more.

I lose track of time again as our tongues fight to gain the upper hand, so to say, but I soon realize that this is a battle I will not win. I submit to his tongue flicks and little bites, chasing him with a few in return. When the kiss finally ends and come up for air, Luke has me pulled tight to his chest with one arm around my lower back, and I have a tangle of his hair wrapped around the fingers of my right hand. Both of us also have our free hand grasping the top edge of our towels tight in our grip so we don't end up losing them. Luke seeing me naked is one thing, but I'd rather not show anyone else who might be looking out their bedroom window.

Luke tucks a wild strand of hair that escaped my bun behind my ear and softly kisses my forehead. "I think this is where we say good night."

My shoulders drop as I sigh. "I think so too."

"You head inside first." Luke steps back and scoops up his clothes from the ground.

"Why?" I ask as I do the same.

Leaning down again, our eyes locked this time, I can see and feel the waves of want rolling off of him. "Because if I don't give you a head start and wait for you to lock your bedroom door, I will be tempted to follow you through it."

"Oh boy." The shiver is back.

"Oh boy is right."

"Good night, Luke."

"Good night, Hailey."

And I'm off.

4
TROOPER

A few days of ignorant bliss is good for a rough man's ragged soul.

It has been six days since our little swim party, twelve days since I arrived at the ranch, and every day since has been better than the one before. Now that's not to say I have dropped the ball and not watching for any potential trouble, but I have yet to see any. I don't know if whoever was watching Hailey is hiding better than I'm looking, or if the agents who were here before were imagining things, but no red flags have been flying anywhere nearby since I drove in.

On one of our now regular after dinner walks around the ranch, I have Hailey tucked under my right arm, and she has her left arm around my waist with a finger hooked in one of my belt loops.

We stop along a row of pines that seem to be as tall as a skyscraper when you look straight up, when Hailey starts asking questions that pop our happy bubble and send us crashing back down to reality.

"Why are you here?" She definitely doesn't start easy.

"Where? Here with you?"

"No. At this ranch in Deadwood. Why are you going into witness protection?"

"You know we shouldn't be talking about that kinda stuff. The kinds of cases that bring people to places like this, they aren't small things." I can't tell her that I was sent here to essentially be her babysitter. I have zero doubt that her claws would come out and I'd get slashed to pieces.

"As much as I like kissing you every night, I'm not stupid enough to think I'll ever see you again after we leave. Hell, I don't even know how long

I'll be staying or when I'm leaving." Hailey spins out of my reach and throws her hands up. "I didn't even know what this place was until my escort pulled in the driveway."

"You shouldn't be telling me this," I say to try and get her to stop talking. I know a little about why she's here, but I don't need to know all the details. If Warren didn't see the need to share every small detail with me, I don't need to know. Or do I?

"Why not?" she asks with a huge sigh. "How would you tell anyone my secrets when I can't even tell you because I don't even know what ninety percent of them are?"

"What does that even mean?" I am so confused. It's like she's talking in riddles. "How can you be put into witness protection if you don't know important things? They don't just hand new identities to anyone."

"I know the gist of why I'm here, I just don't understand why. I don't have anything to do with what the case is actually about. I'm just the main witness's daughter. I'm here because of a man I've never even met."

"So you aren't close to the people involved in the actual trial?"

"I had no clue my biological father was even alive until Warren told me he was in trouble. Warren showed up at my apartment in the middle of the night last year, introduced himself, and told me I had to pack up and come with him because I was in danger."

"When did that happen?"

"July twenty-third. Almost eleven months ago."

Holy shit! "You've been here almost a year?"

"Yup," she pops the p as she sits on the pine needle covered ground. Hailey pulls her knees to her chest and wraps her arms around her legs like she's trying to keep her true emotions locked in. She's now looking up at me like I'm the crazy one.

"That doesn't seem right." Dropping down to sit in front of her, needing to be on her level, my knees rest less than a foot away from her shoes. I run a hand through my hair and try to think of a reason as to why she is being held in protective custody for so long.

"I don't know what's right or wrong. I'm just going with the flow at this point and doing what I'm told."

"Warren is your contact, right?"

"Yea."

"When did you last hear from him?"

"It's been a couple weeks I think."

"And what about Bill?"

"I know he's a former Secret Service agent."

"No," I insist with a shake of my head. "I mean, does he know why you're here?"

"From what he's said, Bill knows a few general details, but doesn't know about our statuses day to day unless he's contacted that someone is arriving or leaving." Her eyes go wide as a new question flies out. "Have *you* heard from Warren?"

I shrug a shoulder. "He called me yesterday after breakfast to check in, but didn't say anything about anyone here."

My brain is running a million miles a second because something is not right about all of this. I may have been out of the bureau for five years, but my investigator senses are tingling just as strong as they were when everything thing back then went to hell in a hand basket. Someone who will be involved in a trial, whether testifying or not, and then heading to witness protection, shouldn't be out of contact with the agency this long. And I have never heard of it taking this long to issue a new identity to someone who is important to a main witness. I need to call him and figure out what is really going on.

5
HAILEY

Needing to know more, I jump to my feet. Luke is quickly up just as fast.

"Is Luke your real name?"

I watch as the wall of secrecy slams closed in his eyes. He doesn't want to continue our discussion in this direction, but that's too damn bad for him.

"Is Hailey your real name?"

Hands propped on my hips, I snap back. "Yes."

His silence lasts just a second too long for my sanity because my bitch switch flips and I lose it. "If you can shove your tongue down my throat, but not even tell me your real name, I never want to talk to you again."

"Fine." And he walks away.

"Chicken shit," I call out as I walk the other way. And if he can walk away, so can I.

I need to see Bandit, so I head for the barn that holds all the rideable horses. The main aisle light is on, so I don't flip any more switches as I beeline straight for his stall.

"What an infuriatingly, annoying man." Yes, I am talking to a horse who can't talk back, but getting the words out makes me feel better.

Yes, I may have been the one who started asking the nosey questions, but he's the one who started digging deeper when he didn't like the answers I was giving to his questions to my responses. I don't think it was too much to ask if what I've been calling him is his real name, especially when I pretty much told him every doubt and concern I've had for the last six months about what I'm still doing here.

I know I shouldn't have asked what brought him here to Deadwood.

Hell, I have no idea what kind of person he is in real life. What if he's really a hard core felon, or just someone wrapped up in someone else's mess like I am? Hell, Luke could actually be a really bad person who has made an immunity deal and is getting a new identity for his secrets about other people who are even worse.

Fuck . . . Have I been making out every night with a criminal?

Shit. Why do I feel myself not actually caring about what brought him here?

Luke, or whatever his name is, has been nothing but sweet and helpful and kind to me. Doesn't that alone earn a bit of kindness in return? Isn't that really what getting a new name and identity is all about? Starting over and building a new life.

Should I care about who he used to be, or just enjoy the unknown remainder of days we have together until we both move on to who knows where and have to act like the old versions of us never existed?

Slam. Slam.

That sounds like vehicle doors closing. I don't remember seeing anyone leave after dinner, so maybe a witness is getting picked up or someone new is being dropped off. Maybe Warren is here to get me.

Heavy footsteps draw my attention again as I hear them clap down the center aisle. Petting Bandit on the neck one more time, I kiss his nose then step out of the stall, lock the door, and turn to see two men slowly walking my way.

Both guys look to be in their mid-to-late twenties, wearing black t-shirts, jeans, and boots that make them look like they could be anyone you'd cross paths with on the street or in a store. There's nothing really special about them, other than the mean scowls across their faces, so I don't recognize them as anyone I've met before. Six foot tall or so, both have brown hair and eyes that are so similar, they look like brothers. I also now notice a dark colored utility van parked outside at the end of the barn. If I had to guess, it was these two who were slamming doors.

"Hey there. Can I help you? Are you looking for Bill?"

"Nope," the first guy answers.

"We already found who we're looking for," the second replies too.

"Who's that?"

"We're here for you, sweetheart." I think the first brother is the oldest, because he always answers first.

"Me?" I hold a hand to my chest as I start taking small steps back. "Why?"

"That's none of your business." This comes from the first again.

"How is it none of my business that you were looking for me?"

My back hits the stall door and I wonder if I can get inside with Bandit to create the biggest barrier I can think of between me and them. No, I can't do that. I don't want them to hurt Bandit. He didn't do anything wrong.

I don't think I did either. At least not to these men.

I need to keep them talking. I don't know why I feel like them talking is useful, but maybe Luke will want to apologize for our stupid fight and come back find me and scare them away. I know he can make these guys go away.

Are they here because of my biological father and the mob family he's testifying against? Did they somehow find out about me and now want to hurt me?

"Why do you need me?"

"That's for us to know." One stops walking, forcing two to take a step back to his side.

"You'll find out when we get you to where we're going next." Two speaks his longest sentence yet. Maybe he does have some balls of his own.

"I can't leave."

"It's gonna happen whether you like it or not."

Just when I get brave enough to try and run away, I don't make it far because both men rush forward, each grabbing me by an arm, and whisk me off my feet toward the van. I try to wrestle myself free, but no matter what I do, they are just too strong. Kicking my legs out, I try to aim my swing at one of them to make them fall, but it doesn't work like I hope. It only makes us sway a step in either direction, but unlucky for me neither loses their footing. They both have a strong grip on a forearm and bicep, sandwiching me in the middle, so shifting my shoulders forward and back does nothing but make them madder.

"Stop fucking wiggling," the one to my left growls as they march me down the aisle. The closer and closer we get to the van, the less doubt I have about my chances of survival if they get me inside of that thing.

"Let me go!"

6

TROOPER

That conversation couldn't have ended any worse than if I tried to convince her to walk off a cliff. What the hell is wrong with me?

I'm falling for a woman I know I can never have a future with. How ironic and unfair is that?

I have been a single man for a vast majority of my adult life, and at thirty-five years old, I finally find someone I click with, but she comes with baggage heavier than a semi-truck hauling a load of bricks. My luck seems to be shittier than an outhouse at a prune eating competition.

Sitting in my room, I wait with the door open, hoping to catch her when she has to pass by to get to hers. Almost an hour passes by but there is no sign of Hailey.

Looking out my window, I can see that the barn lights are on. Maybe she went in to spend time with Bandit. She really loves that horse. If spirit animals were an actual real life thing, I think he would be hers.

Hustling into clothes again, because I had changed into pajama pants to sleep, I am out the door and jogging toward the barn in less than three minutes.

I almost trip and fall face first into the barn when I round the corner and see Hailey being carried toward a dark van down at the other end, but I quickly get my feet back under me and quickly formulate a plan to help her.

Both men are yelling at Hailey, and each other, as well as Hailey being loud and obnoxious with her displeasure of the attempted abduction, so I am able to run down the aisle toward them without being heard heading their way.

Once I'm close enough, I grab the guy to first guy I can, make sure I have a good grasp on the back of his shirt, and yank him with all my strength. Hearing his cry of shock and panic as he flies backward and slams into a stall door headfirst, makes me smile for a nanosecond.

In my attempt to get ahold of the loser to Hailey's left, I accidently grab her arm in the melee of everyone trying to move in different directions. She swings her free elbow back at me, probably assuming I am the guy who is now unconscious on the floor, but I see it coming and step to the left.

"Easy, Tiger. It's me." Hailey and I lock eyes and I swear her fight mode kicks into an even higher gear.

"Luke!" she calls out.

I reach forward again and push the second guy out of reach of her.

What I don't anticipate, and should have, is his strong grip still on Hailey's left forearm, because when I push him, she trips and falls in the same direction. Call it an unintentional panic move, or whatever accident related term you want, but hurting her in the process of helping her is the last thing I wanted to do.

The next fifteen seconds happens in slow motion. As he falls, he pulls her down with him, and in her attempt to not land on top of him, Hailey rolls to her right. This causes her to smack her head on the last stall door and I watch her eyes blink slowly twice and fall closed.

"Hailey!" I call out, already scrambling in her direction. As soon as I'm kneeling by her side, pulling her into my arms and slowly laying her back flat on the floor, I see second guy grab the first in my periphery and half carry, half drag him as he runs for the open door.

I go to reach for my gun, but my hand meets nothing but air when I remember I'm not wearing my side holster or carrying my flashlight. I have no way of stopping them.

Part in not wanting Hailey to be suspicious of who I am and what I'm doing here, I am carrying a smaller pistol strapped to my ankle instead of the normal full size Glock 17 that is typically holstered at my right hip. Before I can even think about reaching for my pistol, the van is moving and the men are gone. Immediately my focus shifts and I switch into Hailey mode. I have something more important to worry about. I need to make sure she isn't seriously hurt.

Checking her for injuries, I only find a small bump on the side of her head from where she hit the stall, and some red marks on her arms from where those two losers were carrying her, but nothing that appears life threatening on the outside. The bruises will be gone in a few days, and the bump will defiantly leave her with one hell of a headache, but those are both things I can help her with.

A groan that's not mine draws my attention to Hailey's face and I watch as she blinks a few times before everything around her comes back into focus. When her gaze finds mine, I see a mixture or terror and relief cross her face.

"Luke," she cries out and holds her arms up toward me.

I lean down and let her grab hold of me tight. I wrap my arms gently around her, one holding the back of her head, the other hand on the small of her back, and slowly raise us up to a sitting position.

"You're okay, Tiger." I hold her as close to my chest as I can without morphing our bodies into one. "You bumped your head and were out for less than a minute."

"Where'd they go?" Her question is muffled into my shirt that she now has a herculean grip on.

"I'm sorry, but they got away." I loosen my hold on her a bit to test if she is dizzy, but when she looks up at me with clear eyes, I know she really will be okay. "When you fell, I ran straight to you and they scrambled right for the van."

"Who were they?"

"I have no clue." Looking around the barn, I spot a chair that got knocked over and reach to drag it closer. "Let's get you up and sitting, then I'll find you something to drink."

"Okay." Her voice sounds so small. Hailey never yells, other than at me when I was being stupid, but her voice is usually strong and full. Right now she is everything but.

We move slowly together to get her sitting up on the chair, then I jog down to the stall at the far end of the aisle that holds random supplies. I also grab a bottle of water from the fridge.

"Take a few slow sips."

As she does, I pat my chest, thinking my phone is in my inner cut pocket, but quickly remember again that I am not in my normal biker MC attire. Not only do I have my handgun stored in the lock box in my truck, but my cut is also tucked away under a blanket in the back seat. I hate hiding it, but desperate times called for desperate measures.

Tugging my phone out of my back pocket, I thankfully find the screen isn't cracked from sitting on it on the concrete floor. Swiping my password in, I go right to the contacts. The line rings four times before his voicemail kicks on.

"This is Warren Gates. Leave a—"

I hang up and dial again.

Four more rings and it goes to voicemail a second time.

"This is Warren Gates. Leave a message and I'll call you back as soon as I can."

This time I leave a message. "Warren, call me back. Something's up. Code thirty."

"What's code thirty?" Hailey asks as she twists the cap back on the now half full water bottle.

"Cop speak for 'officer needs help'."

She jerks back and her eyes would pop out of her head if it was physically possible. "Are you a cop?"

Needing to look her straight in the eyes when I rock her world off its axis and admit to being the opposite of who I have been presenting myself as, I squat down onto my haunches and let my butt rest on my heels.

"Up until five years ago I was an agent with the FBI, but I'm not anymore."

"Who the hell are you?"

"That's a bit of a long story, Tiger." I reach out and rest my right hand on her left knee. "But I will tell you a shorter version now if you'd like."

Eyes squinted now, a mix of anger and exhaustion fill her face. "You better start talking before I scream this whole damn barn down around us."

"I was recruited and joined the bureau right out of college. I got a degree in mechanical engineering, so I thought I'd end up working for a construction company, but life went in a different direction super quick."

"Did your degree help you as an agent?"

"Not really," I can't help but laugh at myself a bit. "My parents were super proud of me joining the FBI, but boy were they not thrilled about their money being wasted on the degree."

"I bet."

"They got over it pretty quick, until . . ." I let my body fall back and land on my ass to try and draw out this next part, but Hailey doesn't let me get away with it.

"Until what?"

"Until eight years later when I was mentally and physically exhausted and quit the bureau to join a motorcycle club."

This time her shock rings loud, filling the barn with silence. The only noise around us is the shuffling and puffing of the horses moving in their stalls.

"You quit to do what?"

"I had a few cases go off the rails back to back, and in one of them I met a biker named Steel. Not his real name, but his club name. He was sent to prison for two years for helping a friend, a charge I tried to have pled down to a lesser charge, but the higher ups went around all the work I did and did whatever they wanted to do instead. That was the final straw. I submitted my letter of resignation the next day and was done at the end of the month."

"And you joined the same biker club of the biker you tried to help?"

"Believe me," I run a hand over my jaw as I think back, "it wasn't easy. But with Steel's recommendation to the club President, and a fuck ton of hard work on my part to prove myself to everyone in the club, I was allowed to Prospect and got patched in as a full Brother a year after that."

"Where do you live then? Near here?" Hailey waves the bottle around. "Wait, if you're a biker, and you're here at the ranch, does that mean you're leaving the club and going into WITSEC?"

I just need to rip the bandage off and throw all the crap at her in one toss. If I stop talking before it's all said, I might chicken out and run away from her again. What a tough, badass, outlaw biker I am. I'd roll my eyes at myself if I was in front of a mirror.

"I'm not here to go into witness protection. I'm here because Warren, the agent who brought you here, called in a favor. He in supposedly in the middle of another trial so he couldn't get here right way to check in on you. He told me that the agents he had watching you previously possibly catch sight of a well-known assassin from the mob family your father is testifying against. I live about twelve hours east, pretty close to smack dab in the middle of Wisconsin, and was the only person he trusted to watch you and make sure you were safe. The plan was to hang out on the ranch, pretending to be waiting for my time to roll around like the rest of you, until Warren's other case is over and he can get here."

"So I am just a glorified babysitting job for you?"

"No!" I try to explain but she keeps going. It's only fair that I let her vent like I just did.

"Did our connection mean nothing to you. Did you flirt with me and kiss me and spend all that time with me just to watch me because it was a favor?"

The tears rolling down her cheeks drive a stake through my already broken heart. I hate that I did this to her.

"No." I shift around and am kneeling at her feet. I grab hold of both of her fisted hands and squeeze. "I had zero expectations of who I was coming here to watch over. I only had a name and small snippet of a story. I didn't even know what you looked like until Bill pointed you out when you were in the paddock with Bandit. But don't get me wrong, the second my eyes met yours, this whole trip became about your safety more than anything else. I didn't care about why you were here, I didn't care about Warren owing me a favor, I only cared about keeping you happy and protected. That's why I couldn't answer the personal questions you were asking. I knew we had an end date out there somewhere and had to hold parts of myself back so I wouldn't be crushed when you disappeared."

"What changed?" Hailey twists her hands in my grip and is now holding mine back. "Just because someone tried to grab me, doesn't mean we'll be able to know each other outside of this place. Once Warren gets your message, I imagine him accelerating the timeline and maybe getting me out of here sooner. Once I'm gone, you can go back home."

"When I came around into the barn and saw those two fuckwads with their hands on you, all my concern for the legalities and bureau bullshit went out the damn window." I tug our joined hands to my lips and kiss her knuckles. "Hailey Elizabeth Kellerman, after we figure out who tried to take you from me, and I take care of them my way so they never take another breath, you are coming home with me. You will start over with me, back in Tellison, and grow to love being an Old Lady in the Rebel Vipers MC. I have zero doubts that we can, no, we will be happy together. I promise to make you happy. Please say you'll come home with me? Try for me."

She throws herself into my arms and I fall back on my ass with her in my lap. "I'm scared."

"Oh no no no, Tiger." I hush her as I hold her close. "What are you scared of? I'll make it disappear."

"Who tried to take me?"

There is no time like the present to start figuring that out. A few feet down the aisle I spy a cell phone half tucked under a stall door.

"Is that your phone?" I ask Hailey as I get us both back up on our feet.

She looks at it as I pick it up. "No. I don't have a phone."

"Must be one of the idiots."

"Probably. I didn't see it before."

There is no lock screen, so I get into the device immediately. First thing I check is the call log. Only two contacts glow back at me. BRO and WG.

Assuming BRO means brother, which I'm assuming was the second person here earlier, I click on the contact for WG to see who else he was chatting with and am struck dumb by the phone number.

"This can't be."

Hailey is at my side in a second. "What's wrong?"

"This is Warren's cell number." I show her the screen. "What was he doing calling one of the guys who tried to kidnap you?"

"I don't know."

7
HAILEY

"We gotta get you inside." Luke picks me up, one arm around my back and the other under my knees.

I can't help but laugh as I playfully smack his shoulder. "Put me down right now."

"No." He quietly carries me to the main house and locks us in his bedroom.

The next few minutes are a flurry of activity as I sit on the bed and watch Luke kick into what I'm guessing is his biker protector mode. I'm swept up into the cyclone of phone calls and information that starts flying at us at warp speed.

Luke first calls someone named Whiskey, who he then tells me is the club President, and asks for help. He wants to pack up all our stuff and drive straight to their clubhouse over in Wisconsin. While I agree that staying here on the ranch doesn't feel safe anymore, I try to tell him that driving eight hundred some miles is a crazy idea since we still don't know what is going on with Warren. It's defiantly suspicious that his number is in one of the mystery man's phone, but what if he's the only shady character here. Maybe the others, like Bill, can help us.

Another deep voice comes over the speakerphone and tells Trooper, I quickly learn that its Luke's biker name, to use to log onto a certain website on the cell phone so he can get remote access to it.

"That's Cypher. He is the club's tech wizard extraordinaire," Trooper explains as he hands me the phone. "Your fingers are smaller and can type faster on the screen."

I listen and type the random mix of letters and numbers and dots and slashes that Cypher reads out loud, and the next thing I know, the phone screen moving on its own and I'm not touching it. I set it down on the nightstand and let Cypher do his thing . . . whatever that is.

"I have a buddy in the bureau that I know I can trust." Luke, I mean Trooper, says into whoever is still on the other end of the call on his phone. "I wanna call him and see what he has to say about Warren."

"Who?" I think it's Cypher who asks.

"Bruce Catter."

"Never had the pleasure of talking with him, but I've seen good things."

"What?" I ask, confused about this new name who has been brought up like he's just another player in a game.

Trooper shakes his head and drops a kiss on top of mine. "I've learned that it's best not to ask the computer spooks about what or who they know."

"Is Bruce a tech wizard too?"

"He is."

"Call Bruce and give him my cell number. We can dig a bigger hole twice as fast if we work together."

Whiskey is back again. "Make the calls you need to, then call ne back. I want to know everything as it happens."

"Ten-four."

After a quick call to this mysterious Bruce fella, we learn that my name is not actually on any FBI active files or connected to the open case like Warren told both of us. They do have a Rutherford Jones, my biological father's real name, not the pseudonym of Travis Johnson that Warren gave me, listed a real witness against a southern mob family, and a bit of the tension in my body melts away. Some, but not all of it. We still don't know where Warren Gates is or what he seems to want with me. If my biological father, whom I have never even met, is a cooperating witness, why was I brought here and put into hiding?

We also learn from Bruce that Warren was put on unpaid leave six months ago and that he should not be pretending he has open cases. In addition to the lies he has been weaving to keep me here in Deadwood for the last year, the tangled web of lies is growing thicker and thicker by the minute.

This mess obviously started back before he was put on leave, so who knows who far back it all goes? There are no details as to why he was put on leave in the file, but the lack of information makes it even more suspicious.

Whiskey answers his phone after the first ring. "You saved me from having to wipe my son's butt, so thank you for the perfect timing of your call."

Both men laugh. "Still potty training the Krew-man, huh?"

"This kid would run around naked all day if we let him. If he poops on the living room carpet one more time, Duchess is gonna make me sleep next door with the dog."

"Whiskey and his Old Lady, Duchess have an almost two year old who likes to pretend he's not potty trained. It's hilarious."

"Just wait 'til it's your turn,"

Whiskey chuckles and Trooper's face flashes pale white for a second, then his color is back even faster as he looks at me. "We'll just do the exact opposite of what you did and our kiddo will be out of diapers in a month."

Now it's my turn to go pale. Our kid? Is he crazy? We don't need to be thinking or talking about babies when we have only known each other for a couple weeks, and I just barely agreed to be with him. Trooper did ask me to move home with him and be his Old Lady, but I don't really know what that all entails yet. I have a lot to learn before he can talk me into giving him babies . . . Right?

"I want to bring Hailey home with me and move her into the clubhouse. Not just because I don't trust anyone here on the ranch anymore, but because I need to make her my Old Lady."

"It's about time you settle down, Trooper. The club would be lucky to have whoever you found." Whiskey lets out a loud whoop. "Start thinking about what cupcake flavor you want. Duchess is gonna be asking the second you get home."

"Who gets cupcakes?" I love cupcakes.

"I'll explain when we're on the road," Trooper says as Cypher joins the conversation again.

"Make sure you ditch your phone the first chance you get and switch to a burner. And drive straight home with only stops for gas."

"I have a couple burner phones in my truck. I'll ditch this one somewhere random along the way."

"And check in every hour," Whiskey adds.

I am up on my feet and head for my room to pull the folded down boxes from my closet. I used these same boxes for my now known falsified move here, so it only seems fitting that I use them to get away. I have five medium size moving boxes and one backpack and everything I own will fit in them with no room to spare.

I start taping the bottoms of the boxes before Trooper even hangs up the phone. I know it's going to be an adjustment calling Luke by his biker name, but in a way I feel like this name fits him better. Not that Luke is a bad name, there is just something about how he responds when someone calls him Trooper. The pride and strength radiates out of him when he responds.

8

TROOPER

Most of my clothes are still in my duffle bags, so packing my toiletries and the rest of my stuff is an easy three minute job.

I quietly, and quickly, carry all my bags out to my truck, then quietly again step through the house headed for my Tiger's room. Just as I shut the door behind me, my phone rings. It's Cypher.

"We got into the email from the cell phone."

"What's the damage?"

"Turns out the two men who tried to take Hailey are brothers and both missing criminals who ran while on bail. Warren was also their stepfather."

"What do you mean, was?"

"He was married to their mother until she divorced him two years ago. They were supposed to grab Hailey and bring her to him."

"And take her where?" I continue to volley questions and answers with Cypher as Hailey dumps and entire drawer of unmatched socks into a box.

"It doesn't say in texts or emails. Bruce and I both tried to find Warren by pinging his cell, but it's offline."

"What if he finds me?" Hailey asks as she tapes her last box shut.

"I won't let him get you." I pull her to stand between my legs as I sit on the edge of the bed.

"You can't promise that."

"Yes I can, Tiger. When I told you that I've got you, I wasn't kidding. I don't know yet what he's trying to do, but I will do everything I can to stop it."

Half an hour later, we stop to fill up at the first gas station we see in

Sturgis. Seeing Hailey's boxes in the bed of my truck sends rush of blood south. God, I wish I could have gotten to get better acquainted with her body, other than the visual still floating in my mind from our night in the stock tank, but anything more will have to wait until I show her her new home.

We load up on some snacks and drinks, enough to carry us over until we cross back into the friendly state of Minnesota, where we have friends in the Saint's Outlaws MC. Just as I'm about to drive away, my cell phone dings with a couple texts back to back.

I haven't tossed this phone yet because my plan is to send it swimming down the mighty Mississippi when we cross over her entering Wisconsin.

Can you check that for me? It's probably one of the guys checking in.

Hailey's face goes pale.

"What's wrong, Tiger?"

"It's Warren." She shows me the screen.

Warren Gates: I know you have Hailey.

Warren Gates: I know you left the ranch.

"It didn't take him long to realize we were gone." I pull the truck away from the pumps and park at the edge of the lot with no other vehicles.

Hailey hands me the phone and I hit the little phone shaped button on top of the screen to call him. At this point in whatever game he is playing, texting won't get me the information or truth that we need.

As the phone rings, I look at Hailey and tell her, "If he tries to talk to you, don't say a word, okay? Let me handle him."

"Yeah," she agrees with a nod.

"Where are you, Luke?" What a delightful greeting . . . not.

"What the fuck is really going on, Warren? Why did you lie to me?"

"Where are you?"

Not bothering to answer his unnecessary question, I get straight to the point. "I know Hailey is not actually in process to be in WITSEC. Neither the FBI nor the Marshalls have her anywhere on an active case file. They obviously know about her, but that's as far as it goes."

"That is none of your business, Luke," he growls. "I sent you there to watch her, not fall in love with her and run away. That wasn't the damn plan." Each word is louder than the one before.

"Well, your damn plan went out the damn window the second I realized you lied to me. I was part of what I now know is a bogus mission because you called me for help. This all started because you needed me, so now I need *you* to cut the crap and tell me the truth, asshole."

"If you won't tell me where you are, I'll just find you myself."

"Good luck, fucker. You're gonna need it."

"You don't know what you've stepped in, Luke. This is bigger than either of us. Your little biker gang can't help you with this. You really don't know who you're messing with, do you?"

"My club has a bigger reach than you could ever—Hello?"

"What happened?" A look of shock and stupor crosses her face. I'm sure I have a similar one too.

"He hung up on me."

For a man who wanted to talk to me so bad, and was angry he didn't get his answers, he sure ended the call sooner than I expected.

9
HAILEY

One state almost done, one and a half to go.

Sioux Falls, South Dakota is the last stop for gas on our journey to Wisconsin. This road trip will two new states to my imaginary map of states I have been to. A majority of where I've visited are in the southwestern part of the United States, but I have a feeling that being with Trooper is going to take me on many new adventures, physically and metaphorically speaking.

Trooper was hoping to make it a little bit further before we needed to refuel, wanting to be over the Minnesota state line, but unfortunately the gas gauge didn't have the range to get us the extra twenty miles that we would have needed.

Trooper shoots me a wink just before he turns to put the nozzle back in the gas pump, when all of a sudden, my door opens behind me and I am pulled out of the truck backward. Before I can even get a full grasp on what's going on, Trooper is shouting a name that sends my body into a frozen state.

It's Warren and he has me in a chokehold, holding a knife to my throat.

"What the fuck? We're in public, asshole."

I watch as Trooper slowly steps to his right, inching his way toward the back of the truck. Now would be a really good time for him to put a little pep in his step. Unless he's seeing something I'm not, which is a real possibility because my captor is behind me, I'd like to get this show back on the road pronto.

"I don't give a fuck," Warren yells back, rattling my right eardrum.

A second man appears, and before I can even think to say anything to warn him, Trooper rounds on him so fast, hitting him over the head with a Maglite flashlight that seemingly appeared out of nowhere.

The two wrestle for a few seconds, but Trooper maintains the upper hand and breaks his neck with a quick twist of his hands. The crack that follows is a sound I have never heard before, and would be perfectly okay to never hear again.

"Warren," Trooper steps a bit closer, his hands are up and facing palms out. "You need to let her go."

"No."

For every step Trooper makes forward, Warren takes one backward, dragging me along with him. When my body froze, I clasped my hands tight to Warren's forearms, hoping he wouldn't jostle us too much and he end up cutting me. I'm still frozen like that, hoping for the same results.

All of a sudden, Trooper stops and I watch horror cross his handsome face. He looks mortified as my world starts to tilt backward. I'm looking at more of the gas station canopy lights than I was before, and that's when the pieces click to form the full picture—we're going down.

The free fall stop with a sudden jolt, and thud, as well as a different version of a cracking sound. This time it is a duller tick, but just as unpleasant to hear.

Realizing that I'm free from the knife and Warren's clutches, I roll to the side and up on my feet to see what tripped us. In his attempted to evade Trooper's advance, Warren miscalculated his surroundings and backed right up to the curb running around the next pump over. He lost his footing and down we went.

Trooper scoops me up in his arms, but I can't look away from the man on the ground, the man who was supposed to be my protector. The man who bulldozed his way into my life with the claim that he was there to keep me safe. He was a liar.

Warren was a liar, but I feel no remorse or sadness with how his life ended. I actually almost feel bad for him—almost, but not quite.

Too bad, so sad for him, his head hit the back side of the curb and the crack I heard was his skull cracking open. I don't think he's breathing any longer.

"I think he's dead." I tell Trooper when he finally sets me down.

He checks for a pulse. "Nope. They're both done."

"They got what they deserved."

"You got that right, Tiger." Trooper pulls me back in for a short but hot as fuck kiss. I'm panting for a breath when he lets me go and leads me to the passenger side door.

"Now what?" I ask as he lifts me up into my seat."

"I hate to do this with you in the truck, but I need to load them up and get us the fuck out of here."

I look around Trooper's torso and see Warren still laying on the ground. "You want to take the bodies with us?"

"I got no choice unless we want someone calling the law."

"That probably would end very badly."

"You're not wrong, Tiger."

"What will you do with them?" I don't know if I really want the answer to my question, but I ask it anyway.

"I'll deal with them when we get to the clubhouse."

"Do I want to know those details?"

"I wouldn't tell you even if you wanted to."

"Fair enough." I swivel in place and sit forward in my seat. "Club business, right?"

"You are gonna be one hell of an Old Lady, Tiger." Trooper buckles my seatbelt and tilts my chin up for a quick peck.

"I love you, Trooper." Apparently my brain to mouth filter is broken today. Ahh hell, who cares? I didn't lie.

"Thank fucking Lucifer that you said it first," he says back with the biggest grin I've yet to see him smile. "'Cause the words were just about to fly outta my mouth too."

"Really?" My heartbeat is out of control.

"I love you too, Tiger."

It doesn't take him long, and thank goodness that it's just after four a.m. and nobody but us is in this gas station parking lot, because Trooper lifts both bodies and literally tosses them into the bed of the truck like they are bales of hay. They land right next to my boxes, and just as quick as he moved them, Trooper unrolls the tonneau cover I didn't notice until now and covers everything form anyone's nosey view.

Once we're back on the road for a bit, I turn to Trooper and ask him a question that's been buzzing around in my head since we left the ranch back in Deadwood.

"Is this what it's gonna be like being with you?"

"What do you mean?"

I wave my hand toward the truck bed, "The bad guys and killing people and being in danger."

"I'm not gonna lie and say it doesn't sometimes happen," he starts while shaking his head. "But no, it's not an all the time kinda thing. And our club doesn't hurt or kill anyone who doesn't deserve it. Ninety-nine percent of the time, who we kill is someone who tried to hurt one of us first. Just like what happened to you."

I stew on what he said and give him a short nod in return. "I can live with that."

"When it comes to club business, or random scary things like you just went through, or when any of the Brothers and I need to do something potentially dangerous and or illegal, it's better that you don't know all the details. And most of the time, you won't have any idea of when the club is doing something potentially illegal. Part of being a biker's Old Lady is knowing that there is danger, but not knowing the specifics because we keep you safe and away from it."

"Why am I so calm about this?" I look over my shoulder and can imagine the bodies hiding under the vinyl. "My life was nothing like this two weeks ago."

"Because Tiger, you are finally where you were always meant to be."

"And where's that?" I can't help but smile as Trooper grabs my hand and kisses my knuckles.

"Right here beside me."

"There is nowhere else I'd want to be."

10
TROOPER

The more I hear about my former friend and mentor, the shadier and dirtier his life becomes. Warren Gates was much dirtier than I could have ever expected. I hate that Hailey had to spend even one day trusting him with her safety, but I am grateful that the circumstances we both went through because of his nefarious lies brought us together.

After we got to the clubhouse, just a few hours ago, and I introduced my Tiger to the few people who were hanging around, I got her settled into our room in the clubhouse for a much needed nap. Once I was sure she was out, I went back downstairs to meet with Whiskey and a few of the other members and club officers. Cypher filled us all in on all the mess that he and Bruce found, while a few of my other Brothers turned the bodies we brought back with us into ash.

Warren was not only working for the one southern mob family, intending to use my Tiger as collateral to get her biological father to not testify against them, his track record with being a mole for several other criminal organizations across the country was a mile long. He has his fingers dipped in a shit-ton of dirty ponds. While we have no way of asking a dead man why he did what he did, knowing that my Old Lady is safe is all that's important to me now.

~

It's the next day and I am chopping at the bit for what I have planned for my better half . . . if only my better half would hurry her sexy booty up and get out of the bathroom soon rather than later.

Tiger finally appears, looking stunningly beautiful as always, and I tell her I have something to show her. "But I need you to trust me."

"I'd do almost anything for you. I love you."

"I love you more."

We repeat the same fight a few dozen times a day. She loves me more. No, I love her more. It's a squabble that neither of us will ever win, and I am okay with it.

I get Hailey downstairs and out onto the front porch of the clubhouse, and this is where I stop her. "I need you to wear this as a blindfold." I pull a folded bandana out of my back pocket.

"Where are you taking me," she asks as she ties the material to cover her dark chocolate brown eyes. "I won't ride on your Harley with this thing on."

"We're not taking the bike out . . . yet," I reply as I grab her right hand in mine and lead her across the parking lot toward the front gate. "But I will get you wrapped around me on it as soon as I can."

The gate is open just wide enough for us to walk through and I continue leading her across the road.

"Are we going to the scrap yard?" she guesses.

"Kinda, but not for long."

The surprise I have for her is only accessible through the side fence of Tellison Recycling and Salvage until I can a permit from the county to put in a new driveway approach.

Directly across the road from the land that the clubhouse is the recycling and metal salvage business that the club owns. And right next to that is a twenty acre plot of land I had purchased a few months back. Until I met my Tiger, I had no idea what I was going to do with it, but the price was too good to pass up.

Seeing her be so at peace with the animals at the ranch, I wanted her to experience that same feeling here in her new home.

As we cross the gravel lot and pass through the side gate, stepping onto the land I own, I tug on the bandana and pull it from her head.

"Oh. My. Gosh." Her jaw is on the metaphorical floor. "What is this place? And there's a barn too. Can we go see it? Pretty please?"

"Not quite yet." I have to tug her back and keep her close for the time being. "I need to check out the support beams a bit more to make sure it's safe before you go inside."

"Looks like you'll finally get to put some of your engineering skills to work," she sasses me and bumps my leg with her hip.

"Sassy tiger." I dive in for a kiss.

"Only for you."

"Right back at ya."

Spinning back around to face the faded red, two story, old hayloft style barn in front of us, Tiger leans back against me and I prop us both up. "What are your plans for that?"

"As soon as it's safe, whether we need to knock it down or just do some work to make sure it's sound, Bandit will be coming to live with us."

Her surprised gasp can probably be heard across the road. "He is?"

"He is."

Her eyes sparkle with unshed tears. "Where is he now?"

"He is still at the ranch in Deadwood, but he's being looked after by the rescue and volunteers who came in to take over after Bill was arrested."

In his digging around Warren, Cypher also discovered a few skeletons in Bill's closet, then passed that information onto Bruce who opened a formal inquiry. He was arrested late last night, super quick, good riddance.

"If Bandit gets to live here, where are we gonna live?" she asks as she leans back into me again.

I point to a flat space of grass a short ways off to our left, a bit closer to the road than the barn. "I put a deposit on a prefabricated cabin last night and the club and I will build it right there. You just need to pick out which floor plan you want."

She melts a little deeper into my arms. "You really thought of everything, didn't you?"

"I tried."

"You succeeded, Luke Emanuelle. You are everything and more than I could have wished for."

I feel the leather of her Property cut as I wrap my arms around her waist. Looking down I see her playing with the horseshoe skeleton key necklace hanging around her neck. I gave her both items last night when I formally asked her, more like ordered her, to be my Old Lady. She cried and said yes over and over again.

Tiger is her name now.

My Tiger is relentless and fierce. I can tell her I love her until I'm blue in the face, I can show her my appreciation for saving me from a lifetime of being miserable and alone, but I don't think she'll ever let me convince her I love her more than she loves me.

She's stubborn, hard-headed, loyal, dependable, and a pain in my ass. But no matter what happens to us from now on, she'll be my forever, and I'll be her rock. She is my light and I'll be her strength even in the darkest moments.

Until my dying day, I will be devoted to one thing—her.

She calls me a real trooper, her savior. But when it comes down to it, she's my savior too.

ABOUT THE AUTHOR

Jessa Aarons was born and raised in the frozen tundra of Wisconsin. She has had her nose buried in books for as long as she can remember. Her love of romance began when she "borrowed" her mom's paperback Harlequin novels.

After experiencing a life-changing health issue, she had to leave the working world and dove back into books to help heal her soul. She would read anything that told a love story but still had grit and drama. Then she became a beta reader and personal assistant to another author.

Jessa is the boss of her husband and their castle. He really is her prince. Thanks to his encouragement, Jessa started putting pen to paper and creating new imaginary worlds. She spends her free time reading, crafting, and cheering on her hometown football team.

Linktree: https://linktr.ee/JessaAarons

DEADWOOD'S KILLER BREW

A PERFECT BLEND COZY MYSTERY

NORY WOODS

BLURB

Starr Kona and her spirited corgi companion, Bean, embark on their first true vacation adventure. As a computer analyst, she had always stayed close to home, but now she wanted to see all the Americas had to offer. Their first stop is Deadwood, South Dakota.

Everything seemed to be running smoothly, that is, until Bean found that pesky dead body. Will her innate curiosity and Bean's corgi charm be the key to solving the case, or will they end up stepping on everyone's toes?

Deadwood's Killer Brew is Book One in The Perfect Blend Cozy Mystery Trilogy.

1

STOUT INN

Starr gathered everything she needed for her and Bean, her five-year-old tri-colored corgi. He sat on his bed watching her intently. His head tilted every time she turned to do something different. Starr, while very meticulous in her work environment, tended to be all over the place at home.

"I think that's it," she announced, glancing at Bean, who was giving her an, *are you sure*, look.

"Yes, I'm sure, I think," she stated, not so confidently.

Bean tilted his head knowingly, which made her laugh.

"Stop being so judgy!" she told him.

Bean stood on his stubby legs and stretched, his fluffy butt rising in the air. Starr absolutely loved that crazy pup. She had taken him because he was the runt of the litter, but he had been so loving when she picked him up. It was as if he was meant to be her dog, no, not dog, companion.

"I checked the weather, and it should be nice this time of year, but it might be a little chilly. We should bring at least one of your sweaters. Which one do you want?" she asked, holding up two sweaters.

Bean trotted over to her. He first sniffed the brown one (it was red, but he couldn't tell because he was color blind!). He didn't mind that one, but she often made him wear a hat with it, which he didn't like very much, so he sniffed the blue one. That one he liked better as it fit him nicely, and more importantly to him, there were no hats involved. He woofed his selection.

"Good choice," Starr agreed.

She folded the sweater and stuffed it in the outside pocket of Bean's travel bag. She double checked that she had everything both she and Bean would need. His food, snacks, bowls, chew toys, and blanket were all neatly packed in the diaper bag she used for his things. She looked at him as he approached her with his battered fish.

"We can't bring that one," she told him.

He dropped it and barked at her. How could she expect him to travel wherever they were going without his comfort fish? His fish went everywhere with him. Yes, it was battered, but it was an important item. He picked it up again and jumped on the bed, dropping the fish into his bag. He then sat and eyed her.

"You are so stubborn. You know that, right?" she asked, hands on her hips. She swore he smiled. "Okay, fine. You win. We'll bring it."

He jumped off the bed victorious as she zipped up the bag. She grabbed both of their bags and walked into the living room, following him. She made sure everything was locked up and then opened the garage door. She dropped the bags on the back seat and looked at him.

"Up."

He hopped inside the vehicle and into the front seat, where he nestled into the soft booster seat attached to the passenger seat. Starr clipped his harness to the booster and made sure he was secure before getting in herself.

She smiled at him. "Are you ready for our adventure?"

He barked happily. He wasn't sure where they were going. He was just happy to be going with her. He had been kenneled before. He didn't mind because he was pampered, but he preferred to be with her. After all, who would keep her safe?

They had been driving for hours. The drive from Denver, Colorado, to Deadwood, South Dakota, was around six hours, depending on driving speed, weather conditions, and stops. Generally, she liked to drive to places as she rarely went out of town without Bean. She found that he could handle traveling in the car for up to ten hours. After that, he whined and complained. Not that she blamed him.

"We're almost there, Bean."

He was thankful for that. They had stopped at the park twenty hours ago. Yes, he knew it wasn't that long, but he had no real concept of time. It was primarily based on his need to relieve himself.

"There's the sign for Deadwood. It's only 22 more miles," she said happily.

The winding road through the Black Hills was stunningly beautiful. Large trees graced the hillside as they made their way to Deadwood. She was sure it would be an interesting time. She had never been there but always thought it would be fun to visit.

"What was that?" Bean thought as a loud roar passed his side of the car.

"It's okay, it's only a motorcycle," she said calmly. "I know they are loud, but they won't hurt us."

Deadwood was a quaint little town. They had modern homes on the outskirts of the city, but then they had a whole separate section that encompassed all the elements of an old western town. She couldn't wait to explore the area with Bean.

"Hey, I think that's it," she stated as they made a turn down another winding road. "Yep, that's it."

Stout Inn was a beautiful two-story house. From what she had read online, there were four bedrooms upstairs, a large living room, a modest dining room, and a kitchen. She had double checked that it was okay to bring Bean, and was told absolutely, but there would be a deposit. She was used to that since most places required an animal deposit when she traveled with him.

"Isn't it lovely, Bean?" she asked, as she parked.

Bean sat back on his hind quarters, wobbly with his short legs. He used the back of his booster seat to steady himself. He noticed the house, but what he was interested in was the yard. He loved to run in the grass at home. He turned to her and barked.

"Okay, boy, let me take you out, and then we will get settled."

She took him to an area away from the house that seemed to be where pets were supposed to relieve themselves. She let him do his business, and once she had cleaned up after him and tossed the bag in the trash, they headed to the house.

"Good day, ma'am," said a woman as she approached them.

"Hello, my name is Starr Kona, and I have a reservation," she replied.

"Why yes, you do. We have been expecting your arrival. I trust your drive was uneventful."

Starr laughed. "Yes, it was. It is quite beautiful out here. The drive through the Black Hills was stunning."

The woman smiled. "Yes, we love it out here. My name is Sally, and this here is my husband Tim. We own the place."

"Nice to meet you," Starr stated as she shook each of their hands.

Sally started to reach down to pet Bean, but then stopped and looked at Starr for approval. "May I pet your dog?"

"Oh, yes, he loves people."

"What's his name?" she asked, as she petted the playful dog.

"His name is Bean."

"That's an unusual name for a dog," Tim stated as he reached down to pet Bean as well, unable to resist the corgi charm.

Starr laughed again. "I know. My co-workers said I should name him coffee since I love it so much. I settled on Bean, you know, for coffee bean."

Starr laughed and then indicated, "We make coffee throughout the day for our guests, but there are also a few coffee shops below as well," Sally told her, rising.

"Good to know. Is it okay if I have my key? I want to get Bean settled in the room."

"Of course."

Starr dug in her pocket and grabbed her driver's license and credit card, handing them to Sally. She quickly ran the card and then showed them to their room. Starr closed the door and unclipped Bean's leash.

"Go ahead, little man, sniff it out," she said with a laugh and plopped on the bed, which she found to be very comfortable.

Bean patrolled the entire room, sniffing everything. He identified at least four other humans who had been in the room. No dogs, though, which he was happy about. Once he had sniffed every area of the room, he made a running jump to get on the bed.

"Oh shoot," Starr said, as Bean's front paws reached the mattress, but his bottom pulled him down. He had a frustrated look on his face. "Hold on, boy, let me get you something to jump up from."

She quickly moved the ottoman from the chair in the corner and placed it in front of the bed. Bean was a little hesitant, but he ran up, jumped from the ottoman onto the bed triumphantly. He immediately went to Starr to lick her face.

"You are welcome." They lay on the bed and relaxed for a little bit, and then she looked at him. "You stay in here; I'm going to get our things."

He didn't like her leaving without him, but was also very comfortable on the bed, and would like his toys and a snack. He didn't complain when she left the room. She trotted down the stairs and saw another couple in the living room. The woman waved her over.

"Hi, my name's Nina, and this is my partner, Monte. We're staying here too," she said excitedly.

"That's wonderful. How are you liking it?" Starr asked a bit uncomfortably, as she knew Bean was in the room, probably getting into mischief.

"Once you are situated with all your things, why don't you come down and have some coffee with us?" Nina suggested.

Starr smiled. "Well, I'll never say no to coffee."

"Sally just made a fresh pot," Nina replied.

"We'll be down in a few minutes," Starr told her and made a mad dash to her car.

She quickly gathered their bags and was back in the room. She filled Bean's water bowl and gave him one of his snacks, which he happily devoured. Once he had lapped up enough water, she clipped his leash to his harness, and they walked down the stairs.

"Oh my gosh," Nina squealed as she saw Bean.

Starr laughed. That seemed to be the typical response to her rambunctious corgi when people saw him. Of course, he absolutely loved the attention. He glanced at Starr, who gave him a nod. He waddled over to Nina, who immediately started petting him.

"I've always loved corgis," Nina said, looking at her partner.

"We can't have dogs where we live," he explained to Starr.

"I understand completely." She took a seat across from Nina. "Where are you two from?"

"We're from Michigan," Monte replied.

"Never been there," Starr stated. Of course, she was only just starting to travel.

"What about you?" he asked.

"Denver," she grinned at Bean, who was now rolling on his back.

"I hear that's a nice place," Nina said, not looking up from her play time with Bean.

"It is nice, a bit cold, but still nice."

Monte laughed. "It gets cold in Michigan as well."

"That's true," she said with a chuckle. She then addressed Nina, "Can you hold his leash while I get a cup of coffee?"

"Of course," she beamed, playing with Bean's ears, which he didn't like.

Starr handed her the leash and then walked into the kitchen. She grabbed a cup from the cupboard that said, *"It's Wild in Deadwood"* with a picture of a man on a bucking horse. She giggled for a moment before going to the coffee pot on the counter. She quickly filled her cup, adding a dash of cream and sugar.

"You should be careful who you talk to," she heard from behind her.

She jumped, startled by the sound. When she turned, she saw Tim leaning against the refrigerator. He had his arms crossed defiantly, which confused her. She took a breath, gathered her composure, and took a sip of her coffee to settle her nerves.

"I'm sorry, what?"

He pushed off from the refrigerator and walked towards Starr. He reached behind her to grab a cup from the cupboard, forcing her to move out of the way. He poured a cup of coffee and stared at her.

"I said, you should be careful who you share your information with. Not everyone is trustworthy," he told her cooly.

She swallowed thickly, unsure how to take this conversation. She heard a loud thump, and then Bean squealed. She turned quickly to see what had happened. Before she left the room, she glanced at Tim, who nodded just slightly.

"I told you so," he responded.

Starr didn't have the time nor inclination to analyze his odd behavior. She needed to check on Bean. She set her coffee on the counter, darting into the living room... and screamed.

2

CHAOTIC ENERGY

Starr screamed as she looked around the room. It was a mess. The end table was knocked over; the lamp was on the floor, and the blanket on the chair she had been sitting on was tangled in the legs of the coffee table. Nina was trying to fix things while Monte tried to grab Bean's leash.

"What happened!"

Nina looked at her apologetically. "I dropped his leash, and he started running around. We both laughed, and then he, I don't know, he must have taken our laughter as approval and just went wild. We tried to catch him, but I think he thought we were playing a game. I'm so sorry."

She stared at Bean, who was now cowering in the corner. Oh, he knew he was in trouble. He had always had chaotic energy around him, but he knew better. He knew how to act with strangers and in other people's homes. She snapped her fingers, and he came over to her, ears all the way back as he practically crawled to her.

"What do you have to say for yourself, young man?" she asked him.

He looked up at her, his eyes contrite. He recognized after the fact that she would be upset with him, but honestly, he felt it wasn't his fault. They were playing with him. They should have been quicker to catch him, and none of this would have happened. As he stared at Starr, he knew she didn't see it that way. He released a whimpered bark that he hoped conveyed his regret... at getting caught.

"You were a bad boy, Bean. You know better," she scolded.

"It really wasn't his fault," Monte told her. "I think we kind of riled him up."

"Well, he knows not to run from people," she replied, still upset, but it was waning. "I should probably take him back upstairs.

"No, please stay and visit," Nina urged.

Starr sighed and looked down at Bean. "There will be no more running around, understand?"

He woofed his response to her and wagged his short little tail, knowing that she was no longer upset with him. As she sat down, he jumped onto her lap. She tapped her chest, and he leaned up so she could hug him. While he wasn't the biggest fan of hugs, he knew she enjoyed them, and he figured he needed to apologize or she would not let him sleep with her on the bed.

"I forgive you," she finally muttered.

He heard footsteps approaching and resisted the urge to bark. It was so hard to do, but he had already gotten in trouble and didn't want to be in more trouble. He felt the sound vibrating in his throat, wanting to get out. Just as he was about to unleash it, he felt Starr's hand pat his back a few times. He shook his body of the urge to go off on whoever was entering the room.

"Is everything okay?" Sally asked with concern. Her husband Tim appeared in the doorway beside her.

"Oh, everything is fine," Nina stated nervously, hoping she had put everything back in the right place.

Tim walked over to Starr and set a cup on the table beside her. Bean felt Starr tense slightly and was confused by it, as he had sensed nothing nefarious about the man. Perhaps his radar was wrong?

"You left this on the counter," he stated politely.

She chuckled softly. "Yes, thank you."

"No problem, ma'am," he replied, walking back to Sally, who had stepped fully into the room.

"I thought I heard some ruckus," Sally stated, looking around the room. She approached the coffee table and straightened one of the doilies.

"I apologize, apparently Bean sort of ran around the room playing with Nina and Monte, but I assure you that will not happen again. He will remain leashed," Starr stated firmly, as she ran her hand over Bean's back, hoping they were not going to be asked to leave.

Sally inspected the room and then smiled at Starr. "I don't see anything damaged, but do try not to let him run loose in the house."

"Will do," Starr told her cheerfully, excited that she didn't have to look for another place to stay.

"Well, we will leave you be," she stated and looked at her husband, who followed her out of the room.

"I was worried they were going to make us leave," Starr said, once the owners were out of earshot.

"I was too, and man, I would have had so much guilt about it," Nina agreed, blowing out a relieved breath.

Lighthearted laughter filled the room as they sipped coffee and talked. Starr learned that the couple was also on vacation because they were apparently very popular travel influencers, which they suggested was why the owners were being so nice to them.

"So, as travel influencers, you just go around and stay at different places?"

Monte and Nina laughed. "Yes, basically."

"And you get paid for doing that."

"We have sponsors," Monte clarified.

"Oh, that makes sense," Starr responded with a nod.

"What made you decide to come here?" Nina asked.

"It's kind of crazy, but I won a trip from my job. It totally surprised me because I had never won anything before, but it was a weekend getaway in Deadwood. I thought, why not stay a bit longer, so I called and asked if I could add an extra day onto it, and they said yes, so here we are."

"How fun is that!" Nina expressed excitement. "Do you have plans?"

"We are kind of winging it. I'm thinking about checking out Main Street tomorrow."

"There are a lot of nice stores down there. They also have various reenactments throughout the day, which are cool and, to be honest, quite funny," Monte told her.

"Thanks, I think we will check them out," Starr stated with a nod.

"Hey, would you and Bean like to be in a video for our post tonight?" Nina asked.

"Um, sure, what does that entail?"

"We'll talk about you as a new arrival at the B&B. Totally easy and simple. We will show you the video first, and if you hate it, we won't post it." Nina assured her.

"Okay, that sounds reasonable. Let me go and freshen up first."

"There's no need for that, but if you'd feel better doing so, that's fine as well," Monte replied.

Starr set Bean on the ground and stood up. "We'll be back in a few minutes."

She trotted up the stairs to their room and closed the door before unclipping him from the leash. He took a few sips out of his water bowl and then watched her curiously as she stared at the shirts she had brought with her, settling on one he had seen her wear many times. Then she reached for his bag and pulled out his sweater.

"If we are going to be on a video, we should look nice, don't ya think?" she said to him cheerfully.

He reluctantly walked over to her as she undid his harness and put the argyle sweater on him. She then quickly changed tops and brushed her hair out. She briefly thought about putting on some makeup, but decided her foundation and blush were fine.

"You ready, boy?" she asked him.

He wagged his stubby tail and looked over to where she had set his leash. She walked over there and picked it up, clipping it on his collar. She stopped at the door and, before opening it, looked down at him.

"You need to behave, Bean, understand?" he woofed his response, and she nodded.

They exited the bedroom and headed down the stairs. Starr had to admit she was a little nervous. She had never done anything like this. Perhaps she should have looked up Nina and Monte's blog to see what kind of content they posted. Well, it was too late now.

"Oh, look how handsome you are," Nina said, kneeling so she could pet Bean, who, like usual, was eating all the attention up.

"We will shoot in here," Monte said. "It's a little windy outside, which will interfere with the sound quality."

Nina rose. "And he doesn't want to spend several hours editing out the background noise," she laughed.

"She's not wrong," Monte agreed with a cheeky grin.

"Would it be possible for me to take a glimpse at your website?" she asked nervously. "I mean, I probably should have done that first," she finished with a shrug.

Nina nodded happily. "Of course." She reached for her iPad and, a few quick strokes later, handed it to Starr. "Have a look-see."

Starr perused the site, which consisted of several video blogs of various places the couple had stayed at. She was shocked to see how many people subscribed to the website. While the videos showed that the couple was legitimate travel influencers, it also made her nervous about the number of people who would see the video.

"Wow, this is impressive," Starr responded, handing her back the iPad.

"What's your Instagram profile so we can tag you in the post?" Nina asked politely.

Starr laughed. "I have one, but it's mostly just Bean."

Once they all exchanged their social media handles and followed one another, Nina directed her to the chair Starr had sat in earlier, but it had been moved slightly so it was near the fireplace. The blinds were open on one side to allow for natural light to come in.

"I promise this will be just a lighthearted chat, so be yourself, and let's have some fun," Nina told her.

"You make it sound easy," Starr smiled.

"It truly is," Nina winked and then glanced at Monte, who nodded. He motioned with his fingers, counting down to one. At that point, Nina started speaking in an exaggerated way. "Hey everyone, it's Nina and Monte, here in Deadwood, South Dakota, and guess what? We have new guests, Starr and her adorable corgi, Bean."

The camera panned to Starr, who was sitting with Bean on her lap. He tilted his head adorably as Starr hesitantly waved. Bean woofed, which brought a string of laughter from both Nina and Monte.

"Adorable, right?" Nina stated enthusiastically, trying to contain her laughter.

As promised, the video itself was lighthearted and low-key. There were no hard-hitting questions, and she was even able to shout out the agency she worked at. Starr could understand why Monte and Nina were so popular. They were both very personable.

"Do you want to watch a rough cut of the video?" Monte asked her.

"Definitely," she replied, eagerly taking the camera he offered.

She laughed as Nina regaled her audience with the tale of how Bean had escaped their clutches and proceeded to bring havoc and chaos. All the while, Bean watched her intently. You could tell that he wanted to jump in to add his two cents' worth, but Starr had kept a hold of him to prevent any further mishaps.

"That was a lot of fun, guys, thanks for asking me," Starr stated as she handed Monte back his camera.

"It was our pleasure," Nina said, reaching to pet Bean again.

"I'm going to work on the edits so it will be ready for tonight's post," Monte told Nina.

"I'll be up in a minute," she told him with a quick kiss on the cheek.

"Bye, Monte," Starr said when he waved at her. "Does it take a lot to edit the videos?" she asked Nina.

She shook her head. "Not really, but he's a perfectionist, so he will go over the sound quality and clean up the images."

"I will keep a lookout for it," she said, looking at Bean.

Nina laughed. "Oh, don't worry, you will know when the video hits." Starr glanced at her curiously, so Nina added, "You will be getting a lot of alerts.

Starr nodded with a smile. "Oh, well, that's never happened to me, so I will try not to be shocked by the notification sound."

"Smart plan. Well, I'm going to go up and double-check the written part of the post. Have a good rest of the evening."

"Thanks, you, too." Once Nina had pet Bean one more time, she darted up the stairs. Starr looked at him. "We should probably go stretch our legs before it gets too dark outside, huh, boy."

He woofed excitedly as she exited the front door with him, almost running directly into someone about to knock on the door. She jumped back, startled as Bean immediately barked at the stranger.

"I'm sorry, ma'am, didn't mean to scare you," the young man said. "I'm just here to drop off an order for Nina Young. Is that you?"

Having regained her composure, she shook her head and glanced towards the sound of footsteps running down the stairs. Nina approached, out of breath. Bean had stopped barking but was still eyeing the man suspiciously.

"Sorry, had my phone off, so I didn't get the alert," Nina stated out of breath.

"Excuse us," Starr interjected politely as the Uber driver stepped out of the way.

"Boy, that sure got the blood pumping," Starr said aloud as they began their walk. She stopped and sighed at the sky and all the beautiful colors. "Now that is what I call a sunset."

3
KILLER BREW

Starr awoke to her alarm going off. She had set it for eight and neglected to turn it off last night. She yawned and rubbed her eyes. She was tired. When Nina told her yesterday that she would know when the video was posted, she was not wrong. Apparently, the video was out at nine, and Starr's phone notified her of every like and comment. She eventually turned her notifications off at midnight.

"You awake, my boy?" she asked groggily. Bean lifted his head, blinking several times. "Do you need to go out, or can we sleep more?"

Bean didn't move right away as he was still sleepy, but now that he was awake, he considered her question. He didn't have to go potty until she mentioned going outside; now he felt he should go potty. She would be upset if he had an accident. He woofed his response.

She sighed. "Okay, boy, give me a second."

Starr threw on her jacket and ran her fingers through her hair before slipping on her Crocs. She probably should have been completely dressed, but she didn't care. She was tired and hadn't had her morning cup of coffee. Thankfully, no one was up when they went downstairs and out the door. Once Bean was finished, she walked him around a little, hoping to release some of his morning energy.

"Come on, Bean, let's go back now. We might as well get ready for the day."

Once they were back in their room, Starr went about getting herself ready for the day, then got Bean his breakfast. Once he was settled in his morning nap, she headed downstairs to get some coffee. This time, when she made it down the stairs, she saw Nina and Monte visiting Tim and Sally.

"Good morning, everyone," she said as she walked over to the coffee pot.

"Everyone just loves the video from last night," Nina stated, enthusiastically.

Starr smiled. "I saw some of the comments," she replied, thinking that Nina was way too happy for this early in the morning.

"There are one hundred and seventy-two so far," Monte chimed in.

"Are you serious?" Starr shook her head in disbelief. There were eighty-nine when she turned off her notifications. "That's crazy." She then laughed. "They are all about Bean, aren't they?"

Nina nodded. "Oh, they love him. They want us to make another video."

"Of the two of us, or just Bean," she asked, raising an eyebrow. She already knew the answer.

"Both of you, of course," Nina answered before taking a sip of coffee. "Where is he, by the way?"

"He's taking his after-breakfast nap. If he doesn't, he will be crabby all day, and I don't want that as we explore Main Street," she replied.

"That's so cute that he needs a nap," Nina giggled.

Starr sat and visited. Apparently, she and Bean had been a big hit. Nina had shown her some of the funnier comments, all of which were about Bean. She was surprised no one said anything negative about her. She always assumed people were terrible in the comment sections.

"I suppose I should get my little man ready for the day. He is probably awake by now," she stated, glancing at the clock on the microwave.

"Have fun today, and take lots of pictures," Nina told her.

"I plan on it," Starr replied, walking to the sink. She quickly washed her cup and set it in the drainer. "See you guys later."

She had been chatting for over an hour. When she stepped into the room, Bean was sitting on the bed. He had a look of annoyance on his adorable face.

"Have you been waiting long?" she asked him, plopping on the bed. She ruffled his ears. "Mama was just visiting with our new friends."

He woofed at her. He had only been awake for a few minutes, but was a tad annoyed she wasn't there. He thought they were supposed to go somewhere today. That's what she had told him, or maybe that was the other day. He got his days confused sometimes.

"Let me get things together, and then we will go explore the area," she told him.

Once she had gathered his bag with his snack and travel water, she was ready to go. She put his harness on, clipped the leash to it, and they were ready to go. They hurried down the stairs, said a quick goodbye, and were off.

"It looks like it isn't too crowded yet," Starr observed as she pulled into the parking lot on Broadway.

She parked and stepped out of the car. The air felt nice. It was warm with a gentle breeze that moved her hair just slightly. She walked around to the passenger door to get Bean out. She slipped her wallet into the inside portion of his bag before placing the strap over her shoulder.

She looked down at Bean. "First stop, coffee. I saw there was one not far from this parking structure."

They walked the short distance to the coffee shop, which was literally right down the street. She didn't see any signs saying no dogs allowed, so she tightened Bean's leash. He looked up at her and knew the drill. Stay close, no pulling, and make no sounds.

"Welcome to Main Street Espresso," a cheerful lady behind the counter said.

Starr smiled and walked to the counter to look at the menu. There were the standard espresso drinks, which she always loved. That's when she noticed the special. It sounded interesting. It was called a Toasty Trio Latte with pistachio, almond, and cinnamon.

"The special sounds interesting. I'll try that, and a Spinach Breakfast Wrap with cheddar and bacon." She looked at Bean, who had that eager look on his face. "Would it be possible to get two eggs scrambled with no seasonings?"

She nodded. "We can do that."

"We're going to look around while we wait," Starr said with a smile.

After Starr paid, the woman asked, "Can I get your name for the order?"

"It's Starr."

She and Bean checked out the store. It reminded Starr of those old-fashioned stores, which of course made perfect sense. She picked up a Deadwood coffee cup, some local coffee, and various candies. By the time the woman called for Starr, she had a handful of items she was barely holding on to.

"I'll get these as well."

Once she paid, she gathered the bag of items as well as their food. She had seen a couple of tables and chairs outside and decided that's where they would eat. She found an open table and wrapped Bean's leash around her chair. She then set the small container of eggs on the ground for him.

"Enjoy," she said with a smile.

Of course, Bean went to town on his eggs and looked longingly at Starr, who was still eating her wrap and sipping her coffee. She would need to be sure to stop by the coffee shop before they headed back to the B&B. She reached down to pick up Bean's bowl.

"Did you enjoy your eggs?" she asked and got several grateful licks in return.

Starr set the bowl on the table and moved her chair slightly so she could see the activity on the street. Bean moved and positioned himself in front of her, observing his environment. The streets were getting full of people, in shorts and t-shirts with cameras around their necks. Deadwood was most assuredly a tourist town, but she liked it.

"How about we go for a walk?" she asked Bean who woofed his response. He was tired of sitting around.

"I think we should go this way," she said, looking to her right. "There is supposed to be one of the reenactments at two o'clock, which isn't that far from now. I'm sure there are things we can look at there."

Bean didn't understand most of what she had said, as she used too many words that he didn't know the meaning of. All he really got was that they were going somewhere. She started walking, so he did as well.

"Oh, look, I think that's Saloon No. 10. I've heard of that. Let me double-check to see if you can go in there." She pulled out her phone and smiled. "It says it's pet-friendly. You just can't be in the upstairs restaurant, but that's okay. Let's go check it out."

They strode across the street and entered the building. It was amazing to say the least. Ripe with all the features of an old west saloon. Of course, everyone loved Bean, who was being a perfect gentleman and reaping the rewards for that behavior.

"Can I offer your pup a treat?" a woman asked, dressed in an old-fashioned western dress.

"Sure, he'd never say no to a treat," Starr laughed.

The woman kneeled and smiled at Bean. "Do you want a treat?"

Bean barked his yes response. What was wrong with this woman? He obviously wanted a treat. He always wanted treats. She outstretched her hand to reveal a bone biscuit. He gobbled it up a little too quickly because now he was thirsty.

"He's such a good boy," she said, rising to her feet.

"Thanks," Starr replied, and then noticed the woman's name badge, "Rose. Bean loves all the attention he's been getting."

"I hope you have a wonderful day, ma'am, and you and Bean come see me again," she stated with a smile before walking away.

Starr couldn't help but notice there was sadness in her eyes. She wondered what that was about. She shook her head. She needed to stop doing that. She was always putting her nose into things, simply because she was curious. It was a bad habit she had been trying to break for years.

"Oh my gosh, Bean, this is so you!" she stated excitedly, picking up a hoodie. "Look, it has holes for your ears."

If Bean could sigh in annoyance, he would. The woman was obsessed with dressing him up. She brought a few of these hoodies to his nose. He knew she expected him to pick one, but on the plus side, if he did pick one, perhaps she would buy him some of those tasty snacks he could smell despite them being wrapped up.

He barked at one. "Perfect."

She tossed it on her shoulder and perused some of the squeaky toys, showing him a couple of them. He picked the one with the loudest squeak because why not? He bounced slightly when she reached the shelf with the treats on it. Now she was getting to the good stuff.

She glanced at him. "They have a lot of treats. We'll get a couple, okay?"

He barked once, just to let her know he agreed to this arrangement. Once they had selected a few, he trotted alongside her to the cashier and then out the door. They walked down the sidewalk for quite a while before she finally stopped.

"This should be where the re-enactment is."

There were already a lot of people around, so Starr found a nice shady spot for them to wait until the show started. The time flew by as Starr visited with people nearby, while others fawned over Bean. That corgi charm was no joke.

"It's about to start," someone nearby said, just as a couple of people walked up, dressed like cowboys.

"The Strange Tale of David Lunt," was announced.

Starr moved Bean close to her as they watched intently. Laughing at the antics of the performers. Apparently, David Lunt was accidentally shot in the forehead, the bullet exited the back of his head, and then he got up and walked away, only to die a few months later.

"That was fun," she said aloud to no one in particular. Once people started to filter away, she looked at Bean. "How about we chill here for a bit before we wander about again."

They relaxed in Outlaw Square. Bean drank his water and then took a nap on her lap, while Starr people watched. Forty minutes later, they were wandering down Main Street again, exploring shops and grabbing a bite to eat at Mustang Sally's. They then watched another shootout and the Boone May Altercation.

"I'm getting tired, how about you?" she asked Bean. "I want to do those pictures tomorrow, and maybe that Jack McCall thing as well."

Bean was indeed tired. They had been walking for a long time. He hadn't had his afternoon nap, and while she did get him a burger, he wasn't counting that as dinner. He wanted to go home and eat.

"How about we head back to the B&B and rest for the night," she said casually.

He barked his agreement. He sniffed the ground as they started walking back towards where the car was parked. There were so many different smells. Then something piqued his interest as they turned towards the parking structure. *What was that?* He wondered. He had to find out. He ran at full force towards the unusual smell.

"Bean," Starr yelled in a panic.

4
DISTURBING DISCOVERY

"Bean," Starr yelled in a panic.

She was in shock. Bean never took off like that. She chased after him, calling his name, but he didn't slow down. He ran behind a parked car, and the panic swelled. She ran as fast as she could, finally reaching the vehicle he had darted behind.

"What the..." She stopped suddenly, realizing she had tripped over a person. She got up quickly and grabbed Bean's leash.

"What's wrong with you, Bean?" she scolded.

He whimpered and looked over at the body, which made her look as well. He started barking at the man, maybe for tripping Starr, maybe to avoid getting in trouble himself. Perhaps it was a little of both. All he knew was that the man smelled funny.

"I'm sorry, mister," she said and then stopped.

At first, she thought maybe the man was drunk and passed out, but he didn't smell of enough alcohol to pass out that hard. Now that she was looking at him closely, she realized that he wasn't moving at all.

"Oh my gosh," she whispered as her free hand flew to her mouth.

She gently tapped the man with her foot and got no response. She took a deep breath and kneeled, bringing her fingers to his neck to see if he had a pulse. She pulled her hand away and tried to steady her breathing.

"I... I think he's dead," she said to Bean.

She stepped back and leaned against the car behind her. She breathed in and out several times before she pulled out her phone to call the emergency operator. Bean tried to sniff the man again, but she pulled him closer to her. She didn't want him anywhere near that dead man.

"There's a dead man behind a car near the Deadwood Parking Ramp," she said as calmly as she could.

The operator asked for more information and then said an officer would be there shortly. She couldn't go anywhere, so she kept staring at the dead man. There was something familiar about him, but she didn't dare move him to get a good look at his face.

"So much for a chill vacation," she grumbled as she stepped to the side of the vehicle.

She couldn't have waited more than five minutes when she heard sirens approaching. That was quicker than she expected. She supposed they didn't want a tourist tripping over a dead body. Oh wait!

"Ma'am," one of the officers said, walking up to her. "Can you tell me what happened?"

"My pup got loose, which he never does. He is well-trained and a good boy, but um, he got loose and ran over here. I ran to follow him, and well, we found him lying there," she glanced towards the dead man. "At first, I thought maybe he was drunk." She turned back to the officer. "Because you know, I can smell alcohol on him. But..." she paused uncomfortably. "He didn't move so I called 911."

"Do you know the man?" the officer asked.

She shook her head. "No, I'm on vacation. This is my first time in Deadwood."

He smiled. "Sorry, this had to ruin your trip."

She sighed as she turned towards an ambulance that had just arrived on the scene. Had this ruined her trip? She wasn't sure yet, but she had a great time up until this moment. She watched as the paramedic turned the man over.

"Hey, I think I have seen that man before," she stated, startled.

The officer turned and furrowed his brows. "One moment,' he said curtly as he walked over to his partner and started talking.

She nodded slightly. She remembered him from the re-enactment earlier in the day. That was surreal. She had never seen a dead body before, let alone one that was someone she had seen before. What were the odds of that?

"He's one of the actors," she blurted out.

The officer looked her way and nodded. "We know who he is."

"I don't know his name," she continued, more talking to herself than the police. "I just remember watching him act. He was funny."

"We need to verify his last show," the officers said to one another.

"Oh, I watched all of them today. He was only in the second shootout a few hours ago. I didn't see him in the last re-enactment," she offered.

They stared at her for a long minute before the one she had talked to earlier approached her. He gave her a warm smile.

"Thank you for your help, you are free to go," he told her nicely.

"Oh, really?" she asked, surprised. On all the cop shows she watched, they usually asked a lot more questions. "That's all you need from me?" she questioned.

"Yes, we are familiar with this individual."

The other officer approached. "It looks cut and dry. He has a reputation for drinking and fighting. Perhaps, he pushed the wrong person."

Starr tilted her head slightly, confused by their response to this man's death. "Does that mean you don't plan on investigating this?"

"No ma'am," the first officer told her. "We have full intention of investigating."

"Yes," the second officer interjected. "And we already have a couple of leads, based on people we know he has had problems with, in the past."

"I see," she responded unsatisfied with their responses to this man's death.

"I assure you, we will follow all leads," the first officer said, seeing her frustrated expression.

She nodded. "Could one of you call me with an updated status?" she asked, not wanting them to ignore the case.

The first officer smiled. "What number can I reach you at?"

Starr rattled off her number and made them read it back to her. She then waited until the ambulance drove off with the man before she and Bean headed to their vehicle. There was something about the casual way the police were treating this case that had her on edge. When she got in the car, she set her leftover food and souvenirs in the back seat and got Bean situated in his car seat.

"What did you think, boy?" she asked as she sat behind the wheel.

He tilted his head, really trying to understand what she wanted him to say. Not knowing exactly, he barked and hoped it would convey that he agreed with whatever she was thinking.

"Yeah, me too. I don't like how dismissive they seemed about the dead guy. I don't care who he is; he still deserves respect," she paused, her lips twisting slightly. "Unless he's a serial killer or something like that, but why would a serial killer be working as an actor in Deadwood?"

She looked at Bean, who was staring at her intently. She was riled up, and he figured it was about the guy who smelled funny. All he knew was that he wanted her to start the car so they could get back to the room and he could eat his dinner. He woofed and glanced at the steering wheel and then back at her.

She laughed. "Fine, obviously you aren't as interested in that man's death as I am." She turned the ignition and started to back out before saying, "But it is actually your fault for bringing me there in the first place," she quipped, only half joking.

She focused on the road as she drove back to the B&B. She could see that Monte and Nina were outside, under the large tree. Once she parked, and she and Bean were out of the car, Nina waved her over.

"Hmmm," she glanced at Bean. "Do we tell our new friends about the dead body?"

Starr saw Monte stand and help Nina up. She knew she had better walk over there before they came to her. She wasn't sure she wanted to have this conversation in the house and would rather be out in the open.

"How was your day?' Nina asked excitedly.

"It was interesting," Starr replied.

"Interesting in a good way or a bad way," Monte inquired curiously.

"I suppose both."

Nina grinned. "Oh, do tell!"

"Well, the day was a lot of fun. We watched the re-enactments, ate, and bought some souvenirs. You know, typical stuff."

"Sounds pretty typical," Monte agreed as Nina kneeled to give Bean attention.

Starr nodded and glanced down at Bean, who was being smothered with pets. "Yep, it was all perfectly normal until Bean made a disturbing discovery."

Nina stood back up. "What happened?"

"He took off, and I chased him. When I caught up to him, I tripped over a dead body," she stated matter-of-factly.

Nina and Monte looked at one another and then went back to Starr. "Are you serious? It was an actual dead body?" Nina exclaimed in shock.

"Yep, I'm pretty sure it was one of the actors from the re-enactments, but the police didn't tell me his name. In fact, they seemed kind of dismissive about the whole thing. I mean, honestly, someone died, and they were like oh, okay, no big deal. He was a drunk and got into fights, so he probably deserved it."

"We need to call the precinct and see if they have any information," Monte said to Nina.

Nina nodded before looking at Starr. "Are you okay? It would be normal to be a bit rattled. I think anyone would be."

"I don't know if I'm rattled or annoyed. I guess maybe both."

"That seems like an ordinary response to me," Nina told her with a cheery smile.

"Thanks, hey, I know you guys are going to call and get more details, but maybe don't put that on the blog. I don't know if the man's family has been notified, and I'd hate for it to look badly on the town."

Monte touched her shoulder. "Don't worry, we won't post anything until we know more."

Starr nodded. "Well, I'm going to get my things and head to the room. This guy is hungry," she said with a slight nod to Bean.

"We understand," Nina said, taking Monte's hand in hers. "If you are feeling up to it, come on down later, and we can have some coffee together."

"I'll do that after he eats and I get him settled." She glanced at Monte, who was on the phone already. "Let me know what you find out."

He nodded. "Will do."

Starr walked away and could hear Monte asking for information about a death that had happened earlier. Starr gathered their things from the car and walked into the house, hoping Tim and Sally weren't there. She didn't want to answer any more questions.

"How are you?" Sally asked, rushing to greet her and Bean. Tim followed close behind her.

"I'm fine," Starr answered, confused.

"We heard that someone was found dead down on Main Street. We knew you went there today," Sally said quickly. She was looking at Starr with wide eyes, waiting for an answer.

"Actually, Bean found the body," Starr replied somewhat reluctantly.

"He did, did he?" Tim stated with a smile.

Starr sighed and took a moment to explain everything that had happened. They listened intently, intrigued by what she was conveying to them. They were a little too intrigued for Starr's taste, but some people were like that. Especially those who are into macabre.

"What an exciting day," Sally said, shaking her head in disbelief.

"Yep, it sure was." Starr looked down, and Bean was staring at her. She needed to feed him. This was way past his dinner time. "I'm sorry, Sally, I need to get Bean upstairs. The poor boy is hungry."

"Oh, yes, yes, of course," she stated sheepishly and stepped out of the way.

Starr quickly got upstairs and released Bean from his halter and collar. He immediately went to his water bowl while Starr got his dinner ready. She set it down for him and then walked over to the bed to sort through their trinkets. She plopped on the bed, and moments later, Bean was up there with her.

"It was quite a day, wasn't it, boy?" she said, running her hand down the fur on his back.

She leaned back and sighed. She couldn't get her mind off the dead man, which was ridiculous since she didn't even know the man's name. She decided that she would go down later tonight, and hopefully Monte could weasel some information out of the police.

5
NOT SATISFIED

Starr woke with a start. Her phone was ringing. She rolled slightly, fully aware of the little fur ball lying beside her, and snatched her phone off the nightstand. She glanced at the number and furrowed her brows.

"Hello?"

"Am I speaking with Starr Kona?" the woman on the other end asked.

"Yes, this is Starr."

"We are calling regarding the incident yesterday and to advise you that we have someone in custody," the woman told her calmly.

"Wow, that was quick, and to be honest, I didn't think the officers would call me with an update," she stated and then laughed. "Then again, they didn't; you did. By the way, who are you?"

"My name is Officer Adams. I work with Officers Baker and Katz. They asked me to give you a call."

"Oh, I see. Well, thank you for calling. Do you know what happened yet?"

"I am not at liberty to talk about an ongoing case, but if there are any changes, I'm sure you will be getting a call back."

"Thank you," Starr stated before hanging up.

She lay back on the bed as Bean rested his head on her stomach. Her brain was moving a mile-a-minute. Was the case cut and dry like the officer implied yesterday, or were they taking shortcuts? She wasn't sure; all she knew was that she was not satisfied.

She looked at Bean, whose eyes were open. "Maybe we should go and do a little snooping of our own."

Bean sat up. He heard go, which meant it was time to get up and get ready. Of course, now that he was up, he realized he needed to go outside. She picked up on his cues immediately. She got his leash and then darted down the stairs. As she went by, she saw Tim and Sally talking in the kitchen. She was saying something urgently while Tim was shaking his head.

"None of your business," Starr mumbled to herself as they exited the front door.

While Bean was doing his business, Starr was deciding on the plan for the day. Logically, she knew she should do nothing, but she couldn't help herself. She was an innately curious person, especially when there was a mystery to be solved.

"I heard they arrested someone," Nina said, offering her a cup of coffee when she and Bean walked through the door.

"That's what Officer Adams told me this morning," Starr replied.

"Officer Adams is a good one," Sally interjected. "She grew up down the hill."

Starr nodded, not sure what to say. "I'm going to go up and feed, Bean. See everyone in a bit."

Starr took Bean upstairs and got his food together. She then changed clothes, putting on one of her new Deadwood shirts. She thought maybe if she looked like a tourist, she might be able to gather more information because performers were taught to be nice to tourists and answer questions. At least, that was what she was hoping for.

Starr and Bean stayed around the B&B for the rest of the morning. She didn't think she needed to leave as early as she did yesterday. While visiting, she had gathered some information from Nina and Monte. Monte had found out the man's name was Benjamin Dawes, but everyone called him Benny. He was indeed an actor and had been dating a local girl, but his source did not reveal her name. Only that she worked in town. By the afternoon, Starr was ready to leave.

"I think I'm going to go grab Bean and head on back to Main Street. Hopefully, no more dead bodies appear," she stated with a chuckle.

"Let's hope not," Nina laughed in return.

"You should check out that outlaw square, see if anyone is talking about what happened," Monte stated eagerly.

"Monte, stop, let her have fun. We'll go check it out later, after people have been drinking," she assured him.

"And tongues are loosened," he replied with an exaggerated wink.

"Exactly," Nina grinned and then looked at Starr. "You and Bean have a wonderful time."

"Thanks, I'm sure we will."

Once upstairs, she changed Bean into his new hoodie, and they gathered their things. She made sure to take him out before they headed down to Main Street. She first grabbed a coffee to go, then scheduled their pictures to be taken later in the day, and then wandered a bit until they ended up at Outlaw Square.

"Where to go, where to go," she mumbled as she scanned the environment.

She settled on a spot near the gazebo so that she had a bird's eye view of the entire square and could see if any of the actors came around. It didn't take her long to notice a woman talking to a man. He seemed upset, and she was on the verge of tears.

"Well, that's interesting," Starr stated out loud.

The man walked away in a huff. Starr watched him, and when he approached a group of tourists, his demeanor changed. He was now in character. Her eyes turned back to the woman who was leaning against the wall, trying to gather herself.

"Bean," she said. He looked up at her. "Do you see that woman over there?" she asked, and saw him look in the direction she was looking. He saw several people over there, so he hoped she'd be more specific. "I'm going to walk nearby and drop your leash, then I want you to go to the woman."

Starr took a deep breath and stood up. She walked a short distance to where the woman was. Luckily, she could see inside the building and pretended to be searching for someone. Meanwhile, she casually dropped Bean's leash.

"Do your thing, boy," she whispered.

She turned just as the woman bent down to pet him. He was nuzzling against her hand and saturating her with his corgi magic. He had a way of doing that. People let down their guard with him. She had noticed that once at a company event. He had approached a woman who had isolated herself. When Starr had come over to tell him to stop bothering the woman, she had cried and told Starr her whole life story.

"Bean, you naughty boy, stop bothering this poor woman," she pretended to scold.

"No, no, he is fine. He's such a sweet boy," the woman exclaimed.

"Are you okay?" Starr asked, seeing she was trying not to cry.

"I'm sorry. It's been a rough day for me," she shook her head. "I shouldn't be telling you any of this. It's very unprofessional. Please excuse me."

She started to rise, but Starr stopped her. "You can't work in this condition. Come with me."

The woman stared for a moment and then followed Starr away from the crowd. They stopped when there were no more prying eyes on them. The woman kneeled and started petting Bean again.

"Is this about the man who was arguing with you earlier?" When she didn't respond, Starr added. "If it is, I can find him and have Bean nip at his ankles."

The woman chuckled and stood up. "No, that's my brother."

"Oh, well, yeah, I probably shouldn't have Bean nip at him then," she laughed, knowing she would never do that in the first place. She was simply trying to break the ice.

"He's angry at me for being so upset about a man he didn't approve of," she stated with a shrug.

"You are a grown woman, so he really doesn't have a say in such things," Starr commented, becoming more annoyed with her brother.

"That's true." The woman looked down and sighed.

"My name is Starr, and this, of course, is Bean. What's your name?"

"Abigail."

"So, what's wrong with the man you are dating?" Starr asked curiously.

"He used to be sort of a troublemaker." She scrunched her brows together and looked at Starr. "He used to drink and get in fights, but he's not like that anymore. He was so kind and treated me so well." Tears started to trickle down her face.

"What do you mean, was?" Starr inquired, worried about where this was going.

"He died yesterday," she stated sadly.

"Oh my, is that the man killed by the parking garage?" she asked tentatively.

"Yes, how do you know that?"

She looked at Abigail's distraught face. "Bean found him. We're the ones who called the police."

The woman grabbed Starr's arms. "Do you know what happened to him?"

Starr shook her head. "No. I... I didn't see anything. We were leaving when Bean found him." Abigail released Starr's arms and leaned against the wall, defeated. "Do you know what happened to him?" Starr asked her.

"No."

There was a long silence. Starr wasn't sure if she should say anything, but honestly, she felt sorry for the girl. She had lost her boyfriend, and she couldn't even get support from her own brother.

"The police said they have someone in custody," Starr offered.

"Yeah, I heard that too, but he didn't do it," Abigail said sadly, looking to the ground.

"How do you know?"

"Because Jax and Benny settled their beef long ago." She looked at Starr, and there was sadness in her eyes. "As I said, he was a different man now. He was trying his best to make peace with everyone he felt he had wronged during his drinking days. He didn't want that life to keep following him around."

"Was he doing the steps or some other program?" Starr asked.

"Yes," she answered with a quick nod. "Benny went to meetings a couple of times a week. That's where I thought he was going yesterday. He seemed kind of upset when he told me he needed a meeting, so I said that it was fine and to come get me when he was done. I kissed him goodbye, and that's," she stopped as tears streaked her face. "That's the last I saw of my sweet Benny."

"I'm so sorry, Abigail," Starr said, gently touching her shoulder. "How long had you two been together?"

"Our six-month anniversary would have been next week," she stated before grabbing onto Starr and crying fiercely.

Starr held Abigail for several minutes, letting her cry it out. She felt terrible for her. Everyone seemed to be judging Benny on his mistakes, rather than the changes he made. He didn't deserve to die, and Abigail didn't deserve to feel so heartbroken right now.

"Thank you," Abigail said, pulling away from Starr. "I appreciate you listening. Most people are avoiding me."

"You're welcome, and I'm sorry people are avoiding you. They probably don't know what to say."

She nodded. "I guess so." She looked at her phone and sighed. "I better go. My shift starts soon." She took a deep breath before kneeling and petting Bean. "Thank you for finding my Benny."

As she walked away, Starr looked down at Bean. "We are very good at info gathering, aren't we?"

He barked his agreement and then followed alongside Starr as they passed several stores until they reached Woody's Wild West Photography. He waited patiently as Starr talked.

"Can he wear a bandana?" she asked.

"Oh yes, we can do that. It would be adorable," the woman at the counter said gleefully. "Have you decided on what you want to wear?"

"I think so."

Starr walked over to several dresses, selecting one, and then picking up the shotgun. She wasn't sure why she wanted to have one in the picture, but thought it would look so cool. She changed clothes and put the bandana around Bean's neck. The woman then led her to the photographer.

"Are you ready?" the photographer asked.

"Yes, we are," she exclaimed happily. "I've always wanted to do something like this."

He smiled. "We get that a lot."

They spent the next thirty minutes posing in different ways, with different backgrounds. Bean was a good sport about it, but did start to get annoyed by the end. Once they were done, they were told to come back in an hour to retrieve their pictures. Starr couldn't wait to see them.

6

TRIAL... AND ERROR

Starr sat with Bean as they waited at Mustang Sally's Bar & Grill. It seemed to be the go-to place to eat. Starr ordered their breaded steak tips for herself and a plain hot dog for Bean. She knew they would be late today because they were going to watch the trial of Jack McCall.

"Here you go, ma'am, enjoy," the waitress said, setting their food on the table.

Starr reached for Bean's bag, pulling out his food bowl and a small baggie that had his evening meal in it. She poured the food in the bowl and then carefully cut up Bean's plain hot dog, mixing it with his dry food.

"Here ya go, boy." She set the bowl on the ground for him. "Don't eat too fast."

She grinned. It was too late. He was already going to town on those hot dog pieces mixed in. Starr ate in silence as her mind pondered what she had learned already. Abigail was a sweet girl, and Starr wanted to believe her account of things. However, she was a girl in love, and sometimes love clouds the truth.

"Is everything okay?" the waitress asked with concern.

Apparently, Starr had been holding a piece of steak on a fork for a while. She hadn't noticed. She had been fixated on remembering everything that Abigail had told her that she had forgotten to eat.

"Oh geez, I'm sorry. Got lost in my thoughts. Yes, everything is wonderful," she assured the waitress.

Once she was gone, Starr started to eat. She was determined to find out more about Benny and what happened to him. She decided to call the police station after they picked up their pictures. She was curious if the man in custody had been released already.

"You okay, boy?" she asked when Bean was nudging her leg. He licked his lips. "Oh, sorry, sweetheart, let me get you some water."

Once Bean was settled and she had paid for their meal, they headed back to the picture place. It turned out that Starr loved every single picture they took and bought the set. She couldn't wait to take them home. As they stepped out of the store, she decided to go a little out of the way so she could call the police station again.

"Hi, this is Starr Kona. I spoke with Officer Adams this morning," she stated to the operator.

"One moment," the operator said before putting her on hold.

She looked at Bean. "I hope our information from Abigail can help them."

"Hello, this is Officer Baker. How can I help you?" he stated curtly.

"Oh, hi," she responded quickly, surprised by his tone. "I was calling to check the status of the case and relay some information."

"Ma'am, there is no need for concern," he stated somewhat condescendingly. "The case is closed. Our suspect confessed."

"Wait, what?" This completely surprised her.

"Yes, he admitted guilt, and is currently being booked," the officer continued.

"Oh, okay," she paused before adding. "I had wanted to tell you that I spoke with the deceased girlfriend, Abagail, and she told me that the man arrested didn't have any problems with Benny anymore. In fact, she said they settled their beef a long time ago. Why would he want to kill him?" she rambled on. "I mean, that doesn't seem to fit the narrative."

"I'm not sure what to say to that other than I can't go into the exact details of the case, ma'am, but I assure you it is solved. I hope you enjoy the rest of your vacation," he finished quickly and hung up.

Starr stared at her phone in disbelief. "Damn, that was kind of rude."

Starr leaned against the wall, holding onto her bag of pictures, wondering about everything. Nothing seemed to fit right. Abigail had been so sure of the fact that Jax was innocent. Could she have been wrong? That, of course, was completely possible. She knew she should let it go, but she felt like she couldn't. She needed answers.

"Okay, Bean, this is the plan. We go to trial, and then afterwards we see if we can find Abigail." She looked down at him. "Sound good?"

He woofed his response, and they headed towards Saloon No. 10 for the capture of Jack McCall. She was hoping to possibly catch Abigail there, but when they entered, it was packed with people. Even if she could find her, they wouldn't be able to talk.

"Bean, let's find a spot out of the way of everyone," she stated as she nudged her way inside.

Within thirty minutes, Jack McCall was captured. Starr couldn't help but notice that one of the men who had captured Jack was the man Abigail had argued with earlier, her brother. If she couldn't talk to Abagail, perhaps she could talk to him.

"Folks, the trial will begin in the Eagle Bar, just down the road," someone announced.

Starr followed the flow of people out of the Saloon and down the street. People were already rushing towards the front benches, but she found a seat towards the back of the room. This way, she and Bean could relax without people crowding them.

"Today, we begin the trial of Crooked Nose Jack McCall, who viciously murdered Wild Bill Hickok. Now we need some volunteers to serve on our jury."

Starr laughed as the jury was selected; they obviously had a type: teenagers and young adults. She had gotten a kick out of every reenactment she'd seen so far. This was no exception. She laughed throughout the production, but every so often she would catch a glance at Abigail's brother. Every time she did, he looked angry. She wasn't sure if that was part of the role he was playing or if it was something else, but she was determined to find out.

"Your dog is so well behaved," the woman next to her said, bringing Starr out of her thoughts.

"Thank you, he's a good boy," she replied, bending to give him some head scratches.

Once the show was over, she kept an eye on her brother. If he left, she wanted to be able to follow him and ask a couple of questions. He was talking to guests and taking pictures. When it looked like people were filtering out, she caught up to him.

"Excuse me, could I get a picture?" she hollered to get his attention.

He turned and smiled. "Of course, ma'am." One of his friends came over and took a couple of pictures of them. "Hope you enjoyed the show."

"I did, it was amazing."

He smiled and nodded slightly. "Ma'am," he said in the form of a goodbye and started to walk away.

"Hey, I wanted to ask you something," Starr yelled quickly.

"How can I help you?"

"You're Abigail's brother, right?" She asked when he returned to her.

"How do you know my sister?" he asked, his tone and vocal inflection were out of his cowboy persona.

"We met earlier today. She seemed very nice," Starr told him politely.

He nodded. "She is."

Starr laughed slightly. "She didn't tell me your name, though."

"It's Jake," he replied reluctantly, but he was back in character again. "You said you wanted to ask me something?"

"Yes, so, um, how do I say this?" she stated, trying to sound like some confused, non-threatening person.

"I find it's best to just spit it out?" he stated, trying not to laugh at her.

"Why were you yelling at her earlier?" she asked bluntly, throwing him off.

"Excuse me?"

"When I saw you, you were yelling at her. She said it was because you didn't understand why she was upset about Benny's death."

"That's none of your business," he said, completely out of character again.

"I was just curious, because it was Bean and I who found Benny's body. They arrested someone already, but Abagail said they didn't have a problem with one another, and I thought I'd ask you what you thought since you seemed to have an opinion on Benny."

Jake glared at her. "Why are you trying to do the cop's job? If Jax admitted to doing it, then he did."

"Okay, I get that, but I wondered why he did that. What was your issue with Benny?"

He stared at her, dumbfounded. Starr could see the anger on his face. His neck was starting to get heated, as evidenced by the flush of red forming there. She could almost see his brain processing what to do next. He was in costume, and she was a guest. He couldn't very well yell at her, not without consequences, so she waited.

He took a deep breath. "I have no real opinion about him at all," he finally said.

Starr laughed. "Yeah, not buying that. You were arguing with your sister about him instead of comforting her about the loss of her boyfriend. That tells me you had a very strong opinion of him."

He glanced around the room and saw a few people watching their exchange. "Look, Benny was a drunk, and my sister was too good for him. Do I care that he is dead? No, I don't. Is that all?"

"Wow, seriously?"

He shrugged. "Look, I need to go; my shift ends soon, and I have to get out of my costume."

"Yeah, thanks." He started to walk away, and before she realized it, she was speaking again. "They say that when you play a bad guy long enough, you become one. Do you think that's true?"

He stopped and looked over his shoulder. He then walked over to her and leaned down to look her in the eyes. Immediately, Bean started to growl. He didn't like the way that man was staring at Starr. He moved forward to try to stop the man's movement.

"I didn't kill him, if that's what you are trying to insinuate," he muttered through clenched teeth.

"I'm not insinuating anything," she stated, not backing down. At that moment, Bean nipped at his boot.

Jake looked down and stepped back. "Benny burned a lot of bridges and had a shit ton of enemies. I wasn't the only one who disliked him."

"I see. Well, who else hated him?" she asked.

"Like I said before, why do you care? Someone already confessed to killing him," he answered, clearly annoyed that she wouldn't drop it.

"I care because I think they have the wrong person in jail, and the cops don't seem to want to figure it out," she replied angrily.

"That's because the man who did it is already in jail, they don't need to investigate any further," he stated, bewildered by her.

"I think if I felt they actually investigated in the first place, I could accept that, but they don't seem to be interested in finding out why?" She was flustered by the situation.

He sighed and relaxed his stance. "I get it, but you should save your sympathy for someone who deserves it."

"Ouch, that's cruel," she gasped.

"I call it as I see it," he replied nonchalantly. "Now, if you are done accusing me of murder, I need to go."

"Yeah," she replied with her own sigh. "Thanks for answering my questions."

"You're welcome. Enjoy your vacation, do tourist things," he stated with a chuckle.

"I have been doing tourist things," she replied with conviction and waved her free hand around the room.

"And we thank you for that."

As he started to walk away again, she blurted out, "Can you give me a name?"

He stopped walking and looked at her in confusion. "A name?" he questioned.

"Yes, the name of someone else I could talk to. You said Benny had a lot of enemies," she reminded him.

"You don't give up, do you?" he asked, flustered by her tenacity.

She laughed and then shrugged. "Nope, not in my vocabulary."

He placed his hands on his belt, likely trying to decide if he should give her any other names. Starr watched him take an aggravated breath, glance around the room, and step towards her again.

"Why don't you talk to Rose? She was his last girlfriend before Abby. She works at Saloon No. 10, but don't tell her I sent you over there; she'll have my hide. Now I really do have to go." He waved his arm to show her that they were the last ones in the building. "And you should head home."

"Thank you."

He nodded and walked away from her. She quickly followed out the door. She had a plan now. She couldn't talk to Rose today, but she would tomorrow. If she remembered correctly, she was the one they met yesterday. She liked Bean, which means she had an in.

7
ROSE COLORED

Starr pulled up to the Stout Inn close to ten in the evening. She was tired but saw lights on in the house. That didn't surprise her. It seemed Monte and Nina always stayed up late. She took Bean potty before going into the house and walking into the living room.

"How was it?" Nina asked with a smile.

"It was great," Starr agreed. "Oh, check these out." She handed over the bag with the pictures.

There was a lot of oohing and aahing as they looked at each picture. She would have to find a place to hang all of those up. She looked down at Bean, who had fallen asleep at her feet. It was a long day for him, but she wanted to talk to them about what she had learned today.

"These are amazing," Nina said, handing the package back to her.

"Thanks."

"What's up?" Monte asked, picking up on her cues.

"So today, I had three interesting conversations. The first was with Abigail, she was Benny's girlfriend, and then after the pictures, I called the cops, and they told me that Jax confessed."

"That's what I was told when I called today," Monte agreed.

"But you see, Abigail said that Jax had no problems with Benny, that they had worked out their past issues. When I told the police, they didn't think it was important."

"That happens sometimes," Monte told her. "Cops get the confession, and then they move on to the next case."

"Yeah, but it doesn't make sense why he would do that if he had no problem with him. I mean, what he just gets it in his head to kill someone, that's a big leap," she said, looking between them.

"Do you think this Abigail person was being honest with you?" Monte asked.

Starr nodded. "She was very sincere and distraught at Benny's death."

"I agree, it is weird," Monte admitted.

"Who was the last conversation with?" Nina asked.

"Abigail's brother, Jake. When I first met Abigail, Jake was arguing with her, so I decided to see if he would talk to me."

"And he did?" Nina asked, shocked.

"Yep, at first he didn't want to, but he did," she laughed and shook her head, remembering his reaction to her. "Let me just explain it all because I really want some feedback to decide my next steps."

"Hit us," Monte stated with a laugh.

Starr spent the next thirty minutes talking to Nina and Monte about everything that transpired. They agreed that it sounded fishy and encouraged her to talk to Rose, especially since she had spoken to her before. They even gave her tips on how to approach the topic, which she was very thankful for.

"I think I'd better get this little man to bed," she said, just as Bean looked up at her with sleepy eyes.

Nina smiled happily. "He looks so exhausted. It's adorable."

"I'll see you guys tomorrow."

"We'll probably be out by the time you leave," Monte told her.

"Where are you off to?"

"Devils Tower," Nina interjected. "But we'll be back in the evening so you can tell us all the juicy details."

Starr laughed and nodded. "Will do, and you guys have fun tomorrow."

"We will," Nina replied.

Starr looked down at Bean. He was waiting for her to stand up so that they could go upstairs and to bed. He trotted beside her, but without the usual pep in his step. The stairs seemed to stretch forever. He then stared at the bed. It seemed so high.

"I got you," she told him, lifting him onto the bed.

As she walked to the bathroom, she could hear Sally and Tim talking in hushed tones. It seemed urgent. They immediately stopped when they saw her. She smiled at them as Tim walked to their bedroom door and shut it, then she heard the hushed voices again.

"Why is everyone in this town strange?" she wondered aloud.

The next morning, Sally and Tim did not mention what had happened the night before. That was perfectly fine for Starr as she didn't want to discuss it. As expected, Monte and Nina had left earlier. She had a couple of cups of coffee, took care of Bean, and was off to Main Street again. She'd be going home tomorrow, so she hoped she could get some answers today. Even if the police weren't interested in the truth, she was.

"Have a great day," she said to Tim and Sally as she and Bean walked out the front door.

She heard them say to have a great day as well, but she didn't respond. Her day was going to involve sleuthing. She just hoped that Rose would be working today and that she would be open to talking to her about her ex.

"You ready, Bean?" she asked as she got in the car. "I'm really going to need your charm today. Rose liked you a lot, and I think if you are your chaotic and loveable self, it will lower her defenses."

She had said a lot of words that Bean didn't understand at all. All he knew was charm. That meant to nuzzle up to people and be super friendly, and he could not nibble or bite. If he did that, he always got treats. So whatever else she said, he was willing.

"You have no idea what I said, do you?" she asked, grinning. He woofed, which confirmed her suspicion.

They drove down the hill on their last full day in Deadwood. She had enjoyed her time, even though she spent all of it on Main Street trying to solve a crime the police said was already solved. Maybe it was all those old detective shows her grandma made her watch that were spewing this craziness, but she would figure it out.

"First stop, coffee and then Saloon No. 10, and we pray that Rose is there," she told him when they parked.

As they had planned, they stopped at Main Street Espresso. She ordered whatever special they had and breakfast. Bean gobbled up his scrambled eggs and was ready to go. He had a job to do that involved treats, but he had to be patient and wait for Starr to be done.

"Alright, boy, let's go see if we can find Rose," she told him.

They walked across the street to Saloon No. 10. It amazed her that almost everything going on was near these areas. She was now quite the expert on where things were on this street. She looked around the room and didn't see her immediately.

"Dang it, I don't see her anywhere. Maybe she's off today."

Out of nowhere, she heard. "Oh my, you brought him back." She kneeled and gave him pets.

"It's our last day here, and he wanted to come by and say hello," Starr stated cheerfully.

"Well, how sweet of you," Rose told him, digging out a bone from her little fanny pack.

Starr laughed as Bean scarfed down the bone. "Do you just keep bones in there all day?"

She grinned. "Everyone knows I love animals, so when one comes in, they send me. So, yep, I have a pocketful of bones."

"That's a great job to have."

"I like it, and I get to pet all these amazing puppers," she said in a sing-song voice to Bean.

"It's the one really great thing about our trip," Starr said, laying the trap.

Rose stood up. "You didn't enjoy your stay here." She seemed upset at that thought.

"Yes, I did for the most part, unfortunately, Bean found," she looked around and whispered, "A dead body."

Rose brought both hands to her mouth to stifle the gasp she had just made. "You guys are the ones who found Benny?"

Starr nodded. "Wait, did you know him?"

Rose looked around quickly to see if anyone was watching them, and then grabbed Starr's arm, pulling her towards a back area of the store. There was a small hallway that led to a room, which Starr assumed was a staff break room.

"Are we alright to be back here?" Starr asked with concern. She didn't want to get the girl in trouble; she just wanted intel.

Rose nodded. "Yes, it's fine, no one should bother us here."

"That's good. How did you know Benny?" Starr asked softly.

"We dated for over a year," Rose replied, looking at her hands, which she was wringing.

"What kind of guy was he?"

Rose looked over at her strangely. "What do you mean by that?"

"I'm sorry, I just heard he was kind of a troublemaker, and you seem so nice and chill, I can't imagine you with someone like that."

Rose stared at her for a moment before talking. "Yes, he was a bit of a troublemaker. He was mostly very protective of those he cared about and hated mean people."

"Mean people?" Starr questioned. This was another perspective on Benny that she did not expect. Who was this guy?

"I just mean that he hated bullies. The people he got in fights with were generally people being mean to others. And before you ask, yes, he was a drinker, but you know everyone is here."

"His girlfriend Abigail told me that he was sober and going to meetings," she offered.

Rose scrunched her brows together slightly at the mention of Abigail. That was interesting. It seemed like maybe the beef was between Abigail and Rose. Rose looked away for a moment; it appeared she was trying to collect her thoughts.

"I'm not saying he didn't have his problems, because he did, but he wasn't a bad person and certainly did not deserve to die," she finally said with conviction.

"I agree." Starr touched her hand. When she looked over at her, she continued. "Did you know this person, Jax, that they arrested?"

Rose nodded. "Yes, he and Benny didn't always agree on things."

"The police told me that he admitted to killing Benny. Do you think he was capable of that?"

She shook her head. "No, Jax was a follower. I can't imagine he would just do that."

"Maybe it was self-defense or even an accident," Starr offered as an explanation.

"An accident I could see, but self-defense no." She shook her head. "Benny would never fight someone who couldn't defend themselves, and Jax certainly couldn't defend himself."

Starr watched her carefully for a moment before speaking. "According to Abigail, Benny told her that he needed a meeting. Are there some local places he would go to? She said he was upset but didn't say why."

She rolled her eyes slightly and caught herself. "I guess you'd have to ask her about why he was upset, as far as meetings, yeah, there are some around."

Starr nodded. She could check those out, but knew they were confidential and that no one there would talk to her anyway, so there was no point in doing that. She looked at Rose, who was picking at her fingernails.

"Do you and Abigail have some kind of history?" Starr asked, which caused Rose to look over at her. "You seem annoyed anytime her name is mentioned."

Rose leaned back in a defensive posture. "I don't trust her at all."

"Oh, I see. Is there a reason for that?"

She narrowed her eyes slightly. "Why are you interested in all of this?"

Starr shrugged. "I don't know. I guess finding Benny makes me a little attached to the case and to be honest, very curious about him."

She nodded. "Well, let's just say that Benny and I broke up because he cheated on me."

Starr nodded. "Is it safe to assume that he cheated with Abigail?"

Rose nodded. The picture was becoming clearer. While Benny was a drinker, his fighting seemed more justified in the sense of defending people who couldn't defend themselves, but he was a cheater, and that was a bad mark on him, at least for Starr, and apparently Rose as well, but did that warrant murder?

8

MISTAKEN

Starr sighed slightly. "I'm sorry I troubled you. Rose. It must be hard reconciling being frustrated and angry with someone who did something bad, and then that person later has an untimely death."

Rose looked at her curiously. "Benny and I were friends. Not at first, of course, because I was angry with him. I couldn't believe he would do that to me, but we started talking again a few months ago. I've known him a long time and missed our conversations."

Starr chuckled nervously at the thought of someone she was dating talking to their ex. "You guys talking again didn't cause problems with him and Abigail, did it?" she asked tentatively.

She shrugged. "I don't know. I guess maybe. We didn't really talk about Abigail that much, and it wasn't like we were hanging out or anything. We would just say hi, you know, in passing, or he would ask how my family was doing, stuff like that."

"I get it. That makes sense."

"He wasn't trying to get back together with me if that's what you are thinking," Rose stated adamantly.

Starr shook her head. "No, I wasn't thinking that. I was mostly thinking how awkward that might be for both of you, but now I see you guys managed it very well."

"I'd like to think so. We aren't teens who block everyone associated with their ex," she stated with a laugh.

This caused Starr to laugh as well. Heck, she knew some adults in her office who still acted that way after a breakup. She looked down at Bean, who was resting at her feet. She then glanced at the clock on the wall. They had been back there for quite some time.

"I suppose I've bothered you long enough," Starr said, which made Rose look at the clock as well. "Thank you for the visit and for being so friendly to the two of us." She stood up and smiled at her. "I wish you nothing but the best, Rose."

Rose stood as well and hugged her. "Thank you for caring about Benny."

Starr nodded as she stepped out of the hug. "Have a wonderful rest of your shift."

"I'll walk you out."

"Oh, that's not necessary. I can find my way," she stated, feeling that she had already taken up way too much of Rose's time.

Rose grinned. "Hey, if they see me with a customer, I won't get in trouble, so you'd be helping me out."

"Ah, well, in that case, please, lead the way," she told her happily.

Rose walked Starr and Bean to the front door and stepped outside. She kneeled again, reaching her hand into her fanny pack, pulling out another bone. He finished it quickly and got on his hind legs to give her kisses, which made her laugh and brought a much-needed smile to her face. That corgi charm is no joke!

Rose stood. "You two have a safe trip home tomorrow, and don't forget us."

Starr laughed. "Yeah, Deadwood has been quite the adventure, I won't be forgetting anytime soon. Thanks again, and I'm sorry for your loss."

Rose nodded and walked back into the Saloon. As Starr was getting ready to walk away, she noticed someone waving at her. It was Abigail. Now, while she was frustrated to learn that Abigail and Benny had cheated on Rose, she was still Benny's current girlfriend, and she wanted to let her know what the police had told her.

"Come on, Bean, let's go say hello to Abigail," she told him as they crossed the street.

"Hey there, you two," Abigail said, happily, giving Starr a hug.

"Hey there to you. How's your day going?" Starr asked, not wanting to get into the nitty-gritty immediately.

"It's been good so far." She glanced towards Saloon No. 10 and then back at Starr. "I didn't know you knew Rose as well."

"Oh, we met yesterday." Starr looked at Bean, "She gave my little man some treats."

Abigail laughed. "Yes, she does that, doesn't she?"

"She seems nice," Starr added, wondering how Abigail would respond to that.

"I suppose she is." Abigail looked around before she whispered. "She doesn't like me, though."

"Oh, really? Why's that?" Starr asked, already knowing the answer.

"She and Benny used to be a thing, but he left her to go out with me. I think she's a bit jealous," she stated with a shrug and a cocky smile.

"Ouch!" Starr replied.

"I'm not saying that to be mean, I was just a better fit for Benny, and he knew it."

"That happens sometimes," Starr said uneasily. She didn't want to have this conversation with her. She liked them both.

"Hey, have you heard anything else about Benny's case?" Abigail asked, effectively changing the subject.

"The police didn't call you?" Starr asked, puzzled by that revelation. She thought the police usually notified the boyfriend or girlfriend of the deceased.

"No, why?"

"I talked to the officer yesterday, and they told me that Jax confessed to killing Benny," she informed.

"Really?"

Starr noticed that Rose's tone said shock, but her body posture said something else. "Yeah, I was kind of surprised, based on what you told me the other day."

"I guess Jax must have said something to set Benny off, and Jax had to defend himself."

This surprised Starr because the other day she was saying how sweet Jax was and that he and Benny had no problems with one another, and now she was accepting that Jax murdered Benny in cold blood. There was something off about this.

"I mean I guess that is a possibility," Starr agreed and then added, "It kind of goes against what Rose thought about the killing."

"You talked to Rose about Benny's murder?" She asked, annoyed

Starr felt Abigail's agitation. "Well, yes, I mentioned it briefly, and she asked to talk to me, so we went into the breakroom and visited for a bit about Benny and what he was like."

Abigail was staring at her in an unusual way. Was she upset that she had disclosed information to her? Rose had a right to know as well. She knew Benny, dated him before Abigail had. Rose and Benny seemed like they were on speaking terms. What was wrong with Starr telling Rose what she knew?

"I'm sorry, are you upset with me?" Starr asked, confused by her behavior.

Abigail fixed her expression and shook her head. "No, of course not. I'm just surprised she wanted to talk about Benny."

Starr shrugged, unsure how to answer that. In all honesty, she didn't like how this conversation was going. Abigail seemed to be all over the place. Starr had relayed her information, and now she wanted to head out and try to enjoy the rest of her day.

"Well, I guess that's it for the case," she finally said. "It's our last day, so we are going to wander a bit and then maybe try to see something other than Main Street," she finished with a laugh.

Abigail quickly grabbed her arm before Starr could respond. "Come with me."

"Um, okay," she replied as Abigail brought her to the back of the building.

"I'm sorry, I didn't mean to grab you like that," she stated in hushed tones.

"What's going on, Abigail?" She asked, moving away from her.

"I need to know exactly what Rose told you?" Abigail asked urgently.

"Nothing really, just that she dated Benny before and that they were friends," Starr answered, confused by Abigail's behavior.

Abigail laughed. "They were not friends anymore. She kept trying to sabotage our relationship. Tried to come between us more than once."

"Really?" Starr asked in shock.

That was not the impression she had gotten from Rose. Had she been mistaken about Rose all along? She came off as kind and sensitive, but maybe she was heartless. Of course, Abigail came off as being totally kind as well. This was a mess she needed to get out of.

Finally, Starr responded with, "Oh, wow, that kind of surprises me. She seemed pretty chill about your relationship with Benny."

Abigail rolled her eyes. "It's not like she would advertise that she was trying to steal him from me," Abigail huffed out angrily.

"Well, she didn't mention anything like that to me," Starr assured her, wanting to de-escalate the situation as fast as she could.

Abigail started tapping her fingers against her lips, clearly upset. Her brow scrunched together as if she were trying to solve a difficult puzzle. Starr was very confused by her behavior. The only thing she could think of was that Abigail was sensitive about Rose and possibly jealous. Or the other way around. She opened her mouth to tell Abigail that she and Bean were going to head out, but Abigail started mumbling to herself in an unnerving way.

"I don't know why Jake would send her to talk to Rose. That makes no sense at all. What possible reason would he have to do that? I thought he was on my side. He's supposed to be on my side. Not hers."

Starr gently tapped Abigail's shoulder to get her attention. "If it's any consolation, I sort of forced him to give me another name to talk to about Benny," Starr offered as an explanation.

"Why would you do that?" Her expression was riddled with sadness.

Starr hesitated for a moment before speaking. "I was kind of upset that the police were just taking Jax's confession without investigating further to see if it lined up. You said he was sweet and had no beef with Benny anymore, so it just didn't make any sense to me. I wanted to talk to someone else, just to see if I could wrap my head around it. Jake finally just told me to talk to Rose, so I did, and after what Rose said, I'm even more confused about what happened."

"And what did Rose tell you about Jax?" Abigail asked coolly.

Starr wasn't sure what was happening. "Um, she said that Jax was a follower and would never instigate a fight with Benny."

"But apparently he did?" Abigail responded.

"Yes, I guess he did." Starr knew she should probably stop with that, but she couldn't bring herself to do so. She continued calmly, "But Rose also said that Benny never fought anyone who couldn't defend themselves, and from her description, it sounds like Jax just did what other people said to do."

"She's so damn nosy. No one asked for her opinion on the matter," she gritted out.

Starr almost hated to say something else because Abigail seemed to be on the verge of a meltdown, but she couldn't let anything bad happen to Rose because she sat with her and answered questions that Starr had asked her. That wasn't right.

"Abigail," she said evenly. "I am the one who was asking questions. Rose was just offering her own theories. She wasn't being nosy. She was just someone who knew Benny and wanted answers. Just like you."

"She is nothing like me!" Abigail shouted and then screamed at the top of her lungs.

"I'm sorry, you're right, she isn't like you," Abigail agreed, hoping it would calm her down.

Abigail narrowed her eyes at Starr. "Rose doesn't know anything about what happened."

Starr watched her carefully. "I thought you didn't know anything either."

Abigail grinned. "Maybe I do, maybe I don't. What's it to you?"

In truth, Starr was now a bit frightened. Abigail's behavior was nothing like how it was the other day. Had she been there at Benny's death? Was she the cause of it? Her current thoughts were leaning in that direction; she just didn't understand why.

"Abigail, were you there when Benny was killed?" Starr asked carefully.

Abigail nodded, just slightly, and in that moment, Starr realized that she had not only made a mistake about Abigail because she was clearly a danger, but she also had made the mistake of putting herself in a situation that was dangerous to both her and her beloved Bean.

"Did you tell Jax to kill Benny?" Starr whispered.

9
UNRAVELING MESS

"Did you tell Jax to kill Benny?"

She did not want to know the actual answer to that question, but the words had come out of their own volition. Her morbid curiosity had gotten the best of her. Of course, now that she had asked the question out loud, she wanted to know the answer.

"Abigail! Did you kill Benny?" Starr asked louder than she intended.

Abigail smirked but didn't say anything. She just continued to stare at Starr in a creepy fashion. It was the kind of look that you see in a lot of horror movies, right before someone gets murdered. Starr would always yell at those people in the movies for staying put, instead of running, yet here she was, frozen in place, asking a potentially crazy person questions about a murder.

"Did you tell Jax to do it?" Starr asked slowly, since she hadn't answered the previous question.

Abigail once again smirked but this time she shook her head. Okay, well, then if she didn't ask him to do it, did he do it on his own? That seemed unlikely based on the information she had.

"Abigail, did you kill him? I need to know," Starr finally asked.

Abigail nodded slowly. She seemed pleased with herself. Starr was in a serious predicament now. She needed to get out of it, but the next thing she knew, more words were coming out of her mouth that she couldn't take back.

"Why would you do that?" Starr asked in complete shock.

"He deserved it," was her simple reply.

Starr swallowed thickly. Everything was unraveling fast. It was a mess of epic proportions. She had misunderstood everything, and now she was panicking. She could feel the fear rising in her. She needed a way to get out of this situation without harm.

"I'm sure he did," Starr responded carefully. She figured that might be the quickest way out of this mess if Abigail thought she was on her side.

"He did," she yelled. "He had been meeting with Rose, conspiring against me. Telling people, I was acting crazy, making people question me."

"You confronted him?" Starr asked, then added with a slight nod, "As you should have."

"Exactly," she stated woefully. "But he couldn't even be honest with me."

Abigail started to pace in front of her. Starr glanced around, hoping that someone would see them and come to help, but there was no one. Even with all the crowds, no one had any idea what was going on, a mere block away from them.

"Is that when he got hurt?" Starr asked softly.

Abigail stopped pacing and stared at her angrily. "He didn't get hurt. He got dead," she replied with venom in her voice.

"So, it wasn't an accident?" Starr asked and immediately regretted it.

Abigail rolled her eyes dramatically. "When he kept saying I was being crazy, I pushed him hard. He fell and hit his head. I grabbed Jax's bottle he had and poured it on Benny. I figured they'd think he was drunk and that it would be considered an accident."

"So, he hadn't been drinking?"

She shrugged. "I don't know, guess not. Maybe he really was going to a meeting, or maybe he was planning to meet Rose there. Either way, I wasn't going to let that happen." She stated irately, while shaking her head."

"Abigail, did you mean to kill him?"

Abigail smirked. "Not initially, but when he kept lying, I didn't care anymore. Then I told Jax not to say anything or else he would end up like Benny, dead in the street."

"You were just going to let Jax take the fall for something you did?" Starr questioned.

"He chose to do that," she replied evenly.

Starr stared at her in disbelief. "Then why act all distraught the other day?"

"It was an act," she said with a dramatic bow. "Honestly, it was one of my best performances."

Starr shook her head. Abigail was indeed crazy. No wonder Benny wanted to get away from her. He was probably talking to Rose to see if she would take him back. But Rose didn't trust him anymore. He was trapped in a relationship with this psycho.

"Are you happy now?" Abigail asked coolly. "Since you needed to know so badly."

Starr stared at her, choosing her words carefully. "Yes, thank you for being honest with me. Don't worry, I won't say anything, Abigail, and I'm leaving tomorrow, so no one will know what happened."

Abigail smiled eerily at her. "No one will know because you aren't leaving."

Bean, picking up on Abigail's changing tone and posture, started to growl. Starr moved her and Bean out of the way, but Abigail kept blocking their path. She was laughing, as if they were playing some kind of game. Starr could feel her heart racing. She needed to get out of this.

"What's your plan, Abigail? Think this through. People know I am here; they will look for me. People saw me talking to you. You will be the prime suspect," she said, trying to reason with a mad woman.

"I don't care," she said as she pulled out a knife.

Abigail lunged at her. Bean reacted quickly, latching his teeth onto her pant leg, refusing to let go. Abigail had no idea that he was an expert at tug of war, and he was not about to let her go until she stopped threatening his mama. He had been calm as she yelled, but he would not abide her trying to hurt Starr.

"Get off of me!" she screamed as she tried to swipe at Bean with her knife.

"Get the hell away from my dog, you freak!" Starr screamed.

Starr pushed her with all her might. Abigail flew backwards, losing her balance. Starr rushed over to her, standing on the hand with the knife. She was still trying to kick Bean off her, but he only held on tighter. Starr could see blood starting to peek through her pants.

"Ma'am, step away from her," she heard as footsteps were running towards them.

"She's crazy and trying to hurt my dog and me," Starr yelled.

The man pulled her away from Abigail while another one tried to grab Bean, who was growling ferociously. Abigail was screaming, making a big show of things. Starr wriggled out of the man's grasp and realized it was Jake, Abigail's brother.

"Do you know what she did?" she asked him angrily.

"Please release your dog," he replied calmly.

"Not until the police come," she insisted. "That woman tried to kill me!"

Another one of the re-enactors looked over at her with pleading eyes. "We're trying to help you. Tell your dog to let go. She's bleeding."

"I don't care if she's bleeding," Starr huffed and then came to her senses. "Bean, release the crazy woman."

He looked over at her. He wasn't so sure about this, but he obeyed. He then trotted over to her and sat at her feet. He still growled at Abigail as the men helped her to her feet. She was putting on an act of hobbling and crying hysterically as if she were the wronged one.

"She tried to hurt me," Abigail said, tears streaming down her cheeks.

"Are you freaking kidding me?' Starr shouted, incensed. She couldn't believe that Abigail dared to say that out loud.

"Abigail, stop it," Jake said to her. He was very calm as he added. "I know what you did. Jax called me and told me everything."

"He's lying!" she insisted.

"He's not lying," Starr interrupted. "She said she killed him because she thought he was going to go back to Rose. She's not right in the head. She needs help."

"What?" Rose said, having just walked up.

Starr turned to her. "I'm sorry, Rose. She was jealous of you. She thought you were trying to take Benny away from her."

Rose walked up to Abigail and pushed her back, causing her to fall again. "You killed Benny. He had done nothing wrong."

"Jake, are you going to let her do this to me?" She asked as she stood. "You're my brother. You are supposed to protect me," she pleaded with him.

"Not this time. You need to get the help you have needed for a long time. I'm only sorry I covered for you all these years," he told her casually. "But not anymore. You killed someone, Abby. I may not have liked Benny, but he didn't deserve that."

She screamed at the top of her lungs and stumbled forward in an attempt to attack Jake. At that very moment, the police arrived. They grabbed her before she could reach him and put her in handcuffs. One of the officers put her in the back of the police car as the other one looked over at Starr. He was the same officer she had talked to when Benny had died.

"You're welcome," she muttered.

The officer smiled at her. "We will need to take your statement."

"I told you there was more to the story and that it wasn't just cut and dry. None of it made sense. That's my statement," she sputtered out angrily and then sighed. "I'm sorry. It's been a day."

"You don't need to apologize, but we do need to go over what happened," he told her.

Starr nodded her understanding. She stepped away with him. She and the officer spoke for a good ten minutes while she went over what had transpired and, more importantly, what Abigail had confessed to her before she went full-on crazy.

"Thank you," he said as he finished jotting down her statement.

"Are they going to take Bean because he bit her?" she asked worriedly.

He shook his head. "As far as I can see, it was clear that he was protecting you from someone out of control. We won't be calling animal control."

She nodded, relieved, and looked at Abagail, who was sitting stoically in the back of the police car. "She can't file a complaint, can she?"

The officer shook his head. "Even if she tried, it would not work." He looked down at Bean, who was sitting calmly, watching all the activity around him. "He's had his shots, though, correct?"

She smiled and nodded. "I make sure my special boy is up to date on everything."

The officer nodded. "Then there is nothing you need to worry about. I know this may sound cliché, but enjoy the rest of your vacation," he said with a smile and walked over to the police car.

"Yeah, sure," she laughed.

Rose walked over to her once the police man was gone and hugged her. "Thank you so much for getting me answers."

As Rose pulled away from her, Starr smiled. "I can see why you didn't want to talk about her. She really had me fooled."

"I knew she was a little unhinged, but had no idea she was like that. I can't believe she killed Benny. Over nothing. He wasn't trying to be with me. I made that very clear when we started talking again that I didn't want to get back together with him," Rose stated with a sigh.

"Crazy people see what they want to see, not what is really there," Starr assured her.

Rose laughed. "So much for a fun weekend in Deadwood."

Starr laughed. "It was definitely an adventure."

"You have to promise me that you will come back. I swear it isn't always this crazy," Rose said reassuringly, hoping it would work.

"I will come back. After all, I need to see more than Main Street," she chuckled. She glanced at Jake, who was talking to the others. "Do you think he knew?"

Rose shook her head as she looked over at them. "No, not about Benny's death, but about her being nuts, yes, I'm sure he knew that."

"I honestly don't know what to do now," Starr stated truthfully.

"I'm off now. Let me at least treat you to dinner. I think I owe you that at the very least," Rose said, with a warm smile.

"Sure, somewhere not on Main Street, correct?"

"Yes!"

Both laughed as Bean looked up at them, confused by their behavior. He wasn't sure exactly what was happening, but at least that woman was gone, and the one with the pocketful of treats stayed, so that was a pleasant turn of events. Maybe she would give him more treats. He hoped so. He deserved it!

10
WINDING DOWN

Starr had a great dinner with Rose. She had learned so much about each other in such a short time, but she was a great person. By the end of their meal, they had decided to stay in touch and proceeded to follow one another on social media. Rose walked outside with her after they had finished their meal.

"I mean it, thanks for everything," Rose stated thoughtfully. "You could have easily done the whole tourist thing and put Benny's death aside, but you didn't, and I truly appreciate it."

"If I hadn't done anything, he would have been in my thoughts constantly," she chuckled softly.

Rose nodded and gave her another hug. "You have a safe journey home, and I mean it. Please come back."

Starr nodded. "I promise. I will."

"Good," Rose replied, and kneeled to give Bean one last pet before she turned and walked away.

Starr helped Bean into the car. They drove up the road to the B&B in silence. It had been a crazy day. There was a part of her that was looking forward to going home, where nothing exciting ever happened, where crazy women didn't try to kill her, where Bean didn't find dead bodies. Where life felt so normal that it almost hurt. If she were truly honest with herself, she would say that she enjoyed solving the mystery of Benny's murder.

"Well, my boy, we did it, now to get some rest before we head home tomorrow," she told Bean as they parked.

She could see that the lights were on in the house, which, of course, was normal. It wasn't that late. She wasn't sure she was ready for all the questions, but she owed it to everyone to tell them what had transpired with Abigail.

"Come on, Bean. Time to converse with everyone," she told him, as she got out of the car and then let him out.

She took her time with him outside, making sure he had relieved himself, and then started towards the door. The minute she stepped inside, Sally came rushing through the kitchen to greet her. Her face was a mix of excitement and concern.

"Are you alright?" Sally asked quickly.

"Yes, I am," Starr replied tentatively.

"It must have been so scary today. I can't believe she did that to you," she continued.

"How do you know what happened?" Starr asked, stepping back from her.

"What do you mean?" Sally responded, equally confused.

"How do you know what's going on in everyone's life. Are you spying on people?" Starr asked her, annoyed.

Tim came out from behind her. "She has a police scanner that she listens to nonstop. I told her to stop doing it, but she is insistent." He looked at her. "Didn't I tell you people would be annoyed with you if they found out?"

"It's for their protection," she told him, and then looked at Starr. "I do apologize if it was intrusive. I worry about people in my home and in the town. I meant no disrespect."

"They give names over the police scanner?" Starr asked, suddenly paranoid.

Tim shook his head. "No, they give descriptions sometimes, which is how she figured out it was you that had been attacked."

"You were attacked?" Nina gasped as she and Monte entered the foyer, where everyone was.

"Yes, sort of," Starr answered and then scrunched her brow. "Okay, no sort of, Abigail turned out to be the killer. She trapped me and tried to kill me, but my precious Bean saved my life." She looked down and smiled at her courageous pup. She sighed. "Why don't we all go into the living room, and I will tell everyone what happened."

"I will make a fresh pot of coffee," Sally said, and immediately dashed into the kitchen.

"That sounds good. I could use a strong cup, right about now," Starr agreed.

Starr and Bean walked into the living room and took a seat in the large chair. Bean jumped on her lap and nuzzled against her hand. His not-so-direct indication that he wanted her to pet him. She smiled down at him, and when she looked up, she could see that Nina and Monte were desperate for her to tell them what happened, but they would need to wait. She didn't want to repeat the story.

Sally set a cup in front of her. "I think I got it just right."

"Thank you," Sally told her and took a sip. It was indeed just the way she liked it.

Monte stood to get him and Nina a cup, but looked over at Starr before moving. "Do not start without me."

She grinned. "I promise I will wait until everyone is present and accounted for."

"Thank you," he said as he rushed out of the room.

Starr sat and sipped her coffee. She felt as if everyone was staring at her, because they were. Sally and Tim were a bit odd, but overall, a nice couple. A bit nosy, but despite that, they seemed like good people. Nina and Monte proved to be a joy to be around. She would miss them when she returned to Denver.

Once Monte returned with two cups of coffee and sat next to Nina, she began. "Well, as you all know, my plan was to visit with Rose, because Jake had said she was Benny's girlfriend before Abigail."

"Oh, yes, Rose is such a sweetheart. Loves animals," Sally interjected, but Tim placed his hand on her leg and smiled at her. She returned his smile and then looked at Starr. "Please continue."

"You are right, she is a sweetheart. I think she and Bean are now besties," Starr said with a laugh. "Anyway, that visit went very well."

Starr went on to tell them everything that Rose had said, and then how things progressed with Abigail. There was a lot of commentary that primarily centered around why Starr didn't bang Abigail's head into the side of the building and take off, but they all seemed to appreciate how she was able to get all the answers out of Abigail, and that Bean had been such a good boy, protecting her.

"Needless to say, I'm glad we finally found out the truth about what happened," Starr finished.

"Do you think Jax knew what she was going to do?" Nina asked curiously.

Starr shook her head. "No, I think Abigail probably asked him to come with her, told him it was for protection because she feared Benny. I'm sure he wasn't expecting her to kill him. When things escalated, he was probably scared. I know I was. But a night in jail was all it took for him to come clean. I'm sure there is more to the story."

"I'll try to get more details," Monte said with a nod. "We're here until the end of the week."

"We will let you know what we find out," Nina told her.

"I can also let you know, if you don't mind me emailing you," Sally added sheepishly.

Starr smiled. "I don't mind at all."

"Hopefully, you can come stay with us again," Sally told her. "It's not always this crazy."

Starr laughed. "Yes, that's what Rose said as well. In fact, she made me promise to give Deadwood another try. I told her I would."

"That's good to hear," Sally stated and rose. "We will let you all have some visiting time."

"Thank you, Sally," Starr answered, picking up her empty cup. "I'm going to grab another cup of coffee. Nina, can you hold Bean for me while I do that?"

"Of course," she reached for his leash. "Come here, you brave little man," she told him, running her hand down his back.

Starr walked into the kitchen and leaned against the counter. Now that things were winding down, she wasn't sure what to do with herself. She felt exhausted, but knew that it was way too early to go to bed. She supposed she would have more coffee and then figure it out. She filled her cup and then walked out to the living room.

"Starr, we were wondering if you and Bean wanted to shoot another video before you leave tomorrow," Monte asked, when she set her cup down and reached for Bean's leash.

"Sure, why not. Are we going to be talking about the murder or just hanging out?" she asked.

"Just hanging out," Nina immediately replied. "We don't want you to talk about anything you don't want to talk about."

Satrr nodded. She appreciated that. "Are we gonna do it in here or outside?"

Nina and Monte looked at each other and then at her. "Outside," they said in unison.

Starr waited while Monte and Nina set up where they wanted to shoot the video. Once they were ready, they began. It was once again a very light-hearted video. They didn't mention the murder, only that you never knew what to expect in Deadwood and that it was always an adventure. Then the rest was focused on Bean's crazy antics.

"That will be a great post," Nina told her with a laugh.

Monte glanced at Starr. "Want to see the video?"

"Sure," she said and took the camera. She found herself laughing, mostly at Bean, who was being his total chaotic self. "That boy is a nut!"

"I'm going to go work on editing," he replied before looking over at Nina. "Tell her what we talked about."

"Oh, yes, I almost forgot."

"What's going on?" Starr asked, hesitantly. She wasn't sure how many more surprises she could manage without losing her mind.

Nina watched Monte walk away and then smiled at Nina. "We were talking about how personable you and Bean were, and wondered if you wanted help getting a blog going of your and Bean's adventures. We could totally help you set it up."

"You mean be influencers like you two?" Starr asked, astounded that they would even think she could do something like that.

"Well, no one starts as an influencer. They build a following talking about things other people don't even know they are interested in until they see it," she laughed.

"I don't know." Starr was confused by this conversation. She then added, "I don't think I am that creative."

"Well, you would start small, maybe posting some crazy videos of Bean. He is such a cutie pie. Everyone will love him," Nina told her, watching Bean jump around the yard. "Hey, hand me your phone for a minute."

Starr did. She watched Nina shoot a short video of Bean chasing a butterfly. Starr had to hold in her laughter as he became frustrated at not being able to catch the thing fluttering around his head. When she stopped the video, she showed it to Starr.

"Now, you take the video, add some background music and maybe a little commentary, and post that," Nina told her, as if what she was asking was so simple.

"I don't know how to edit videos," she explained, trying to get Nina to see that she'd be terrible at this.

"There are a lot of programs geared at helping people get started. Monte could help you find the right program for your system, and I could help you with content. We'd also share on our page as well," she told her in her typical energetic fashion.

"I guess, I could try, but I really need to think about it," Starr said, biting her lip slightly. "I may not even have the time to learn how to do this thing properly."

Nina handed her one of her cards. "This is all my information. When you are ready, we will be there to help you."

Starr looked at the card and flipped it over, which had a message that said, " You can do it", in what she presumed was Nina's handwriting. She smiled and put the card in her pocket. She wasn't sure if she would do it, but she was happy that Nina thought she could.

"I'm so glad we had the chance to meet each other," Starr told her, hugging her.

"Me too." Nina pulled away from her. "Now, listen, even if you decide not to do a blog or videos or anything, still reach out. We want to know that you and Bean are doing okay."

Starr nodded. "I will."

"Perfect," Nina stated happily. "I'm going to go help Monte get the post ready for tonight, but be sure to come see us before you head out tomorrow."

Starr nodded as she watched her walk away. Even though her trip was a bit on the wild side, she had met some great people along the way. She walked with Bean for a bit and leaned against the fence that outlined the property. The sun was just starting to set. It reminded her of the beauty in the world, which led her back to Benny.

"Benny, I hope you know that you had people who cared about you and are sorry you passed. I hope you can rest in peace." She looked down at Bean, who was watching her. "Let's go inside and wind down. It's back to the big city tomorrow."

He woofed and stood, ready for their next adventure. He had fun and met some great people who liked to give him treats. He also got to eat a lot of people's food, which was a plus. While he enjoyed all of that, he was ready to go home and get back to normal.

EPILOGUE

Starr walked down the hallway to her bedroom, stopping to smile at the pictures that lined the wall. They were the set of old-time photographs she had taken in Deadwood, just four months ago. She tilted her head slightly. Had it really been four months since her adventure in South Dakota? She shook her head, knowing it was.

She approached the bed and took a seat on it. She patted the mattress, and Bean jumped up there immediately, plopping down beside her. She instantly started petting him as she looked at the desk, where her computer sat, eyeing her, judging her.

She sighed and looked at Bean. "Should we do it?"

He tilted his head, not sure what they were doing, but whatever it was, he was on board. He woofed excitedly, hoping they were going somewhere, preferably somewhere where he could obtain treats.

"Alright, let's do this," she stated, trying to motivate herself.

She stood up and walked over to her desk, logging onto her computer. She pulled up YouTube and stared in fear before she made a few quick clicks. She was now on another page. It was a channel she had created a couple of months ago called *Bean on the Scene*. She had twelve videos sitting in the queue.

She had been talking to Monte and Nina since she left Deadwood. They had been working on videos together, but she had also gotten an update about the case, which had been resolved. Abigail had pled guilty, but because she was not right in the head, she was sent to a psychiatric hospital for the criminally insane. She wouldn't be getting out anytime soon. She quickly dialed Nina's number.

"Hey there," Nina answered happily. "Are you ready?"

"I still don't know. I'm nervous," Starr admitted.

"Don't be," she heard Monte say. "The videos we worked on are amazing, and once you post them, we will share them as well."

"Okay, hold on." Starr took a deep breath and then clicked publish on the first video.

"Hey, everyone... My name is Starr, and this is my rambunctious little man, Bean, short for coffee bean. Ya see, I'm a bit of a coffeeholic but don't tell anyone," she said with a whispered laugh. "Anyway, these videos will mostly be of Bean and our escapades. Now, our first adventure was in Deadwood, South Dakota, and if you follow Nina and Monte, you know it was a wild ride to say the least. My Bean was on the scene and found... a dead body!"

Starr waited with bated breath as the video continued, telling the story of their trip to Deadwood, without naming names. Interspersed were some of the shots that Monte had taken that were not used in their videos. It ended with the video that Nina had shot the last night they were there.

"That's it, everyone. Please, if you like this content, give Bean and me a follow. Now hopefully, we don't run into any more dead bodies, but if we do, don't worry because Bean will be on the scene!"

"It's done, and I can't take it back," Starr stated, only half joking about removing it.

"People are going to love it, and it's been shared on our channel as well," Nina announced over the phone. "Now watch for the reactions."

Starr blew out her breath. "Thanks for everything. I hope people like it."

"They will," Nina assured her.

"Post another video in a couple of days and then go to weekly," Monte told her. "In the meantime, we can work on some of the other videos you shot to get them ready to be published."

"Thanks, guys. I appreciate all your help," she said sincerely. "I'm going to take Bean for a walk so I won't sit here staring at the post waiting for anyone to reply," she said with a nervous laugh.

"Have a good walk, we'll talk in a couple of days," Nina told her before hanging up.

Starr rose and turned away from the computer. Honestly, she could not sit and wait and wonder if people would care about her silly little video. For now, she would walk and turn her phone off.

"Come on, Bean, let's go have some fun!"

Keep a lookout for Book Two in the Perfect Blend Cozy Mystery Trilogy, coming later this year!

AUTHOR NOTE

I hope you enjoyed getting to know Starr and her amusing little corgi, Bean. Bean is inspired by my daughter's corgi, Jedi, who is a character that could span hundreds of books. I have three books planned for this series and will start the second one in a few months. I have one other book ahead of it that I need to finish.

I want to take a moment to thank the creators of the Stay or Go in Deadwood Anthology for letting my little cozy in there. I can't wait to read the rest of the stories!

AUTHOR BIOGRAPHY

Author T.M. Witko lives on the Standing Rock Indian Reservation with her children. They are accompanied by their crazy dogs (Jacqui, a German Shepherd mix, and Jedidiah, a tri-color Pembroke Welsh corgi). She and her family enjoy attending pow wows, traveling, and living a quiet life.

Ms. Witko is a licensed clinical psychologist, a full-time writer/editor, and one of the co-founders of Winyan Press, LLC. She is a multi-genre author who writes Romance, Suspense/Thrillers, and Young Adult Fiction. She has recently ventured into the cozy mystery genre under the pen name, Nory Woods, which was inspired by her late mother.

Social Media Contacts

Facebook Group: https://www.facebook.com/groups/923658484383307

Website: https://authortmwitko.com/

Mailing List: http://eepurl.com/g7to8X

HOW IT BEGAN

MELISSA NAATZ

The story, all names, characters, and incidents portrayed in this production are fictitious. No identification with actual persons (living or deceased), places, buildings, and products are intended or should be inferred.

ALSO BY MELISSA NAATZ
CONTEMPORARY ROMANCE

One Summer Knight

The Things We Break

How We End

Fantasy Romance

The Forgotten Life of Ella Moon

CONTENT WARNING

This story contains themes of teen pregnancy, abortion (non-graphic), emotional manipulation by a parent, underage drinking, drug use, teen sexual content, mentions of body-image expectations, and heartbreak. Please read with care.

THIS IS WHERE IT BEGAN.

1

"Wyatt, table three needs to be bussed, and we need more ice at station two again. I think there is something wrong with it," my older sister Morgan called as she did a quick after-lunch inventory of the bar.

"Yeah, yeah," I responded over my shoulder. It wouldn't matter if table three sat dirty for another half hour, and station one, which was right next to station two, had plenty of ice. Besides, no one was going to be in until after the show.

The show was a reenactment of the shootout between the famous and fan favorite Wild Bill Hickok and the lesser-known Davis Tutt. It was the same every Saturday, Sunday, and major holidays. At one p.m., they set up a table in the middle of Main Street. Paul Linberg, who was also the funeral home director, played Wild Bill Hickok. There would be a disagreement over a card game, and Wild Bill would have to shoot and kill the infamous Davis Tutt.

It wasn't a fan favorite because people were so eager to know about Davis Tutt or they loved Wild West history. No, it was because of who played Davis. Bodie Vega.

I didn't know if that was Bodie's real name. My father seemed to think it sounded made-up. But Bodie swore he was named after a ghost town in California. Vega was stepdad two's last name, and Bodie thought it sounded more like an actor than Bodie Henderson. And I believed him. Why would he make up a name?

He was eighteen and had blown into town with four other boys this spring. He had a California tan and a bright white smile. At first, he was stocking shelves at The Family Mart, then Paul thought he'd be perfect to play Davis Tutt. Apparently, Davis was a handsome man. And so was Bodie.

The scene was set, and the actors took their places. I could recite every word Paul yelled out. I knew the steps Bodie would take. I knew the exact moment Bodie, dressed in Davis's period white shirt and brown pants, would flip the table. Then Paul, dressed as Wild Bill in a long black duster and a sweat-stained shirt, would beg Davis not to do this.

Everyone who lined Main Street hung on every word Bodie said. They watched as he so brilliantly played the role of an arrogant gunslinger from the 1800s. But it was the next part I hated. Even though it was when Bodie shone the brightest. When those standing around gasped in surprise.

When Wild Bill shoots the very handsome Davis Tutt in the street, Bodie would stagger around saying his famous line, "Boys, I'm killed," and die there on the street. Not on the porch of the courthouse where the real Davis Tutt died, but none of the tourists would care. They were here to cheer for the hero.

As he lay there in the scorching July sun with the crowd cheering for Wild Bill, I wished the script would change and Davis would win. Shoot Wild Bill dead. Then he'd be the hero. Fathers would be happy to have a hero dating their daughter. Mothers wouldn't use words like "Don't let a pretty face fool you." Or "You're too pretty to fall for that silly boy."

And Bodie and I could ride off into the sunset. Rewrite history.

"You really think he's going to stick around come winter?" Morgan came up behind me, a bus tub full of table three's dishes on her hip. "And what? Go to prom with you?"

I watched Bodie stand and bow. He was tall and lean. His sun-bleached hair curled at the base of his neck. He wore his cowboy hat low on his brow and smiled at all the people who came up and dropped tips into his hat. He'd wink and flirt with the pretty girls, hoping for an extra buck or two. He'd give them that fake Southern twang he thought gave his character a more realistic feel.

"I'm not going to prom." I didn't take my eyes off him. Paul was reminding people to come back at three to watch *The Death of Wild Bill*. A couple of girls lingered, one typing something into Bodie's phone. Probably her number. I didn't like it when he let them do that. But the pay was shit, and the tips were how he fed himself and put gas in his truck. The truck he'd kiss *me* in, not the giggling girl who waved as she joined her family.

"If you say so." Morgan watched the crowd disperse. "The crowds are getting smaller and smaller every year. Even your golden boy isn't helping."

Bodie had been hired to help bring in a younger crowd. And he did. The problem was that most sixteen-year-old girls didn't drive themselves to

Deadwood, South Dakota, in July. And it wasn't Bodie's job to save my family's bar or this city.

"Girls, get ready for the rush. Morgan, station two needs ice," my father called as he came in carrying a plastic crate of beer.

"I told Wyatt to fill it." Morgan nudged me with the bus tub.

"And now I'm telling you," my father said.

"He'll be gone by September, mark my words," Morgan called as she walked away.

That had been the first thing everyone said to me when it became known that Bodie and I were a "thing." Then came the constant questions—why an eighteen-year-old boy had landed so far from home. Rumors bred more rumors: he'd run from something, maybe a record, left behind a baby mama, owed someone too much. All lies.

I knew why.

Bodie said he wanted to see the world. California was great, but he had never seen the Atlantic Ocean or Lake Michigan. Never ate a hot dog in Times Square or climbed the Empire State Building. He wanted to see all of that and more. He and his friends were going to travel all summer, then head back to California before winter. But they ran out of money, so here they were.

And I knew he wouldn't leave without me because he told me he wouldn't.

He promised he'd take me back to California with him. Rescue me from this small dying town. He said it's golden in California. The sun shines, and the people have big-world thoughts. It's the place where happily ever afters were invented.

"I'm going to sweep out front." I grabbed the broom and stepped into the afternoon heat.

Halliday's stood as my father's pride and joy. He'd come to Deadwood as a ranch hand, fallen in love with my mother, and never looked back. Our last name appeared in an old-timey font across a piece of plywood nailed to the front. My dad, Ferris, leaned hard into the whole Wild West theme. From our family name to the ones he gave my sister and me—Wyatt Cassidy and Morgan Jesse. Both pulled from the Earp brothers and other western "heroes." Honestly, we should count ourselves lucky he didn't go with Virgil.

I busied myself sweeping the boardwalk in front of the bar, smiling and greeting people as they hurried by. I did my best not to watch Bodie as he finished up. But it was hard not to. I bit back my smile as he sauntered up to me.

"Well, well, Miss Wyatt Halliday. Aren't you a sight for the dead?" Bodie teased in a false twangy accent as he leaned against the post. The gunshot wound was still bright red against his shirt. It would stain the skin that pulled tight over his ribs. "Is that a new dress?"

I looked down at the period clothing we had to wear in the summer. "Why, yes, it is." It was blood red and had a black silk and lace corset. I'm not sure what it said about our parents that they would let their teenage daughters dress up like whores and spend their summer in a bar. But that was my life.

"Do you like it?" I moved the broom so he could see the whole thing. The way it hugged the new curves I had gotten this spring. Everyone said I looked like my mother. I had her full lips and blue eyes. Her sharp cheekbones and blonde hair. I was lucky, or so my sister said. I got my height and my boobs from my father's side. Or at least that's what my mother said.

Bodie stepped closer, his hand resting on my hip. "I do. But do you know what I like better?" His accent was gone.

"What?"

Sweat dampened his shirt, and his hair was plastered to his forehead. But that didn't stop me from letting him pull me closer. I could feel the heat of his body through the cheap fabric of my dress.

He ducked his head, his mouth brushing the curve of my jaw. "I like it better lying on the floor of my truck."

I never knew what to do with the ease he had when talking about sex. Everything about it still felt new to me. We'd only done *it* for the first time a month ago. Bodie was my first. I wasn't his.

That didn't mean I was completely clueless. I'd gotten close with boys from school, always stopping before it turned into an awkward moment of fingers in the wrong place and eagerness ruining it. Morgan warned me boys often finished before girls even had the chance to feel anything.

But Bodie was different. He knew where fingers belonged. He knew how to kiss, and things never ended until we both had finished. That's the part of sex people never talk about. The good part. They make sex sound like some horrible thing that once you've tried, you never want to do again.

I feel bad for them.

"Wyatt." This time it was my mother who was calling my name. I quickly stepped away from Bodie.

"Wait." He reached for my hand, pulling me back into him. "What time are you done?"

"Five." I could hear my mother asking Morgan where I was.

"And then?" he asked as he kissed my wrist.

I stepped closer to him. "Then I think I might go meet this cute boy from Minnesota. He's got a fast car and told me he'd take me anywhere I want to go." That was true. I left out the part that it was his dad's car. And that he wanted to have sex in that car. He was cute in that rich boy type of way. Just like the girls who giggled for Bodie.

"You know those girls mean nothing to me." He pressed those words into my skin. His green eyes looked almost golden in the bright afternoon light. "You know it's only you I want when all the dust has settled." He tilted my chin towards him and kissed me in front of my parents' bar and all the girls he'd just smiled and winked at.

"Wyatt Cassidy." My mother's voice was sharp and closer than I wanted it to be. I stepped away, pressing my fingers to my lips.

"Mrs. Halliday." Bodie slipped back into character.

"Bodie, don't you have something better to do than my daughter?" My mother crossed her arms over her chest. This was playing out like some sideshow. My mother dressed in period clothing with her blonde hair slipping from her braid. Bodie with his gun slung low on his hip, his hat pulled down low. Me in the middle.

"Yes, ma'am." He smiled and tipped his hat. "Miss Wyatt, I hear Minnesota has had a terrible outbreak of the clap. You might want to be careful."

"Oh, for god's sake. Go." My mother pointed to the road and grabbed my arm. And just like we were in some period drama, my mother dragged me back through the swinging doors, and I watched Bodie disappear into the crowd.

"How many times do I have to tell you to stay away from that boy?" My mother pushed me into the bar. "You want to end up like me? Stuck here slinging beer for tourists? Your dreams dead and dried up like this town?" She tossed a rag at me. "Wash down table three."

That wouldn't happen because I had bigger dreams than she did.

And I had Bodie.

2

"So this boy from Minnesota?" Bodie took a long drag of a joint in the setting sun. We were in the back of his truck, parked at the edge of a field. Since Bodie lived with four other guys and we couldn't fuck in my parents' house, it was here. In a quiet field with the sun setting. Just like a movie.

"A *rich* boy from Minnesota," I corrected him. I sat up and rested my cheek on my knees, watching the dragonflies dart around in the pink glow of the sky. "With a fast car." Apparently, that was what girls from Deadwood were looking for. A fast car.

"Sorry, a rich boy from Minnesota with a fast car. He didn't show up?" He ran a finger down my back. I was in nothing but a thong and his button-up shirt. His jeans were unbuttoned and low on his hips. The stain from the dye packet was dark on his skin. He had picked me up after work, Morgan yelling that I better be home before Mom and Dad.

Not that they'd care. They wouldn't be home until after last call and would be too tired to give a shit where their daughters were.

"No, he showed up." I moved to straddle him, his shirt falling open. His hooded eyes traveled up my stomach, coming to rest on my breasts, then to my mouth. "I just decided I like broken-down villains better than fast cars."

"Fast cars will only get you so far."

"What are you, a poet now?" I tossed my long hair over my shoulder, letting my gaze roam over the tattoo. It was in script across his ribs. *I pray you do not fall in love with me. For I am falser than vows made in wine.* "Is that why you have this quote? Because you're a poet?"

"Nope. I got it because love can be deceitful."

There was so much I didn't know about him. He rarely talked about his life in California and never mentioned his family. He had let it slip he had a brother, but I didn't know if he was older or younger. If his parents were dead or alive. My father said he would never let his daughters road-trip across the country.

That's because if he did, who would work at his bar?

"Is your love deceitful?" My mother loved to warn me about boys like him, insisting they only wanted one thing and when they got it, they left. She was wrong—Bodie got what he wanted and kept showing up. So did Hunter with Morgan.

I was beginning to think my parents really didn't understand sex.

"Maybe?" Bodie murmured.

I never asked if there were others. Whether on nights I couldn't get away or nights he hung out with his friends, if he found other girls like me—half-dressed in the back of his truck. Whether he ever called the numbers saved in his phone or the ones scrawled across stray scraps of paper.

"Maybe you're deceitful." He squinted through the smoke of the joint. "Maybe when I'm not lookin', you're chasin' after boys from Minnesota with fast cars." His words came out in a puff of gray smoke.

I could have a summer full of boys with fast cars. They came with their families. Smiled and winked at me as I set burgers and Cokes in front of them. They whispered which hotel or campground I could find them at.

"Maybe I should be. Stop wasting my time with a small-town boy that plays with toy guns." I matched his tone.

Bodie crushed out the joint and sat up, brushing the hair from my face. "I would not like that." He pushed the shirt aside, kissing my shoulder.

That counted as the closest he'd ever come to saying *I love you*—telling me he didn't want me to leave or that he missed me. I'd already told him I loved him. The words slipped out one night after too much cheap whiskey and a sky full of stars.

He didn't say it back. He just kissed me like the whole world narrowed down to my mouth and the stars above us.

That night had felt different. We weren't clawing at each other, desperate and breathless. He went slow, pressing his mouth to the places his hands usually claimed. And I think that's what love looked like. But I still wanted to hear those words.

The promise.

"Then why won't you say it?" I whispered, afraid now that it was just the sex that he wanted. That he was like all the summer boys who just wanted to use me. To consume the package they thought I was. "Will you pray for me to take back the words I already said? The confession I already made?"

His green eyes were dark in the setting sun. "Would you take them back? Can you say it without whiskey on your breath and laughter in your voice?"

He ran his thumb over my bottom lip. My heart raced up my chest and into my throat. "Can you?" I needed to hear the words. I wanted the universe to hear them.

"Yes. I love you," he whispered. "Now you say it."

"I love you more."

"Promise." He pulled away; his voice had a sharp edge to it. An edge that made my heart race and body crave to cut itself.

"Forever."

He laid me down on the blanket, kissing my stomach and then the insides of my thighs. He pressed his promises into the curve of my breast and the rise of my hip.

I would forever remember how pink the sky was the night he confessed his love. How the breeze felt warm on my skin. I would remember the way he felt as he pressed into me. The way the words *I love you* sounded as they fell from his lips.

I would forever remember the promises whispered in the setting sun.

3

I shuffled into the kitchen. It was Sunday, which meant Mom and Dad didn't have to be down at the bar until four. It should've been a time for us to be a family, to have breakfast and talk about our week. Maybe do something all together that didn't involve the bar.

But it wasn't.

"What time did you get in last night?" Morgan was loading the dishwasher.

"Late." I poured a cup of coffee and added almost as much vanilla-flavored creamer.

"Like how late? And gross." She turned her nose up at the pot filled with stagnant water. The musty smell filled the kitchen. "Can you please rinse your dishes?"

"That's not mine." I sipped the now lukewarm coffee. "I got home before you." Not much before. But it was still a win.

"Yeah, but I'll be nineteen soon, and you're not. Mom and Dad set your curfew to midnight."

"And you're not my mother." I put the creamer back in the fridge. Bodie had dropped me off somewhere around two. Mom and Dad weren't home yet.

"But *I* am. What time did you get home last night?" My bleary-eyed mother walked into the kitchen. Her face had been scrubbed clean, and her hair was still in a braid.

"A little after midnight," I lied. Morgan flashed me a warning.

"So the fact that your father and I saw a truck that looked like the one

Bodie Vega drives turning off our road at two fifteen was a coincidence?" My mother crossed her arms over her chest.

"Yeah." I didn't look at her, choosing instead to turn my attention to a sale flyer for a clothing store in Rapid. "Nikes are on sale, and I will need a new pair for school."

"Was he here all night?" My mother didn't let up.

Morgan rinsed the pot and quietly set it in the dishwasher.

"No." I knew where this was going. My mother was well aware of what time I got home and who dropped me off. I glared at Morgan, who gave me the "what, it wasn't me" look. I returned it with a "bullshit, it was too" look.

"How many times do I need to tell you to stay away from that boy? He's trouble."

"No, he's not." Another warning glance from Morgan.

"Oh, and you know what trouble looks like? How long have you known him? Two months? Boys like him only want one thing, and when they get it, they'll be gone."

"Okay," I said, feeling good about the fact that I had given him that *one* thing and he was still there. Strike one against my mother's logic.

"Okay?" My mother pushed off the cupboard and walked over to the counter I was sitting at. Morgan was still doing the dishes. "Have you had sex with him?"

"Mom!" I feigned disgust. My mother had been very open about the consequences of having sex. She told us every day about how we'd end up knocked up and living a small life in South Dakota. Or that we'd end up with a strange STD that would make our future children go blind. She never spoke of love or when it was finally okay to have sex. Just that we should never have it because it would only lead to our downfall. She knew this because it had led to hers.

"Oh god." My mother threw her hands up and cursed at the ceiling. "You would be the daughter to fall for a pretty face. I wanted better for you."

"What's that supposed to mean?" I shot back at her. My mother, Vail, never hid how she saw me. To her, I only had my looks. I wasn't smart enough for a good college. I didn't have Morgan's drive. So, according to her, my only way out came from my face... or from marrying rich. And the only reason a rich man would ever look twice at me?

Because I looked pretty.

"It means that I don't want you knocked up and stuck in this town. The whole world is waiting for you. Do you want to end up like me? Busting your ass for every penny you have? This is not the life I wanted for you."

"Don't you want better for Morgan? She's screwed Hunter plenty of times."

"Don't drag me into this. I wasn't the one getting in two hours past my curfew," Morgan snapped at me.

"Of course I want better for her." My mother rubbed her face. "But it's you I'm worried about. You have a silly idea of what love looks like. He doesn't love you."

"How do you know? Did you ask him?"

"Did you?" my mother threw back.

"Yes. And sorry to disappoint you, *Mother,* but he loves me."

My mother's laughter filled the small space of the kitchen. Morgan shook her head. She had warned me early on to just let Mom win. Let her be right about everything she was wrong about.

But I wasn't Morgan, and Mom wasn't always riding her ass about being more. Not making her mistakes. "I'm not you. And Bodie is not Dad. So stop making me pay for your mistakes."

"You watch your mouth, young lady," my mother snapped.

"Why? What are you going to do, ground me? That would mean you'd have to be home, and we both know that will not happen." I was tired of this conversation. Tired of having to pay for some stupid mistake my mother made nineteen years ago. I didn't make her fall in love with my father. I didn't make her stay in the town. I didn't make her give up her dreams of being pretty for the world.

"Wyatt Cassidy, don't you take that tone with me."

"Whatever." I rolled my eyes as I left her and my sister to discuss all the ways I was failing at some test I didn't even know I was taking.

I would not end up like my mother because I wasn't a quitter. And Bodie wouldn't make me give up my dreams because he wanted to stay here and play some role.

My story wouldn't end like hers.

4

"Wyatt, we need more ice at station two," my mother called through the door into the kitchen.

I slammed the dishwasher door closed and stalked over to the large ice makers. My mother hadn't grounded me. She had done something far worse. She was playing the role of a mother. First, she cut off my access to Bodie by giving me dish duty at Halliday's. Then she drove Morgan and me home—and stayed.

I scooped the ice into the bucket, wondering how long she could play the role of "concerned mother." Which was affecting more than Morgan and me. It left my father to either close the bar by himself or have to pay someone to help him.

"This silent treatment only proves you are not mature enough to handle the consequences of sex."

I jumped at the sound of her voice so close.

"Wyatt." My mother pushed her way between me and the ice machine. "I know you don't understand this, but I've seen boys like Bodie. You forget I grew up in this town. I know what the summer boys are like."

I continued to scoop ice into the bucket. I'd heard all the stories, if not from my mother, then from those who knew her growing up. She was the beauty queen with a bright future. Some guy from LA had scouted her. She was going to be an actress that the world would adore. Then she met my father, one of those summer boys.

"As soon as he gets what he wants, he'll be gone."

"And what is that?" I slammed down the lid of the ice machine, wondering why we were still having this conversation about some magical thing that I held that Bodie was going to steal from me. This wasn't a fairy tale. "Because if it's sex, too late. I gave that to him willingly." I turned to leave.

She grabbed my arm, yanking me back to her. "Is that what you think?" She let out a bitter laugh. "My god, you are a silly little girl."

"And who raised me that way?" I tugged my arm out of her grip.

"No, I raised you to be smarter. It's not sex he wants; he can get that from any of the stupid tourist girls. He wants your future."

"My future?" I rolled my eyes. That was dumb even for my mother. "And how is he going to get that? Magic?"

My mother laughed again as if I was too stupid to understand something as common as men and sex. "By breaking your heart or, worse, knocking you up."

Bodie was the one who had been overly careful. He'd driven me to Planned Parenthood to get on the pill and always had a bunch of condoms. "He doesn't want kids."

"Of course, he doesn't, and when he knocks up some girl, he won't have a kid, but she will. Wyatt, I mean it. Stay away from that boy. He will take everything you give him and will not give you anything but a broken heart. And believe me when I say your first broken heart will bleed into every part of your life. You will never forget it."

"You're right," I snapped. It wouldn't be Bodie who had broken my heart. My heartbreak was because of her and my father. It broke the first time they didn't show up for a stupid middle school choir concert. Then the time they couldn't celebrate my birthday because they had to work. It broke every time I wanted a moment of childhood. One family dinner. One holiday where the bar didn't come first. He couldn't break my heart because she already had. "I remember every time you and Dad broke my heart."

"You think you are the first teenage girl to think her parents are horrible." She ripped the bucket out of my hand. "News flash, little girl, you're not. And your childhood was far from heartbreaking. You need to grow up and see the truth behind those pretty green eyes and dimples. He will break your heart, and when he does, don't come crying to me." My mother shoved open the doors that separated the bar from the kitchen.

"Don't worry, I won't," I said to the swinging doors. I went back to stacking the red plastic cups and dirty chipped ceramic plates into the dishwasher trays.

Morgan set a bus tub of dirty dishes down and started helping me load the plates. "She's going to make me give you a ride home tonight. Play your cards right, and you could be seeing your beloved tonight."

"How?" I didn't look at her.

"It's Hunter and my anniversary, and I am not spending it babysitting you." Morgan shoved the tray into the dishwasher. "You cover for me, and I cover for you."

"Meaning?" I started loading another tray of plates, the ketchup and mustard pooling underneath.

"Meaning since you can't be trusted with time, you invite Bodie over tonight. Hunter and I will leave the house for you two. And as long as we are both back in our beds before Mom and Dad get home, they will be none the wiser. Deal?"

I glanced at her. She was spraying the bloated French fries down the drain. She never did anything for free. "What's it going to cost me?"

"Nothing. Yet. Just make sure your cowboy is long gone before midnight." Morgan let the spray nozzle hang between us. "I'm putting my neck on the line for you, so don't fuck it up."

"Why?"

"Because I'm tired of the silent treatment." She smiled and turned to walk away. "And I can't handle Mom trying to be our mother. It's weird."

I snorted out a laugh. I think that was the worst part of this punishment. We were too old for a mother. We had been figuring it out ourselves since I was ten and Morgan twelve.

The damage was already done.

5

And just as Morgan predicted, our mother couldn't bring us home tonight; Candy, the other server, had called out sick. And since it was Friday night and my father couldn't handle the crowd himself, my mother had to work. But she gave Morgan strict instructions that I was not to leave the house. She said nothing about Bodie coming over.

"Where the hell are they? I told Hunter nine thirty." Morgan glanced at the clock through the back door. She was leaning against the porch post I sat at the base of.

"Hunter was never the best at telling time." I kicked at the overgrown weeds that surround the never finished back porch. "Remember the Halloween of your sophomore year?"

Morgan thought for a moment and smiled. "That wasn't his fault we were late." She sat down next to me. "I heard Mom and you fighting today."

I picked at the long grass that was as high as the porch. Morgan and I weren't the only things neglected around here. "She thinks Bodie is going to suck the future out of me."

"I think that's your job," she teased, bumping shoulders with me.

Everything I knew about sex I had learned from Morgan. She had sat me down and explained what would happen and then showed me a photo of a cock so I wouldn't be shocked when I saw one. She told me where things go and where they shouldn't go, no matter how much the boy begged.

"She said the same thing to me about Hunter." Morgan looked out across the yard to the dark woods. Hunter, who was giving Bodie a ride, was supposed to park at the abandoned farm next to ours and walk over.

"So did he?"

"Yep. Because I wanted him to. She forgets we are not her, and just because she didn't want to marry Dad doesn't mean that I don't want to marry Hunter. I'm fine with that future."

"I don't know if I want to get married," I confessed. I didn't know how marriage worked. My parents were held together by a bar and an unplanned pregnancy. I saw marriage as something done out of necessity, not want.

"You're telling me that if the very cute Bodie Vega asked you to marry him tonight, you'd say no."

"You think he's cute?" I looked over at her. She had pulled her long brown hair up in a ponytail. She had my father's eyes and nose but my mother's mouth and petite stature. This would be the first fall she and I wouldn't be together because she was leaving me for college.

Morgan rolled her eyes. "Yeah, if you're into that boy-next-door look. You shouldn't be, though. You need someone like you. Pretty. The type of man that everyone notices when he walks into a room. That's not Bodie."

"Now you sound like Mom." I thought Bodie was more than boy-next-door cute. Yeah, he could play that part. But Morgan hadn't seen him drunk on whiskey with his shirt off and his jeans slung low on his hips, belting out some stupid song with his friends. In that moment he lost all that softness and gained an edge that I was drawn to.

"Never say that again. I think Mom is right, though. I don't think he'll stay. He has the same look that she does. It's like a caged animal." She jumped down onto the overgrown flower garden my mother had wanted. It was almost ten o'clock. "I think it best if he does leave, because you'll outgrow him." Morgan checked her phone again.

"No, I won't." I sat up and stretched my back. "You're sure Mom and Dad are going to be at the bar all night?" I let the conversation drop. She was very much like my mother sometimes. Stubborn.

"Yep. The softball team will be in at ten. Where the fuck is Hunter? I told him not to be late."

"Who's late?" Hunter appeared suddenly. Morgan squealed as he wrapped his arms around her.

"You are, asshole." She slapped at him.

Bodie stepped out of the shadows. He looked so young in the low light. Sometimes I forgot he was only eighteen. He lived an older life. An adult life filled with rent payments and budgeting for electric bills and groceries. My parents might never be home and made questionable choices about our work apparel, but the lights always turned on.

"I'll be back at twelve fifty. Don't be late," Hunter said as he scooped Morgan up, hauling her into the darkness. "Let's go, woman."

Morgan called, "Be good, Wyatt," before the darkness swallowed her.

"Hey, you." He stood in front of me.

"Hey, you," I whispered. How would I outgrow someone who made me feel like this? Like I was more than a pretty face.

What did Morgan know?

6

It was almost midnight. My head rested on Bodie's stomach; my legs were propped up against the wall. The faded yellow curtains fluttered in the moon's soft blue wash. I wanted to believe he'd stay—that whatever this was, it was more than sex. But in the quiet of my childhood room, doubt floated to the top. It sat like oil on water.

"Can I ask you something?"

When he didn't answer, I turned to see his eyes closed, his lashes dark against his cheek. His hair was a tangled mess. The lean muscle that now wrapped around his ribs flexed with each breath he took. Bodie would turn into a man people would notice. How could Morgan not see his beauty? "Bodie?"

"I'm listening." His voice was heavy with sleep.

"What will happen to us?"

"When?"

"When I go back to school. I still have two years left." When I said it out loud, it sounded so childish. Why would he stick around? He was eighteen, free to do as he wished.

Bodie ran his hands through my hair. "Nothing."

All of this felt out of place in a room that still held so much of my childhood. The sex. Bodie lying naked on a bed with a frilly canopy. Me in just a thong I had to hide from my mother. "You're going to stay?"

"Why wouldn't I?"

"Because. The show ends on Labor Day and..." My head started spinning with all the reasons he should leave.

"I know when the show ends. I'll go back to The Family Mart. Charley'll give me my job back. Paul said I could live in the studio above the playhouse. I only need to make sure the back drive is clear for Thursday night rehearsal, make sure the sidewalk is clear and the pipes don't freeze."

"Are you sure?" Until Bodie, I had never known what it was like to be so close to someone that you breathed the same air. To want to be that close to them. I had only known him for a couple of months, and yet he felt like a part of me. A part that couldn't be removed without causing me to bleed out.

"Come here." He tugged me closer to him. I rested my chin on his shoulder. "We have a plan, remember?" He laced our fingers together, kissing the back of my hand. "We are going to get a place on the beach. I'll surf and live off my hot model girlfriend. We'll watch the sunset and wonder what all the small people in Deadwood are doing."

"Do you really mean that?"

"That I'll surf and live off my hot model girlfriend? Yes."

I laid my head on his shoulder. "That we will leave together." I wanted to leave Deadwood. But I had no idea how. The only times I ever left were on school field trips or to Rapid for bar supplies. I didn't know how tall the mountains were or how blue the ocean was. I didn't know what came after the South Dakota border.

"Wyatt." He sat up, pulling me up with him. "This isn't just a summer fling. If I wanted that, I have a phone full of numbers. That's not what I want. I want someone to see the world with. Someone who's okay with sleeping in the back of my truck or on a beach. It won't be easy, but I'll be right here with you chasing that sunset." He ducked to meet my gaze. "Maybe I should ask you if you are okay with that?"

My heart raced with the thought of packing up everything I owned and chasing Bodie Vega across the country in search of our happily ever after. I started planning how I could be done with this childhood. A childhood I was outgrowing fast.

"Wyatt." Morgan burst through the door. "Mom is on her way. Bodie, hurry." She gathered up his clothes.

"What?" My brain was still making future plans.

"Candy called and said the softball team went to One Eyed Pete's. Mom left early. Bodie, Hunter is waiting for you. Hurry!" Morgan threw his clothes out the window.

"Morgan!" I shouted.

"Mom will be here in like two minutes." Morgan's voice was pitched higher.

"Shit." I scrambled out of bed, not sure what I should do.

"Bodie, hurry." Morgan held the curtain aside as Bodie climbed out onto the back porch roof. It wasn't the first time he had done that.

"He needs clothes."

"They're outside. Where he should be. Now help me clean this up." Morgan moved around my bedroom, picking up my discarded clothing.

I rushed to the window to watch Bodie jump to the ground. Hunter handed him his clothes.

"Bodie, wait!" I yelled.

"Wyatt, Mom." Morgan hurried to clean up the pizza.

"What?" Bodie watched the driveway as he slipped on his pants.

"Yes." Yes to all he had asked me. Yes to our future.

He smiled up at me, his words cut off by the headlights in the driveway and Hunter dragging him into the darkness of the woods. He wasn't taking my future; he was my future.

I slipped on my shirt just as my mother opened the door.

"What the hell?" She glanced at Morgan and me. Morgan still had her shoes on and was holding the cardboard circle from the pizza. My mother surveyed the room. "What's going on? Morgan, why are you wearing your shoes in the house? And why is the back door wide open?"

"Um..." Morgan looked at me.

"We were fighting." I blurted out the first thought that came to me. "Over who was going to eat the last piece of pizza," I said. "She threw it in the woods." It was the worst and only thing I could think of.

"God, Wyatt. Shut up." Morgan turned on me.

"Well, it's true. I made it, so... why should you get to eat it?" I shouted at her. "Plus, it was my pizza. Mom bought it for me." I reached for the stupid cardboard.

"You don't need to eat it all. I only wanted one piece." She yanked the cardboard back; the crust flew across the room. We were both trying not to laugh.

"Girls, enough!" my mother shouted. "Just clean up this mess. And Morgan, you know better than to wear your shoes in the house." My mother shook her head as she walked out of the room.

"Do you think she saw them?" I asked.

"No. And this was my pizza." She looked at the grease-stained cardboard.

"Yeah, well, sex makes me hungry."

"Shut up." She smiled at me. "Me too. That's why I bought the pizza."

7

July left with a storm that knocked out power for most of the town. Then August rolled in, bringing with it a sticky heat and something else. Something I had been too afraid to admit. But now, almost two weeks later, I couldn't ignore it anymore. It started out as exhaustion and had bloomed into me rushing to the bathroom to vomit every morning.

It would end with the test sitting on the bathroom counter. Mom and Dad had gone to the bar early and Morgan was still asleep. I sat alone waiting through the longest five minutes of my life. There was no way I was pregnant. I was on the pill. We were careful. It had to be the flu or something. Bodie said his roommate was sick last week.

That's all it was.

The timer ticked down to nothing. I closed my eyes and whispered a prayer to whatever god listens to the damned. All night, I'd gone over every reason this couldn't be happening. Girls like me didn't end up pregnant. Pretty girls with futures planned out didn't end up like this. Plus, I was on the pill.

I'd thought about calling Bodie so he could be with me. But this was just a scare, a warning to be more careful. So, two of us worrying over nothing was silly. I stood, the test lying alone on the cluttered counter.

It would all be fine.

I flipped it over.

And then it wasn't.

The world shifted and spilled all the plans I had into the nothingness of uncertainty.

I slid to the bathroom floor; the panic crawled up my chest, making it hard to breathe. How had this happened? I was on the pill and when I forgot, we used protection. We were careful. I was only sixteen. Bodie was only eighteen.

We had plans. A future that didn't include me being pregnant.

The test had to be wrong.

It had to be. I just had my period. Didn't I?

My mind raced, trying to remember the last time I had my period. I sorted through life events trying to place a date or something that would remind me of when I had it. To prove the test wrong.

Was it in July? No. Shit, think. I squeezed my eyes shut. The trip to Rapid in June. Yes. I remembered because I'd forgotten tampons, so we had to stop. I breathed a sigh of relief.

But it was August, so that meant...

"Wyatt, I have to pee. You've been in here long enough." Morgan pushed into the bathroom. "What's wrong? Why are you on the floor? Did you drink too much again?"

I looked at the counter where the test sat. She picked it up. It took a heartbeat for her to register what it said. "Oh god. Oh god. Wyatt. Is this yours? Of course, it is. Who else's would it be? Oh god, what are you going to do?"

I did not know. I still didn't believe it myself. Maybe if I closed my eyes and waited, it would go away. Whatever this was would all be gone when I opened them. But it wasn't, and Morgan was still standing there holding the proof.

"What am I going to do?" I sobbed into my knees.

Morgan sat down next to me, pulling me into her arms. I couldn't stop the tears that came out in a raw sob.

"It's okay." My sister held me tight. "It's okay," she whispered over and over again.

I clung to her, fearful that if I let go, I would lose what little grip I had. I was so scared, not of what my mother would say. Not of the disappointment I would see in my father's eyes. But of what Bodie would say.

How would I tell him our future was no longer ours?

8

I said nothing to Bodie about it. Not after the one o'clock show when he kissed me. Not when he picked me up or when he asked where I wanted to eat. I didn't know how to say it. I didn't know how to make it my reality.

I felt empty and drained as I stared through the dirty windshield of his truck. I hated my body and the fact that there was something else growing in it. Something taking all my energy. My sleep. Everything. It would take my life.

"I'm pregnant." The words slipped out of my mouth before I could think them.

"What?" He looked over at me.

"I'm pregnant," I said again, this time a little louder, my gaze focused on the bug splatter. The yellow and clear liquid splashed on the glass.

Bodie slowed the truck, pulling it over and slamming it into park. "This isn't funny."

I started laughing. "I know." It didn't sound like me. The person who said those words sounded crazy.

"Are you serious?" He yanked my arm so I'd look at him.

I was too numb to respond with anything other than a nod.

"How? I mean..." He looked at the steering wheel. "I thought... You said you were on the pill."

"I was. I am."

"Then explain to me how the fuck this happened?" he shouted.

His accusation broke the weird trance I was in. "If you don't know where babies come from, then I can't fucking help you."

"You think this is funny?" he shouted at me.

"Yes, Bodie, I find this all very fucking funny. I find it funny that I am going to get fat and my body will morph into something I don't recognize. That my life as I know it is going to end."

"Your life?" he spat back at me. "What about mine? I'll be stuck here working some dead-end job because of you."

"Me? I don't remember doing this to myself. I seem to remember you being a very willing participant in the act of fucking me." I didn't expect him to be happy. But I didn't think he would blame me. Like I woke up one day and thought being pregnant at sixteen sounded like a lot of fun.

"But you didn't stop me. You didn't warn me that this could happen."

"Oh, my god, I didn't warn you. You're eighteen, Bodie. You've been fucking someone since you were fifteen. I would've thought you knew what could happen." The tears had stopped, now replaced with anger and hatred.

"You did this on purpose." He pointed at me. "You think this is going to make me stay. You think I'm going to give up everything because some small-town whore gets knocked up. Joke's on you, honey."

I slapped him before I could stop myself. How dare he think that this was what I wanted? It was my life that was over. "Fuck you!" I screamed before I got out of the truck. We were four miles from town. I could walk it. It might do me some good, seeing that in a few months I wouldn't be able to see my fucking feet.

"Where are you going?" Bodie called after me as he stepped out of the truck.

"Why the fuck do you care?" I yelled at him.

"Wyatt, get in the truck." He pointed to it.

"No." I kept walking.

"I mean it. I'm not chasing after you."

"Good. I wouldn't want you to." I didn't need his pity or him.

"We are four miles from town, and it's getting dark. Get in the truck. Now!" he shouted.

"Fuck off! I wish I never met you." I turned and started walking. The sun setting across the field was turning the sky a brilliant pink.

"Same." I heard him slam the truck door, the wheels kicking up gravel as he sped off.

I kept walking, sand and gravel filling my shoes. Silence pressed in from every side. Not a soul for miles. I took a few more steps, until the weight of it all dragged me down. I sank into the dirt when the exhaustion finally caught me.

I had never felt so alone and so lost in all my life.

My parents hadn't been around enough for me to wish my mother were here now to dry my tears. Or for my father to tell me I was going to be okay. I never thought I'd needed them. But right now, I wanted someone to care. Someone to tell me what to do.

I wished time would stop even for a moment. I would lie down and watch the sky fade from pink to night. Watch the stars claim their spot in the heavens. If it paused, I could have a moment to catch my breath. To come to terms with what needed to be done.

If time would just stop for moment. But that was the wish of a silly little girl. And I was no longer that silly little girl.

I don't know how far he got or how long I sat there. At some point, I heard tires on gravel, then his truck door slam shut. Bodie's footsteps came toward me.

"Wyatt, please get in the truck." The edge had left his voice.

"No." I didn't move as I watched the warm breeze move through the tall grass of the field. When I thought about my life, I never thought about kids and a house. I never thought about diapers and formula. It was just a blurry idea of a bright life in a city far away from here.

"Please."

I turned to face him. The cuffs of his jeans were tattered and his boots scuffed. He had a Miller High Life T-shirt on. A Blue Star Ranch baseball hat pulled down low. He looked like a kid. I realized my father wasn't a kid. He never said those things to my mother. Never blamed her for the shit that happened. Not for the leaky roof, the slow days at the bar. The flat tire. My father was a man, and Bodie was just a boy.

I turned back to face the field, realizing I would have to do this on my own. "Go away. You've said what you wanted to. Now leave me alone."

Bodie sat down next to me in the dirt. He pulled me into his arms. "I'm sorry. I shouldn't have said those things. I am so sorry," he whispered into my hair.

The tears started again. I don't know where they kept coming from. My body felt dry and wrung out, and yet the tears still came. They came in sobs that felt like my chest was going to rip open. I wished it would. I wished it would spill out—the thing that was growing in me.

Bodie pulled me onto his lap. We clung to each other in the setting sun, both wishing this was just a nightmare.

~

We sat in his truck. Him on his side and me on mine. I didn't know if we could bridge the distance between us. I pressed my forehead to the cool glass. Reality had finally stepped in. My brain was sorting through what would need to be done. I wouldn't let my story end like this.

I wouldn't be like my mother. I wouldn't raise a child as some second chance to live out my dreams.

"I'm not keeping it." I didn't look at him, afraid I'd start crying again, not for the decision I had made, but for how alone and scared I felt.

"Thank god."

"I don't have any money, and I can't go to my parents."

"I'll get it. I'll have to work with Jon. It should take me a couple of weeks. Will that work? I think these things need to be done soon, right?"

"Yes." We'd talked about this in school; it had been a point of contention with the community. Now I knew why. This wasn't a decision to be made in the open for the world to discuss.

I turned toward him. The glow of the setting sun made his eyes look so green. I wondered if I looked as scared as he did. "Can you come with me? I don't want to do this alone."

Bodie slid closer to me. "Of course."

I let him pull me close. I closed my eyes and listened to the sound of his heart beating. Let my breath match his. I let the sounds of the world around me lull me into believing that it would be okay.

For so much of my life, I had never thought about what was next. I always thought what was supposed to happen just happened. Things just worked out. You fall in love with someone who loves you back. You find where you belong. Everything neatly falls into place.

But now I know the truth.

Nothing was certain. Especially dreams made in the faded light of a sunset.

9

It had been a week since I told Bodie. He'd left town to work with his roommate Jon in Wyoming. Some rancher needed help moving cattle. He'd be back this weekend to do his shift with Paul. I didn't know what it would be like to see him after all that had passed between us.

Would he still give me that smile? Would he still tell me he loved me?

"You think he'll make it back in time?" Morgan stood next to me in the doorway. Paul and the crew were setting up for the weekend shootouts. Bodie wouldn't miss that.

"Yes." I leaned my head against the doorway. I was tired again, even after going to bed at seven last night.

A couple of girls my age were laughing and taking photos with a wooden cowboy statue. They made funny faces and peace signs, tilting their heads for the perfect angle. It's funny how one thing can change the way you see the world. Now I wanted to be those girls.

Carefree.

"I hope you're right." Morgan pressed her back against the opposite side of the door frame, fanning herself with the menu.

"He'll be here." I watched the girls go into the candy store. Their parents followed close behind. I wondered if I had parents like that, if I would be where I am today. If I'd have had a mother that applied sunscreen to my face or a father that held the door for me would be like this. Sixteen and pregnant.

"And if he's not?" Morgan asked.

He had to be; I didn't have another plan, and I didn't have any money saved up. I didn't get paid to work at Halliday's, and I spent my tips on stupid things like cherry lip gloss and a push-up bra.

Paul and the rest of the actors began setting up. The first one would be the shootout between Davis Tutt and Wild Bill. I searched the actors for Bodie. Paul stepped out in his tan jacket, the one he wore in the show where he dies. That wasn't until three. It was only one o'clock. He was supposed to do the shootout with Bodie.

Morgan must have noticed too because she pushed off from the door. "Paul," she called, stepping onto the covered sidewalk. "What are you doing? *The Death of Wild Bill* is at three. It's one. Aren't you supposed to be murdering Bodie?"

"There's been a minor change." Paul walked over and rested his arm on the porch post. "Bodie's gone."

"What do you mean, gone?" Morgan asked. "For just this show, right?" She glanced quickly at me.

"Nope. Left on Sunday. He and the boys packed up and left. Bodie didn't even collect his last paycheck. Didn't leave a forwarding address either." Paul spat on the ground. "We didn't have time to train anyone else, so we just cut that show. Which is fine. We were losing the kid come September." Paul spat tobacco onto the ground again. "He was friendly with you, Wyatt. He say anything? Say where we should mail his last check?"

"No." It was suddenly too hot, my corset too tight. The sun was too bright. The orange juice I'd drunk this morning soured in my stomach. I rushed back into the stale air of the bar and pushed into the bathroom just in time to retch over the toilet I hadn't cleaned very well. I tried to bite back the sob, but it came out with another heave. He was gone.

He was gone, and I was alone.

I sat back on the sticky floor, pressing my back against the wooden divider.

Morgan pushed into the small stall. She crouched down next to me. "It'll be okay." She ripped the toilet paper from the roll and wiped the tears from my face.

"He can't be gone. He promised me." I looked at her, hoping she would tell me Paul was wrong, that Bodie would be here. He had to be here because he'd promised. "We had a plan. He was just going to work until he had enough money. He has to come back, Morgan. He said he loved me. He promised."

Morgan caressed my cheek. "He's not coming back."

"Why? He said he loved me."

"Because sometimes love isn't enough." She pulled me into her arms.

"Girls, what are you doing? We have customers..." our mother yelled as she stepped into the bathroom. I could see it in her eyes that she knew. "Which one is it? Morgan?"

"No," Morgan said softly, looking at me.

"Goddammit, Wyatt, tell me you're not. Tell me you are not pregnant," my mother hissed.

I couldn't get the words out. They were caught behind the tears.

"Shit." She pressed a finger to the spot between her eyes. "How long?"

"I don't know."

"Well, think," she snapped.

"Mom, stop," Morgan snapped as she rubbed my back.

"This isn't the time for soft words. These things are time sensitive. Think."

"A month. Maybe?" I fought the urge to puke again.

"There is still time. Morgan, go get your sister some water." My mother stepped aside. "And don't tell your father."

Morgan stood and reached for the door. My mother grabbed her arm. "I mean it, Morgan, not a word to your father. Do you understand?"

"Yes." Morgan slipped out, leaving me alone with my mother.

"Is it Bodie's?" she snapped.

"Yes."

My mother cursed under her breath. "Does he know?"

I nodded, tearing at the toilet paper Morgan had given me. "He left. He said he was going to get money. But Paul said he left. He's not coming back, is he?" This was where I needed my mother to play the role she never had. I needed her soft words. I needed her to tell me it was okay. That she would make it all better.

"No. I told you this would happen." My mother paced the floor. "Who else knows?"

"Just Morgan."

"Let's keep it that way. And you are sure it's only been a month?"

"I think. The last time I last had my period was in June. I don't remember getting it in July. Oh god." I leaned back over the toilet and heaved, but there was nothing else to come up. My stomach tightened, but nothing would come.

Morgan came back into the bathroom with a red plastic cup of water. She kneeled by my side, brushing the hair stuck to my sweat-slicked brow. "Here." She helped put the cup to my mouth.

The cold water felt good on my throat. But as soon as it hit my stomach, it came up violently.

"Morgan, take her home. Tell no one about this. Not Hunter, not anyone, do you understand? Put her to bed. Wyatt, you stay in bed. I'll tell your father you have cramps."

"What am I going to do?" I let Morgan help me up off the floor.

"What I wish my mother had done for me." My mother didn't say another word as she opened the bathroom door and stepped back out into the life that had been forced upon her.

She didn't need to say it.

I knew what was next.

The harsh reality of the sunrise.

AUTHOR'S NOTE

Thank you for reading *How It Began*.

This was where Wyatt's story started. If you're ready to see how it unfolds, keep reading for a sample of *How We End*.

You can purchase *How We End* wherever books are sold or directly at **www.melissanaatz.com**.

For updates, exclusive content, and first look at upcoming releases, join my newsletter at **www.melissanaatz.com** and follow me on social media **@melissanaatzauthor**.

I'm so grateful you're here.

ABOUT MELISSA NAATZ

Melissa Naatz writes emotionally driven contemporary romance about complicated love, second chances, and the moments that shape who we become. Her stories focus on the chapters between the beginning and the happily ever after—where love is messy, honest, and hard-won.

HERE'S HOW IT ENDED.

WYATT

October 8

I've hated sunsets since I was sixteen. There was nothing magical about them. The world didn't soften, and promises of love weren't honored because the sky turned pink. No one rode off to their happy ending. The only thing that came after a sunset was the harsh reality of the sunrise. And maybe that was why I loved Las Vegas so much. From the Strip, the neon outshone any sunset. It glowed with all the possibilities that Las Vegas held.

"When will you be back in LA?"

Richard pulled my attention from the view. From the penthouse of the Starlight Sands, you could see the entire Strip. It was my favorite view. "I don't know. Why?"

"Because." Richard took my chin, tipping my face to the light. He was searching for all the imperfections he could fix. "Your age is starting to show. You could use a little filler here and here." He ran a fingertip from the corner of my eye to my jaw.

Dr. Richard Valentine was a high-profile plastic surgeon from LA. His rich and famous clientele kept him too busy for a relationship. At least that was what he claimed on his profile. There were plenty of escorts in LA, but he didn't fuck where he slept. And I had a reputation for keeping my life very private. Which meant his little secret wouldn't be splashed all over the gossip page of the *Los Angeles Times*.

"*My* age?" So was his. Richard was in his mid-sixties, an average-looking man who had a little too much work done to his face. His skin had lost its firmness, his hair was thinning, and a little filler wouldn't fix his short performance problem.

"Yes, *your* age. What are you now, thirty-six? In another year, you're going to need a breast lift," he said, cupping my left breast, ducking slightly to examine them. "They're losing their firmness."

"I'm thirty-five. And my tits are fine." I stepped away, pulling my robe closed.

"I don't pay for *fine*. I pay for perfection."

Nothing that came out of Richard's mouth surprised me anymore. I would be concerned if he didn't have something to complain about. I knew when I took him on as a client how particular he was. When I was twenty, he could find nothing wrong with me or my tits. I opened the bedroom door, ready for this session to be over. Richard was exhausting, and not because of his sexual prowess. "Well, Mr. Valentine, as always, my time with you was..." I looked him up and down. "Short."

Richard scoffed, tugging on the sleeves of his designer shirt. "I'm not here to please you. I'm here to enjoy the company of a beautiful woman." He stopped in the doorway, looking me up and down. "I can have average for free. If you can't live up to my expectations, I'll have to find my entertainment elsewhere."

He was right about one thing: I was getting too old for men like him. "I don't care." I smiled before calling to my bodyguard, "Jackson, please show Mr. Valentine to the door."

"You'll care when you don't have my monthly ten grand coming in." Richard stepped through the door, taking the suit coat Jackson held out for him. "I've recommended you to a friend. Gabriel. Show him a good time."

"My tits aren't too saggy for him?"

"He has much lower standards." Richard checked for his wallet. "Call my office."

"Mr. Valentine." Jackson motioned for the door. "Cassidy, Margo is waiting for you."

I walked into the large living area of the penthouse suite to find Maverick's PA sitting cross-legged on the couch, her laptop in her lap.

"God, what a fucking asshole. No wonder he has, like, ten ex-wives," Margo said, not looking up.

"It's only three. How long have you been here?" Margo was my scheduler, part-time accountant, PA, and condom orderer. She, along with Jackson, was an employee of Star Light Inc. and Maverick Sands.

"Long enough to hear Dickie is a one-minute lover. Is he always that loud?"

"Louder," Jackson said, coming back into the suite. "Do you need anything else, Cass?" he asked, gathering up his things.

"No, last client of the night. Thanks, Jackson." I waited for him to close the door. "Why are you here so early?" Ten o'clock was prime time for Maverick to need a babysitter.

"Maverick had a *thing* at the Golden Serpent." Margo rolled her eyes, her face lit by the screen of her laptop. "He should have named that place the viper's den." She glanced up. "He wants me to go over the next couple of weeks with you."

Only Maverick would have his PA schedule time with this whore. "You want a drink?"

"No, still on the clock. What was Dickie's issue this week?"

Some men had normal kinks like being pegged or edged, but Richard liked degradation, not as a kink, as a personality trait. "That if women want equal treatment, they should do equal work." I made a tequila soda before flopping down on the couch. Last month he was going to solve the abortion issue by putting girls on birth control when they hit puberty.

"Does that include the bedroom?"

I laid my head on the back of the couch. The crystals in the ceiling reflected the light back like stars. "I wish. He could do a little more work there. But that was better than listening to his almost two-hour tangent about his ex-wives and how they never worked. Which then rolled into my career choice and how I took the easy way out. I mean, how hard could it be to have sex for a living?"

"What did you say?" Margo was half listening as her fingers flew over the screen on her phone.

"Nothing. He doesn't pay me to think or have an opinion." Those were his words. The actual sex was the easiest part of my job. It was all the shit before. The *foreplay* of pretending I gave a shit about what men like Richard Valentine were talking about. Or that I was turned on by a sixty-five-year-old man who took the easy way out and had surgery instead of exercising.

"The confidence with which some men speak is something that should be studied." Margo finished typing on her phone before tossing it down. "As much as I would love to hear all Dickie's theories on women, I have my own dick I need to talk to you about. Maverick has a few events he wants you at. There's this hockey thing next week, and then the annual Maverick Sands Halloween party. He wants his 'best girls' at both."

~

How We End continues Wyatt's story—where love, survival, and sacrifice collide in the neon glow of Las Vegas.

How We End

Wyatt Cassidy Halliday knows exactly what the cost of desire is.

At thirty-five, the high-end escort has spent half her life trading beauty for survival beneath the neon lights of Las Vegas. But time is a ruthless dealer, and Wyatt feels her value slipping with every sunset.

Julian Silver has it all—fame, fortune, and a career most could only dream of. Now, at thirty-four, the star winger for the Las Vegas Desert Coyotes is battling injuries, whispers of retirement, and the quiet fear that his best days are already behind him.

They were never meant to be anything more than a transaction—just a temporary escape from lives that no longer fit.

But when the life Wyatt has built collides with the future Julian is fighting for, they're forced to face a devastating truth: love doesn't come without sacrifice—and some sacrifices may cost them everything.

Get your copy were e-books or sold or at www.melissanaatz.com

FINDING HOPE IN DEADWOOD

V.J. LEE

BLURB

I ran away from my wedding to the last place my ex, Nico Marino, would ever look for me—the place where his best friend died in his arms: Deadwood, South Dakota.

I will tear the world apart to find Hope Walker, even if it's the last place on earth I want to be. To win her back, I'll return to the place of all my worst nightmares.

Finding Hope in Deadwood

PROLOGUE

Hope Walker

Six months earlier

I was smiling so big and bright, I thought my face would split in half. Even though the last year has been tough on my relationship with Nico Marino, I was walking down the aisle to marry my best friend and the man of my dreams.

Dad was glowing with pride as he guided me toward my future. Nico was staring at me. The badass had tears in his eyes, but my feet faltered, and I came to a stop. My best friend and maid-of-honor rubbed her face, then gave me a pitying look. We could read each other's facial expressions, and hers said sorry. She tried to stop this from happening.

Nico's brows furrowed as he stepped down from the stage, walking purposefully toward me. Incense mingled with heavy perfume and spicy cologne. Colorful light streamed through the stained glass as people whispered.

None of it mattered as my eyes locked onto the person standing next to my sisters as a last-minute bridesmaid. I hadn't wanted her to stand up for me, but Nico begged and pleaded that it would be the last thing I would ever have to give up for her.

"Love, don't make me carry you back to that altar. You better not have cold feet," Nico half-teased, half-worried. His big, tattooed hand reached for me, but I stepped back. My dad stepped in front of me, blocking Nico.

Heather stood there, her red lips curling into a devious smirk I had grown accustomed to. Her blonde hair was styled the same way as my midnight-black locks. I had grown used to her copying my style. What stopped me in my tracks was the white dress she wore, not the blush bridesmaid's dress I had painstakingly picked out. She wore a wedding dress so similar to my wedding gown—only cheaper and poorly fitting. Instead of the single blush rose the other bridesmaids held, she had a bouquet that matched mine.

This is why no one had seen her while we were getting ready in the bridal suite.

The rage inside me was intense, making me shake violently, barely able to stand on my expensive heels. I couldn't help but look at her feet, wondering if her shoes matched mine. I'd bet my left tit they were almost identical.

Heather Starr was the only thing Nico and I fought over; otherwise, our relationship had been perfect ... until her brother died. Nico had promised Dorian he would look after and care for Heather. Then she permeated every part of our lives.

He reached toward me, making me step back again, shaking my head. My shaking hand came up, pointing at Heather. "Explain now."

Nico turned and looked up at the stage, his black brows meeting his hairline. My fiancé was a handsome man with black hair slicked back for the wedding. His eyes were almost black and as cold as a winter's night, unless they were on me. He was tattooed from his neck to his feet. He instilled fear in people and ruled his various businesses with an iron fist, without apology. Right now, he looked as if he were seeing Heather for the first time.

His spine straightened as Heather smiled at him and gave him a little finger wave, then spun back around to me. "It's just a dress. Please don't make a fuss."

"Don't make a fuse?" My voice was getting louder. "She's wearing a white dress when I had to work my ass off to get her the same dress as the rest of the bridal party."

"So, what?" He shrugged his broad shoulder. "It shouldn't affect us continuing with the ceremony," he stated.

Oh no, he didn't. It looked like we were doing this right here, right now. "It. Is. A. White. Dress!" I yelled.

His flinch was caused by how loud I got. "I can see that, love."

"Everyone with a brain knows you don't wear white to a wedding! Not to mention, it looks like the Temu version of my dress, and she's holding a bouquet of flowers instead of the single rose the rest of my girls have. Did you not notice? You let her walk down the aisle to stand onstage as if she were the fucking bride!" A few people gasped at me for using foul language in the church, but I had no fucks left to give at this point.

"Let's get married, and we can discuss this afterward, okay?" He sounded desperate now.

I shook my head, my eyes widening as I watched Heather walk toward us. Nico turned and followed my gaze. He gritted out, "Not now, Heather," between clenched teeth.

She didn't stop until she stood in front of us. "Hope, you were acting so hostile over the last few weeks. I was worried you weren't going to show up. I figured I'd get this dress ready in case you were a no-show. Isn't my dress nifty?" She batted her blue eyes at Nico while speaking to me.

"So, you figured if I didn't show up, you'd marry Nico?" I asked, clutching my bouquet so tightly I could feel the stems breaking.

She shook her head as Nico rubbed the back of his neck, knowing my words were true; he just hadn't wanted to admit it.

My dad knew not to intervene ... yet. He stood beside me in silent support.

"I figured if you ran off, we could at least have a fake ceremony to save face for both families." She smiled as if she were my saving grace.

"I was in the bridal suite getting ready. If you had been getting ready with the rest of us, you would have known I was here. Nico is the love of my life, and I was ready to spend the rest of my life with him."

Nico's head swung back to me. "What the hell do you mean 'was ready'?"

I let out a long, weary sigh. "You know how I feel about her. When Dorian died, I was okay with you moving her into the apartment above our garage so you could watch over her. I was upset you gave her a key to our house, but I let it go, because she was grieving. Then she started showing up in our kitchen, only in her underwear, and I asked you to tell her to stop." He opened his mouth to speak, but I held up a hand to stop him. "You did tell her, but it lasted less than a week. When she showed up in our room while we were being intimate, I asked you to move her out and take her key away. You told me she was depressed and needed access to you. I explained I was not comfortable with the way she touched and looked at you—that she was madly in love with you—and what did you tell me?"

He looked down, then away. "I told you to be patient."

I nodded. "I distanced myself from you and her for a while, but I realized I love you and want to be with you." He smiled at me, but I shook my head. "What happened at our engagement party, the one you talked me into letting her help with?" He didn't say anything. "Let me refresh your memory. She replaced all the framed photos of us on the tables with pictures of you and her, and when our couple's video played, it showed only you and her. The only picture of me in the entire place was one from when

I had been out in the garden all day pulling weeds. I was covered in grass stains and dirt—that was it."

"I was only trying to be part of the celebration," Heather whined.

"It wasn't your celebration. Nico, you told me to let her have this, and after the wedding, you'd cut ties. Well, here we are at the wedding, and she's trying to marry you. I told you she was in love with you. Isn't that right, Heather?" I asked.

Her shoulders straightened. "So, what if *we* are in love?"

Nico's eyes widened as I laughed. "I told you she loves you. Now, the question is: who do you choose?"

"What do you mean? I choose you. I love you. I don't love her," he said. Heather deflated as the last word left his full lips.

"Then your choice should be an easy one. Either make her leave or I will."

He didn't say a word, and that was answer enough. He still couldn't bear to hurt her, but it was okay to hurt me, the woman he supposedly loved. I took the ring from my finger and walked toward Heather. Taking her hand, I slipped the ring onto her finger. "I wish you both the marriage you deserve."

I could feel my father following me as I left the church.

1

Hope

Six months later, I found myself settled in Deadwood, South Dakota. When I walked out of my wedding, I had no idea where I was headed. Luckily, my cousin Hadley had recently moved back to South Dakota and into a bigger house, now that she had her baby. The house she had been renting on Airbnb was available, and she offered it to me. The fact that I didn't think Nico would follow me to Deadwood after what happened here to Dorian was just the cherry on top.

Her husband, Dakota, helped me get a marketing job at the largest casino in Deadwood. I was earning money, but I missed my family and, God help me, Nico. I didn't miss Heather at all.

When I talked to my parents or sisters, they knew I didn't want to hear anything about Nico and Heather. They could be married by now, for all I knew. I did find out she booked a ticket to Italy on the same day we were supposed to go on our honeymoon ... to Italy. The devious little twat was planning to crash our honeymoon.

It was the start of summer in South Dakota, and the heat was beginning to rise. I was wearing shorts and a tank top, with my black hair pulled into a high ponytail as I walked down Main Street to Main Street Espresso/Big Dipper.

The scent of coffee hung heavy in the air this morning as I walked up to the counter. "Hey, Hope, what can I get for you this morning?" Sarah asked.

"Let me get the Miel and a breakfast wrap."

She smiled brightly at me. "You got it." I was looking at my phone when

I felt a presence behind me. I stepped to the side, and they moved with me. Looking up over my shoulder, I saw Hank in his navy-blue police uniform. We had grown close when I met him at one of my cousin's barbecues.

His smile was contagious as he winked at me. His light brown hair was spiked, and the way he filled out his uniform was almost sinful. "Hey there, gorgeous. Got time to sit and have coffee with me?"

I smiled up at him. He was well over six feet, and at my five-foot-six, I had to look way up at him. "I always have time for you, handsome."

With our drinks and food in hand, we went outside and sat down. "How's work?"

He swallowed a bite of his sandwich. "It's been the usual drunk tourists and DUIs. Mrs. Gentery is always calling about Mr. Jones's rooster."

I hadn't been here long enough to know who he was talking about, but I enjoyed listening to his stories. We had become fast, close friends. "Sounds exciting."

"Better than dealing with shootouts every day."

I held up my cup so we could toast. "Less deadly, too."

He laughed. "That's true." We sat watching people walk by. "How are you doing?" He always asked me this question, proving he truly cares.

"Eh, still processing. It's hard to wrap my head around the fact that I was going to spend the rest of my life with someone, and now we're nothing."

"You just disappeared without letting him know where you were. Do you think you should get some closure? Or hear more of what he has to say?" he asked.

"He had the chance to speak when I told him to choose, but he couldn't. That said it all," I shot back.

Hank chewed on his lip, but didn't say anything until I told him, "Spit it out."

He set his arms on the table and leaned in, speaking softly. "You told me he was with his friend when the motorcycle crash happened." I nodded. "Heather was on the back of the bike and in the hospital for a month."

"Yeah?" I asked, wondering where he was headed.

"As police, we don't always arrive at a deadly crash involving strangers; sometimes they're loved ones or friends." He tapped the side of his head. "It messes with your head, and we have to see a therapist to help us cope. Did he go to therapy?" he asked.

"No, he spent most of his time by her bedside, caring for her every need. He worked right beside her in the hospital. I brought food, helped with showers, and took care of whatever else needed attention. I treated her like a little sister, but I told him she was madly in love with him. He didn't want to hear it." I watched some tourists walk by in their new cowboy hats, laughing and talking, before I continued my story. "When Heather was discharged from the hospital, she had physical therapy, and he was too busy taking her back and forth and moving her into our home. He refused to set boundaries with her, fearing she would hurt herself, and she used that to her advantage." I sipped my drink, savoring the honey and cinnamon.

"I've been in therapy for a few things I've been through and have had to deal with on the job. It helps ..." he let his words trail off.

"I'm sorry."

He shook his head. "Thanks, but I was thinking if he had just gone to therapy, he might have been able to cope with the guilt, learn how to help Heather, and keep boundaries."

I let out a long-suffering sigh. "Yeah, but now it's too late."

He shook his head. "It's never too late to get help."

"Well, it is for our relationship." As the words left my mouth, my heart squeezed with pain. I missed Nico with every fiber of my being. You don't just stop loving someone who held your heart. It would take time, and right now, I still don't even want to try dating anyone. It wouldn't be fair to them, because I compared everyone to Nico. He was my everything, and even though he chose Heather, he had been good to me long before the accident. Then everything changed.

I wanted to believe I was strong and had moved on, which I had—sort of. Still, I found myself crying over the loss of us. Sometimes, I'd tear up over a scent or a commercial we'd laughed at, and even certain foods would bring back memories, making my eyes leak.

Nico entered my life, loving me in a way I thought no one else could. He held open doors, took my hand, and kissed my forehead. He playfully slapped my butt as we climbed the stairs. He rubbed my feet and bought me anything I looked at twice. He understood my moods and knew how to comfort each one. He showed me affection, no matter where we were or who was around. He constantly told me how much he loved me. We would have silly conversations and deep, meaningful talks.

I appreciated everything he did for, with, and to me, and I showed him my love by caring for him and meeting all his needs. I would rub his tense shoulders, cook his favorite meals, clean the house, and work hard to give us a better life.

Although I didn't like Heather at first, I accepted her because they grew up together, and I thought he saw her as a sister, even though I could see how possessive she was of him. Then Dorian died, and everything came crashing down. It was as if my needs meant nothing; our talks dried up, and he rarely came home until he moved her in above the garage. Then he'd go straight to her.

I felt my hand being squeezed as I met Hank's concerned gaze. "Hey, where'd you go? I lost you for a minute there."

My lips curled into a sad, wistful smile. "I was stuck in better days for a minute, but I'm all good now." I changed the subject. "Have you found out anything about my situation?"

He shook his head. "No, I've been stopping by your place whenever I'm on call, and some of the others have been doing the same. No one has noticed anything unusual. Have you seen anything on the cameras I installed?"

"That's what's weird. I've had two more deliveries of some of my favorite things, but the camera's constantly glitching or getting blocked. If I didn't know better, I'd think it was Nico, but I'm pretty sure he's happily married to Heather now and has no idea where I am. Plus, after trying the chocolate-covered strawberries the first time, I don't believe it's him."

"Call me if anything escalates." He stood, taking both of our trash. "I need to get to the station."

I stood and hugged him. "Thanks for watching out for me. I need to run home and get ready. Our new boss wants to meet with marketing today."

Hank laughed as he pulled away. "All two of you?"

"Yep." He went his way as I headed home to change into a nice work outfit. Yes, it may be Deadwood, South Dakota, but I still dress for success.

~

With my navy knee-length skirt, cream-colored silk blouse, navy heels, and my hair up in a neat twist, I got out of my car and walked to my office.

My good friend and the only other person in marketing, Kara, met me in the hallway, linking her arm through mine. "Omg, I just talked to Judy, and she said the new boss is devastatingly handsome, but seems cold. He introduced himself, then told her to bring marketing in for a meeting. Do you think we'll be fired? I can't lose this job; I just got my own place."

I patted her hand. "You've been here longer than I have, so if anyone leaves, it'll be me. Plus, you've worked in other departments, so I'm the obvious choice to go." I still had savings, but finding well-paying work here was difficult.

Kara snapped her fingers. "That reminds me ... they're shorthanded in payroll. I need to help with that before the meeting. According to Judy, the new boss knows I'll be late and approved it."

"See, you're safe; he probably wants me there to fire me," I explained.

She pulled me into a warm hug. "He'd be a fool to fire you. You've been the driving force behind the social media marketing that's brought us a huge uptick in hotel stays."

"That doesn't mean anything. You'd better go. We'd hate for checks to be late, pissing off the new boss."

"Well, from what Judy said, he has several casinos all over, including in Vegas. I think he knows what he's doing." She headed down the hall to HR as I made my way to the conference room where we held our meetings.

When I pushed through the door, my mouth dropped open. The long conference room table was loaded down with food and desserts, but not just any food and desserts—everything looked like all my favorite things.

If I were getting fired, I was going to eat my weight in all this yummy goodness. I grabbed a plate and filled it with bruschetta, macaroons and jalapeño poppers, thinking I'd save some of the other goodies for my way out.

There was no way I was going to let the new boss see me shoveling food into my face when he walked in, so after grabbing a strawberry lemonade, I turned toward the window and watched a group of big horn sheep laze about.

I was so busy with sheep-watching and filling my mouth with the best bruschetta I've had in forever, I didn't hear the door open or close.

"Nice to see you enjoy the food." Those words in that deep, familiar voice made me whip around.

Nico leaned against the door, arms crossed over his chest. The ass looked better than ever. He now sported a black five o'clock shadow. His black hair was as dark as I remembered, and his equally dark eyes devoured me from head to toe.

2

Nico

My lips curled into a smirk as I watched her forest-green eyes widen in shock at seeing me. Then she spat out the food in her mouth onto the plate in her hand, as if anything that came from me were poison.

I chuckled. "That wasn't very ladylike, my love."

Her little chin jutted out, and her eyes narrowed. "I'm not your anything." She stepped toward me. "How'd you find me?" she asked.

I held up three fingers.

"What's that supposed to mean?"

I wanted to go to her, pull her into my arms, and kiss the sass right out of her mouth, but I knew that if I left this door, she'd bolt. "It took me three days to find you and track you across the country. It would have taken three hours, but your family kept me running in circles."

She grinned at that. "When I handed Heather my ring and stormed out of our wedding, it was clear I was done with you. You should be at home taking care of your precious little Heather. I'm sure she's not too happy you came looking for me." She narrowed her eyes at me and pointed a finger at my chest. "They said the new owner—you—owns casinos all over. Since when?"

Reaching out, I took her finger and kissed its tip. She jerked her hand back and stepped away. "Since always. You knew my company dabbles in a bit of everything."

"But casinos? How did I not know about them?" she asked, her little nose crinkling in confusion. God, I wanted to kiss it—her. I missed her more than words could say, but I knew I needed to bide my time and win her trust back. I fucked up majorly, and I needed to prove she was mine and I was only hers. "Then again, I guess I didn't know as much about you as I thought. Maybe it's a good thing I left."

"Love," I started, but she sent me a glare that had my dick trying to turtle back into my body. "You know me. No one knows me better."

She shook her head, then fell into a chair. "I thought I knew you before her."

She looked so defeated. I did that to her; I made the love of my life, the person I consider my heart, not only run from me, but also give up on us. "I fucked up." She raised a brow at my words. I ran my hand down my face. "I thought I was fulfilling Dorian's last wish. I promised I'd take care of Heather."

"What about what you promised me? Is it okay to break all your promises to me just to keep his?" She nodded. "Good to know." She stood up. "Move."

"Why?"

"So, I can go turn in my resignation." Her pretty eyes narrowed on me in a deathly glare.

I had to stop myself from smiling. "No." There was no way I was going to let her leave this room before we hashed this shit out.

Hope crossed her arms over her chest and jutted out her chin. She was so damn adorable when defiant; it made me hard just watching her stance. "Nico, you can't keep me here against my will or force me to work under you."

My blood heated at the thought of her under me, and a low, sexual grunt escaped my mouth. "It doesn't have to be under me. It can be over me or bent over ..."

She pointed at me. "Do not finish that sentence. You made your choice, and it wasn't me. Now let me leave, or I'm calling the police and reporting you for kidnapping or unlawful detention or something." She fumbled in her handbag.

"Looking for your phone to call Officer Grant?" I asked.

Her eyes widened. "How ..." Then they narrowed on me. "Have you been watching me? You stalker, psycho."

"You think I showed up here only today? I've been here for a bit, and even you must admit it's a small enough town to learn people's habits. Especially when those people maintain rituals, like coffee at a specific time with a certain cop or runs along the Mount Moriah Cemetery trails three times a week, looping five times, then going to have a giant cinnamon roll." I raised a brow, silently challenging her to refute it.

Her breathing quickened, her little nostrils flaring. "That proves my point. You're stalking me! You can't force me to work for you here."

I stepped in close to her. "Tell me something, love. Do you plan to run again? I didn't realize how much I enjoyed the chase until I started chasing you." I brought my hand up, running the back of it down her arm. I didn't miss the goosebumps that popped out along her arm or the way her pupils dilated.

She swatted my hand away. "Don't fucking touch me!"

"Is that any way to talk to your boss?" She opened her mouth, most likely to tell me she was quitting, but I wasn't having it. "It doesn't matter where you go. I'll buy any company you work for and become your boss. Your choices are simple. Work with and for me here, or become my wife, and you won't need to work at all."

I watched her deflate before my eyes, and my heart clenched. "I don't understand why you're doing this. You made your choice, and it wasn't me. Now you want to pursue me to the ends of the earth. I figured you and Heather would be happily married by now." She snorted. "Hell, I figured you two would have used our wedding venue to get married."

The sheer devastation in her pretty eyes made my heart clench in my chest. I could make a million excuses or tell her I had no desire for Heather at all, but she wouldn't believe any of it. "I fucked up." She looked at me with wide, surprised eyes. "I never crossed any physical lines with Heather, but I may have crossed others by giving her my time and attention that should have gone to you, or by running to her whenever she needed something. At first, I didn't think it was cheating, but I've learned it is. I may have promised my best friend I'd take care of her, but I should never have put her wants and needs above yours. You're the one I was about to swear to love and cherish until death do us part, not her. I only promised Dorian to watch over Heather, and I took it too far. I'm so sorry I hurt you. It was never my intention."

"It's hard to believe the great Nico Marino, the badass, is apologizing. I appreciate ..."

I sighed, rubbed a hand down my face, and asked, "But?"

"But I can't forget. You prioritized someone who wasn't me. I learned that Heather had bought a ticket to Italy on the same day we were to leave for our honeymoon. If she had shown up with no hotel room and asked to share the villa we had rented, would you have let her stay?" I shook my head and opened my mouth to deny it, but she wasn't done. "Don't lie."

"I would have then, but not now. Now, I understand."

She raised an eyebrow. "Oh, you understand now, do you?"

I didn't expect her to fall into my arms when I apologized. I guess I really didn't know what to expect, but one thing I knew for sure was that she could never resist my tattoos. I get hard thinking about all the times she licked and kissed each one. Slowly and deliberately, I remove my cufflinks, then undo the buttons at each wrist, watching as her breathing changes and she swallows several times, licking her pink lips.

"W ... W ... What are you doing?" she questioned in a raspy voice.

I grinned at her. "It's hot in here. Don't you think?" I kept rolling up my white dress shirt sleeves over my tattooed forearms. "And to answer your question, I do understand now. I wish I had opened my eyes sooner." I crossed my arms over my chest, watching her eyes follow the movement.

It took her a few seconds to look up at me. "Why did you allow her to wear a wedding dress to our wedding? You should have stopped her from coming down the aisle in a cheap copy of my dress. She had been copying everything I did up to the wedding, and you said nothing." The hurt in her eyes about killed me.

"My love, the reason I didn't stop her was that I didn't notice her. I was so wrapped up in my own head, worrying about whether you were going to walk out on me or toward me, that I didn't notice anyone, especially not her. I didn't give a fuck about what she was wearing, because I was never attracted to her. So if she changed her hair or clothes to match yours, I never would have noticed, because she was not and never will be you. You are it for me."

She sliced a hand through the air as if swatting my words away. Seeing no ring on her finger gutted me. "Funny how your actions since Heather came into our lives don't match your words. If I were it for you, you would never have left me hanging over and over again for her. So excuse me if I'm not buying the bullshit you're trying to sell me."

Hope grabbed her bag and stepped toward me. "Do you know why I picked Deadwood to run to?"

I knew the answer, but I didn't want to say it out loud, because voicing it made it real. Real in the sense that she chose this place, because she didn't think I'd follow. "I have my thoughts on it." I could feel the muscle in my jaw pulse as I clenched my teeth.

She came up to where we were almost touching. "Because this is where Dorian died, and I didn't think you'd ever come back here." With that, she shoulder-checked me hard enough to make me stumble, giving her time to reach the door and swing it open. She dashed out and down the hall.

The second I got my bearings, I was running after her. I didn't give a damn who saw me or what the fuck they thought of me.

The moment I burst out the door, I almost slammed into Hope, who stood there as if she had turned to stone. Before I could figure out why, she swore, "You've got to be fucking kidding me!"

My eyes shot up to where she was looking.

"Heather, what the fuck are you doing here?"

She rubbed her rounded belly. "The baby and I missed you."

3

Hope

The air was ripped from my lungs, leaving me not only speechless, but also immobilized.

Once I could unlock my frozen muscles, I speed-walked to my car, not looking back as I pulled out of the parking lot.

I couldn't speed down Main Street, but if I could, I would have floored it. My mind was racing a million miles an hour, thinking about everything I needed to do to take off. I knew Hadley would pack up anything I didn't need right away and either put it in storage or ship it to me once I got settled. There was one thing I knew for sure, and that was that I wasn't about to stick around the small town of Deadwood and watch the two of them become a family of three.

It wasn't until I pulled into my driveway that I realized I had been crying the whole way home. I thought I had spilled all the tears I had left for Nico because of Heather, but I was wrong. My heart, which had just begun to mend, cracked wide open again, as if it were bleeding out through my chest.

I had to pry my fingers from the steering wheel and force myself to move. On the doorstep of my house was another basket of things I loved. Without hesitation, I called Hank to come pick it up. He explained he was on another call and would get to me as soon as possible, but he told me not to touch the basket.

I side-stepped the offending basket, seeing what I could only imagine were my favorite double-chocolate banana muffins. I knew that's what they were, because every time I got something on my step, it was my favorite. At first, I thought it had been Nico, but one bite of a chocolate-covered strawberry had me rushing for the toilet. Those particular treats contained heavy-duty laxatives, and then there was the cheeseball and crackers. I handed those right over to Hank, who, after some testing, found out there was a deadly amount of sleeping pills in them. Then there were the cookies with antifreeze. And that was just a few of the things. Now my favorite muffins. Why did it have to be all my favorite things? Because it was ruining everything I liked!

Nico would never try to poison me, or so I thought. I never thought he'd get Heather pregnant, either.

There was no time to dwell on what-ifs; I needed to start packing right away.

Without much thought about where I was going or what I'd need, I pulled out my suitcase and started throwing stuff into it, along with all my important papers. Hadley would send me the rest once I got settled somewhere.

If Nico and Heather were here, I knew one thing for sure: I wouldn't be.

With my suitcase in one hand and my phone to my ear with the other, I headed down the stairs, thinking how much I was going to miss this house and Deadwood.

Right as I hit the last step, Hadley picked up, but I said, "Let me call you back," without explanation.

Nico stood in my living room, a muffin from the basket heading toward his mouth. Before I could think better of it, I dropped my suitcase and rushed to him. I slapped the muffin away from his beautiful lips.

"What the hell, love?" he asked, startled.

I pointed my finger at his face. "First, I am no longer and never will be your love. Second, why the hell did you break into my house? I should call the police on you."

He let out a huff of breath. "You mean you'll call your boyfriend?"

"How did you get into my house?"

He bent down and picked up the smashed muffin. "I have a key, and your security is shit. You'd think your boyfriend would install a better system for you." He was fishing for anything he could find out about Hank and me, and I wasn't going to give him shit.

I tilted my head to the side. "What do you mean you have a key?"

He was now looking at the muffin as if it had personally offended him. "Your cousin Hadley has the place set up with a property management company." He picked up the biggest part of the muffin from the floor and left the rest.

"I'm aware."

"I bought the company. It seems I'm now your landlord." His smile was salacious.

I crossed my arms over my chest. "Under code 42-32-32, a landlord or landlord's agent shall give the tenant reasonable notice of the landlord's intent to enter and enter only at reasonable times, usually twenty-four hours' notice."

"You've learned a thing or two from *him*." He set the muffin on the coffee table and brushed his hands together to remove the crumbs. "I entered your home, because I thought you were going to hurt yourself."

"You have a higher opinion of your place in my life than you should. The moment you let Heather wear that dress to our wedding, I no longer gave a fuck about you or her. So go back to your baby momma and leave me alone." I walked over and opened the door, but the ass went to my suitcase and picked it up.

"If I don't have a place in your life, why are you running away?" He tapped the side of his head. "If you were over me ... over us, you'd stay and deal with me." I walked back to him to get my suitcase, but he wouldn't let go. Our hands touched, sending electric shocks up my arm.

Before I could think through my answer, I found myself saying, "I'm going on a business trip."

He grabbed my arm and pulled me into his muscular chest. "Did you forget I'm your boss and I know you don't have a business trip?" Then he pulled me even closer. Before I could take a breath, his lips were on mine.

In my head, I was shoving him away, but in reality, I was kissing him back. I even opened up to him so we could twine our tongues. The man could kiss, and he did it well. I missed his mouth on me, not just on my mouth.

Before I could protest, he lifted me and wrapped my legs around his waist. I could feel his hardness pressing against my soft folds.

"God, love, it's been too long." His voice was rough with desire.

His deep voice pulled me out of my sexual haze. I pushed against his shoulders, meeting his gaze. "What about Heather? Aren't you two together now?"

"There is nothing going on between us, and there never will be anything."

It confused me. "But Heather implied the baby was yours."

"Why are you talking about her? It's been six long fucking months, and I need to be inside you." He started kissing my neck. This was so wrong, but the chemistry between us had never been the problem. Heather had been.

As I was enjoying his mouth on my neck, I tried to remember why this was a bad idea when there was a pounding on the door. "Don't answer it," Nico groaned into my neck.

"Hope! I know your home! Open the damn door!"

I released my legs from his lean hips, he moaned in displeasure. Once I extricated myself, my head cleared. I needed to put as much space between us as possible. It had only been six months since I had left him, and my heart was still madly in love with him.

Before I could reach the door, it swung open. Hank pushed through, glaring at Nico as if Nico had kicked his puppy. "Just come on in, Officer Grant," Nico said.

Hank held up his keys. "I have a key to let myself in whenever I need to." He smirked, then winked at me.

I rolled my eyes and mouthed "ass."

Hank's eyes swept the living room as I put myself back together. I needed to keep my distance from Nico. He had a way of dragging me back into his life, and I wasn't going to be anyone's second choice—not again, anyway.

Hank's assessing cop's eye didn't miss a thing as he zeroed in on my swollen lips and raised a brow at me. He shook his head, walked over to the remains of the muffin on the floor, and then toed it with his boot.

There, beneath the leftover muffin mess, was the glint of silver. Nico bent forward, looking at the mess. "Is that a fucking razor blade?"

"Wow, maybe I should ask for you to be my new partner," Hank deadpanned, then turned to me. "I told you not to touch that basket." He pointed at the basket of muffins on the coffee table.

Before I could say anything in my defense, Nico stepped in front of me. "It was me. When I showed up and saw it, I brought it in, but when I was about to eat one, Hope knocked it from my hand." He turned, pulled me into his arms, and kissed the top of my head. "You saved my life."

"You're our number one suspect, and you have been since all of her favorite things started showing up here," Hank told him.

Nico slowly turned around, locking eyes with Hank. "I would never do anything to put my love in danger."

"And a lot of men go on the news begging for their wife to return or for whoever has her to please not hurt her, because she's his life. When in fact, she's buried under the deck he just built."

"That was specific," Nico said. "I love Hope and came all the way to Deadwood, a place I hate with all my being, to win her back."

Hank stepped into Nico's personal space. "Exactly. Hence all her favorite things being delivered with an extra side of malice."

Nico stepped in so close the two men were chest to chest. "Tell me,

Officer Grant, if I love her, why would I put razor blades in her favorite muffins?"

"I don't know. Why don't you tell me why you paid more attention to another woman than to your fiancé when you had her? Maybe you think that if you can't have her, no one can?"

That drew a growl from Nico. "Like you? As if you have a chance with someone as perfect as her."

"If she were so perfect, then why'd you give your affections to another woman?"

I couldn't take it anymore. I stepped between them, pushing against their chests. "Enough, both of you! Stop the dick measuring and let's figure out who's trying to kill me. It's progressed slowly from laxatives to freaking razor blades. What's next, a gun blast to the face?"

Nico's body tensed under my hand, then he pulled me into his hard chest. I could feel him shaking. "This isn't helping us find who is doing this," I said calmly, pulling away from him.

"I know who my number one suspect is," Hank said through gritted teeth.

"And I know who mine is," Nico countered.

"I will bring you down, scumbag."

"Not if I bring you down first, Officer Asshole."

Hank snorted. "You can't get in the way of an investigation."

"I'll do my own private one."

I screamed. Both men looked at me like I'd lost my mind, and maybe I had. "It wasn't either of you assholes, but while you two are going after each other, the person who wants me dead is still out there."

Hank's hand instinctively went to the butt of his gun. "How do you know it's not him?" he jerked his chin toward Nico.

I opened my mouth to answer, but Nico beat me to it. "Because I fucking love her."

Love not loved. The stupid butterflies in my stomach started kicking me with steel-toed boots. I couldn't let his words soften me the way those kisses had. Fuck, I was screwed if I stayed here around Nico.

4

Nico

My lips curled into a smile. I had no idea how lucrative this little casino in Deadwood would be, but the numbers from summer alone kept them afloat through the winter months, and all the marketing Hope had done had brought in a huge uptick of locals gambling. She was freaking amazing.

The fact that someone was trying to kill her had me calling in my own team of experts to find out what the hell was going on. She was too kind, too good for anyone to want her dead.

The door to my office was pushed open so hard it banged against the wall. "I'm sorry, sir. I told him he couldn't barge in," Judy said, trying to stop Hank from entering my office.

"It's fine. After all, he is an officer of the law. He wouldn't be barging in without good cause or a warrant." I cocked a bow at him.

Judy closed the door on her way out as Hank fell into the leather chair in front of my desk. "I'm here to talk."

My heart raced. "Did you find out who's targeting Hope?"

He ran a down his face. "Not yet, but I'm working on it." He pulled out his phone, tapped the screen, then slid it across my desk. "Someone has been blocking the cameras' signal at Hope's, and the software used to do it is from one of your companies."

I took the phone and looked. "And? Anyone can buy this software. That doesn't mean I did anything."

He took his phone back. "I don't think you did, but this software was a prototype. There can't be that many people with it. I can get a warrant and spend months going through the records, or you can pull them for us. Off the record, I don't believe you have anything to do with trying to hurt Hope."

"Interesting. Just yesterday, you had your hand on your gun, ready to bring me in. What changed?"

"I saw the way you looked at her and how you tried to protect her. It's my job to trust my gut and take everything in with a critical eye. I could see how much you still love her."

I nodded. "Thanks. There's nothing I wouldn't do for her. She's my everything."

"And yet you chose someone else to give your time and attention to."

"I did. I felt guilty about Dorian. I had blinders on when it came to Heather."

"Do you still have blinders on?" he asked.

"No."

He leaned forward. "Then why did it take you so long to get your ass here?"

I didn't know how much to tell him, since no one knew I had found her sooner or later, or why I had waited so long. I decided to bite the bullet and put myself out there. "I spent the time in therapy. I had to learn that Dorian wrecking his bike wasn't my fault and that I had more than repaid my debt to him regarding Heather. I did the work, I'm still doing the work, and I made myself a better man for Hope."

He bit his lip. "Good, that's what I needed to hear." Then he pulled out a small black device.

"What's that?"

He twisted it around in his hand. "This is a dash cam we found near the crash site." He pulled out a flash drive. "And this is what we were able to retrieve from it."

I was confused as hell about what he was talking about. "The crash scene case where your buddy died was closed, but this was found, and I feel it changes things. There's nothing I can do about it, but maybe you can."

"I don't understand?"

He jerked his head toward the flash drive. "You will once you watch what's on it." He got up and headed to the door. "This will help you even more in your recovery. Consider it more therapy."

"Why are you helping me? I thought you wanted Hope. Wouldn't it be easier to keep me out of the picture? Not to mention, this could put your job on the line."

He turned, pressing his back against the wooden door, and crossed his broad arms over his chest. "I think you misunderstand the relationship I have with Hope." He held up his left hand, waving his ring finger, which was tattooed to look like a ring. "I'm married to the love of my life, and he loves Hope like a sister, just as I do. I know she still loves you, and I'm giving you the last piece you need to heal yourself. All I want is for her to be happy. No one deserves it more."

"What about the gifts being left for her?" I asked.

"We're still working on it, and I do have a theory. Once you watch that video, I think you'll understand. I have to follow the law and the rules ..." He left the part about me not having to hang in the air.

"What do you want in return?" I asked, knowing there was no way he was doing this for nothing.

"If she doesn't choose you, disappear and let her stay here." For him, it seemed that simple. I could see that in the short time Hope had been in Deadwood, she had made an impact on him. Knowing my love, I knew she had affected many others, too.

"And if she does choose me?"

He snorted as if it were the funniest thing ever said, then raised a shoulder. "Then you both stay in Deadwood, and maybe I can learn to tolerate your nasty ass."

He left me at my desk, staring at the flash drive. I had forgotten Dorian always rode with a dash cam on his bike.

How did I forget that?

There had been a lot going on that day. Heather had been an especially huge cunt, whining about everything and wanting to ride on the back of my bike, even though she had been told a million times that the only woman on the back of my bike would be Hope. She was bitching about everything and nothing, so we took a ride into Deadwood to get some food and play some poker, hoping to quiet her down.

Heather wanted me to buy shit for her and would hang onto my arm wherever we went, no matter how many times I told her to knock it off. I also remembered how pissed off Dorian was with her and how he had been getting ready to ship her ass off to someplace with a padded cell.

It was strange that I had suppressed memories of his growing concern for Heather's mental well-being. He was truly worried she might hurt someone—me or herself.

I wasn't surprised my hand shook as I plugged in the flash drive. I had done so much therapy to stop blaming myself that I was afraid this would set me back. I took a deep breath and opened the file.

We had stopped at the Sinclair gas station, and I had run in to piss.

"D, just leave," Heather hissed. "If you leave, he has no choice but to bring me along."

"H, that ain't gonna happen. Get the fuck on the back of my bike. The only person who rides with Nico is Hope, and you ain't her."

"Come on, he won't leave me here. I really need to ride with him, not you." Her whine was so shrill it could pierce an eardrum.

"Get your fucking ass on this bike, or I swear to everything holy, I'll put you over my knee and tan your hide right in front of Nico."

She let out a scream. "God, I hate you!"

"Feeling's mutual."

The sound of his Road King starting up filled the office. Soon, the camera was swaying all over the place, as if the bike were swerving. "Settle the fuck down, or you're going to dump us," Dorian yelled.

"Pull over and let me off so Nico can pick me up."

"NO!"

The bike was swerving like crazy, and I knew that Dorian rode it well, so Heather must be causing it.

"You're going to make me spill the fucking bike. If you fuck up my bike, I'm done with your crazy ass."

"If I can't ride with Nico or have him, then we both go down," Heather screamed.

"Stop fucking hitting me, you crazy-ass bitch!" Then the bike veered into the other lane. Dorian must have overcorrected. It went back over too far and hit loose gravel. Then the camera flew.

The only sound in my office was my heavy breathing. Heather had been the reason for the accident. I was still trying to process when I remembered arriving on the scene. As I pulled Dorian into my arms, he said, "Take care of her."

At the time, I thought he meant for me to take care of her, but now, given the way he had growled those words, I understood he meant something different. I had fucked up the best thing that ever happened by taking care of Heather, when I should have put her in a fucking psychiatric ward. Dorian's death was entirely her fault.

Cold dread ran down my spine. If she could kill her own brother, who else could she kill?

Before I even realized what I was doing, my hand picked up my phone and called police dispatch. Before the dispatcher could say a word, I was yelling, "I need to talk to Officer Hank Grant. It's a fucking emergency."

"Officer Grant is on a call."

I rattled off Hope's address. "Get someone there now."

"What's the problem, sir?" she asked.

"I don't fucking know, but it could be a murder if you don't get someone there right fucking now!" I didn't wait for her to respond before hanging up and running out of the building. I noticed the strange looks, but I didn't give a shit. I had a horrible sense of dread riding me hard.

I had left Heather at the rental house when I found out she had followed me here, but now I'm not so sure she had. I feared she had been here all along. During therapy, they told me to distance myself from her for a bit, because it would help both of us. I had paid for her to travel and hadn't seen her for a few months.

What if she had been here the whole time? I got in my car and took off, not giving a shit about running red lights or getting pulled over. I wanted the cops to follow me.

There was no way to tell whether my gut instinct was right, but I wasn't taking a chance with Hope's life. I called her repeatedly, but it kept going straight to voicemail.

5

Hope

The first thought in my head was why I was on the floor and why I couldn't move my arms or legs. My eyes wouldn't open, and my head pounded with a drumbeat so painful that my eyes started to water. My throat was dry, and my mouth hurt. I forced myself to lie perfectly still as what had happened rushed back to me. Even though I felt like I was going to throw up, I forced myself not to move a muscle.

I had been doing laundry when I heard a knock at the door. I went to the peephole and looked through, but no one was there. I pulled out my phone and saw that no one had triggered the camera. It had to be another one of those fucking deliveries of my favorite things.

As soon as I unlocked the door, it was pushed open, and I fell to the floor. Someone in all black jumped on me and put a rag smelling of sweet, freshly cut hay over my nose and mouth until the fight left me. I tried to scratch and hit, but they were covered from head to toe, and with them sitting on my arms, I couldn't do much.

I refused to move, trying to gather as much information as I could about who had brought me down. I knew whoever it was had been behind the favorite things basket. I opened all my senses.

Whoever it was had been watching a trashy reality show.

They were currently chomping on my favorite chips.

They burped like a drunk in a barroom.

And don't get me started on the amount of flatulence coming out of their ass.

My hands and feet were wire-tied. There wasn't much wiggle room in my hands. I could feel the circulation leaving them, but my feet weren't too tight. I thought I could use that to my advantage. I peeked out through my lashes, trying to keep my eyes closed as much as possible.

There on my couch was someone all in black, wearing a ski mask, eating my truffle oil chips and drinking my diet Dr. Pepper, laughing at the stupidity on my TV like they didn't have a care in the world. Acting as if they hadn't just broken into my home and tied me up.

They looked like they had a big beer belly and muscular arms and legs, but through my lashes, everything looked distorted and weird. They didn't seem very tall as they sat on my couch, their feet on my live-edge oak coffee table. The black boots they wore had soles at least four inches thick and looked three sizes too big.

I wasn't sure what I was going to do, since I couldn't really move. I lay there for a bit more, trying to get myself together as the drug wore off. I willed myself to move and prayed I wouldn't throw up when I heard a strange, deep voice with an accent somewhere between British and Southern. "Fuck this, I'm not waiting any longer." The person got up and picked something off my table. It had to be the peach roses I kept there.

Suddenly, my face was drenched in gross flower water as thorny roses rained down on me. I sputtered and coughed. "Good, you're up now. We can get this over with." The voice was all wrong, sounding strange to my ear.

The rose thorns dug into my skin. The water smelled of algae as I spit it out. "What do you want? My purse is over there. Take anything you want, but please leave me alone," I begged, nodding toward the side table by the door where my purse sat.

The person snorted. The only parts of their skin showing were their mouth and eyes. They had to have contacts in because their eyes were a menacing black. It was like looking into an emotional void. They smelled like they had taken a freaking bath in Axe body spray, which made my eyes water and tears run down my cheeks.

"Aw, I see you're so scared you're crying." The person patted my cheek—hard. Then reached a hand between my legs, cupping my pussy. "Did you piss yourself?" they asked in that strange, fake voice.

"What do you want?" I asked.

"I wanted you not to dirty up our town with your whorish ways, take jobs from locals, or spread your legs for our fine officers, but here we are."

Confusion made my brows draw together. "What are you talking about? I haven't slept with anyone since I got here."

The person didn't pay me any attention as they strode over to the table and picked up a basket, swinging it from one finger. "You need to understand that you made me do this. I didn't want things to get messy, but you refused to eat all your favorite things. Now I need to get my hands dirty. Good thing I have these gloves." Something about the way they said nifty had me wracking my brain, wondering why it sounded so familiar. They over-enunciated the t and y.

They came over to me and sat on my chest, making me grunt in pain. Not because they were heavy. I thought they'd be heavier. No, it was because my hands were behind my back, and I could feel the bones in my wrists protest in pain.

"You're going to break my wrists," I gritted out through pain.

They shrugged. "That's the least of your problems." The person picked up a chocolate-covered strawberry and smiled. "This had to be the first and last thing you tried. Did you shit your pants?" They threw their head back and laughed.

I could see where this was headed and clamped my lips shut.

"We start with the chocolate-covered strawberries, then the cheeseball, which will help you sleep while you shit yourself. If you survive that, we move on to the snickerdoodle cookies with antifreeze. If you're still kicking, we finish with the muffins, and you know what's in them. If you still won't succumb, I'll put you out of your misery and mine with my own hands."

I had to ask, "Would you kill me simply for moving here and trying to thrive?" Then I sealed my lips.

"I've done worse. It's funny that even your officer can't help you."

I shook my head to make clear he wasn't mine, but I was afraid to open my mouth again.

"People like you come into our small town, take our jobs, take our men, drink our coffee, and pretend to fit in, but you don't and never will."

I wasn't the only out-of-towner to put down roots here, and I hadn't heard of anyone disappearing or being murdered. This felt personal, though I didn't know why. Maybe when I took the job at the casino, I had bumped someone else off the position, but Kara would have told me if it had pissed someone off; she was in on all the good gossip.

I never cut in line at the coffee shop.

I made sure to be polite to everyone, including the tourists.

At work, I brought goodies and went out for drinks at Saloon 10 with everyone. I bought my fair share of rounds.

Maybe whoever this was had a thing for Hank and was jealous of my relationship. I knew it wasn't his husband, Mathew, because Mathew loved me, maybe even more than Hank did.

The person on my chest pressed down even harder. I could feel the bones in my wrist starting to give way, and on instinct, I bucked as hard as I could. They went flying over my head, but there was nothing more I could do with my hands and feet wire-tied.

Whoever this fucker was, jumped up and kicked me in the ribs several times. I could hear bones cracking. Then they jumped back down on me with all their weight, and I felt the bones in my wrists give way. The scream that came out of me was one of severe pain, which I couldn't hold back any longer.

The moment my mouth parted in that scream, a chocolate strawberry was shoved into it, and I spat it back out. So the fucker on top of me pushed down on my ribs, and I had no choice but to gasp.

This time, when the strawberry was shoved into my mouth, they held my mouth shut. "You don't have to chew it. The chocolate will melt and run down your throat, and that, my friend, is where the laxatives are."

I could feel the chocolate melting and tried everything not to swallow.

The person sitting on me had one hand over my mouth, then started bouncing, making the pain in my wrists and ribs increase tenfold. Tears streamed down my cheeks as I tried not to swallow, but I was about to choke or pass out.

You always think you know what you'd do in a home invasion until you're the one on the floor, with a mouthful of a strawberry covered in chocolate-flavored laxative, two broken wrists, and God only knows how many broken ribs.

"I tried to use polite violence, but you wouldn't take the bait. Now there's no more politeness left in me." I could see their lip curl into a vile, evil grin.

The person reached over and pinched off a chunk of the sharp cheddar-pecan cheeseball, then brought it to my lips. I couldn't even smell the cheeseball, because of how much body spray this fucker had on.

Gloved fingers squeezed my nose shut. I held my breath as long as I could, but with the strawberry in my mouth and no air coming in through my nose, I had no choice but to get air to my lungs, or I would pass out. I gritted my teeth and opened my lips just enough to get a little air in.

The fucker grabbed my lip, pulled open my mouth, and, as quick as lightning, released my nose, grabbed the piece of cheeseball, shoved it in my mouth, then covered my mouth with their hand.

With the strawberry and the piece of cheeseball with pecans on it, and with a hand over my nose and mouth, I had no choice but to chew and swallow.

"There, that wasn't so hard, was it? This can go easy or hard. Your choice. I've got nothing but time, since I've been making fake calls across the city, sending your cop on wild-goose chases. No one's coming to save you, because I know for a fact that Hadley and Dakota are in Colorado visiting her uncle."

I was unsure whether it was the pain or the drugs taking effect, but my vision began to blur at the edges. It felt like I was underwater, slowly drowning.

Before I lost consciousness completely, the weight on my body lifted as everything went dark.

6

Nico

I was flying down Main Street, blaring my horn at stop signs and ignoring all traffic laws. I had one single-minded focus: to get to my Hope. I prayed a cop would pull in behind me and follow me. I made call after call to 911, but was told all officers were busy with other calls and that if it wasn't an emergency, they would get to me when they could.

"Someone could be dying right now!" I screamed.

"Sir, please don't scream at me. It won't get you anywhere. Do you know for sure that this Hope Walker is in danger?"

I didn't know for sure, but I wasn't about to tell them that. My heart was racing, and a cold sweat had soaked my shirt and covered my brow. "Yes."

The dispatcher let out a long-suffering sigh, as if she knew I was lying. "What kind of danger is she in, sir?"

My hands gripped the steering wheel so tightly I feared I'd pull it right off. I couldn't explain the fear, but I knew deep in my soul that something was seriously wrong. Hope and I always had that special connection. "I'm begging you to just get to the address I gave you!" I hit the end button on my steering wheel and laid my hand on the horn as I flew past casinos and tourists crowding the sidewalks.

I was getting glares and shouts, and people were flipping me the bird as they had to jump out of the path of my car, but the only thing on my mind was Hope. I finally found Hope in Deadwood, and I wasn't letting her go ever again.

All the ways I had not only let her down, but also hurt her were playing like a movie in my head. When she wanted me to choose between her and Heather, I didn't pause to think. I paused, because I couldn't understand how she could ever think she wasn't my one and only.

My therapist showed me how wrong I was, that my actions toward Heather spoke louder than all the love-yous I gave to Hope. I had stopped showing Hope I loved her, and I only told her I loved her, which broke something in me, because I had failed her so badly. The fact that I didn't realize that sooner killed something inside me; I was too much of a dumb ass to see it, and my head was twisted up with some stupid promise I thought I was making to my best friend.

I realized too late that Hope was the only one I needed to prove anything to. I'd spend the rest of my life showing her how much she meant to me, even if it meant watching her from the shadows as she moved on with another man. There would be only one woman for me, and that was my Hope.

Two blocks away from Hope's home was where I decided to park, hoping the element of surprise would work to my advantage. I got out of my car and prepared the keys to Hope's back door.

As I made my way to her house, the streets were quiet, and the warm summer breeze carried a pine scent. Everything looked normal, but something felt off. That warm summer breeze did nothing to ease the cold dread running through my veins.

My senses were on high alert, listening and watching for anything amiss, yet all was calm along the Ponderosa Pine-lined street.

There were no strange cars along the road, and I would know, having watched her home and everyone who came and went so many times in the last few months. I kept looking over my shoulder to make sure no one was watching me.

The keys in my hand rattled as my hand shook. It took me three tries to get the key into the lock. As quietly as possible, I turned the lock, feeling the tumblers click. The sound was as loud as a shotgun blast.

With my breathing ragged, I waited for a sign that someone had heard me, listening for footsteps approaching the back door. When there was nothing, I slipped through the back door and took off my shoes before going any farther.

With only my socks on, my feet were silent on the wood floors. My heart pounded so loudly, I was afraid it would be heard, and I stopped every few feet to listen. I could hear her murmuring, then a pained gasp. The house, which normally smelled of vanilla, now carried a strange, sweet scent.

I snuck around the kitchen wall into the living room, and what I saw had my blood turning from ice to molten lava in my veins. Some asshole was sitting on my woman, trying to force-feed her.

I didn't think I just pushed myself off the wall, and with everything in me, I punched the fucker right in the side of the head, knocking him out cold and sending him off Hope. I wanted to check on her, but I needed to detain this guy first.

After I looked around, I noticed an open black duffel bag by the door. I grabbed it and found duct tape, wire ties, a hammer, and a huge butcher's knife. Before I could turn around, a sharp pain shot through my left shoulder. I turned, and the fucker had a knife raised to strike again, but I knocked it away and punched the fucker in the face. They went down with a thud, so I wasted no time wire-tying them up.

With the stinging burn in my shoulder and warm blood trickling down my spine, I turned to Hope. What I saw made all my worries for myself vanish. She was unmoving, with food smeared across her gorgeous mouth. I picked up the knife from the floor and cut the ties on her feet, but when I reached her hands, they were so swollen I didn't know how I could cut the ties without hurting her even more. Her wrists were also bruised beyond belief. I didn't know much about medicine, but I knew a break when I saw one.

There was no way the giant butcher knife would fit through the small gap between her wrists without causing her more harm. I pulled out my pocketknife, but I was still afraid it was too thick to cut through the binds. I knew that when Hope and I lived together, she kept a box cutter where she recycled our cardboard.

I went out to the garage and found all her boxes broken down. Right there on a shelf above the boxes was a pink box cutter. I grabbed it and went back to my Hope. I pushed her onto her side and slid the thin blade into the small gap between her wrists, sawing slowly, with more care than I had ever taken with anything in my life. With each sawing motion of the box cutter, time seemed to slow to a stop.

I knew my own wound was bleeding heavily. I started seeing black spots in my vision and felt woozy, even swaying, but I refused to go down before I could help Hope.

After what seemed like an eternity, the wire ties came apart. With as much care as possible, I brought Hope's arms around and placed them on her chest as I laid her on her back, then took two fingers to check for a pulse. It was slow but steady, and I let out a long, strung-out breath.

With a quick look around, I found Hope's phone on the coffee table, along with a basket of goodies, all of which I knew were her favorites. I quickly used her face to unlock the phone and found Hank's number. Fuck dispatch. If he cared about her the way I was sure he did, he would come.

I held my breath as I stroked Hope's hair.

After three rings, he answered. "Hope, I'm a bit busy."

"It's Nico. Someone broke into her house and attacked her. She's hurt, and the attacker is tied up and unconscious on her floor. I need an ambulance here now." I could hear my voice weakening, but I refused to succumb to my injury until I knew Hope was safe.

"Fuck, I'm on my way and dispatching an ambulance." He didn't bother with a goodbye.

I flopped my ass down on the hardwood floor and leaned my back against the wall so I would stay as upright as possible. Once I was as settled as I could be, I pulled Hope into my lap, making sure not to jolt her broken arms too much.

As soon as I had her wrapped in my arms, I heard how ragged her breathing was. Fear wrapped around my heart and squeezed. I was growing cold and lethargic, which didn't bode well, but I refused to leave Hope alone.

I kissed her head. "Please stay with me. Dear Lord, if one of us needs to go, please take me. Hope is all good and light, and I almost dimmed that light, so if anyone should die, it should be me." I rested my chin on her head. "Love, I love you so much and have fucked up a million times over, in a million different ways, when it comes to you. No one should ever be more important than you. If we both make it out of this, I'll show how sorry I am and spend every day making it up to you. Even if you don't want me, I'll never take another woman as mine, because there is only one. I'll take care of you from the shadows. Please don't die." I felt tears burning down my cheeks before I realized I was even crying. I couldn't recall the last time I'd cried.

Every time I blinked, my eyelids stayed closed a little longer. I knew I was losing too much blood, but I forced myself to stay awake until help arrived. When I first saw Hope with Hank, I was pissed he was taking care of her, something I should have been doing, but had lost the right to. Now, I was so thankful she had him in her life, knowing he would bring help. If they could save one of us, it needed to be her. She deserved to bring her love, light, and hope to Deadwood.

The pain in my shoulder had gone numb, but I could feel the blood pouring down my back, growing cold and sticky. I gritted my teeth and used my weight to press my back against the wall, putting pressure on the wound.

It took all my strength to keep my eyes open, but I pulled Hope into my arms a little tighter and refused to let go. If it was my time to die, I was going to make sure she was the last person near me.

Finally, I heard sirens in the distance, but I wouldn't let my eyes close ... not yet.

The door burst open, and I never thought I'd be thankful to see Officer Hank Grant, but now I felt my body relax as my hands gripped Hope even tighter.

"Hey, man, you're going to have to let her go so we can assess," Hank said, trying to take her from me, but I couldn't and wouldn't let go. "The EMTs are here. I need you to let her go so they can take care of her ... and you, too. Please, Nico, release your fingers so we can get her help." Hank was on his knees beside me, begging.

I tried to open my eyes. I really did, but I couldn't. "I can't let go."

"What happened? Can you tell me so we can help Hope?" he asked. When someone else tried to come near me, I pulled her into my chest, crushing her against me. Hank raised a hand, stopping the other guy.

"I ... I ... don't know for sure. Her hands were tied behind her back. They're swollen and bruised. I think they're broken. She's breathing funny, and I think that fucker over there was trying to force everything she didn't eat from the baskets left on her step. I don't know what's in her system." My eyes were barely open, but I tried to look at Hank through my lashes. "You can't let her die." My voice slurred, and my hands were slipping. "I was stabbed in the back."

"I promise that if you let her go, I will personally ensure she receives the best medical care available." He was trying to take her from me.

My hands gripped tighter. "I love her so fucking much. I screwed up with her. I need another chance. Please help." I wasn't sure whether I was asking for his help to save her, to save me, or to get her back for me.

"Let me go! Nico, help! You promised you'd take care of me. You can't let them take me in. What about our baby?"

"Heather?" My brows furrowed in confusion at what she was doing here and why. And what baby? Then pure rage surged through me. I let go of Hope, letting Hank take her from me, but I latched onto his arm. "Don't let her go. Make sure she pays for what she did to Hope."

"You can fucking guarantee it." It was the last thing I heard before darkness claimed me.

7

Hope

The beeping was driving me crazy. Why was my mouth so dry?

I turned my head and saw Hank in a chair. He wore a navy T-shirt and jeans. His head was back, his eyes closed, but the moment I looked over at him, he was sitting up. He had dark circles under his eyes and his hair was sticking up all over.

I looked down at the casts on both my arms.

"You have broken arms and a couple of broken ribs. They had to pump your stomach, but nothing serious. Thank God Nico got to you in time."

I took a deep breath, wincing at the pain. "Nico?"

"Don't ask me how he figured out it was the psycho bitch, but he did. He pulled her off you, but he got stabbed in the back for his efforts." He got me some water and held the straw to my lips. He had to pull the water away from me. "Little bit at a time."

Maybe it was the meds in my system or the pain with every breath, but it took me what felt like forever to put the pieces together. "You mean Heather?"

"Yep. She came to your house to kill you. When we were dragging her away, she kept screaming, 'No one could have him.' Meaning Nico. Then she screamed that she was pregnant with his baby and that we were going to kill her baby. She screamed that we were child murderers at the top of her lungs all the way to the station."

There was so much information to process in my drug-addled mind, and the stench of antiseptic and copper, like no amount of scrubbing could take away, reminded me of how much blood had been spilled in these halls and made me nauseated. Now that I think about it, the person in my home seemed strange yet familiar, and the way the assailant said "nifty" reminded me of her. I couldn't decide whether it was a woman or a man. "Is Nico going to bail her out? It is his baby."

"It's not."

"Why do you say that? I saw her at work. She was holding her stomach and said the baby missed him. He didn't deny it." Of course, I took off while he was still stunned, but still. Then Hank's words about Nico sank in. "Nico got stabbed? Saving me?" Hank nodded. "Is he okay? Can I see him?" I tried to move, but he put a hand on my shoulder, pushing me back down.

"You haven't been released yet, and he isn't here. He had to be flown to Rapid City by a flight-for-life aircraft."

The words hit me straight in the chest.

Did he hurt me? Yes.

Did that make me hate him? For a while, maybe.

Did I still love him with every breath I took? Hell yes, and I needed to see him.

As I was struggling with my own thoughts, Hank got up, went to a big black bag by the door, and put on some disposable gloves. He pulled out some padding. "This is a fake belly. Heather wore it with this." He reached in and pulled out a muscular suit. "It made her look like a muscular man with a beer belly. We believe that's why Nico knocked her out, but then again, he may have known going in that it was her."

"He knocked her out and took a knife on my behalf?"

He stuffed everything back into the bag, took off his gloves, and tossed them in the trash. "He did. I gave him information we couldn't investigate, and he ran with it. He saved your life." He ran a hand through his hair and fell back into the chair. "As much as I want to hate him for what he did to you, I'm grateful he saved you. Heather had made several fake calls to keep the police, fire, and medical busy on wild goose chases all over the city, both in town and out. If Nico hadn't made it to you ..." He shook his head, a pained look on his face.

"I need to see him, please."

"He's in surgery now. As soon as they release you, I'll take you to Rapid City."

Tears filled my eyes as I let everything that had happened wash over me—how close I had come to dying, and that it was Heather who had been trying to kill me all along. But above all else, Nico had put his own life on the line to save me. I wasn't sure where Nico and I were headed, but I knew I needed to be there just in case.

The thought of him not making it or of a world without his dominant, sexy energy held no appeal for me.

~

Later, I refused to stay in the hospital for another moment, and Hank and Mathew promised to keep an eye on me as we drove for an hour to Rapid City so I could see Nico. Mathew had friends at the hospital he was keeping in touch with.

When we got to the hospital, the woman at the information desk, seeing how I looked, tried to get us to go straight to the emergency room.

Once she realized I had just come from Monument Health in Deadwood, she directed us to Nico.

In the waiting room on his floor, the nurse told us the surgery was a success, but he was still unconscious. She then explained that only family could visit him. Before she finished her sentence, I heard myself say, "I'm his fiancé."

Mathew smirked.

Hank rolled his eyes.

The nurse looked at my ring finger, but I couldn't wear a ring because my hands were in casts and my fingers were swollen.

Mathew stepped forward. "Connie, it's fine. I'll vouch for her." Matt was ten years older than Hank, with a trim silver-and-black beard and intense, kind gray eyes. He was bald and a firefighter.

Connie shrugged. "Fine, you can see him, but if he wakes up and doesn't want you in his room, you will leave." She held up a finger and pointed at Matt and Hank. "You two can't go in. Stay out here or go to the cafeteria."

Matt nodded. "Thanks, Connie. You're the best."

Connie took me back to Nico's room and left.

He was too big for the little hospital bed, his tattoos peeking out from the hospital gown. He was extremely pale, with tubes in his nose, an IV in his arm, and monitors beeping.

The warmth spreading down my cheeks had me swiping at the tears that were falling. Tears I had no idea were pouring forth.

I went to his side and tried to take his hand with my cast hand. "What the hell were you thinking? Why would you put yourself in danger for me? I thought you wanted nothing more than to keep your promise to Dorian and protect Heather." His hand twitched, but there was no other movement.

It took a bit of leg maneuvering, but I managed to push the chair close enough to the bed to sit and hold his hand.

"In the months leading up to our wedding, you hurt me so many times by putting Heather ahead of me and my wants and needs, but seeing her standing at the altar in that wedding dress broke something in me. I love you, and I don't think it will ever change, but I can't be second best and won't be. We need to talk when you wake up. If what you said about not even seeing her in that dress, because you were too worried about me not walking down the aisle is true, maybe, just maybe, it changes things, but only if we talk and work through them. We can't do that if you don't wake up. Please, Nico, wake up."

~

Someone's hand was caressing my head. I jumped, my heart pounding. "Hey, it's okay," Nico said calmly. His voice was hoarse. I must have dozed off, but I was wide awake now.

"You're awake. How do you feel? Do I need to get the doctor? Do you need water?"

He smiled at me. "I feel like I got stabbed in the back, but I'm lucky to be alive. I don't need a doctor, because he just left, and you slept through it. I'd love some water."

I got him some water, and after setting it down, he asked, his eyes filled with so much tenderness, "How are you? When I saw you on the floor, I thought I was too late." His voice broke at the end.

"I was scared, too. Did you know it was Heather when you knocked her out? I didn't realize it was her."

He laid his head back on the thin pillow, so I lifted the head of the bed a bit. "Hank gave me the footage from Dorian's dash cam." He stopped, as if remembering. When he spoke again, his voice was ragged with grief. "When I was holding him as he lay dying, he told me to take care of her. I thought he meant for me to care for her. I took that care too far and hurt you."

I felt tears pricking behind my eyes and my nose burning with emotion. I couldn't speak, so I nodded.

"Turns out she was the cause of his death ..." His emotions choked him up. "She wanted to ride with me no matter how many times Dorian or I told her you were the only woman to ride on the back of my bike. She tried to kill them both, just because he wouldn't pull over on the side of the road so I'd pick her up. She killed him, and his last words weren't for me to care for her, but to take care of her for what she did to them."

The gasp came out of me raw and ragged. "How could she do that to her own brother? If she wanted to kill herself, that's one thing, but Dorian was a wonderful guy who didn't deserve a sister like her."

"Too late now. When I saw that video, something clicked in my head, and I had a sixth sense that she was the one going after you. After you left, she did, too. I thought she had finally given up on me, so I focused on therapy and becoming a better man for you. I sold the place where we all lived and bought a new place, brand-new and ready for you to decorate when you came back, because there is no life I live without you in it. Little did I know she followed you here."

I tried to push a strand of hair that had fallen out of my bun back, but I only ended up smacking myself in the face with my cast. Nico reached up weakly and pushed it behind my ear. "You are the most gorgeous woman in all of existence." I had no makeup on, a messy bun, and was wearing sweatpants and a huge T-shirt, because it was easy to get in and out of, yet he still looked at me like I was the only woman in the world. "She hurt you, because of me, and I will never forgive myself for it."

"It's not your fault she's sick. Your fault here is not seeing her scheming sooner and choosing her over me, because of your promise to Dorian. At first, I respected your choice to care for her. Even when you stopped listening to me, I still wanted to believe it was just your sense of duty to your dead friend, and I got that. But the wedding was the last straw."

There was pain in his features, whether from his injuries or from his heart. I wasn't sure. "Even if there's no hope of us getting back together, there will never be anyone else for me. I may have fucked up, but my love for you will never dim. No matter how long it takes, I hope you'll see how much I love you. If you do give me a chance, I'll spend every day proving it to you."

"Nico, a lot has happened, and I don't know how I'm feeling right now." The words had no sooner left my mouth than his phone buzzed with the same unknown number that had been trying to call for the past couple of days. "You should answer that. I think it might be Heather. I'll go give you some privacy."

"Don't go." He picked up his phone and put it on speaker. Sure enough, it was the jail. After Nico accepted the charges for the call, he put it on speaker.

"Nico, thank God. You have to get me out of here." When Nico didn't respond, she continued, "It's what Dorian would have wanted."

"No, I'm done with you." His tone left no room for argument.

"You don't mean that. I had nothing to do with what happened at Hope's. Please come get me out so we can talk." She was sobbing.

"Why did you pretend to be pregnant with my child?" he asked, not taking his eyes off me.

"I was only trying to protect you. If she thought we had a kid together, she wouldn't cling to you so much."

"Hope is the only person I want clinging to me forever. You need to stop calling me. I'm not bailing you out, and you can bet your ass I'll be at every court hearing to make sure you never get out. I didn't stop you from hurting Hope, but I will stop you from ever hurting her again. I'll put every dollar I have into making sure you rot in there, not only for Hope and me, but for Dorian." The conviction in his voice sent goosebumps down my spine, and if I was being honest with myself, it was pretty hot.

In a voice barely above a whisper, she said, "You don't mean that."

"I do."

"I didn't do anything to her or to you," she added. "And I would never hurt my brother."

"If you weren't there, how'd you know I was hurt?"

"It's a small town. I heard it from some of the cops."

Nico sighed. "I call bullshit, and I have proof it was your fault the bike wrecked. The case may be closed, but I will never let it rest, even if I have to sue you in civil court. Now, princess, settle in and enjoy your stay. You're going to be there for a looooong time." He hit the end button on his phone, then let his head fall back as if he were too exhausted to go on.

"I'll let you rest."

Before I could even turn around, Nico reached out and grabbed my shirt. "Please don't go."

I let out the breath in my lungs. "Nico, what do you want from me? I appreciate you saving me, but it doesn't change anything between us."

"I know how much I fucked up, and even if you can never forgive me, I still want to be part of your life, whether as your boss or from a distance." He tugged my shirt, pulling me back toward him a couple of steps. "I've been working hard on myself, and I understand how badly I hurt you. I need to make things right, even if you don't want me."

I sat back down in the chair by his bed. "Nico, I will always and forever love you, but you hurt me beyond measure. It's not only how you acted with Heather; it's that you brought her into my world, which caused everything to happen. I can't even eat my favorite things anymore."

He brushed his knuckles along my fingers, peeking out from the pink cast. "Then I'll take you to new places so you can try new things and find new favorites. If you want to stay here, I'll stay with you. If you want to leave, I'll follow. If you need to move out of that house, because it holds bad memories, I'll get you a new one. Wanna move out of state? Then I'll help." The desperation in his voice, layered with the roughness of his pain, made my heart twinge.

"I'm not leaving Deadwood. I will not be terrorized by Heather into leaving my home or my job."

"Then I'm staying, too," he told me.

"What about your other businesses?" I had to ask.

"I'll video conference and fly in when I need to. I don't want to leave you ... even if you don't want to see me. I'll stay in the shadows of your life." He looked drained.

"Get some rest." When I said that, he tensed. "I'll stay with you, and once you're out of the hospital, we'll sit down and talk," I told him. He relaxed into the bed, his eyes closing almost instantly. Even pale and tired, he was still the most handsome man I'd ever seen, and I couldn't deny I still loved him. But could I give him another chance? That was the real question.

8

Hope

Nico had stayed in the hospital for a week, and after we sat down and talked, I wasn't ready to take him back yet. But he swore he would show me how sorry he was and how much he cared for me.

I allowed him to stay in my home during his recovery so I could be there to help him. I knew he could afford a health care aide, but I wanted to be the one there for him.

I'd go to work, and when I came home, there'd be a hot dinner waiting for me, made by Nico himself. He'd pack me a lunch and have my coffee ready in the mornings.

On the weekends, we would travel around the state, trying new favorite foods. I discovered that one of my new favorites was Indian frybread tacos. He also refused all calls from Heather and hired a lawyer to sue her for Dorian's wrongful death.

Having him back in my space, I expected it to feel strained or weird, but we fell right back into our comfortable groove.

One sunny Sunday, about three months after Nico got out of the hospital, he came out to the backyard where I was watering flowers. He sat hesitantly on one of the chairs on the deck. "Hope, I need to give up the rental on Paul Street in Lead."

I turned, raising a brow in question. "How's that my problem? Don't you own the housing management company? I'm sure you can find another one."

He rubbed the back of his neck. "I was hoping to build a home ... for us.

Your dream home, anything you want." When I kept looking at him without saying anything, he fell silent, then rushed on. "We could have two separate living spaces if you want."

Nico has continued his therapy here in Deadwood, and we have even done some couples counseling. He shows up every day, showing me how much he cares. He knows how much he messed up with Heather and is trying to make amends. He even befriended Hank and Mathew, and to my shock and awe, they like him. They have threatened him repeatedly, saying they would make him disappear if he ever hurt me.

Nico has been the perfect roommate and friend.

I turned the water off and walked to him. Instead of sitting in the chair beside him, I sat on his lap, looping my arms around his neck. "If we move into a new home, I want it to be because we're married."

"Are you fucking serious?" His eyes were shining so brightly I couldn't hide my smile.

I put a finger to his lips, stopping him from going on. "But we take things slow while the house is being built. If there are any signs you're slipping away again, I'm done for good. I'll leave, and this time you will not find me."

"You still love me?" he asked.

"You know I never stopped, but you hurt me. We will continue with couples counseling or no deal."

His smile took up most of his face. "Anything! Is it too soon to ask if I can kiss you?"

I leaned in close. "It's not, and you may, but no naked yum-yum time until at least our next three counseling sessions. All the things you've been doing for me continue."

"Whatever you need and want, but if I slip, call me out. Don't just run off. I got a taste of hell without you in my life, and I never want to go through it again. I found Hope in Deadwood, and I will never let you go again."

"Deadwood gave me hope, too, and I don't plan to leave."

The End

ABOUT THE AUTHOR

V.J. Lee spends her time writing characters you will both love and want to punch in the face—full of heat and action, from her home in the beautiful Colorado mountains, when she's not traveling or shoe shopping. She lives with Mark, the best husband on the planet, and has two sons and three grandkids. You can find all her works on her website vjleeauthor@wordpress.com

If you enjoyed Finding Hope in Deadwood, follow me so you don't miss upcoming stories.

Dedicated to Hillary Crawford, my amazing editor: we found each other after losing hope, and I'm so thankful you came into my life when you did. You are exactly what I needed and helped me more than you realize. I'm so sad this is our last story together. We started out as strangers who got scammed, but it's proof that everything happens for a reason — you were exactly who and what I had been searching for. We may no longer be working together, but we will be lifelong friends. I love you, lady, and wish you all the best life has to offer. You have come so far and done so well — I'm proud of you. Don't forget me.

The second dedication is to anyone who made mistakes and found hope. I hope you find what you're seeking in love. To my husband Mark, the best husband ever, I love you most.

Thank you to all the authors and organizers of Wild Deadwood Reads for letting me participate in this incredible event and share my story with you. Also, thank you to my excellent editor, Hillary Crawford, my Alpha reader, Monica Bird, and my beta readers, Shana Colbert and Deanne Fenton. You guys are the best.

FEROCIOUS PROTECTOR

VIA MARI

Ferocious Protector

1

BLAKE

The Gulfstream touches down at the private airfield right outside of Deadwood, South Dakota on a beautiful sunny day. Nice perks of having a very wealthy crime family protecting this land and the investments they've made in the casino, restaurants and other shops in town.

If anyone had told me six months ago I'd be working for a crime family, protecting their family interests instead of staying in the military, I'd have said bullshit. But life changes on a dime and family priorities and making the kind of bank this gig pays comes first now.

Damian and Dereck walk next to me and toss their go bags and gun cases into the trunk of the black SUV. "You guys always get the private plane and nice car waiting for you kinda treatment?" I ask, placing my duffle next to theirs before closing the back.

Damian slides into the driver seat and Dereck takes shotgun as I get into the back. He turns in his seat. "The Larussios, Prestians, and Carringtons have a lot of enemies and want to keep their families safe. You take good care of them, and they take good care of you."

I lean back in the leather seat and snap the buckle into place. "That I will do. I'm happy there was a position open and that Beckett put in a good word for me."

Dereck motions to Damian to take a right as we hit the main highway. "You've more than proven you have the skills. Let's hope we don't have to put some of that training to use on this trip. I'm sure Beckett's given you the scoop, but we've had a hell of a time keeping the Chicago boys out of this territory. They want this land, the casinos, bars and restaurants in the worst of ways. We keep stomping their ass, but they keep coming back for more."

"When are Matt, Sheldon, and Jay heading our way?"

They exchange a look. "You never know with those guys. They keep a pretty busy schedule, but they said they were going to try to make it. We'll see if that materializes though. They've had trouble locally lately."

My phone buzzes and I read the message. "Beckett said he and the others will meet us at Wild Deuces." Damian gives me a grin in the rearview. "Sounds good. We're officially off the clock until the wedding, unless all hell breaks loose. I'd say it's about time for a cold beer and the Wild Deuces has the coldest beer in town. Besides, Kenny the owner is a great friend of Coles. He has a few rooms reserved for us on the hotel side."

I nod, texting Beckett back. "Sounds good. We could use a break. You two have been working me to the bone. The military drill sergeant I had wasn't as bad as you."

Damian laughs. "You'll thank us later if you get in a jam, but in all honesty, we didn't teach you anything skill wise you didn't already know, just what you have to watch out for in our line of work. It can come at you differently than the military."

Traffic picks up as we get closer to town and pass small shops lining the road up and down. Damian pulls into a side street that takes him around the back of the shops and pulls into a parking lot. He gestures to the entire area. "Kenny's been adding on little by little. Last year he expanded this whole backside. It used to be more parking lot than he needed, and now he's got another bar area and big dance floor, and just the right amount of parking outside."

"Same place he took a bullet a few years back?" I ask, hefting my gear out of the back as they do the same.

"One and the same. He doesn't let that stop him one bit, but Cole and the other guys keep a pretty close eye on the situation. You never know when the Chicago assholes will show up and start a fight."

We walk through the back door and a slightly rotund woman with kind eyes and graying hair swishes toward us in a long apron that says Kenny's Wild Deuces.

"Kenny told me you guys were coming into town for the wedding." She gives Damian and then Dereck a big hug before eyeing me up. "And just who is this strong strapping stranger?" she asks with a twinkle in her eye.

I extend a hand. "I'm Blake. Beckett and I go back a long way."

She pushes my hand aside and walks into my arms while the guys try not to laugh at my surprise. I give her a hug as she squeezes my waist. "Dear lord, that's a lot of solid muscle there."

I grin. "Alright, the guys said we could get a cold beer, coldest in town they said." She smiles widely. "You'll get more than that. You guys take this table right here, and I'll get some burgers, fries, and some cold beers."

The guys slide into seats at the round table with laminated menus. "When Lettie says sit and stay a while, we sit and stay a while," Damian says.

I slide in beside them and get a look of approval from Lettie. "I'll be back soon."

Damian taps her arm before she leaves. "Sounds like Cole and the guys are going to meet us here shortly."

She beams. "The gang's all back together again. Alright, then I'll add some more burgers and beers. I know how much you guys need to eat."

A group of men and women walk through the door looking around. The minute I spot Beckett with them I stand and walk toward the group, with Dereck and Damian on my heels. Beckett gives me clap on the back type of hug. "Man, it's been a minute. I'm real glad this job is working out for you and that you could come out with the guys for the wedding."

Damian laughs. "Well it's not like we could leave our new wet-behind-the-ears recruit hanging out by himself."

Beckett laughs. "Meet Blake everyone. That wet-behind-the-ears recruit can hit a mark with one shot from eight hundred meters any day of the week. He's never missed a target yet."

Damian claps Cole on the back. "Just giving him a little shit, buddy. Good to see you guys, and ladies," he says.

Cole holds hands with a very pretty dark-haired woman. "This is my wife, Krissy." He gestures to the couple next to him. "This is Garrett and Lacy. You may recall Beckett telling you about the trouble we had at their wedding."

Beckett puts his arm around the blonde standing next to him. "And this is my soon to be wife, Jules," he says, holding up the hand of the woman standing next to him. "And this is one of the ladies' best friends, Patti." I'm listening but it's hard to track while taking in the little blue-eyed blonde named Patti standing next to the friend group.

Her eyes meet mine and her cheeks flush pink while the pulse on the side of her neck rapidly beats. "Nice to meet you, everyone," I say, without taking my eyes off the woman who without saying a word has managed to capture my attention in this very crowded room.

2

PATTI

I swallow through my emotion. Mr. blue eyes and sandy brown hair with all that muscle needs to keep his eyes to himself because I swear my heart's going to beat right out of my ever-loving chest. But he doesn't do anything of the sort. Instead, he takes a good long look at my boobs, before heading down my legs and right to my painted toes.

The big, muscled brute's eyes meet mine and he gives me a sexy little smirk. I swear I may be dressed in shorts and a thin blouse, but somebody needs to turn the heat down in this bar or I am absolutely going to die.

I turn, trying to get away from that insistent gaze, but the minute I do and start following the others, the heat of his gaze on my ass just makes me that much more self-conscious as I walk in front of him.

Damn that man.

The others get situated around the large round table. Blake gives me a smile as he holds a chair out next to PJ who's given me a set of wide eyes and is trying very unsuccessfully not to grin.

I settle in while he adjusts my chair. "Thank you," I whisper while giving my friend a well-deserved glare. Sure, she thinks it's funny now, but it wasn't so funny when Mason came to town. Besides, this is not going to be like that. She and Mason are made for each other. I on the other hand am sworn off men. Give me a live band, a few dances and drinks, and I'm happy to go home alone. And this one, he's got womanizer written all over that cute-ass face.

Lettie walks toward us carrying a large tray and Cole and Garrett stand, meeting her across the room to take it from her arms. She turns and heads back to the bar while the guys bring it to the table. Cole and Garrett set it down. "Here, pass the food around and I'll go get us some drinks," Cole says.

Krissy starts handing out plates of burgers and fries from the tray that takes up half the table. "Lettie's going to break her back one of these days if she doesn't slow down," she says, watching her husband walk back to the table with a big tray of beers. He sets them down on the now empty food tray and passes them around. "Lettie bet me ten bucks I couldn't make it back to the table without spilling a beer. You're all my witnesses," he says, grinning as she swishes across the bar heading our way.

Lettie eyes the beer tray with open suspicion. "Pretty good. You did a lot better than I thought you would. I had visions of you sloshing it all over the place and falling on the floor. It was really quite a mess."

He shakes his head laughing at her. "You owe me ten bucks."

Lettie laughs. "I think we'll let it ride. Next time, you'll probably land on the floor." Everyone laughs at Cole who grins good humoredly. "Are you almost done for the night? Pull up a chair and join us."

She wipes her hands on her apron. "Good lord, I wish. We need to hire some more people, especially on Thursdays and Fridays. Lately, we've been getting just as much business on those days as we do on the weekend."

Krissy puts her hand on Lettie's arm. "You don't work so hard. Tell Kenny he needs to get some more help. I'd come in and work, but those babies keep me busier than you'd know. Today's the first day we've been able to slip off by ourselves for a while. We're looking forward to the wedding reception. Babysitters all lined up for the entire weekend and everything."

Lettie smiles. "I'll be back to check on you. In the meantime, PJ, you know where the beers are. Help yourself if I'm in the back." She eyes Cole. "Don't let Cole carry anymore tonight. His luck probably won't hold up. Then we'll be down a best man."

At the mention of best man, Damian holds up a beer. "Cheers everyone. Who would have thought we'd be at so many weddings in Deadwood when Cole came out to see Kenny that first year? Cole, you started a chain reaction my friend."

Damian looks at Blake. "Drink beer my friend, do not go near the water."

Blake laughs as I watch the dimple on the right side of his face. "Thanks for the warning. I'm staying far away from the water then," he says, confirming exactly what I tracked him for. Just another free spirit playboy, the type who likes to get in your pants and then jump in his truck and run.

His eyes meet mine and lower to my chest.

Not in your dreams, asshole.

3
BLAKE

A couple more beers in and the table starts loosening up. Someone selects a popular dance song from the old timey jukebox and couples start moving to the floor, while Damian and Dereck head to the bar leaving me all alone with the blue-eyed angel who looks as sexy as sin.

I stand and hold out a hand. "Care to dance?"

Patti looks up at me from her seat with those wide eyes. "Hard to say no when you're already halfway there."

It's hard not to grin. "You've caught onto my plan. Don't worry though. I won't bite, at least for the first dance. Besides it's broad daylight. Harmless, right?"

Her eyes narrow but she puts her hand in mine and allows me to guide her to the dance floor where her friends are laughing, and all make room for us to join next to them.

I don't miss the look PJ and Lacy give their friend or the wide eyes she sends back. I'm finding it hard to miss anything about this woman. And I do love the way her hips begin to sway back and forth in those tight-fitting little denim shorts.

She's not as oblivious as she wants me to believe. That blush on her cheeks and twinkle in her eyes tell me more than she probably wants me to know. But I notice the guys at the bar, the ones sitting around the tables and the slot machines too. They all have eyes on the woman in my arms.

Patti must be more than used to being pursued with a face like that and a body made for sin. The men in this town have to be lined up waiting for a chance to dance with her. But she seems unaware of their interest at all.

The song comes to an end, and a slower one comes on almost immediately. My colleagues draw their women to them. I hear Patti's sharp intake of breath as my hand snugs against her lower back, holding her closer while trying to keep her at a somewhat respectful distance. Only because I don't want to scare the blue-eyed doe away.

The warmth of her breath brushes against my chest as we move, and the silkiness of her hair lies against the hand at her waist as I move her around the dance floor.

Garrett's wife, Lacy, the tall one with red hair, suddenly stops dancing, talking animatedly with Garrett and Cole. They both turn at the same time, and it's not hard to spot the riffraff who just walked through the door, heading straight toward Lettie standing at the bar.

Cole, Garrett and Mason move in sync, meeting Damian and Dereck as they all head toward Lettie. "Stay with the ladies," Cole says to the rest of the group. Beckett's eyes go to the back door. The scuffle up front is not a bad distraction for someone who wants to grab the ladies while the men are busy up there. Beckett and I have seen that maneuver more than once in multiple situations.

Lacy looks at me and Beckett. "Should have known the Chicago boys wouldn't stay away. I swear no matter what we do, they just keep coming. It's like they have an endless supply of ugly who are willing to do anything they say."

A tall dark-haired guy with a hat comes in the back door. "You guys know him?" I ask, cause that man hasn't taken his eyes off Patti and he's making a beeline straight our way.

"Tucker has a thing for Patti, and doesn't like the word no," PJ says, placing a protective arm around her friend.

Patti's eyes meet mine. "He moved to town over the holidays. We dated a few times, he wanted more, I said no."

From where I'm standing it doesn't seem that Tucker has gotten the message. He doesn't even bother looking at me or Beckett, just walks straight up to Patti. My jaw clenches, but this is a free country, and he hasn't done anything wrong, yet.

"Don't see you around here during the daytime much," Tucker says.

Her mouth tightens but still, she's coolly polite. "A friend came to town. We're just catching up," she says, taking my hand as Tucker sizes me up.

His dark gray eyes narrow. "Were you cheating on this asshole over the holidays with me?"

Her blues eyes flash. "Look, I've never cheated on a soul in my life. You just don't take no for an answer. You were a nice guy but wrong for me. That's all Tucker, now can you just leave it be?"

He shakes his head. "I'll catch up to you soon, Patti," he says, and that sounds pretty damn threatening to me. I step between them. "You heard the lady. She's not interested. Don't come around her no more."

Tucker tosses his head back in a loud dramatic laugh. "You have any clue who you're talking to like that, asshole?"

My eyes widen. "I'm talking to the man who just got told no and better get on his way."

"Or what? You and one of your mobbed-up bodyguards are going to try and make a move? Rough me up? Pretty sure you don't want a piece of me, city boy. Go back to where you came from."

In one quick move, I have his shirt bunched up in my hand. "Leave the lady alone or next time, you won't get the warning so nicely." I lower my voice so only he can hear. "Get the fuck out of this bar. It's private property and you're no longer welcome here."

Tucker raises a fist but I'm not in the mood to give him a pounding just for being a douche. I catch his fist in my hand, twist his arm and then the other behind him as I walk him to the back door. "Leave the lady alone. Last warning," I tell him as his face turns red. But he doesn't take another swing, and instead walks straight toward a souped- up big red Ford and climbs in. I watch as he guns the engine and peels away, while typing his license plate into my phone.

Because I have a feeling I'm going to need to learn a lot more about this man named Tucker.

4
PATTI

My heart is still pounding as Blake walks back over to me. Beckett is watching Blake and the commotion up by the bar, but he knows the guys up front have numbers on their side.

Blake, however, did not need backup. "My lord the way he put Tucker in a hold and kicked his ass out the door," PJ whispers to me. "Shut up," I whisper hiss.

Lacy laughs. "Patti Ann, one of these days your flitting around is going to get you in a world of trouble. You know you have to settle down one of these days."

I huff. "Not likely. I said I do one time, and that was the last time I'll ever do it again. Lying, cheating sack of .... "

Blake joins us and I stop talking mid-sentence.

He scans the front and sees that the guys have escorted the riffraff at the front out the door. "First day in Deadwood is turning out to be mighty interesting," he says, turning those gleaming blue eyes on me.

"I can fend for myself usually, but there's something about Tucker. He makes me feel cringy every time he's around. So, thank you."

"Anytime, Patti Ann."

My mouth gapes. "Nobody calls me that."

He grins. "Well, I just heard Lacy call you Patti Ann. Tell me I didn't."

I huff. "That's different. The only time she ever calls me that is when she's trying to pretend to be my daddy. It's a joke."

The handsome devil smirks. "Well, I like it. It suits you, Patti Ann."

My cheeks heat as he shifts in front of me causing me to glance down at his crotch. And of course he catches me looking. Damn that man.

"I don't know about anyone else, but I could go for an ice-cold beer," I say, turning and heading back to the table, glad that I took the entire week off from the veterinarian clinic to spend it with my friends before their big day next Sunday.

Damian and Dereck exchange a look as they return to the table. "What was that look all about?" I ask as everyone settles in.

Cole answers. "We recognized a few of the Chicago crew. They told Lettie they were just sending a message. They were trying to sneak in and out but found us here in broad daylight instead. It took them by surprise."

Lettie walks over with a tray of beer and the guys jump up, helping her balance it and set it on the table before passing out the round. Her cheeks are red. "Those assholes make me madder than hell. They think they can just waltz in here anytime they want. Is it ever going to stop?"

Damian turns so he can meet her eyes. "It's one of those situations where you hold the enemies at bay, but you don't want to squash them completely because you don't know who's going to take their place because they might be worse. The Chicago boys know their boundaries. The Larussios gave them more than a warning last year, but if they come looking for trouble this summer, they're going to get another message a whole different way."

Krissy arches a brow at Cole. My friends aren't letting them get away with not telling us exactly what's going on. Lacy narrows her eyes at her husband and his friends. "What message did they leave?" she asks.

Damian and Dereck exchange another look involving Cole and Garrett this time too. "You might as well tell them because if you don't, we're not going to get a wink of sleep tonight," Garrett says, putting a playful arm around Lacy.

Cole sighs. "The message wasn't any different than other years. The boss says sell now and save yourself and your employees a lot of headaches."

Lacy drinks an entire glass of water down. "I swear those Eldridges and Chicago boys, they are never going to stop. What's it going to take to get them to leave Kenny alone. They no doubt heard about the weddings and have come back to town to cause a whole mess of trouble we don't need. I swear they make me so fighting mad."

PJ looks at Lacy. "Don't let them get under your skin, you know that's half of it for Jake Eldridge. He just doesn't want you to be happy."

PJ clinks glasses with Jules. "But Jules and me, we are not letting any one of those fools spoil our special days. Come next Sunday, we're going to be walking down that beautiful path we set up at Cole's, right into the arms of the men we love." She looks at each of the bodyguards. "And I expect every single one of you to keep those Chicago boys at bay. Don't you let them interrupt our wedding, understand?"

They all smile, and Mason draws her to his side and kisses the top of her head. "Nothing is going to happen, you can count on it." Beckett puts a possessive arm around Jules. "We've got the best sharpshooter around sitting at our table tonight. They come anywhere near that wedding and Blake here's going to send them packing."

Blake grins. "Count on it," he says, holding up his beer in solidarity with the crew.

I turn to Blake. "Military?"

He takes a sip of his beer. "Yes, ma'am."

It's really none of my business but now I'm curious, and it's not because he's been flirting with me all afternoon. "Home on leave, and then stationed where next?"

"No, actually done with my tour and working full-time with these guys," Blake says, gesturing with a nod to Damian and Dereck.

I glance at them. "And where are the little ladies at?"

"They couldn't make it but sent along a couple gifts," Damian says. "I wish it would have worked for them to come out with us. Usually, it does."

Blake stands. "I'm going to head up to my room and catch a little nap. Didn't sleep at all on the flight in. You guys want to meet up for supper tonight?"

Cole stands and shakes hands with his friend. "Sounds good. And thanks for coming. We appreciate it. Krissy and I are going to head to the house for a while. We'll spend a little time with the kids and then meet you here about six-thirty for supper? There's a live band that plays every Friday and Saturday night. It's pretty good. My guess is Kenny and Eileen will be around later, too."

We all finish the last swallow of our drinks and stand as the couples gather their things.

I remove my purse from the back of the chair. Mr. handsome with a whole lot of muscles leans down slightly. "I'll see you tonight."

I meet his eyes. "Maybe."

He leans in so close I can smell that woodsy scent of his skin just like on the dance floor. "It wasn't a question, Patti Ann. I'll see you tonight. Wear a pretty dress," he says, leaving me to watch his fine ass walk away and climb the stairs to the hotel rooms above.

5
BLAKE

Once in my room, the shower is my first stop. I toss my clothes to the floor and get under the water, letting the pelting rain hit my muscles to wash away the aches of two days in an SUV and another day on a jet while I imagine that pretty little thing downstairs and give myself some much-needed tension relief.

Patti Ann is the hottest woman I've ever seen but doesn't even act like she knows. A late Friday afternoon nap beats the hell out of the days we've been spending dealing with enemies of the Larussios out in Vegas.

I may not have worked for the family long, but I know they wouldn't have this big of a crew out here if they didn't have vast interests in and around this town. It has to be worth a whole hell of a lot of money for what they pay because I'm making more now than I ever have and these guys have been with them a whole lot longer than me.

My phone beeps and I glance at the screen, smiling at the picture of my nephew before I set the alarm to go off in an hour. As long as they're taken care of, the work doesn't matter.

I doze off, dreaming of the blue-eyed blonde who has me rattled more than she should after an afternoon of flirting.

When the alarm goes off, I'm already almost awake. Ready to eat and to go see if Patti Ann decided to wear a pretty dress just for me. The minute I'm freshened up , I tug on a fresh pair of jeans and a black t-shirt and pull on my boots. A rough hand through my unruly hair and I'm ready to go.

I meet Dereck coming out of the room a couple doors down from mine. "Where's Damian?"

He gets in step with me. "Don't know, my friend. He said he was going to take a nap before we went our separate ways. I'm sure he'll be down in a while."

We're halfway down the steps when the rest of our crew and the ladies walk toward the same table we occupied a couple hours ago. I look past everyone though, unable to focus on anything except that sexy little thing in that pretty pink dress that she wore just for me. My cock shifts against the inseam of my jeans. He likes that dress, those bare shoulders and long gazelle-like legs too.

I close the distance between us holding her eyes captured in mine. I don't say a word while her friends all watch me. "A seat?" I ask, holding out a chair for the beauty.

"Thank you," she says demurely while her friends try their best not to smile but fail miserably at the job. The others begin taking their seats, talking amongst themselves as Lettie arrives at the table. I lean towards Patti Ann. "You look beautiful in that dress."

Her cheeks flush noticeably even in the dim lighting of the club. It makes my dick hard. I hold her gaze. "What would you like to drink? I'll order."

Those baby blues meet mine. "Strawberry margarita, please." She crosses her leg under the table, and it brushes mine. I lean in close. "That will get you whatever you want, love."

Patti Ann swallows, drawing my attention to the creaminess of her throat, and the pulse beating on its side. Lettie's hand on my shoulder draws my attention. "What would you like to drink? It's Blake, right?"

I smile at the grandmotherly lady who always seems to have something friendly to say. "That's right. I'll take one of these,"—I point to a domestic beer on the laminated menu—"and Patti Ann will have a strawberry margarita."

Lettie's eyes light up like it's Christmas. "Oh, Patti Ann will, will she?"

Patti Ann blushes. "Lettie," she whisper hisses.

"Oh, don't mind me. My life's mission is to get her partnered with someone who isn't a damn fool." She looks up and grimaces. "Looks like one of the damned fools just walked in where he isn't supposed to be."

My eyes track to the door and sure enough Tucker's back, and this time he doesn't look so steady on his feet. "Your ex doesn't seem to take the word no or don't come back too well at all."

Patti Ann scowls. "I swear, every week he seems more determined than the last. Let's just see what he does," she says although every guy at this table knows he's got one thing on his mind stumbling in here like that.

And he proves everyone right, when although we give him the space to do the right thing, he doesn't. He stumbles in and around the tables, making his way toward our table by the dance floor.

I watch carefully as he points a finger at me. "You, I came to warn you. This little bit..." I'm up and have him by the throat before he can say another word, walking him backward and toward the door. It won't do to mess up Kenny's club.

I hear one of the guys ask if I need help, but I'm too focused on this douchebag to answer so Beckett does it instead. He laughs. "Blake doesn't need any help. He's got this."

The minute we're outside he shrugs out of my grip but only because I let him. He leers. "She may toy with you a little bit, but after three dates she'll toss you out the door." He waves a hand. "You ask any guy in this town. She's a cold, frigid little bitch!"

My fist hits him square in the mouth, and he'd go down, right to the ground if I didn't catch him as he sways. A big guy walks out of the bar. "Where do I get a ride share for this guy? He's drunk off his ass."

He laughs. "Toss Tucker in the back of my truck. I'll get him home. Fucking loser harassing Patti again?"

"Yeah, he was. Earlier today, too."

He puts the tailgate of his truck down. "Toss him in, buddy. Hope Patti's okay. Nobody in town likes this fool."

I extend a hand. "Name's Blake. Thanks for the help. I'm a good friend of Beckett. He works with Cole and the guys."

He gives me a smile and a hard shake. "Name's Randy. Any friend of theirs is a friend of mine." He looks down the street as a police car turns onto Main Street with a light on. "I'm going to get out of here now. All you know is some guy offered to take a drunk man home. I'll get him home safe but keep my name out of it."

"Roger that," I say, walking back inside and heading to the table. Patti Ann looks up at me. "You okay?" she asks.

"I'm always okay, love. I sent Tucker home with some guy I met outside. Said he was heading that way."

Patti Ann chews her lip. "He's gonna come back. When he's been drinking, he just does not give up."

I lean over and whisper in her ear. "He's not going to be able to find you tonight, love, because you're going to be in my room upstairs, screaming my name all night long."

6
PATTI

I swear my heart's racing so loud everyone at this table can hear, but yet not one person is paying us any mind. They're all focused on the menu and laughing at something Krissy said to Cole that I didn't even hear.

Garrett and Mason get up when they see Lettie setting up our drinks at the bar. They get to the bar before she has a chance to pick it up and bring it to us themselves. She trails behind them. "I swear you guys act like a bunch of mother hens. I've been doing this a long time. And I'll have you know I've never spilled a drop, well, except the one time, and that was a doozy. Beer, sticky syrupy drinks all over this place."

Lettie laughs along with the rest of the group at her joke. "All right, enough of that memory. Let's get your orders going. Kenny's in the back helping on the grill. I swear we need some more help every day of the week. This place is just getting busier and busier."

The couples put their heads together and start giving Lettie their orders. Blake leans in. "Have you decided what you want?"

My cheeks feel like they are on fire. I almost spit out, *you, upstairs, right now*, but that would not be ladylike at all. Damn this man. I am no wilting violet but that handsome mug, muscled body, and gentlemanly charm is just too much. "You don't have to order for me," I whisper, meeting his eyes.

"You'll find I seldom do anything I don't like. Tell me what you'd like to eat, and I'll order."

Alrighty then. I've always liked a take charge kinda guy, and well, he's that and a whole lot more. "Grilled chicken salad, ranch on the side, please."

His eyes don't leave mine as Lettie reaches us. "Patti Ann is going to have the grilled chicken salad, with the ranch on the side, and I'll have the smothered pork chops, mashed potatoes, salad and drench it in ranch."

I laugh, because I swear Lettie's got a grin so big her face is going to split. "Lettie," I whisper hiss. I just know she's going to try and do some of her matchmaking.

She leans down. "I'd try to get this one on my hook. Looks like a good catch. A real keeper."

The others are still talking amongst themselves but PJ, who's sitting beside me, doesn't miss it, and neither does Blake. "I'm hardly the fishing kind, Lettie. You know me, I'm a catch and release type of gal."

PJ jabs me in the ribs from the right. I turn, gaping at my friend who gives me narrowed eyes like I said something wrong. I shrug. "Well, it's the truth. It's not like I'm about to get snagged in somebody's net again. I have a hell of a lot more self-worth than that," I whisper.

She shrugs. "Not all men are the same. Look at your friends around the table."

Blake leans in. "Good advice. Our song from this afternoon is on. Dance with me until dinner arrives." He stands and draws me to my feet. "It would be a shame not to dance in that pretty little dress."

I blow out a breath. I swear, this man is coming on way too strong, and I am seriously all female right now. One who feels like she's coming into heat the way his eyes keep roaming over my body like he'd rather have me for dinner instead of dancing.

And when his arms go around me this time and he holds me close, there's no doubt in my mind that I'll be going home with him tonight.

7
BLAKE

Dancing, dinner, more dancing. Patti Ann moves in my arms as though she fits like a glove. Another slow song comes on and when our friends head back to the table I keep her on the floor, drawn close so I can hear every little breath she makes.

My lips hover over her ear. "I want you in the worst of ways. Are you ready to leave?"

Her eyes meet mine. "So ready, I was ready an hour ago," she says, smiling mischievously at me. Patti Ann is enough to keep any man interested both with her body and her intelligent wit, and so much more. "Let's get your purse. I'm on the second floor."

If I thought this was going to be awkward, she doesn't make it that way at all. I keep a hand on her lower back as we walk back to the table. She puts her purse across her shoulder and looks at her friends. "We're going to head out. We'll see you tomorrow."

The guys' eyes meet mine, and the ladies all have smiles on their faces, but other than that we don't get the business I thought we might. My hand stays possessively on her lower back as we walk past a table of men who have been eyeing her ass all night long.

She's quiet on the way to my room. I'm sliding the key card into the reader when Patti Ann touches my hand. She swallows before saying a word. "I don't do this a lot. Every once in a while, but not after just meeting someone. I just feel safer because you're a friend of Beckett's and not just some stranger who blew into town."

I tilt her face with the tip of my finger. "Never once did that cross my mind. The attraction between us. You could light a fire with the sparks. You're safe with me, Patti Ann."

I open the door and let her in. She scans the well laid out room. "I haven't been up to the rooms. It has that lodgy feel, with all the wood trim and this bed made out of logs," she says, running a hand over the smooth round wood of the footboard.

"Beckett said Kenny remodeled a few years ago and updated the rooms. The guys have stayed here before. It's a comfortable room. Would you like a drink? I don't have much up here but water, but you're welcome to a bottle."

Her eyes meet mine without answering my question as she walks to the window and pulls the curtain back just a little to look out. "Great view of the main street and beyond. I didn't realize you could see right toward the historic area."

I close the distance between us and slide my hands around her waist from behind, whispering in her ear. "Turn around, love. I've been waiting all night to kiss those gorgeous lips that have been taunting me since we met."

She inhales a deep breath and spins in my arms as my hand nestles beneath her hair and on her nape. Her silky strands spill down her back as I draw her to me, capturing her lips in a kiss meant to please because Patti Ann is as anxious for this as me.

Her fingers find my buttons as I find the zipper to her dress, letting it slide to the floor. My eyes glaze over the magnificent creature standing before me, left only in the sexy little heels that I plan to have wrapped around my back or my neck for the remainder of the night.

A couple hours after we're sated and gone to sleep, the slow downward movement of her hand causes me to wake. "Finding what you need, love?" I ask sleepily.

"And then some. You were mumbling in your sleep."

"Dreaming about you."

She laughs that melodious tinkling laugh in the darkness of the night. "I love that answer," she says, kissing my chest and spattering kisses following the path of her hand. I let her play for as long as I can take, but she should know right away that I'm in charge of her pleasure. In one swift move I catch her off guard and swing her around. She exhales a deep half laugh. "Blake!"

"Quiet, love, let me have what I want." Patti Ann doesn't argue, instead she purrs with pleasure giving and taking the way love is supposed to be. Damn this woman is perfection. And that's exactly the same thing I'm thinking about when we're sated again and I fall into a deep sleep.

In the morning, I run down and grab us coffee and sandwiches. The door clicking behind me as I return to the room causes her eyes to flicker. "Sorry, didn't mean to wake you."

"You went for coffee? I think you're too good to be true." She turns her phone on, and it beeps continually as it powers on. "That's a whole lot of messages," I tease. "Let me guess, the ladies checking up on you, wanting the scoop?"

Patti Ann blushes. "How did you know?"

I shrug. "Just a guess."

She scowls as she continues going through her messages, visibly shaken as she sits up in bed, pressing the silky sheet to her chest in an attempt to keep herself covered.

I set her coffee and sandwich on the ledge that doubles as a desk in the corner. "That look. What's wrong?"

Her lip tightens in a grimace, and she hands me her phone. I read every single one of the threatening messages, misspelled and garbled probably in a drunken rage but all say as clear as day that Tucker's not going to stop, and that his involvement with the Chicago boys runs deeper than anyone here knew.

"Damn, I'm sorry, Patti Ann." I start tapping buttons. "I'm putting my number into your phone." Then I call my phone from hers. "There, now you have mine too." I glance up because she's quiet.

A tear slips from her eye. "Thank you. Never, never did I or anyone else think he could be tied in with the Chicago boys or the Eldridge crew. I mean, it just seemed like he was a decent guy who moved to town over the holidays. There's a lot going on here during the holidays, all the parties and stuff. We ran into each other a few times and hit it off. Went on three dates, he wanted more, and I didn't."

"Wanted more, sexually?" Anyone not completely satisfied with Patti Ann in bed is just not doing it right. Because we've gone all night and I still want more.

She blushes. "Um, let's just say I didn't think we were very compatible in that area or any area for that matter. It kind of makes sense now though. He kept asking me about Cole and his land.

"I never saw the connection until today. He didn't want me; he was after the land. I swear the Chicago boys will try every trick in the book to get what they want. And they want land and business in this town."

"He's lucky I didn't leave his sorry ass on the street where he almost landed. We better let the others know about his connections though. I can give the guys a call."

She nods. "Or, we could run out to Coles. You ride horses?"

"I love horses. It's been a minute though. Don't get too many chances moving from base to base."

Her eyes meet mine. "Let's head out there then. He has a ton of property not too far out of town. He only bought so much property because strangers were trying to buy it up who wanted to turn the surrounding area into something we don't want it to be but we all love it out there."

"I've heard it's a nice property. Beckett told me about it on one of our calls when he was buying a piece of Cole's land, and built a big, beautiful house on it for him and Jules.

Patti Ann tilts her head as she speaks. "Mason and PJ don't live too far away; they have a nice horse farm not that far from Cole and Krissy. PJ loves horses. She tended bar and worked at Cole's ranch, but once Mason bought their own, she only helps Lettie every once in a while and spends most of her time training. People come from miles around to get her to train their horses."

"And where do you live, Patti Ann?"

Her eyes widen in surprise. "Umm, a little way out of town, but not that far, about a mile and a half. Why?"

"Because until I get to the bottom of Tucker, you're not going home alone. You're either staying with me or I'm coming home with you. Which will it be?"

8
PATTI

How the hell am I supposed to argue with that because right now not one relevant argument is coming to mind. "You're used to being in charge. Something they teach you in boot camp?" I ask.

Blake smirks and settles onto the bed, drawing me to him. He kisses my lips, and I swear those annoying little butterflies start dancing in my belly again. When he releases me, he pushes a piece of dangling hair from my face. "Why don't you eat and get showered up? I can call the guys while you're getting ready, then take you by your house to change clothes before we head out."

I look at my dress he's saved from the floor and folded over the chair in front of the desk. "Yeah, showing up in that little number would definitely cause a stir. Not that they didn't know what we were up to anyway, but still. A change of clothes sounds good."

"You can pack a bag while we're there. We can stay at your house if you need to, but I'd rather stay here since he won't know where you are."

I reach up and kiss his lips. "Thank you. I kind of like your take charge personality. It comes off more as thoughtful caring than overpowering and bossy, you know. It's a refreshing change."

He laughs, standing and walking to his sandwich, then unpeeling one and handing it to me before taking a bite of his own. "I would have given you the coffee too but then that sheet you're hanging on to might slip exposing those lovely breasts. That would be a damn shame."

My cheeks heat. "A real gentleman during the day." I take another bite of my sandwich, trying to keep my mind off of all the ways he was not in the slightest a gentleman last night, ravaging me until he made me scream his name.

He walks to his coffee and takes a sip. "If there's something about last night you didn't like, you should tell me now because if not I plan to do the very same thing again tonight."

"Oh, do you now? And just what makes you think you passed the test for another date?"

"A test?" Blake asks after finishing the last bite of his sandwich and swallowing. "Is this a real thing or something you just concocted for me?"

"Ha! I'll have you know I have some pretty high standards. I don't date. No dates. Just a few dances with some local guys in the last few years, maybe a drink and a roll in the hay. Dates, they require a multitude of effort and tests."

His eyebrow arches. "So, we're considering last night a date or a roll in the hay?"

My eyes meet his sparkling, blue eyes. "I'm still thinking."

"I ordered your drink, your dinner, we danced, I asked you to wear a dress for me and you did. It definitely constitutes a date. And at the risk of moving too fast I want another. How about we go horseback riding and find a place to go swim today. Beckett sent a message and said we should meet everyone out at Cole's."

"Oh, you do like to take control, don't you?" I ask as the butterflies continue to dance in my belly as he looks at me with mischief in his eye.

"You have no idea how much I like control, but I plan to show you a little bit more tonight. Now go get in the shower before I carry you in there and have my way with you again."

I laugh, popping the last bit of sandwich into my mouth. "You are trouble with a capital T, but yes, let's go to my place, I'll change and grab a bag, and we then can head out for the day. It actually sounds like a lot of fun."

"Date number two," he calls from the room.

The minute I'm under the water common sense starts to take hold. This thing is moving way too fast. He's not from around here. I shouldn't have worn that damn dress, no matter that I loved the way his eyes heated up when he saw me walk in.

Still, no dates. That was the rule, and I do not break my own rules, ever. No dates, just a few one-night stands averaging one a year. No matter what the town gossips want to say about me, at least I know my heart won't get shattered again.

But my body and brain already know there's something far different about Blake. It's not just his good looks, or the way he dances or takes me in bed. It's all of him, his gentlemanly ways, his take charge personality, and lord help me all of it rolled into one delicious man. How in the world am I supposed to resist this?

My good sense finally kicks in. Because he's here for a few days, for a wedding, and then he's going to be the one saying it's been fun, see you later.

I inhale a deep breath, finish washing up and towel my skin dry before wrapping my hair in a towel and getting a fresh one to cover myself with. I've clearly gotten far too wrapped up in this man. Time to remedy it before he gets the wrong idea.

I'm all set to tell him just that but when I come out, he's nowhere to be seen. I gather my clothes and get dressed. I've just put my heels on when he walks back in the door. With a huge arrangement of flowers.

My heart pounds in my chest. Who is this man and why is he absolutely messing with my head?

Blake closes the distance. "I went downstairs to make a call. They were selling them in the lobby, fundraiser of some sort. I thought you might like some," Blake says, taking an unused coffee carafe on the desk into the bathroom and returning to the room with it filled with water.

He dumps the little freshening packet into the water and cuts the band from the flowers with a pocketknife before placing the delicate blooms gently into their new home.

Every word I was going to say is gone, wiped from my feeble memory, because not one man in my entire life has ever bought me a flower, not one, not two and certainly not the bouquet sitting before me as pretty as can be. My voice cracks. "I love them. Thank you."

He kisses me gently on the lips. "Let's go, we have the whole day ahead of us."

9
BLAKE

Patti Ann gives me the lay of the land as she drives. "Last house on the end of this road is mine."

She drives up to a cute little bungalow style home. "Very nice," I say as she pulls into the driveway in her white Jeep Renegade.

"It was my aunt's before she passed away. I spent a lot of time here growing up and it seemed like it was just meant to be. The memories were great, and the price was right."

I follow her to the door but grab her hand before it touches the knob of the partially open door. "Wait, it's open."

Her voice shakes. "Someone's been here."

My protective instincts kick in. "Stay behind me. They were probably here last night, but let's just be sure." I draw the pistol from the back waistband of my pants, and her eyes go wide. "Precautionary in our line of work. Nothing to worry about. Just stay on my hip."

Patti Ann nods but her eyes are still fearful. An invasion of your personal space can do that to a person. When I come face to face with Tucker again, he and whoever he's working for are going to deal with me because I know for damn sure it wasn't Tucker. Not in the condition he was in last night.

Her small hand grasps the back of my shirt. I find it oddly comforting to know she's right there, doing exactly as I asked, wanting me to keep her safe.

I walk through the lower level, scanning the small dining and living room, decorated with a mismatch of new and old before heading up the stairs. I scan the loft-style space, which looks to have been recently remodeled from two bedrooms to a large suite with a walk-in closet. After checking everything, making sure to touch nothing, I gesture to the closet. "Why don't you change and grab a bag while I call the guys. Once you're dressed, we can call your sheriff. He'll want to sweep for prints and the like so try to open doors by the sides not the handles if you can."

She looks around. "Doesn't look like a thing is out of place. Still, it's creepy to think that someone was in your home."

I don't doubt it feels creepy to say the least. She goes into her closet and comes back out with tears running down her face.

That look makes my blood pump hard. "What's wrong?"

Patti Ann crooks a finger, and I follow her back into the walk-in space. She points into the drawer where a ton of folded lacy panties lie and points to a note. "Don't forget who you belong to."

I pull out a pair of panties on the opposite side of the drawer, and a fresh bra. "Go put these on and change your clothes. We're leaving, right now."

She nods, grabbing a pair of folded jeans from one of the shelves and a top from a hanger before walking toward the adjacent bathroom. It's not long before she comes out with a makeup kit, pulls a pair of socks and pointed brown boots on, grabs a couple more changes of clothes, a dress from the hanger and a pair of sandals and a purse, and pushes them into a bag. "That's all I need. Let's go."

"I'll drive."

She gives me a look.

"Just in case we're followed." She nods, handing me her keys. The minute we're back in her Renegade and she's securely fastened I connect with Cole. "We're on our way out to your place but wanted to let you guys know before we call the sheriff that someone broke into Patti Ann's place last night. He also sent her some messages that make it evident he's working with the Chicago boys."

"Damn. I'll let everyone know. We can meet out here and decide what we want to do about the situation," Cole says.

Patti Ann inhales a deep breath as I disconnect with Cole. "Guess I better call it in. I can't believe I didn't even suspect Tucker of being part of the Chicago boys. How stupid!" she says, connecting with the local sheriff's office.

The minute the sheriff gets on the phone she explains the situation as I plug Cole's address into the GPS on my phone. She covers the phone. "He wants to know if we can meet him here." I shake my head. "Tell him we have to be out at Cole's but if he has any questions for us, he can meet us out there. Just leave your key somewhere."

She relays the information to him and hangs up a few minutes later.

"Thanks for your help, yesterday and today. You must think I'm a wilting violet who can't protect herself but I'm really not. I'm just mad that he got the upper hand. Now that I've got his number, I'll be more alert to the potential danger, you can count on that."

Patti Ann may think she's going to go up against Tucker and his guys by herself, but she's not. I'm going to be dealing with them, whether the little lady likes it or not. "Let's see what happens. My guess is it wasn't Tucker. Like I said he was too drunk and pretty knocked out. His cronies probably wore gloves, could have even sent those messages, but we may get lucky. If not, we're going to have to flush them out."

Her eyes go wide. "What do you mean?"

I mean what I said. "Flush them out and get rid of them. I'm not leaving you to fend for yourself with men like that walking right into your house. That's not who I am."

10

PATTI

I hear every word he says but the only ones that really stick in my mind are I'm not leaving you to fend for yourself. A sharp reminder that as much as I like this man, he is leaving after the wedding whether we call this a roll in the hay or a date. It really doesn't matter, because Mr. handsome will be on a jet plane and out of my life sometime after next weekend's wedding.

Blake drives us out to Cole's and by the time we arrive the whole gang is there. Damian and Dereck walk to the vehicle and talk to Blake quietly. I take my time getting out, giving them time to talk before he joins me at the door and walks with me up to the massive house that Cole started building about five years ago before he even moved to town.

Krissy meets us at the door holding a toddler on her hip. "Come on in, don't mind the toys, just step around them and try not to slip on anything with wheels. You know little boys and their toys," she says, laughing as she leads us toward a big country kitchen with a large rectangular table where most of the gang are already seated.

They slide closer on the bench seats to make room for us. "I just made a fresh pot of coffee and there are some sweet rolls in that box," Krissy tells Cole, who grabs it and brings it to the table.

PJ gets up and grabs the glass coffee pot and brings it to the table while Krissy sits the little one down in a walker. Krissy does a quick head count and starts pulling cups out of the cabinet and I help her bring them to the table and hand them out before Krissy brings some more.

Lacy takes a big bite of a sweet roll and holds it up to Garrett so he can take a bite. "Good, huh," she says. "Cole was just filling us in on what happened last night and out at your place today. What the hell with Tucker. You're sure he's running with the Chicago boys?"

I pour a coffee for myself and one for Blake before passing the carafe off to Jules. "Yeah, the messages they left couldn't have made it any clearer."

Mason looks down the table at me. "We knew if they were coming back this summer it would be right in the middle of our wedding, but we sure as hell didn't suspect Tucker of anything like this." He looks at Beckett across the table, but Beckett looks guilty about something. "What, what was that look?" I ask.

Beckett looks sheepish. "We actually had Tucker checked out when you first went out. Ran a background on him. Not one thing came up suspicious, everything he said checked out. Independently wealthy and there was nothing to doubt. Until now."

I'm surprised, but the fact they cared enough to look into him for me means something. My eyes meet each of my friends. "I didn't realize you guys did that. Thank you. Maybe that was the plan to send someone in who would pass all of your scrutiny and tests. I mean, it's not like they haven't tried everything else."

Krissy takes a seat, and Cole holds out his arms for the little one and gives him a smooch on the cheek. "Well, he's on our radar now. Sheriff Cates just sent me a message. He and his deputy were just at your house. They're on their way here."

The doorbell rings and Krissy gets up. "You want to get his stuffed monkey and blanket from the living room while I round up everyone for the babysitter?" she asks Cole.

"Sure thing," he says, standing from the table and hefting the little one onto his hip to go in search of the stuffie in the next room.

When Krissy and Cole returns, Krissy smiles. "I love them to death but all day Saturday and Sunday this weekend and next, all to ourselves with a double wedding planned for our friends, yes, please."

"I asked Blake if he wanted to go for a horseback ride, is that okay with you?"

Krissy nods. "You know you're welcome to take the horses out anytime you want, Patti."

Lacy clears her throat. "It's Patti Ann."

Krissy, PJ, Jules, and Lacy start laughing while my cheeks flame. I hold the mug to my face, but the way Blake turns to look at me is not helping at all. Thankfully, a car door outside draws all of our attention back to the matter at hand.

Cole goes to answer the door, and Krissy passes around the box of pastries again. When it comes to Blake, he takes another one. "Would you like one?" he asks.

I shake my head. "No, I'm full after the sandwich and the donut." He grins sinking his teeth into his raspberry pastry. "Energy." No doubt he burns a ton of that up in his job because I know for a damn fact there's not an extra pound on that man anywhere.

Sheriff Cates walks in jostling a set of keys. "Morning everyone." He eyes the men at the table and settles on Damian, Dereck, and Blake. "Whenever you bodyguards come to town, trouble seems to follow."

Cole gestures a hand to a spare spot at the long table. "Take a seat if you want, Sheriff. I'm sure you remember Damian and Dereck, but this is Blake. New member of their team and a good friend of Beckett's."

Sheriff Cates settles into his seat and Krissy pours him a cup of black coffee. "Thank you," he says. "I don't have good news. We didn't get any fingerprints."

Blake's jaw tightens. "I didn't think you would. They wanted her to know they had been there." He turns to the others. "Left the door open and a note that said don't forget who you belong to."

Lacy gasps. "Cole told us all what was going on but left that part out."

Cole shakes his head. "First time I'm hearing about it, ladies."

Sheriff nods. "We sent it out to the lab, hoping to get a trace on something but it's doubtful. Best lead we had was Tucker and he was still passed out at his place. Asked around and Bill from next door to Kenny's said he saw some strange guy helping him into the back of Randy's truck. Randy said he dropped him off and put him on the couch last night, described what he was wearing, and he was still there in the same clothes today." Sheriff Cates looks at Damian, Dereck and Blake.

None of them have anything to say, just go about drinking their coffee and chewing on their pastries.

Sheriff Cates uses a different approach. "Any idea who gave him that shiner and dumped him into the back of Randy's truck? He said he couldn't remember what the guy looked like it all happened so fast."

Everyone at the table shakes their heads. "Better ask Tucker, Sheriff Cates. Maybe he'll remember."

Sheriff Cates smiles. "Yeah, that's the answer I thought I was gonna get." He stands up. "I've got some extra deputies called in for the wedding next week. I'll have them out on the points, just in case there's trouble."

Cole shakes hands with him. "We appreciate you doing that, Sheriff. We're hoping for a peaceful wedding for these four, but I can't say having more protection hasn't crossed our minds."

"Anyone coming to town I need to know about?" he asks. The real question isn't lost on anyone. Do the Larussios plan to attend the wedding, and if so, will that bring in the Chicago boys and the Eldridge crews?

"Hard to say at this point, Sheriff," Garrett says as he heads for the door.

"Alright then," he calls back over his shoulder. "Try to stay out of trouble until we get this sorted."

Damian and Dereck try quite unsuccessfully to hold back grins as he walks past the window outside and toward his SUV. Damian gives Cole a grin. "He's a nice guy. You have it lucky compared to some of the places we've been."

Cole shrugs. "His goal is the same as ours. Peace. We like it that way but no matter if the Larussios plan to show or not given what we know about Tucker we can be assured the Chicago boys have a plan to mess with us."

Mason's jaw tightens. "Then we make damn sure they don't get anywhere near the wedding. If the sheriff plans to have his men out on point, then we have our people in strategic places where we know they're coming in. But my guess is they'll either start coming in tonight or right in as the wedding is in motion."

Blake looks at Beckett. "You want a best man, or you want to make sure you can actually say I do?"

Beckett hefts out a sigh. "There's no one better to spot them or take them out. That's for damn sure. I'd feel a hell of a lot better knowing you're our cover out there with your special type of skills."

Blake nods. "I didn't bring my special rifle though."

Beckett laughs. "I just cleaned mine up, they're ready and waiting for you. Just call it intuition," he says.

Cole grins at his friend. "I've got plenty of ammo and stuff here, too. The guys keep them in our bunker below ground. I'll get them brought up to the basement."

Blake nods. "Looks like I'm all set then. I just need the lay of the land."

Krissy nods. "We have people coming to help me clean midweek, but I still need to pick up all the toys before that and get a ton of things done."

"We'll all help," I tell her.

"Of course we will," PJ says. "We just appreciate you two letting us get married here. It's going to be perfect."

Krissy smiles. "We're so excited about it. I want everything to be just right."

"When will they come to get the property out back set up?" PJ asks.

"They'll be here later, but you are not going out back until it's all done." Krissy waggles her fingers at both of them. "Neither one of you. Don't even try to peek. It's going to be a wonderful surprise."

Jules and PJ give each other a knowing glance. Kenny and a few other people in town we know very well will make sure everything is catered and absolute perfection.

Cole gets up and gestures a hand. “Why don’t we go outside and get out of their hair, grab some horses and take a ride?”

Blake turns to me. “I’ll ride out with them and get plans made and then be back for you.”

His eyes meet mine and it’s hard not to blush. “Okay.”

11

BLAKE

The minute we're in the stables Cole turns to us. "I sent the Larussios a message. Tommy and his men are going to come in and give us a little help. Carlos sends his best and said they would have the place covered. In the meantime, it sounds like they have intel about the Chicago boys. It does sound like they're getting ready to head our way."

Cole leads a beautiful long-legged brown American Quarter Horse out of the stall, while Garrett caresses the nose of a Tennessee Walking Horse. Cole gestures to the Tennessee. "Black Beauty is Krissy's. She'd love to go for a ride. I got her for her comfortable ride after Krissy had the first of the babies."

Beckett and Mason seem comfortable in the stables and head to the end to get two more horses, bringing them both out before petting them and getting them ready to ride.

Beckett hands me the reins of a rich brown American Quarter Horse. "This is Miles. He'll sit still for as long as you need him to, but he'll run like the wind when you say go."

The minute Miles and I are acquainted and we're all ready to ride, Cole leads the way outside where we mount up. He points to the rolling hills for as far as the eye can see. "All this land, the Chicago boys and developers wanted to buy up. They wanted to doze down all these beautiful pines and hardwoods and put up more concrete. That's never going to happen on our watch," he tells me.

"I had these trails put in the first year we were here, and Mason and

Beckett are having some put in that will connect way out there." He points in the distance.

Garrett laughs. "Probably a good time to tell you that Lacy and I are going to be looking for some property too."

Cole squints, looking at his friend. "You don't say?"

Garrett looks sheepish. "Don't you say a word to one of those females. If you do, Lacy will have my hide. We're trying to get pregnant."

"Well shit. Scope out what you want. You know the rules. You ever want to sell, it comes back to me first. Otherwise, there's plenty here for all of us. We'd be thrilled to have you as neighbors."

Mason laughs. "Yeah, it's not like we're sitting on top of each other. He and Krissy have three hundred acres left after we picked our spots."

Cole laughs. "Well, it didn't hurt that Carlos Larussio trusted me, and I was able to pick up another large-ass parcel he was working on acquiring, too. Money well invested if you ask me."

I tip my hat as the sun hits me square in the eye, before heading into a trail of dense pines that cuts the glare of the heat. Cole points at some of the cameras and security devices around the property, acclimating us as we ride.

The minute we get in the clearing, he points. "Over that range, it slopes down to the highway. They'll be expecting someone at that point. I'll take you farther out, where you can see them coming a mile away but they won't expect you to be."

The ride doesn't take long and the minute we get there it's clear to see why he picked this location. I dismount and keep the reins in hand, walking underneath the brush but with a clear view of an expansive piece of highway headed into town. "One hundred percent agree with your choice, Cole."

I'm planning to take Patti Ann out for a ride, then after supper with everything that's happened, we should all plan to hang out here tonight. I'll take first watch. Damian, Dereck, you wanna keep your eyes peeled after that and then I'll take it again tomorrow morning?"

"Roger that," Damian and Dereck say at the very same time.

"Good. You mind if Patti Ann stays at the house with you tonight?" I ask Cole. "After what happened last night, I don't want her staying by herself."

Garret turns on his horse. "You two seem to be getting on nicely. Lacy and the ladies have been burning up the cells ever since you two laid eyes on each other. I may lose some serious money over this bet."

"They have a bet going on?" I ask half laughing.

Mason's eyebrow raises. "You think I'm kidding? Those ladies have a bet going on for everything and you can be damn sure that Lettie's on the phone every few hours stirring the pot. She is the worst matchmaker you will ever meet, but there's not one of us here who wouldn't do anything for her. She's got a heart of gold."

Beckett joins me as the others head to the house and I'm putting Miles in the stall. "Hey, we've known each other a long time, right?"

"We have," I say, patting Miles on the nose and feeding her a handful of hay.

He looks down at his shoes, which is so not Beckett.

"Just spit it out if there's something I need to know. We've been through too much, seen too much not to be straightshooters."

"Yeah, I know. It's just I've never seen you so taken with a woman."

My jaw tightens. "Spit it out, Beckett."

Beckett's eyes meet mine head on. "She's a really nice girl, but she's been hurt really bad. Douchebag of an ex who thought cheating was his right. She doesn't really date, Blake. More guys in this town than she knows would give their next paycheck to take her out and she refuses them all. Every once in a while we hear about a hookup, but anything real, she's running far away, you hear?"

I clap him on the back. "Look, we're having a good time. Neither one of us is looking for anything serious. But I'm not leaving her to deal with this shit alone, right?"

12
PATTI

My back rests against the barn as I listen to the men talk about me and my love life. What the hell does Beckett know anyway? He's only heard little pieces from Jules, and only the pieces I've told her, not the real stuff, the stuff that completely shattered me to pieces.

My eyes close as I try to suck in a deep breath. It's fine though, at least Blake and I are on the same page. Having a little fun and nothing else. That, I can live with. No expectations and no shattering heartache down the road.

I slide around the other side of the barn as they walk toward the house, watching them as they go. I slip into the big barn and find Daydream. A beautiful American Quarter Horse, my favorite of all time. "Come here, Daydream. You wanna go for a ride?" I ask, patting her long velvety nose before feeding her some hay.

Daydream noses my hand as I bring her out of the stall. "You and me girl, we're going to go for a little ride. We need a little bit of freedom; some wind under our sail."

The long-legged American prances energetically as I get her ready. She's as prepared for this ride as I am, but my guess is she's not as keyed up as me. Because every neuron in my body is screaming with the indignity of what's happened to me before and what Tucker and the Chicago boys are trying to do to me now.

I stroke Daydream as I mount. "Good girl, let's ride," I tell her, loosening up the reins as she soars over the terrain and towards the pines and plentiful hard woods in the distance. The minute we hit the open plains I let Daydream take over, pounding the ground beneath us under the big blue sky until we're both ready to turn back and all the emotions of the day have calmed.

Blake stands by the barn watching me as we return, slowly moving toward him as Daydream continues to cool down. He places a hand to his head to shield his eyes from the sun. "I wondered where you went. Krissy said she saw you slip out with Daydream," he says as I dismount.

I give him my best smile. He and I are such similar creatures. We should enjoy each other while he's in town. "I wanted to give her a little run. Let's grab a couple of the others and I'll show you around the trails. You don't get better trails than these," I tell him as I pat Daydream to make sure she's completely cooled down before removing her riding gear, putting her in her stall, and offering her some water.

"Did you and the guys come up with a plan?" I ask.

"We did. After dinner tonight I'm going to head out to a place Cole showed us where I have a good view of the main highway. Damian and Dereck will relieve me later and then I'll take over again in the morning. We'll run it that way all week so they can go to the wedding."

"Here I was going to save you a dance."

Blake draws me to him and kisses my lips, causing the butterflies to dance around like I've never been kissed. "I'm going to collect on that dance, just a little later than we planned."

We walk the fresh horses out and mount, riding slow in a comfortable silence, just taking in the beauty of the land as I take him through some of the best trails South Dakota has to offer.

I point to a place out on the ridge. "One of my favorite spots. You can see the prettiest sunsets."As soon we reach the top of the gradual slope he nods, taking in the view for miles of treetops and lush land. "I can see why you like it so much."

His cell phone buzzes. "Excuse me. Blake here."

He pauses for a moment. "I see. We're not too far out. That's not fucking good. We'll head back right now. Get the gear ready and I'll head out to the point earlier than planned."

I gesture to the phone as he slips it into his pocket. "Cole?"

"Beckett. Apparently, the guys intercepted a call between Tucker and some of the Chicago boys. They'll be riding in on bikes with a crew from Chicago. My guess, they're going to be looking to cause trouble and rumble."

"Damn. You can't just go out there by yourself, Blake. What are you going to do against a whole pack of bikers, I mean, are you planning to shoot them all?"

"You let me do the worrying. Right now, we need to get back to Cole's. Krissy is having dinner moved up to a late lunch. We're going to grab a bite to eat while we get ready. And I'd like for you to stay with Cole and the rest of the crew tonight. I don't want you by yourself."

I nod. "After what happened, I don't want to stay by myself. I'll ask Krissy if I can stay."

"Already talked to Cole."

My eyes narrow. "Yeah, that take charge button doesn't have a pause, does it?"

He grins but those devilish baby blues light up with amusement. "No, it does not. I'm one of those dying breeds. I like to take care of the woman in my life."

Damn those butterflies all to hell, they just will not quit dancing when he's looking at me like that and saying things that just make me want him even more.

I turn away before my cheeks give me away. "Come on, I'll race you back."

A couple of Cole's men are at the stable when we arrive. "We can take care of the horses. Sounds like Cole's in a hurry to get everyone together up at the house," one of them says as I slide down and hand him the reins. "Thanks," Blake tells them, placing a hand on my lower back as we head back to the house.

"You think we should call the sheriff?" I ask just as we get to the door.

"My guess is we'll handle it ourselves with some backup from Larussio's men, but we'll see if the plan has changed with the trouble headed our way."

13
BLAKE

Cole and the guys have a property map spread out on the table while the ladies help some others place mountains of smoked beef brisket, barbeque glazed chicken, potato salad, corn on the cob, cornbread, and a huge bowl of bright red watermelon chunks onto a large rectangular table set up against the dining room wall. I pass the ladies, giving them a grin as I head toward the table the guys have taken over. "Looks and smells delicious. That spread is making me hungry all over again."

Patti Ann laughs as she joins the women. "I don't know where he puts all the food."

I give her a wink as I settle in by the guys, before giving them my full attention. "Get me acclimated. Where's the point I'll be at?" I ask, scanning the property map.

Beckett puts his finger on it, and Cole draws a bright red circle where the house is. "They're going to be doing one of three things if not all. They'll be causing trouble in town to get us divided, you know they're going to hit the house since the wedding is here. And if I'd have to guess, they're going to do both simultaneously tonight and tomorrow with crews running night and day."

. . .

I draw a red circle around the area Wild Deuces is at. "How far out are Tommy and his crew?"

Cole looks at his phone. "Tommy just texted. They'll be landing in about an hour. They've got all the firepower we need."

I glance up. "Soldiers and enforcers flying under the radar?"

Garrett rubs his fingers together. "I'm sure they pay a lot of money to get passed through inspections and it doesn't hurt they fly private strip to private strip. Don't ever think the Larussios don't have control of all that stuff."

My eyes scan the document looking for all the potential spots. "Glad I'm working for them."

Cole laughs. "Damn straight. They'll get the men here and more if we need it. This town, it means something to them. It's not just about the money. They've built a connection with the small business owners of this community. They brought them back from bankruptcy and our friends and neighbors have more money coming in than they ever have before and it's because of the Larussios' business savvy. Discounts on booze, food, you name it, being aligned with them gets the businesses a discount."

PJ brings her cell phone over to Cole. "Mason's on the phone."

He takes it from her hand and his jaw tightens as he listens. "Thanks Mason. Keep us posted on the group chat. Don't worry, we've got this covered."

The minute he hangs up he immediately connects with Kenny. "This is Cole. Things may get rough tonight. I want you to head to that plaçe we talked about. No, listen to me. If they can get to you, they put fear into the whole town. Get your wife and go, now. We'll take care of everything else."

. . .

He disconnects and looks up at us. "Mason's been there keeping an eye out on Wild Deuces and he's seeing a few more strangers straggle in than he likes. They haven't made a move yet, but it's making him uneasy. Our goal is to keep everyone safe. The Chicago boys want Kenny. Revenge, a way to flex their muscle to the other business owners, but we're not letting him get hit again," Cole says.

Beckett and I, we've seen this maneuver more than we'd like to have seen it. I put a finger on the red circle and draw it to the other. "Getting Kenny and his wife out of the picture is a good move. If they can't get him, they'll go after the patrons, use them as hostages to draw us out. We need to get in front of that, fast."

Beckett and I know this drill like the back of our hands. "Mason will be our point man on the inside. Cole, Garrett, you'll head to the bar to help Mason." Not one of them looks okay with that plan but Beckett doesn't back down. "Not one of those bastards will get up this road to this house with Blake and me on the gun." He looks to Cole. "We don't have near enough firepower for town."

Cole looks at me and lowers his voice, but the ladies are busy talking animatedly about the wedding and are paying us no mind. "I want the ladies in the basement. I swear every year they just keep coming with new and more threats."

Good thinking. "That meal they just set up. Let's get it downstairs and protect those women, then we get to our stations."

Damian gestures for me to look to my phone. I glance down at the text he sent. *We have a crew of bikers heading into town to ride interference. They'll be able to handle town if you want to keep Cole and Garrett with the women.*

I look up at the group. "Looks like the Larussios are coming through again.

They have a motorcycle crew heading into town to help. They'll deal with the Wild Deuces if you both want to stay here and cover the house."

Cole and Garrett both nod in agreement. "Mason is there, we trust him to run point with whoever the Larussios send and to report back."

I start circling the areas and calling out the plays. The sons of bitches are going to regret sending enemies into town to take over Deadwood. Because that's not how this is going to go down.

We take the large metal containers of food the caterers left and help get it set up downstairs. Cole gestures to the spread. "Grab a plate and follow me." We pile our plates and follow him to an adjacent room in the basement to eat and assess the firepower he's got stored while getting prepared for the enemy out of earshot of the ladies.

Cole has weapons laid out on a long table in a room lined with multiple shelves of equipment. "Take what you need guys," Cole says.

I eat and grab one of the radios off the shelf simultaneously and the other guys follow suit. I find Patti Ann pushing food around on her plate while listening to the other women talk.

I take her aside. "This button, any time you need me, you push it. This device lets you send a message the same way you would through a cell device, it just circumvents the towers. I don't think we'll need it, but just in case things go south, you'll be able to get message. Beckett and I are going to stop by his place and grab a couple rifles that we're used to on the way out to the point." Chances are the cells will work just fine, but just in case.

Patti Ann's eyes raise to meet mine, and she lifts up on her tiptoes to bring me down for a kiss before placing a bag full of packed up food into my hand. "Please be careful. You still owe me a dance."

14
PATTI

Krissy, Lacy, PJ, and Jules all look as on edge as I am as we wrap the remains of the catered dinner into containers and put them away in the fridge in the adjacent room and Cole and Garret go outside to explore the perimeter. "I like the way you set the basement up. Super nice freezer too," I tell Krissy.

She nods. "Thanks. It's so nice to have the extra fridge and freezer space. Cole likes to have everyone over and if you haven't noticed by now these guys can eat a lot."

"Oh, I've noticed." Although in all the time I've known the guys I never really realized it until I met Blake. Suddenly I'm noticing every single thing about him. Not just how much food he requires to feed those rock-solid muscles of his.

Lacy laughs. "I bet you have, Patti Ann. We've never even seen you blush before. In all these years."

My face breaks into a grin. "Seriously that man."

PJ and Jules exchange a look.

"What is that look for? Shouldn't you two be talking wedding stuff, not snooping your nose into my business?"

"We just happen to know that exact feeling. Those guys come to town and sneak right into your dreams, then into your bed and into your heart."

"Yeah, well, into my dreams and definitely into my bed, that I can deal with. Long-term commitment and heartache, that's off the table for me."

Jules meets my gaze. "They're not all bad. Beckett is a great judge of character. I don't think he'd associate with a loser."

"Well, me and other men typically have a different opinion of what a loser looks like. And how many men go around actually telling their friends they cheat?"

Krissy arches an eyebrow. "Good point. My brother was a loser. He may not have cheated, but I never thought he could do what he did until it happened."

My heart constricts for my friend. Her brother was such an asshole. We all remember the stories about why she came to Deadwood and the story about how she met Cole and when Kenny was shot by the enemies these bodyguards all now protect. The scars that asshole left her with are there for life. "Right, you just never can tell. Right now though, we need to make sure we're prepared in case things go south."

PJ looks up. "These guys are not going to let that happen. They are excellent at their jobs and they're going to have plenty of backup if the Larussios are sending in Tommy and the boys."

"Yeah, those guys don't mess around, that's for sure. I remember what happened the last time they came to town. No doubt Sheriff Cates is going to have his hands full the next day or so."

PJ laughs. "No doubt he will between Cole and the guys, Tucker and his antics, the Chicago boys, and now if we've got an MC club riding into town, he's not going to know which way to turn."

"Lettie will settle him down with a big piece of pie and a smile," Lacy says, causing everyone to smile. "She's always trying to matchmake us and doesn't see that Sheriff Cates has a thing for her, right under her nose. She's oblivious."

My phone buzzes and I glance down at a message from Blake. "Things just got changed up. The motorcycle crews are heading into town, but they're not just our guys. Beckett's going to stay on the point tonight first shift instead of me, but they don't know Damian, Dereck, and I so we're going to head into town to help Mason. You ladies will be safe with Beckett on point and Garrett and Cole with you."

15
BLAKE

The four wheelers are already covered, and at this point in the game I don't want to cause any unnecessary distraction. "Damian and Dereck said to meet them at your place."

Beckett nods to the four wheelers we brought up the trail from his house and covered with branches and leaves. "You could take one but ..."

I recall the trail. "No. It's not far through the woods. I'll head out now and meet them by foot. Keep your phone on. Damian said the Larussios want us to let the bikers get into town, but not up to the house."

Beckett nods, scoping in his rifle. "Roger that. Stay on the line."

"Will do." His house isn't too far heading through the woods, and the lush greenery of the trees and undergrowth provide the perfect cover as I make my way there. The black SUV is parked not far from the house, staying under cover.

I give the back window a rap before opening the door and pull my pistol as something stirs in the forest. Damian laughs. "Damn. You've got good reflexes, Blake. It's just Dereck. We didn't want to be sitting ducks and get caught from behind by the enemy."

"Roger that," I say, sliding into the backseat while Dereck opens the front passenger door and gets into the vehicle. "You have everything you need?" Damian asks.

"I'm all set, let's move out."

Damian avoids the main highway, takes a few long-ass country roads and comes into town from the other direction. Damian meets my eyes in the rearview. "There's a chance someone could recognize Dereck and me, but they won't recognize you. Let's sit apart. We'll let you out before we get there and you walk in, alright?"

"I'm good with that, but what's the play here?" I'm not really the watch and see type of guy. A few months ago, my job would have been to take out the threat before it becomes reality, but the Larussios must have a reason for wanting us to wait.

Dereck turns in his seat. "You'll learn with the Larussios that information is the most valuable asset. My guess, they want to see who's coming and why before we take them out. Always a secondary play with these guys. Even when we take them, they don't want them dead if we can help it, they want them scared enough to talk when Tommy and his boys get to them."

I suck in a breath. "Roger that." I open my door. "You have a signal for when enough is enough?"

Damian laughs. "Nope, I have no doubt you'll know when to step in. Until then, let the show play out, keep any civilians from getting hurt, and only one caveat. They strike first, unless it's something we can't ignore."

I get out and close the door behind me, walking briskly across the crosswalk to the little shop across the street, scanning the area as I make my way toward Wild Deuces. There aren't many bikes on the street, and nothing that screams invasion or anything of the sort.

Mason is sitting at the bar, talking with Lettie. I walk in and don't acknowledge either of them, instead taking a seat toward the middle at a table set up for two. One of the waitresses behind the bar with Lettie sees me and comes over to take my order. "Coffee and a piece of apple pie."

She smiles. "If this is the first time at the Wild Deuces, you're gonna love that pie. We make everything from scratch back in the kitchen."

"I'm sure I will." She walks back to the counter and my eyes scan the entryway first in the front and then in the back. My gaze wanders nonchalantly over to a group of four bikers sitting by the large stage Kenny just put in last year.

A dancer is on the stage in a bright red costume twirling on a pole but there's nothing about the four men that gives me any concern, at least not yet. They're minding their own business just having a couple beers with a huge plate of nachos in the center of the table.

Damian and Dereck walk in and take a seat not far from the door. A good spot to see both entrances and be able to react quickly if things erupt at the bar. The waitress who took my order heads over and places my coffee and pie in front of me. "Enjoying the show?" she asks, gesturing to the stage.

"Sure. Local talent?" I ask.

"Marla. She dances every Saturday night before the live bands start. Warms up the crowd."

I smile. "Thanks for the coffee and pie. It smells delicious."

She gives me a smile and heads over to Damian and Dereck's table to take their order but they're not really paying one bit of attention to her but instead watching the front door as five huge bikers walk in.

I bring my cup to my lips watching carefully, ready to move in a second if needed. The bikers scan the area and land on the bikers sitting at the table by the stage. The tall one with tatts running down the length of his bare arms gestures with his head toward the bar. They walk in sync, and my hand moves to the gun by my side, keeping it out of eyesight but ready if needed. The waitress who took care of us doesn't seem afraid, meeting their eyes and greeting them with a friendly smile like the one she gave me not moments ago. But Lettie, her posture is concerning. She's moved to the front of the counter, and I already know she's pushing that panic button under the bar that Beckett told me about.

She clearly either doesn't know them or knows they're in here for trouble. My phone beeps but I don't take the moment to look down, watching instead, not taking my eyes off the situation in case it escalates fast. I'm not taking any chances with how fast Kenny got shot some years back in this very bar.

But now they've caught the attention of the group of bikers sitting at the table, who were just minding their own business, and now, all hell is breaking loose.

And now I know exactly what the enemies play was, distract and separate us. I know it before five more bikers walk in that door and the big burly guy grabs Lettie by the collar of her shirt drawing her closer to him.

I'm moving at the same time and speed as Damian, Dereck and Mason, with guns already out. "You let her go or your friends are going to be scraping you off the ground."

The one with hands on Lettie gives me a big toothy smile. "We're just having a little fun. A little warm up before next weekend," he says.

"Turn around and get out."

He shrugs. "See you tomorrow, ladies," he says, turning and following the rest of his men right back out the door.

The minute they leave my phone beeps with a message from Patti Ann who has forwarded a message from Tucker. "I'm coming to get you."

"How far out is Tommy and his crew?" I ask Damian.

"Should be here in about a half an hour."

"I'm heading back to the house." I gesture around the club. "This move they just made. Nothing I haven't seen a ton of times, different place, but same play. Patti Ann got a text from Tucker basically telling her he's heading her way while we're babysitting bikers. You stay here and cover this mess. I'm going to let Beckett and the others at the house know and then head back and make sure they don't get to those ladies."

Damian's thoughtful for a moment but he doesn't second guess me, not that I'd listen if he did. He flips me the keys to the SUV. "Take the keys and keep us posted. We've got things covered here until Tommy and his boys get here."

16

PATTI

A text from Blake makes me feel better. I know Beckett's on point and he and Blake have the same skills and background but still, I'll feel a hell of a lot better when I know Blake is back.

Lacy paces after she reads the text aloud for everyone. "There's no way they're getting through Beckett, Garrett and Cole." Then she paces some more. "I swear, every year they come at us harder than the last though. They wanted my house and when I wouldn't give that up, they were not happy, and Eldridge, I swear it's his ego that runs his actions and nothing else. He's not going to be happy until I'm miserable."

I don't tell them, but that's what scares me the most. These guys year after year keep coming and they may be working for the Chicago boys trying to take territory from the Larussios but part of what's driving them is personal, and now Tucker is playing their game.

My phone rings and I answer it the minute I see Blake's name come up. "You okay?"

"Yes, we're still downstairs, and Cole and Garrett are still outside. They've been keeping in contact with Krissy and Lacy."

"Alright, I'm on my way back. I'm going to take up point. I don't mean to scare you, but I think the real attack is coming to the house. Lucky for us, what was going to be an ambush and a surprise by the Chicago boys probably just got fucked up by Tucker's ego."

"Okay, tell me what you want us to do."

"I don't want you to do anything but stay put. Do not leave that basement, for anything. You have the weapons we left you. You know how to use a gun, Patti Ann?"

My hands sweat with even the thought. "Never held one in my life. Lacy and the others, they're hell of good shots. Lacy grew up with a rifle in her hand."

"Good. Stay by them, you have them show you the basics real quick. You don't need to use it to keep the enemy at bay."

I walk to the other end of the basement, around the corner where the freezer and the refrigerator are to have a little privacy. "You okay?" I ask.

"I'll be a hell of a lot better when this mess is done and I've got you in my arms for that dance you owe me."

"Me too," I whisper. "Stay safe."

"Don't you worry about me. You do what I asked, understand?"

"Okay but keep in contact?"

"Of course."

I disconnect and immediately miss the connection with Blake. Nothing like this has ever happened to me. Why I'm letting this man who is going to be in my life for such a short time get under my skin so fast and deep escapes the hell out of me.

The ladies look up at me from the sofa covered with a cartoon print and a multitude of stuffies in front of a big screen as I walk back into the room. "Blake wants you to show me the basics of holding and using a gun."

Lacy narrows her eyes at me. "He does?"

"Uh-huh. Says I don't need to know how to shoot to keep the enemy at bay."

She observes me for a minute. "True but did you tell him you don't have to worry about it with us down here. Tell him that I won rifle shot four years in a row?"

I grin. "No, I most certainly did not mention all your rifle skills when I'm as inadequate as hell. Show me how to at least hold the damn thing," I say.

She stands as the other ladies watch with a mixture of emotion. It's not every day that we have to talk about guns to protect ourselves. "Come on," Lacy says.

17
BLAKE

The minute I'm close enough, I park the SUV and cover it with brush opting to hike into the trails instead of drawing attention to the fact that Beckett and I are out here. I give him a text to let him know I'm joining him and then make my way through the forest and undergrowth to get to the place I know he's going to be.

I give him another buzz, just to let him know I'm there before I reach him, grab the rifle, and slide in next to him on the ground. "You see anything yet?"

"Nothing but the bikers who went through. They raise a lot of hell at the bar?"

"No, didn't get the chance once they put hands on Lettie, but we were right about staying out here together. Next time, no disrespect to anyone, we're doing it our way."

He nods. "They won't have a problem with it once they see what we can prevent from up here."

I gesture in the distance, looking through the scope of my rifle. "Ten bikes, and three SUVs, all heading our way. They get up that pass and there's going to be nothing but pandemonium at the house."

"Let's not let them get up here then," Beckett says.

"Roger that buddy," I say, getting my sights locked in. "I'll start from the back; you work your way back to me."

"On my mark, ready, aim, fire."

My bullet hits the front left tire of the back SUV sending him swerving while Beckett takes out the lead motorcycle, sending it sliding across the highway and two more with it. One bullet after another, methodical, all our training homed in on the job we have to do to keep the people up at the house safe.

The highway below is a disaster area, bikes and SUVs strewn everywhere. The men on bikes are going to need the hospital, but some of the guys from the SUVs have made it out and taken up position behind the vehicles that aren't engulfed in flames.

I don't take my eyes off the sons of bitches. "Now we wait. No one makes it up this hill." If we had reinforcements, they'd be flanking them from behind but right now it's just me and Beckett on the line.

My cell beeps and I grab it with one hand. "Damian confirms that Tommy and the crew have arrived at the Wild Deuces and that everything is in hand. That may be good for tonight, but there's no way they don't have something more planned for tomorrow, and all week long."

Beckett nods. "These guys think they're going to hang out behind their trucks all night and take pot shots at us and whatever unfortunate soul who tries to travel by?"

I laugh, because they don't know Beckett like I do if they think that plan's gonna work. We've driven more enemies out of larger and more equipped vehicles than this with a couple well placed shots and that seems like exactly what's on his mind as well as mine.

"Let's get this done before some well-meaning traveler heads onto the road." Beckett doesn't move his head. "On my mark, ready, aim and fire."

Both of our rifles go off at the same time. We know right where to hit them when we need them to explode. They would have done themselves a favor by peeling out of here with their vehicle intact instead of trying to take us out. We're far too well concealed and that was never going to happen.

The last of the vehicles explodes, and only two men emerge. They don't aim at us and instead head to a couple bikes lying on the ground, get on them, and ride away leaving their buddies strewn along the way.

I pull out my cell and give Cole a call. "We've got a mess out on the highway. A shit ton of enemy bikers and SUVs were headed up this hill. Two got away on bikes but the rest them, hard to say from here what condition they're in, but they're not going to be heading up that hill to hurt the ladies, that's for damn sure. We had to take them out. You want us to call it in or..." I pause as he talks animatedly. "Roger that. We'll stay here until we know it's done."

I pocket my cell. "Tommy's got a clean-up crew on the way. Cole said he'll let Damian and Dereck know what went down. Looks like we're going to take turns covering until Damian and Dereck get back, and probably through the week," I tell Beckett.

He grins. "Just like the good ole days, right?"

"Same damn thing, different location. Who would have thought when I took this job that I'd be protecting a hill of ladies?"

He laughs. "Don't be surprised if Carlos doesn't call you up personally and offer you a job."

My eyes narrow. "You mean to stay on in Deadwood after all this is done?"

"It wouldn't be the worst. You've been looking for a place to set up the family. You know, give them roots in a community instead of bouncing from place to place. It's a great place to raise a family, and hell, we'd all be neighbors. Something to think about."

18
PATTI

I keep checking my watch, then my phone. The times may be synced but that doesn't stop my minding from checking them both to see how much time has passed and if only to will my cell to ring. But it doesn't. Hour after hour, until my heart just can't take it anymore. I send out a message: Where are you?

Blake's response is immediate: Trying to get to sleep but thinking of you.

My heart swells. I smile big as I type out a message: Am I in a sexy little nighty?

His reply makes my cheeks heat: No love, you're totally nude.

My fingers hit the keys excitedly: You're making me blush over here. When are you coming back?

I'm here for a while. These guys don't like to lose. They'll be back with more firepower.

My heart sinks. I send him another message: I need to hear your voice.

My cell rings almost immediately. "Hey, love."

"How can I miss you after only a few hours?"

He laughs softly. "I was just thinking that very same thing about you not a few minutes ago. You know what they say about chemistry. When it's right, it just happens."

I exhale a deep breath. "I know, but I don't date."

"Yeah, so you've said, and I've heard. Not all of us guys are terrible, Patti Ann. I think there's a few good men left out in the world. Well, as long as you like the possessive, protective type."

"And you do like to be in control. Don't forget that."

He doesn't downplay that little detail. "It's a fact."

I don't state the obvious that shortly after the wedding, he'll be on his way, and we'll never see each other again. "We should enjoy it while it lasts."

He's silent on the other end of the phone for a minute. "Damian and Dereck will be up to give us as few hours' break, and then they'll go get some rest. We'll probably run it like that between now and the wedding. I'll call you when I wake up."

"Night. Stay safe out there." I can almost see that sexy smile in my mind.

"You be good, Patti Ann."

I disconnect and Cole walks down the stairs and gives Krissy a kiss. "I'm going to grab something to eat and cold to drink and then I'll send Garrett in."

I go the refrigerator and pull some leftovers out and heat a plate up in the little microwave next to the refrigerator. "Water or coke?" I call out to the next room.

"Coke please. Something to keep me awake."

I bring back a plate for him and Krissy gives me an appreciative smile for allowing her a few more precious moments with her man before he has to head out again. He takes a seat on one of the couches and takes a big bite of the sandwich I put together. Krissy sits next to him. "Are we going to need to change plans for all the people coming in through the week, hair and makeup, and the wedding next weekend?"

He finishes chewing and exhales a loud sigh. "Not if we can help it but we're going to have to play it by ear. It's going to depend on just how determined they are and how cautious we're going to be. We're going to find a way to get these four married though. Beckett and Mason aren't having it any other way."

PJ and Jules smile, because I don't think they can wait much longer to say I do. "Blake said Damian and Dereck are going to come back and give him and Beckett a break from that point."

Cole nods. "I told him he can use one of the spare rooms but he's going to stay out by the stables in case something comes up. I'll grab a sleeping bag from the laundry room before I head out."

My face falls and although I didn't intend my friends to see it, they do not miss much. Lacy puts an arm around me. "You, my friend, have been struck by cupid fast and hard."

"It's nothing but lust my friend, pure physical lust, nothing more for either one of us."

She rolls her eyes and joins the others as I follow behind. "We were just going to curl up on the couches and watch a movie. You want to watch it with us?"

Cole laughs and gives Krissy a kiss on the lips before heading around the corner and returning with a rolled sleeping bag under his arm. "That's my cue to get going."

She smiles at him and waves him out the door. "Be safe, I love you," she says as he makes his way to the steps.

"Love you too. Enjoy your chicky movie ladies." And then he's gone.

We've just turned on the movie when Garrett walks down the stairs and Lacy hits the remote to pause the movie and closes the distance between her and Garrett fast, giving him a smooch that causes his cheeks to heat. "Wow, maybe I should go back out and try that again."

She laughs. "Patti *Ann* made you a plate when Cole came in. "You hungry?"

Garrett laughs. "I could eat but thirstier than hungry." He goes to the next room and comes back carrying three bottles of water and begins downing them one after another until all three are gone.

"Good lord, you were dry," PJ says.

"The sun was out and even after it went down it's still dry and windy. I'm good now," he says, taking the plate Patti heated up for him and eating while he stands. Once he leaves the ladies settle in for more movies. I engineer a yawn, using the back of my hand to cover my deceit before making a lame excuse about being exhausted before heading to a makeshift room here in the lower level. All in hopes that all of them will follow suit so I can sneak out and do exactly what I want to do.

I lie in bed silently fuming, wishing the ladies would hurry up and go to bed. But they just talk and talk and talk.

The fourth time Lacy says goodnight and then just starts up another conversation causes me to punch my pillow in frustration. Hurry up, or he's going to be in the barn and already asleep by the time I get there, and I know I'm not going to have the heart to wake him. That right there should tell me that I don't just want to snuggle into him.

My eyes pop wide open when finally, the doors down here all close and after a little bit of shuffling around, there's not a sound at all.

I slip into my tennis shoes and grab a hoodie to cover up my braless state and sneak up the stairs wearing a pair of sweats and a cami. Not the sexiest of attire but it will suit my purposes just right.

A quick look in both directions and I don't see either Garrett or Cole. I make a dash to the stables hoping that no one catches me but surprisingly getting caught doesn't weigh that heavily on my mind. Getting to Blake, to hold him in my arms, that does.

I open the door and creep into the stables, holding my phone for a source of light and scanning it across the back of the largest stable. A hand goes over my mouth and an arm goes against my waist drawing me to a very muscled body that I would know anywhere by now. "Looks like I have you right where I want you."

My face breaks into a grin as he draws me back into the night. His mouth kisses my neck, teasing and caressing that sensitive skin. "You like being my captive."

I reach around to draw him to me, kissing him with abandon and a recklessness that I've never felt before. "I want you so much. I could barely stand it." Blake doesn't need a bit of encouragement. He has my hoodie and cami off, unbuckling himself and caressing my bare skin before sliding my sweats to the ground. He lifts me and slides into me in one long thrust, hitting the end of me to join us as one and give me exactly what I need.

19
BLAKE

Night after night we fall into the same comfortable routine. Beckett and I on point, guarding and making sure the house is protected until getting a break from Damian and Dereck. Spending nights with Patti Ann rolling around in the hay and holding her close, talking with her like I've never opened up to another person before.

I know Beckett and Mason are anxious to get married, but there's a part of me that just wants to slow time down, because once they get married, who knows where the Larussios will send us.

The alarm on my phone buzzes against me. I watch Patti Ann sleep for a precious few moments longer than I should. I kiss her gently on the lips. "Wake up, love."

Her eyes flutter and then open. "Morning," she whispers.

"It's early but I need to get back to the point. I'm going to walk you back to the house first." She starts to protest just like every morning for the last week, but I stop it with another kiss. "I'll walk you."

She smiles. "That control thing. It's not all bad." I smack her playfully on her beautiful ass. "I want you where I know you're safe when I'm not around."

Patti Ann doesn't argue and helps me roll up the sleeping bag. I reach over and brush the hay off her clothes, letting it fall back to the stall floor before brushing myself off and giving her a kiss. "I'll see you after the wedding this afternoon or at latest tonight. Send me a few pics of you in that pretty little dress I know you'll be wearing."

She blushes and I swear it goes straight to my crotch. How this woman has gotten to me in just about a week is beyond me but she's all I think about now. The horses whinny as we leave the stable. I put my arm around Patti Ann and walk her back to Cole's place. She turns as we get to the door and reaches up on her tiptoes to give me a kiss. "Text me when you get back to your spot and you're safe."

Well damn if that doesn't cause my chest to clench every morning she says that. She's the first person to be worried about me as I head off to battle. Except of course my sister, but that hardly counts.

Although what I have to do is clear, I have so much more on my mind because I've never wanted one damn thing in my life the way I want Patti Ann, and I don't just want her for a week, I want to make her mine. For good.

Damian and Dereck turn as I sneak back up to the point right before nine. "You guys want to go get a few hours of sleep before the wedding?"

Damian squints. "I was going to say yes, but let's see what's coming in the distance." He doesn't need to say another word.

I see the glints of sun striking steel before grabbing my rifle and looking through the sights. "More motorcycles but no SUVs this time."

Dereck laughs. "Guess the Chicago boys didn't want to lose any more of their fancy rides, but they don't mind sending in their MC clubs to take a beating."

"What do you say we end this before it starts?" I ask, far less concerned with repercussions of explanation than wanting them to get anywhere close to the house or to Patti Ann.

Damian nods. "Let me check with Tommy. See if he has a crew nearby. We're going to have to make this fast. It's broad daylight and it's going to look like an unprovoked attack."

He gets on the phone, but something doesn't feel right. Beckett and I have had that same feeling a few times in our lives, and our intuition hasn't served us wrong. "Stay here. I'm going to double back to the other side of the house. Once you get the go ahead, take the fuckers out."

"Hold up," Dereck says. "We should get the clearance before we split up. So the others know where we are."

I put a finger to my lips. "The important thing is they don't know where I am. Stay off the radio about me, and give me the keys to the UTV."

I race down and uncover them, jumping into one and taking it around the backside where Patti Ann showed me just the other day. It comes into the back of the trails that hook up with Mason's and from there I should be able to cover the backside in case anyone decides to come up.

Garrett and Cole may be tough as nails, but they're too close to the house and not going to think the bastards will come in through the brush.

We made them desperate taking so many men out this week. And if I were them, this is the way I would come in, and just as I'm nestled in on my belly, scanning the terrain, I see a shadow, one slight movement, and then two and then three.

20

PATTI

The morning flies by with caterers arriving to lay out an early morning breakfast buffet, people setting up tables and a little archway on the lawn, and hairdressers from town showing up to do our hair and nails.

We admire each other's dresses as we get ready for the quiet little wedding, glad that the men finally agreed to let the people in with additional security, although I'm not sure any of us is too comfortable with Tommy's men hanging around. They may be on our side, but they look scary as hell.

Lacy adjusts the strap on my light green dress. "I think we're all way more anxious than PJ and Jules. They're the ones getting married today."

"I know, I'd be a nervous wreck. It probably helps that it's being held here and not with a ton of strangers, you know? Well, except the thick-necked goons in the zoot suits."

Lacy nods, touching up her lipstick after downing a glass of orange juice. "I know, neither of them wanted anyone but all of us and of course Kenny and family, and Lettie. They said the dance tonight down at Kenny's will be enough celebration for everyone in town. They wanted to keep their vows private and small. I hope things go well and we can make the dance happen."

"I wasn't surprised they didn't want a bachelor and bachelorette party though. Not after what happened at yours."

Her eyes go wide. "We got lucky the guys were all on their A game that night. That's for sure." Her eyes scan across the room. "Speaking of, Garrett just came in for a bite to eat. I'm going to see how he's doing."

"Sounds good. I'm going to check on our brides-to-be." I walk in behind Jules and PJ who are checking out their dresses in front of the mirror. I tuck a straggling strand of hair into PJ's updo, and they both turn to show me their beautiful white gowns. "You both look so stunning that I could just cry."

Jules' eyes widen. "Don't you dare. I'm having a hard enough time not getting soppy myself. And with all this eyeliner and stuff on my face, I seriously would be a mess."

"Did Mason get back last night? I didn't hear anything at all once I got to sleep."

She rolls her eyes. "Well, sneaking in after rolling around in the hay night after night will take it right out of you."

My face splits into a grin. "I wondered if the guys on patrol knew and just didn't call us out."

She nods. "Oh, they all knew. Not much gets past these guys when they're on patrol. Mason got back again late last night and slept here with me once Tommy and his boys took over."

Krissy rings a little bell on the catering table. "Last call for breakfast before it's heading to the refrigerator." She looks at Jules and PJ. "I still can't believe you are both getting married today."

PJ rolls her eyes. I've never seen my friend look as dressed up or as completely in love as I do today. She inhales a deep breath. "Stop already. I honestly can't wait to say I do. That man, he has become my entire world. Well, with the exception of all of you."

I laugh. My friends are all so happy, and for the first time in a very long time, I find myself wishing I was part of a couple too. And that's something I thought would never happen again.

It's hard to believe the time has come when Garrett walks into the great room, which has turned into a room full of feminine chaos. "The pastor has arrived and everything's ready."

PJ and Jules both inhale a deep breath. Krissy leads them out the door while Lacy and I lift and carry their beautiful trains as we head outside to views of blue skies, green grass, forest, and rolling hills. The pastor is waiting at a pulpit under a large white archway not too far away with Mason and Beckett standing in tuxes waiting for their loves.

The way they look at them makes the butterflies in my stomach dance as my best friends in the world walk toward their forever loves. Once they're in position, Lacy and I take a seat with Garrett and Cole, watching as our friends vow to love and cherish each other until death do them part.

The minute the pastor says, "You may now kiss your brides," gunfire erupts in the distance and instead of kissing them, Mason and Beckett get their brides to the ground and cover them with their own bodies.

Cole and Garrett have Krissy, Lacy, and me down on the ground in less than a second. "Stay down!" Cole yells as more gunfire erupts in the distance and a flash of fire lights up the sky.

21
BLAKE

I keep the assholes getting closer to the ridge in my sights while monitoring the wedding processions, hell-bent on not letting them ruin Mason and Beckett's special day with their soon-to-be wives while not putting them in danger either.

It's a fine balance, watching carefully, making sure not one of those men climbing up that hill have even the slightest chance to get their weapons up in the air.

The minute Beckett and Mason kiss their wives I start taking the enemies out. One by one they fall. They may not be dead, intentionally, but they don't have a chance in hell of getting up and causing any harm. Tommy's boys are going to have plenty of men to interrogate and hopefully lots of intel to glean.

Damian's voice comes over the radio on my hip. "All of the targets in front of us are down. We hear fire behind the house."

"Roger that. Twelve bastards trying to flank us from the back are down. Tommy and his boys are going to need a big-ass cleanup crew. All of the friendlies are safe."

"Son of a bitch. Roger that. I'll call it into Tommy."

"I'm going to stay here until they get here, and I know no one else is laying wait to take out our crew."

"Roger that."

I watch carefully through the scope, scanning the distance, not worried about the wedding party who the guys have moved into the safety of the house double time, but instead making sure the enemy doesn't have a secondary move on the hill.

The radio crackles at my hip. "Enemies are down. Reinforcements are in place. I'm on my way to you."

Damian walks in through the same path I took, carefully navigating the terrain but knowing I've got his six.

The minute he reaches me he extends a hand. "That was some damn good shooting. You had those fuckers pegged."

"I think Tucker was with them but can't be sure. He was wearing a hat."

"We'll have Tommy and his boys check it out, but in the meantime, I've been asked to take over here and get you to the plane."

My eyes narrow. "What plane?"

"The Larussio jet."

"You want to give me a clue what's going on?"

Damian shakes his head. "Wish I could. All I know is they want you on that jet and you need to leave now."

"I'm going to go and say goodbye to Patti Ann, then I'll go."

Damian sucks in a breath. "Sorry, Blake. It doesn't quite work that way. You need to go now. The Larussios have a jet out on the private strip, and they want you to go now. Apparently, they're in route and plan to meet you somewhere between here and Vegas."

"That's a pretty large spread. I've heard stories about mobsters meeting you out in the middle of nowhere and those stories don't end so well."

"You did good work here. That doesn't usually end with you in a body bag."

22
PATTI

My friends eye me with sympathy. I hate it. I wish they would at least say something instead of looking at me with those sad eyes of regret. This is why I don't do romance. Because I'm just always destined to be sitting in this bar with my friends and no one special of my own.

One week exactly, and not a word, a text or anything from Blake. After he probably saved all of our lives, just to disappear. It doesn't even make sense to me. I may not have thought we were going to end in the fairy tale romance, even though I had already started to hope that we would, but I didn't expect him to bug out without a word, or to ghost me like the plague.

The town may have settled back down, all the enemies rounded up by Tommy's men and taken to who knows where, but that doesn't make the pain in my heart go away. The same slow song that was playing when Blake first took me in his arms comes on and instead of wanting to dance, it just makes me sad.

I take another long sip of my beer, bound and determined not to let on how much that man ended up meaning to me. Lacy gives me wide eyes and a little grin. I narrow my eyes at her. Whatever she's up to, it's a hard no. No doubt she and Lettie have cooked up some scheme to play matchmaker again.

A tap on my shoulder while watching all of my friends suddenly start to smile causes me to turn and look up at the bright blue eyes burning into me from above. My breath catches. "Blake."

He holds a hand out. "I believe this is our dance."

The butterflies swarm in my belly so hard I think I might die, but he takes my hand and draws me up, bringing me so close my body begins to heat. "Let's dance and we'll talk."

I let him lead me to the dance floor and he holds me close. "I'm sorry I didn't have a chance to say goodbye. The Larussios told me to get on a plane asap. Phones got confiscated for a while. As you can imagine those men are pretty serious about no one being able to locate them or track anyone with them by phone."

"What happened? The guys told me what you did. You literally saved so many lives, Blake."

He nods, moving me to the slow and sultry beat. "It's what me and Beckett did for a long time. That kind of training doesn't just go away just because you're in a new place."

"What happened with the Larussios?"

He laughs. "They offered me a different job."

I step back and glance at him, but he draws me closer again. "They want me to work here with the guys. Apparently, there's a lot more going on in this town than anyone else knows. And they're dedicated to keeping it protected from the Chicago Mafia and the men and MC clubs they sent."

My blood begins to thrum. "Does that mean..."

His eyes lock with mine. "What I didn't tell you is that I have a family and they're the reason I changed jobs, needed to make a little more money. My sister's husband was in a bad accident. He had just transferred into the job so didn't qualify for insurance yet. He's doing better, but it's been a long, painful slow road. I've been helping the two of them and my little nephew with all the medical bills and living expenses while she's been staying home and taking care of both of them. I can do that and a whole hell of a lot more with what the Larussios pay."

I give his lips a kiss. "The part about the family surprises me but you helping them out, that doesn't surprise me one bit. I bet you're a great brother and uncle."

He grins. "Well, I'd like to think so, but Jace, my brother-in-law, wants to work. He's feeling stronger but of course it has to be the right fit. So, I went back home to talk to them about moving here after I met with the Larussios. They're off the grid right now which is why I kept communication null."

My eyes lift. "I'm not sure I fully understand. Is he able to work?"

He laughs. "Well, it would take the right job. Physical stuff is still out of the question and will be for a year or two more, but my brother-in-law just happens to be a genius with numbers, investment management, and anything business related. He was just starting to go through offers when I broached him with a proposition from the Larussios."

My eyes go wide. "Really? That takes a lot of trust."

Blake grins. "It does and it's a smaller world than you think. Apparently, his old investment firm handled a few of their small, let's say shadow accounts. Ones that are public record and are intended to keep the others less likely to be looked into. My brother-in-law found a discrepancy in the numbers and was told to sweep it under the rug. He instead let the Larussios know, which is the reason he had just started on with another firm right before he got in the car accident and was living off the grid."

"It is a small world indeed."

He draws me closer whispering in my ear as he turns me in the dance. "And wouldn't you just know that at the same time, they found out that I was moving to Deadwood, South Dakota. And that there was space on the property I bought for them to come live while we build a couple nice houses."

I swallow past the emotion. "You're moving here, to Deadwood?"

His hand rests around my nape. "My heart, it's here, with you, it never left the town limits. I left that here with you."

A tear trickles from my eye, and then the other, before he's gently wiping them away, kissing my lips. "It may be far too early to say it but I'm going to do it anyway. I love you Patti Ann, and I know you feel it too. You're mine now. Tell me I'm right."

My heart feels like it wants to explode as I put my arms around his neck. "I love you with all of my heart, Blake. So much I could barely breathe the entire time you were gone. I've been yours since day one."

EPILOGUE

Lettie walks to the table, handing each of us a bottle of beer. She leans close. "You see those bikers up front? They've been sitting in the same seats every Saturday night. I'd put money on it that the one with those deep green eyes and longer hair has the hots for our Marla."

Jules laughs. "Time for another one of Lettie's pools."

Lacy smiles at the group. Well count me in, but I'd never bet against you, Lettie. So, now that PJ and Jules special day is over, I can tell you our good news."

All eyes turn to Garrett and Lacy. She looks like she's going to explode if she doesn't tell us right away. "We're pregnant!"

Lettie lets out a whoop and the entire table roars in a cheer. "Oh my gosh. I knew it would happen soon enough, but I honestly didn't have a clue," Lettie says, clucking like the mother hen that she is.

"Well, it is pretty hard to keep anything from you," Lacy says.

. . .

Blake reaches across the table and gets the attention of the guys. "Three o'clock, coming in through the back door." All eyes turn as four bikers with bats walk through the club, daring anyone with a look to even stand up from their chair. The leader walks to the stage and grabs Marla's hand, almost dragging her from the stage.

The guys are up in a flash, but they're not the first. The biker with bright green eyes who's been sitting at the front seat, watching her dance for the last four weeks doesn't miss a beat.

AFTERWORD

Thank you for reading this story, and for supporting the Deadwood anthology. We appreciate you so much! I'm most known for my novel-length steamy romances, but love writing these shorter romances too. You can find them on most major platforms and on my website.

Xoxo, Via

ABOUT THE AUTHOR

International best-selling author, Via Mari likes to keep her readers on the edge every step of the way, fanning themselves as the action unfolds and the heat rises. Her books, no matter the genre or subgenre, exemplify extreme romance and feature the most handsome, intense, powerful men who will stop at nothing to protect the women they love.

AFTERWORD

Thanks for reading the 2026 Wild Deadwood Reads Anthology!

We hope you enjoyed this collection, and we'd love for you to post a review on your favorite book retailer's site.

www.ingramcontent.com/pod-product-compliance
Lightning Source LLC
LaVergne TN
LVHW050910080826
845145LV00001B/39

* 9 7 8 1 9 6 8 0 1 4 0 9 4 *